Praise for
If You Lived Here

"Love, in its various incarnations, is the central theme of Sachs's tale—big love that's revealed in small signs and little gestures."
—*Star-News* (Wilmington, North Carolina)

"Poignant. . . . A well-told story, with appealing characters, delightful moments, and a satisfyingly real ending." —*Charlotte Observer*

"Sachs's descriptions of Hanoi are precise and vivid."
—*Columbus Dispatch*

"*If You Lived Here* is filled with dramatic moments. Author Dana Sachs deserves to be listened to." —ThingsAsian.com

"Anyone who's adopted internationally will recognize the emotional arcs that Dana Sachs charts so eloquently in *If You Lived Here.* But this book is for anyone who appreciates what good fiction does: capturing human beings in all their angularity. Sachs is an expansive and generous writer who gives us, at all times, the pulse of life being lived. She's the real deal."
—Louis Bayard, author of *Mr. Timothy* and *The Pale Blue Eye*

"It should come as no surprise that, after writing *The House on Dream Street*, one of the best accounts of contemporary Vietnam, Dana Sachs would write *If You Lived Here*, an uncannily moving novel of the Vietnamese experience in America. What is most admirable of all the things Sachs does right is her willingness to show how different cultures can be from one another; her empathy, however, establishes how beside the point such differences ultimately are. Forster said, 'Only connect.' Dana Sachs is a one-woman power grid, her book electric company."
—Tom Bissell, author of *God Lives in St. Petersburg* and *The Father of All Things*

"This book is gorgeous and, more important, compelling. In it, the very worst and the very best happen. Behind every event is the heart and genius of this novelist, alive at every moment to the pleasure of life." —Rebecca Lee, author of *The City Is a Rising Tide*

"*If You Lived Here* is a moving story of friendship that bridges cultures and challenges traditional notions—of women of the American South, women of Vietnam, and of the ways in which these two cultures meet. Shelley and Mai are refreshingly real and complex characters, and Sachs conveys their emotional lives and their remarkable journey with patience, compassion, and exacting insight." —Dao Strom, author of *Grass Roof, Tin Roof*

"*If You Lived Here* is a big literary novel, ambitious in its melding and merging of home and homelessness, love and divorce, motherhood and sisterhood, loss and joy. It is about forgiveness in an age when forgiveness is the green plant in a forest fire: it needs protecting. This book shows us our own lives, our own world. It has the power to make us see each other as we are."
—Clyde Edgerton, author of *Solo: My Adventures in the Air*

© Todd Berliner

About the Author

DANA SACHS is the author of *The House on Dream Street: Memoir of an American Woman in Vietnam*, which *Publishers Weekly* praised as "engrossing and engaging" and which the *Orlando Sentinel* called "genuinely beautiful." She has published numerous translations of contemporary Vietnamese fiction. She lives in North Carolina with her husband, Todd Berliner, and their two sons.

If You Lived Here

ALSO BY DANA SACHS

*The House on Dream Street: Memoir of
an American Woman in Vietnam*

WITH NGUYEN NGUYET CAM AND BUI HOAI MAI
Two Cakes Fit for a King: Folktales from Vietnam

If You Lived Here

DANA SACHS

HARPER

NEW YORK · LONDON · TORONTO · SYDNEY

HARPER

A hardcover edition of this book was published in 2007 by William Morrow, an imprint of HarperCollins Publishers.

FIRST HARPER PAPERBACK PUBLISHED 2008.

Interior artwork by Bui Hoai Mai
Designed by Susan Yang

The Library of Congress has catalogued the hardcover edition as follows:

Sachs, Dana.
    If you lived here: a novel / Dana Sachs.—1st ed.
        p. cm.
    ISBN: 978-0-06-113048-9
    ISBN-10: 0-06-113048-6
    1. Undertakers and undertaking—Fiction.   2. Children—Death—Fiction.   3. Grief—Fiction.   4. Wilmington (N.C.)—Fiction.

    PS3619.A284 I34 2007
    813'.6 22
                                                2006046603

ISBN 978-0-06-113049-6 (pbk.)

08   09   10   11   12   NMSG/RRD   10   9   8   7   6   5   4   3   2   1

TO MY PARENTS,
WHO MADE IT SEEM SO EASY

If You Lived Here

Shelley

I'd guess that Marinos have been burying Rivenbarks for seventy years. I can't compare funeral customs here in Wilmington, North Carolina, with funeral customs anywhere else, but I can tell you that Rivenbarks usually ask for the minister from First Baptist, flowers from Will Rehder, and an open bar. Sometimes they read Psalm 23 and sometimes they read Psalm 121. It's hard to know what they'll request for a burial like this one, though, because there's nothing routine about the death of a child. This afternoon, on the first really beautiful day of spring, four-year-old Oscar Rivenbark fell from the third branch of the magnolia tree in his backyard. The ambulance managed to get him to the emergency room within about fifteen minutes, but he died before the paramedics could wheel him in.

My husband, Martin, and I run Marino and Sons, the biggest funeral home in the area. Between the two of us, we have over forty years of experience. Still, we struggle when a child dies. Outsiders probably imagine that my world is all catastrophe, but most of our cases come from heart attacks, hospice, and Brightmore, a retirement community a few miles away. It's not like there's a fatal car crash after every prom.

I get the news of the accident from the police blotter, so I'm prepared when the boy's aunt, Gracie Rivenbark, makes the first call to our office at about five. I click open the calendar on my desktop and ask, in a voice that sounds both competent and sympathetic, "When would Tara and Mark like to come in?" I try to get the parents involved as soon as possible. I'm here to help them with their grieving, and grieving starts at the moment of death.

Gracie says, "Hold on." Behind her, I hear the murmur of various voices, a volley of muffled questions, silence, then a few more moments of tortured debate. Sudden death produces a kind of bafflement in people. It confuses and startles them. They forget where they are, their name, the year. And then, five minutes later, they can become extremely lucid. In my dealings with the bereaved, I never rush them.

"Would tomorrow afternoon work?" Gracie asks. "Around two?"

"That's fine," I say. This case demands particular sensitivity, not just because the boy was young, but because his parents are young as well. Even Aunt Gracie seems to be conducting this business for the first time, ever. When you bury old people, you often deal with other old people, and they're likely to have organized a funeral before. As gently as possible, I tell her, "I'll need them to bring in a few things when they come."

Gracie says, "A few things?"

"An outfit. Something he might have worn to church, or even something he loved to play in." Gracie confers again with her relatives. The door to my office squeaks open and I look up to see my husband, Martin, slip inside. He's wet haired and red faced from the gym and he's holding today's mail. He doesn't know what's happened yet. When he looks at me, I squinch my eyes shut, then open them again, signaling, This is a bad one. I scrawl "Rivenbark—4 ys. old" on a notepad. After a lifetime in this business, Martin doesn't respond to news of death in any obvious way. His flinches are microscopic: a twitch at his mouth; an alteration in his breath; the slow, slow blink of his eyes. Cases like this one have always been hard on him, and they seem to have gotten harder lately. I dread the thought of what's ahead for us.

"Why do you need clothes?" Gracie asks.

"Well," I explain, "we'll need something for the burial." Martin sits down in the armchair, starts to go through the mail, then abandons it on his lap. Even the new issue of the *Atlantic Monthly* fails to interest him. He watches me. Martin's fifty-four this year, twelve years older than I am. His parents and grandparents were all morticians and he started going out on retrievals in his early teens. In comparison, I'm fairly new at it. I got my license a few years after I married him, so that's not even twenty years. I impress Martin, though, because the sadness never really gets me down. It came as a surprise to both of us, actually, that I could marry into this business and adapt so well. How could you know, when you're a kid, that you have the perfect personality to become a mortician?

Gracie Rivenbark says, "I'll go through the closet this evening."

"That'll be fine," I tell her. "And, we'll need a couple of pictures, too, in case the family wants to make a display for the service."

"A display," Gracie murmurs.

"And his Social Security number."

"Okay." Her voice sounds light and wispy. I've got to get the poor thing off the phone.

I make my final point. "And Tara and Mark should feel free to bring their other children to the meeting, too."

Gracie says, "I'll tell them."

And then, in the background, I hear sobbing. It is desperate, rhythmic, utterly bereft. I hold the phone in my hand, listening, staring into my husband's eyes.

At that moment, I forget myself. "Is that Tara?" I whisper.

Gracie says, "Yes."

Martin's head falls back against his chair. I close my eyes. It's been months since we have buried a child and in that time my own life has changed significantly. The sound of an anguished parent affects me more deeply now. I suppose that's because I'm about to become a mother myself.

Martin and I have tried for years to have a baby. At forty-two, it feels as if my chances of giving birth are about as likely as my chances of winning the U.S. Open. There comes a point in your life when your expectations about your future have to shift a little and so, a few years ago, I began to consider adoption. It wasn't an easy route to follow. Martin already has two sons from his first marriage. Abe and Theo were five and four, respectively, when Martin and his first wife, Janet, divorced. Over the years, his attitude toward starting a new family has ranged from overt anxiety to a kind of acquiescence that looks like defeat. The prospect of adopting complicated his emotions even more because he wondered if he could love an adopted child as much as he loves the boys he has already. Eventually, he did agree, but he's never gotten very involved in the process. At worst, I think he tries to pretend it isn't happening. At best, he acts like an easily distracted sports fan, watching my race for a baby from a comfortable seat in the stands. I'd like him to be wild with excitement, like I am, but I don't complain. Lots of dads take a while to come around. It will mean even more when he does, finally, fall in love with our baby.

I've had a lot of low moments over the past few years, but, for the first time in my life, motherhood actually seems imminent. Eight months ago, we received our referral, for a little Slovakian girl named Sonya. She's one year old now, fatherless, and was left at an orphanage by her mother. Eight months ago, I couldn't locate Slovakia on a map. Now, I know Slovakian emigration law as intimately as I know the procedures for filling out death certificates here at home. I've completed every single form for our girl, and I have nothing left to do but wait until it's time to go and get her. Every morning I wake up and wonder, Is today the day I'll get the call? When, earlier today, I received a voice mail message from our caseworker, Carolyn Burns, I saved it and played it back for Martin, twice. "Could you call me?" she asked. "As soon as you have a chance?"

But it's five-fifteen already and I haven't been able to reach her. After I hang up the phone with Gracie Rivenbark, I call the county coroner's office to find out when the boy's body will be released. Martin has gone downstairs to check with Bennet, who does most of our embalming, about a schedule for the next few days. After a few minutes, though, he wanders back in. Taking his seat in the armchair, he picks up his *Atlantic Monthly* and opens it. He's been sluggish like this for months, accomplishing exactly the amount of work that's necessary, but very little more. It's a subtle change. He looks as healthy and confident as ever, but tough cases—and the death of a four-year-old would certainly count as that— have become especially hard on him. At times, he will simply retreat, lingering in places he rarely used to linger at all: bed, the bathtub, my office. He will limit his contact with clients and spend a lot of his evenings out on our porch, drinking tea and reading, or just staring at the sky. I guess it scares me, a little.

"I'm checking the inventory for caskets," I announce, squinting at my screen. We don't keep more than a couple of child-size models at any given time, but I can see that we have a two- and a three-footer in stock. Luckily, neither is pink—one is white and one is blue. I say, "We might not have to special-order."

Martin asks, "Did you hear back from Carolyn Burns yet?"

I scowl. "No. She gets pleasure out of making me wait." Over the years, I've fallen into the habit of depicting adoption agency officials as witches, or thieves, or petty heads of state.

Although he looks unconvinced, he's clearly amused.

"Well, it seems like that to me," I assert, but at least I'm laughing now. It's a sign of my optimism that I can joke about our adoption. Martin grins. He has an astonishing ability to read my moods and know exactly how to respond to them. Mostly, though, it's the sweetness in his face that helps to relieve my stress. He doesn't look so different to me than he looked at thirty-two, when I first met him. Sometimes, in the glare of a summer graveside service, I'll gaze at him across the expanse of mourners and see him as others might—average height, graying hair, skin pale, body a little thick around the middle. My mother calls him a fine-looking man, which is a perfect demonstration of how easily her feelings sway her. When she first met him, and hated the fact that I had fallen for a mortician, she called him "Eeyore." Once, when she was really upset, she even referred to him as "Dr. Dead." Now that she loves him, she says he's "fine-looking," "a real catch," "Mr. Right." The truth is, you wouldn't notice him in a crowd. You'd only notice him if you accidentally ended up next to him at a dinner party or on a plane. Fifteen or twenty minutes would go by with you entangled in some unexpectedly enthralling conversation about Sumatra or bowling or compost. You'd come up with the most arcane bits of information—things you didn't even know you knew—and you'd be surprised by the breadth of your knowledge, and by how smoothly it combined with his, and you'd begin to feel that the two of you were among the most fascinating humans on the planet and, quite suddenly, you'd think: Hey, this guy is kind of cute.

We sit. I compose a memorial card for a funeral taking place tomorrow night. Martin reads. I glance at the phone every so often, willing it to ring. Finally, without looking up from his magazine, Martin says, "Let's walk down to the river."

I glance at my watch. I've completely forgotten that Theo's band is playing downtown tonight. "Oh, God," I say. "Then we'd better hurry."

Wilmington lies on a peninsula that spans the distance between the Atlantic Ocean and the Cape Fear River in the southeastern corner of North Carolina. It takes more than forty minutes to walk from our place on Market Street all the way to the river, but on an evening like this one, it's crazy to get in a car. Within five minutes of leaving our house, I feel better. I feel happy, even. I'm almost ready to believe that sometime in the next few weeks, we'll actually have our child. I take Martin's hand. I like to imagine Sonya here with us, the newest member of our family, lounging in her stroller, sippy cup in hand, admiring this orange sunset. We're ten miles from the ocean, but I can smell the salt in the air and see, on people's front porches, the seashells, chunks of coral, and driftwood they've carried back from the beach. Our little girl will enjoy, I think, this Wilmington spring, this flowering drama of dogwoods and redbuds, lace-draped cherries, lavender wisteria, giddy azaleas, peaches and plums. I believe that she will be happy here.

It's nearly six-thirty by the time Martin and I get to Level Five, a downtown rooftop bar that overlooks the river. I don't see Martin's son Theo, but he's sure to arrive any minute. Last summer, Theo founded the band, Carolina Waikiki, as a joke. He'd been playing bass in a jazz fusion group for years, but when they got an unexpected gig at a tiki bar in Kure Beach they bought some thrift-store Hawaiian shirts and Theo pulled out his old ukelele. For some reason, the group tapped into an unknown market for Southern-tinged Hawaiian music, not only here in Wilmington but also up in the mountains, in Charlotte, and in Raleigh. Audiences go wild when they hear "Little Grass Shack" sung in a Carolina drawl, and the band has developed the kind of avid following that Theo had previously only dreamed about. Martin's son is now considered the best ukelele player in our part of the state. They've even traveled up to Richmond.

We find a table at the edge of the roof and order hamburgers. Martin gets a scotch and I decide to try one of the piña coladas, which look like Slurpees to me. From where we sit, you can see the great gray hulk of the battleship *North Carolina* berthed below, and the shadowy woods of Brunswick County stretching to the west. The view is nothing but river, trees, and the scattered lights of cars heading out of town.

"We've got to work late tomorrow," I remind Martin. "I'm going to make *halusky s kapustou* for the staff." It's a bland but filling Slovakian specialty—potato dumplings and sour cabbage. I've been trying to perfect it so that when Sonya arrives, she'll have something to eat that's familiar.

On the other side of the bar, Theo emerges through the door, tottering under the weight of an amp. Martin waves, then leans across the table. "Listen," he says. "I want to give you something."

"What?" It's not my birthday or anything.

He reaches down to his jacket pocket and pulls out a *National Geographic*. Martin often goes around with a rolled-up magazine in his pocket, so I didn't even notice this one as we walked downtown. "I found it a while ago, not that long after we got Sonya's referral," he explains. "I wanted to give it to you when we were closer to traveling, and we seem pretty close to traveling now."

"I guess." My eyes are on the magazine. You can tell it's an old one because the cover design looks slightly different from how it looks on recent issues. The pages are crinkled and stiff, too, like something that has, over the years, become damp and dry many times over.

Martin carefully opens the magazine to a page marked with a Post-it, then turns it toward me so that I can read the title: "Slovakia's Spirit of Survival."

"I don't know how much you'll learn from this," he says. "It came out in 1987."

I pull the article toward me, gently turning the pages to reveal pictures of farmhouses and villages, a beer hall, the Danube River, our daughter's native land. "I'll learn so much!" I gush. A woman who has just received an enormous diamond from her husband could not feel more elated. I don't actually need a lot of information about Slovakia; I've got books and books already. What I needed was a sign from Martin that he is with me now, that he and I are making this leap together.

We look at the pictures. "This is perfect," I say, imagining him digging through thirty years' worth of moldy boxes in our basement to find it. I know a few people who constantly clip out articles from the daily paper to send to friends, scrawling "Read This!!" and "FYI!!" across the margins. But, in my opinion, such behavior is kind of boorish. Martin is not like that at all. He's a voracious, but private, reader. Sometimes, though, if he senses a need, he will search until he finds a perfect piece of writing to address it: a poem, a story, a cover article from *National Geographic*. Once, not long after Rita, our receptionist, lost her husband, Martin gave her an essay about sea lions he'd found in an old issue of the *New Yorker*. I can't say exactly how the topic of sea lions could help Rita through that period, but it did. She said it was the most perfect thing she could have received, at the most perfect moment.

"How long did it take you to find this?" I ask.

Martin smooths down the pages with his fingers. "A couple of hours, I guess," he says. Then he laughs. "Actually, I ended up reading a lot of things I didn't need to read. I guess it took more like a week."

I have a box in my bedroom closet where I keep the articles that Martin has given me over the years. I keep his letters, too, and various cards and photographs that I love. But nothing so precisely reflects the history of our relationship, our initial infatuation, and our continuing affection for each other as the dusty pages that he has torn out of magazines and given to me from time to time, imperfectly stapled or clipped together, often rumpled or torn or oddly folded. "Remember the time you gave me all your *Geographic*s with stories about India in them?" I ask.

He smiles. "Of course." We barely knew each other then, but, one day, Martin brought me six different issues of the magazine in a brown paper bag. Together, we went through them, page by page, looking at pictures, reading captions, constructing a whole country through our conversations, disputes, and ruminations on what life might be like over there. Suddenly, "India" wasn't just a name on a map, a promise of risk and adventure. It was *this* particular woman, standing in front of a train station, a basket of oranges on her head. It was *this* road, *this* palace, *this* field. For me, the idea of travel had only been about going and doing. Martin saw the world in terms of its content. He might not go anywhere at all, but he read, he asked questions, he listened, he tried to understand. He wanted the things he saw and did to have meaning. For Martin, every single minute of life was valuable and precious, and that way of being in the world felt completely new and compelling to me. I was crazy for him then, and still am, really. I can't imagine going through this life of mine with anyone else.

Martin says, "I couldn't believe that a twenty-year-old girl from Wilmington would think of traveling all over the world by herself."

I grin. "I didn't actually do it," I remind him. It's not a sore subject, but the truth is, perhaps, a little less exciting than the idea of me he once created in his head. "I married you, remember?"

More than twenty years have passed, and I have no regrets about the fact that I chose this adventure over that one. I pick up his hand and kiss it. He looks sheepish and shy. I think he's always felt guilty that I missed my chance, that I decided not to travel because of him. The truth is, I would still rather fantasize about India with my husband than actually go there. He smiles at me. "So, we'll go to Slovakia together."

We toast, piña colada clinking against scotch, but I find it hard to speak. I keep hold of his hand, rubbing it against my cheek, gripping his fingers. I don't think I could love him more than I love him now. From across the bar, the first few notes from Theo's ukelele drift toward us, then the rattle of the drums. Theo, all lilty voice and puppy charm, begins to sing. "Promise me, promise me, promise me, do, here where the waves begin to sigh. Don't leave me, don't leave me, don't leave me, please, my lovely darling Hokuikekai."

On Friday morning, I stay home for a while to make the *halusky s kapustou* for our staff, six of whom I've scheduled to work tonight. From four-thirty to six-thirty, Martin will run the viewing for eighty-nine-year-old Catherine Simmons in the small chapel's viewing room and, at seven, in the main chapel, I'll hold a memorial service for Bladen Hughes. I imagine that the Simmons viewing will bring in fifteen or twenty people at most, but we could see a couple hundred for Bladen Hughes, who was a Rotarian and raised millions for the renovation of Thalian Hall. You have to be ready for a large crowd, in any case. In my years in this business, I've noticed that a single death can affect a wide and often surprising range of people. Unlike a wedding, for which families compile a guest list that shows their varied allegiance to the outside world, a funeral demonstrates how outsiders feel toward a family and its loss. Grief is very democratic.

Our house sits on the far side of the funeral home property, separated from the main building by a parking lot and a stand of oaks. The house has been in Martin's family for seventy years and the inside wall of our bedroom closet still has the pencil marks his mother made over decades of measuring her children's growth. Ever since Martin and I began to try to have a baby, I've looked forward to the day I'd add my own child's measurements to that wall. It's been so many years, though. Your sense of hope drains incrementally, a drop at a time as each month goes by, as each pregnancy ends in miscarriage, as each new attempt at conception fails. It happens so slowly you almost don't notice. The change is profound but inconspicuous. You keep on acting as though you're having a child, but you start to lose your ability to believe it. The chart inside your bedroom closet evolves from a happy promise into a constant reminder of something you still don't have.

As soon as I get into the kitchen, I pull five pounds of potatoes out of the bag in the pantry, then a can of plum tomatoes and another one of corn. Tomatoes and corn aren't in the recipe but they're part of my plan to perfect it. I'm glad that Martin has gone over to the office already. He teases me about the quantities I cook. You can barely find room for a box of spinach in our freezer because of all the extra casseroles, quarts of soup, and third trays of brownies left over from the day I only needed one or two. I agree that all of us, except maybe Rita, our receptionist, could stand to lose a few pounds, and that so many crumb cakes and quiches won't replace any loved ones anyway. Still, we living like to eat. I remember that I'm alive when I bite into an apple (although I seem to feel more alive when I bite into a piece of fudge). That's why we fill the homes of the grieving with stew and pie. That's why I cook. I concentrate on the sizzle of bacon, the knock of my knife, the sudden overbearing smell of cumin. I make my life tiny, nothing but frying pan and stove, sizzling onions, a piece of steaming potato pressed hot against my tongue. This is my narrow universe. This is me, I think, alive.

When the phone rings, I am opening the can of tomatoes. I don't move immediately. Instead, I stare down at the can, a trickle of watery juice already pooling on the metal top, and I know it's Carolyn Burns. I turn off the stove, throw a clean dishrag over the dumpling dough, walk to the phone, and answer it.

"Shelley? This is Carolyn Burns. Southeastern Adoptions." After all these months, the woman still refuses to acknowledge the essential nature of our relationship, that I, like all her clients, am desperate for her calls. She could simply say, "It's me!" and we would know who she is.

I close my eyes, willing *this* call to be the good one. I spin my finger in the air like fireworks. "We've been hoping to hear from you!" I bubble.

"Yes," Carolyn Burns says, and that single word marks the shift in tone from cheerful efficiency to something more sober and sympathetic. And so I know. "Shelley, I'm sorry. I have some very bad news."

No, I think. "I have to have Sonya here by her birthday," I announce, not merely to Carolyn Burns, but also to myself, to God, to baby Sonya, over there in Europe. My voice sounds absolute, but in my heart I know that things can only go wrong in this business.

"I'm so sorry. The birth mother decided that she wanted to have a Slovakian family adopt her child."

"She can't do that."

"She still has some legal rights, apparently."

I lean against the wall, then let myself slide down until I'm squatting, hugging my knees. "I was just about to travel," I whisper. I press the nail of my thumb into the tip of my index finger, trying to concentrate on that pain instead of this one.

"I'm sorry," she says.

"Is there any hope?" I ask.

"Well, another child is available. A little boy from Vietnam."

"I'm talking about Sonya. My daughter. Is there any hope?"

She doesn't answer immediately.

"Tell me."

"There's one possibility. The birth mother has agreed to meet with you. She's willing to let you try to convince her that you're the best family for her child. You'd have to leave as early as tomorrow, though, because she plans to decide in the next few days. I should warn you: You don't have much of a chance."

I have spent so many months imagining my trip to Slovakia: the journey from Wilmington to New York and Prague and then, finally, Bratislava. I imagined the anxious hours on the plane, just waiting to meet my daughter, and then the journey home, juggling bags and bottles and a little girl. I never imagined traveling all the way over there and then coming home without her.

"I need to talk to Martin," I tell her. "There's so much going on right now. We expected to have a week's notice before we traveled. We have to arrange for extra staff."

"If it's any help, your husband doesn't need to come. But talk to him. If you decide to try it, call me within a few hours. I can make the arrangements for you to leave tomorrow. You could meet with her on Sunday."

"So, I'm supposed to beg her?"

"It's a little more rational than that. But, yes. Essentially."

By the time I get to the office, the little body of Oscar Rivenbark has already arrived, making it an awkward time to speak with my husband about flying to Bratislava tomorrow. Rita observes me carefully as I walk through the front door. Maybe she can tell that I've been crying. Maybe she can tell that I'm panicked. Maybe she's just wondering why I stayed home to cook and arrive now, two hours later, empty-handed. Sometimes you can't speak, though. Sometimes you can't explain to anybody that you burned the dish you were perfecting, that you've thrown it in the garbage, that your heart is nearly broken.

"Where's the slow cooker?" she asks, eyeing me over the top of her bifocals.

I don't stop. Somehow I manage to announce, "We're ordering pizza."

I find Martin and Bennet in the preparation room, getting ready to do service on the little boy. Because the death was accidental, the coroner has autopsied the back of the head and the chest, checking for signs of a stroke or heart attack that might have caused the initial fall. These days, Bennet does most of our embalming, but, because juvenile cases are both technically and emotionally challenging, he needs one of us to help.

"Did you hear anything from the coroner?" I ask. I am aware that I will have to hurry if I have any chance of going to Bratislava, but there's something so sad about this little body on the table that it's hard to figure out how my own problems fit in here.

Bennet squats in front of the one of the cabinets. "They won't have a report until tomorrow," he says. I admire his steadiness. It amazes me sometimes, when I watch him work, that the kid is only twenty-seven. He looks pretty much like he did when he was sixteen—soft, slightly pudgy, John Denver in his "Rocky Mountain High" days. Around the office, he's sometimes silly, but he turns solemn and professional when he works. We recognized his talents years ago, when he was still in high school and, out of curiosity, he started taking late-night service calls with Martin's boys.

Even at sixteen, he had a polite attentiveness that calmed the bereaved. Emergency crews often commended his maturity and good sense. Abe and Theo did the job adequately, of course, but they weren't enthusiastic and they couldn't handle the hours. We all felt lucky when Bennet went into the business. Martin and I hope he'll take over when we retire.

Bennet swivels toward Martin, looking up. "I'm going through the cavity fluid, but I'm not sure what we need. Do you think the weight is less than forty?"

We glance at the preparation table, trying to judge. The way the body looks at this moment confirms my support for open caskets: It takes a great leap of the imagination to connect this small gray form with the bright pink flash of energy that must have so recently animated it. The contrast between the two can make you believe in the soul. It can make you believe in transcendence.

Martin stands closest to the body. He says, "Yes, but get eight ounces anyway. We'll do some direct injections."

I walk over to him, just to be close. He looks worn down and flustered. "How you doing?" I ask. It's a ridiculous question, of course. A boy lies dead on this table. In my mind, a little girl, our daughter, is drifting away. But I have to try to make things normal.

"I'm okay," Martin says. He sounds very far away. Almost idly, he picks up one of the little hands and begins to massage away the splotches of blood that have pooled beneath the skin. "I measured the length of the body. If the family wants it, we can use the three-foot casket we have in stock."

Martin seems determined to continue, but is disorganized, aimless. His hands look awkward as he tries to make firm circles on the sallow skin. I look at my watch. I don't have to meet the Rivenbarks for several hours. I say, "Hey, let me finish this up with Bennet. Can you go upstairs and see what's wrong with Excel on my computer?"

"You can't figure it out?" he asks, but he looks relieved.

I say, "Please."

Martin washes his hands and takes off his coveralls while I put mine on and pull a hairband around my hair. I walk over to the preparation table and untangle a couple of stray twigs from the little boy's curls. As Martin turns to go upstairs, I say, "I'll do a shampoo, too."

Bennet and I work to music. He's always the DJ and he has eclectic tastes. For a while, we listen to the soundtrack from *All That Jazz,* then switch to Joy Division, and then, because we've all become fanatics for Hawaiian music, he puts on a little Don Ho. I swab and set the features of the little boy's face, aspirate the abdominal cavity to remove gasses and the contents of the stomach. I make an incision in the neck and push my finger inside, searching for the carotid artery, then pull it out a few inches to connect it to the tube that will inject the embalming fluid. When I'm ready, I turn on the pump. Sometimes, if a person suffered through months or years of illness, the introduction of embalming fluid will transform a scrawny body into what, in slightly different circumstances, would seem to be a picture of health. On Oscar Rivenbark's body, which was healthy and young, the effect is more subtle, like the inhalation of breath. The tinted fluid brings color to the pallid skin. Slowly, the boy begins to look, well, if not more alive, then more presentable to those who will force themselves to look at him. Bennet and I have to pause for a moment, just to watch.

Before I became a mortician, I worried, as a lot of people would, about my ability to handle the more disturbing aspects of this profession. But, like people who work in medicine, you get used to the gore very quickly and you focus on the more intellectual, and even spiritual, aspects of what you're doing. When I prepare a body for burial, I gather hints about the life that person lived. Experience does not always reveal itself in a literal way, of course. Many people endure heartbreak, for example, but I have never actually seen a broken heart. I have never seen a pulled leg, a bent mind, a twisted tongue. I have seen the results of suffering, however. A body's size hints at excess and deprivation. Skin can reveal the myriad ways in which people drag themselves to ruin. Scars give clues of pain, not only physical but emotional as well. Sometimes, I discover the vestiges of happiness, too: the grooves a wedding ring will make on a finger after decades of wear, toenails painted in zany colors, bunions that developed, perhaps, from many years spent dancing. I know very few of the people I bury, but I detect their secrets. I see the odd tan lines, the hidden tattoos, the scars in illogical places. I am the last human being who will ever wash this face or run a damp cloth across these ankles. To the extent that I have a relationship with God, it's in my capacity as a funeral director.

Eventually, of course, Martin wanders back in. He stands at the foot of the preparation table looking unsure about what to do next. "What's wrong with my Excel?" I ask.

"I just had to restart the computer," he says. His eyes rest on the body of the little boy. His voice sounds vague and distracted.

Bennet and I stand on either side of the preparation table, scrubbing grime from the little fingers. If you didn't know better, you might think we're manicurists at some kind of pricey spa. Martin doesn't move and, after a moment, Bennet looks at me, his face full of concern, then says awkwardly, "Shelley tried out that new shampoo. I think she's right. It's better." He runs his fingers through the still wet hair, as if to prove his point.

But Martin has frozen. I would do anything, I think, to make him happier. And so I decide, without any vacillating, really, that I will not abandon him and leave tomorrow for Bratislava. "Honey," I whisper. "Go take a break or something." When he looks up at me, his face is hopeless. I think, Don't weep.

After all the evening's visitors have gone home, after we eat our pizza and wash it down with beer, I wander out to the bench behind the building where the drivers come to smoke. From this spot, tucked between the storage rooms and the back of the garage, I gaze up at a narrow slice of sky. Each experience of sadness has its own particular sharpness, but the pain I feel right now comes from too many different sources, making it blunt and indistinct.

Martin steps outside and sits down beside me on the bench. Back in his street clothes, he looks more composed and steady, like someone you could count on. He sets his hand on my knee. Everyone else has gone home. We have nothing to do but go to bed so that tomorrow we can come back and do more of the same.

The Hughes memorial, despite the crowds, has gone off without a hitch. The Simmons viewing had a moment of tension when the deceased's two daughters got into a spat over the dress they'd chosen for the burial. As for Tara and Mark Rivenbark, they somehow managed to complete all the arrangements for tomorrow's burial of their son. They could barely speak. His eyes were wild; her eyes were dead. That's one advantage of this business. When you're really down, you remind yourself that your own problems are not so awful, really.

"I wish I smoked," I say. I lean over and pick butts off the ground, then toss them into the sand-filled flowerpot I leave out here as an ashtray for the drivers.

I have let my hair down. Martin's fingers begin to weave through my curls. "That would solve everything," he tells me.

For a while we just sit there. He leans against the building and I lean into his arm. It's hard to find comfort in his presence just now, but I try. After a few minutes, he says, "You're holding me together these days. I'm sorry."

I take his hand. I am scared to see him cry, so I make my voice sound light and reassuring. "It's too hard sometimes."

He says, "When I was a kid, one of my dad's friends killed himself. He'd been diagnosed with terminal cancer and I guess he didn't want to go through it. Right before the Duke-Carolina game he shot himself. Did I ever tell you about it?"

"No." Martin has so many stories of death, but he's not a raconteur.

"In his suicide note, he wrote that he'd like his family to schedule the memorial for three o'clock on Saturday, which was right when the game started."

"Do you think he knew that?"

"Of course. He and my dad were Tar Heel buddies. They drove up to games together every season. So he was testing everybody: Would they go to his service or watch the game?"

I'm not sure what Martin's getting at. "That's crazy," I say.

"My dad thought it was funny. He took it as a final little poke, one buddy pulling a prank on the others. So they went to the service, but they took a radio with them. Every now and then, the minister would pause so one of the mourners could announce the score."

"Your dad had a weird sense of humor."

"He just had a way of accepting everything, without absorbing it too deeply." He sounds irritable now, as if he's looking for a path out of his own morass and I'm not being helpful.

"We all have to find our own way to deal with things," I say. I could remind him that his father used to drink a fifth of bourbon when he came home every night.

Martin says, "I'll be better tomorrow."

This kind of talk makes me impatient. I accept that he can't handle the Rivenbark case alone, but I don't want to hear him lie about it. I sit up, then turn to look at him. "We lost the baby," I say. I can hear that my voice sounds accusatory, and I'm sorry, but he needs to know the extent of the day's disasters.

"What do you mean?" My announcement seems to jolt him. I start to cry.

It doesn't take long to explain what happened, because I leave out the crux of it, the fact that I might have gone and begged, but didn't. "I never really believed we'd get her," I say, which I didn't realize until right this minute.

For a long time, he holds me. Then we sit for a while longer. We can't manage to stand up and drag ourselves back home. It's hard to close a day like this one, the last day that we could hope to adopt this little girl. I feel as if I'm living in some in-between time, as if moving at all would constitute the final acceptance that we've lost her. Martin makes no move to get up, either. He tips his head against the wall of the building. "We'll get a child," he promises.

Talk like that used to comfort me, but I have trouble believing it now. "We might not," I say.

"We will." I hear in these words an attempt to conjure up the old Martin, the strong one, the one with endless reserves of strength and solace.

The night is warm and breezy. Martin raises a finger and points up through the branches of the dogwood trees, the blossoms glowing pale yellow in the darkness. He says, "One. Two. Three, over there." It's a game we sometimes play, counting stars.

"Four," I tell him. "It's a paltry night."

2

Xuan Mai

My mother didn't approve of wasting time. On winter nights in Hanoi, while my father and I played Chinese chess and my older sister, Lan, went off to visit friends, my mother would mop, or practice her French, or boil leftover bones for soup. My father often said he'd never expected my mother to become such a competent housekeeper. She had grown up the only child of the richest landowners in her village, a pampered girl destined for even greater wealth and privilege. She could have married a high-level official, or gone to university in France. But my parents grew up in revolutionary times, when you couldn't think of much but war. Instead of living a life of comfort, my mother became an orphan, then a soldier, and, now, an industrious homemaker in barren Hanoi. Instead of studying French literature in Paris, she learned to wring three dinners out of a sack of water morning glory, a handful of dried shrimp, and a few scoops of rice. My father himself taught her how to mop.

From my father, I inherited the ability to relax; from my mother, the need to feel guilty about it. And I do still feel guilty, after all these years, that my own life, unlike that of my parents, has become so luxurious. I have my own business here in Wilmington, an expensive SUV, a house without a mortgage, a Jacuzzi bathtub. My mother is long gone now, and I am long gone from my life in Hanoi and everyone I ever knew there. After twenty-three years, though, I still sometimes glance across my store and imagine my mother standing there, tapping her foot impatiently. My business impresses her, but she doesn't like to see me doing nothing. She crosses her arms impatiently and I hear her say, "Nobody put a man on the moon by wasting time."

But my job is not rocket science. If I vacuum every day, my customers will come. If I don't, they'll come anyway. I don't run a hospital in this town. I run an Asian market. People come here to buy persimmons in season, frozen duck, garam masala. I keep my shop very clean. I wish that my mother could see the high marks I receive from the city health inspectors. (We didn't even have health inspectors in Vietnam!) I am the purveyor to Wilmington's immigrant population, Latinos included, and the brave Caucasian cooks who decide to try "international" for dinner. I do an excellent business, and five days a week I sell take-out lunches, too, but none of this keeps me on my hands and knees every minute. In the afternoons, I usually get a lull between the lunch crowd and the commuters who stop by on their way home from work. Sometimes, I go over receipts then, or take an inventory, or call Far East Distributors to see if they have taro powder or some other item my customers can't get at Wal-Mart. I like the quiet in the store then, and the way the sun streams through the blinds, making stripey bands of light against the palettes of rice in the corner. If I'm not busy, I watch *Oprah*.

Today, she is asking, "Is Your Spouse Also Your Friend?" and, though that's not an issue in my life, I still find it diverting.

The guest is a psychologist. He uses a questionnaire and claims he can predict with 90 percent accuracy whether a marriage will last. He holds a sheet containing answers to the questions he asked O.'s partner, Stedman, in advance.

I'd like to hear, but my employee, Marcy, has begun to argue with her mother. "Will you let me live my life already?" she demands.

Her mother, Gladys, says, "You make big mistake."

"I need quiet!" I yell at both of them.

For a moment, silence, then Marcy wanders over to watch with me, Gladys close behind.

The guest asks O., "What is Stedman's favorite music?"

O. cocks her head as if she's thinking, but you can tell she already has her answer. "Marvin Gaye," she announces.

The guy checks the sheet, then looks at O. apologetically, as if *he'd* gotten the wrong answer. "Actually, it's the Bee Gees."

O. looks appalled. "The Bee Gees!" she cries. The audience moans.

Marcy pulls her hair back and twists it into a messy bun held in place with a pencil. Apparently, that's high fashion these days. "The Bee Gees. Cool," she says.

"Bee Gees uncool," I tell her. I don't know the Bee Gees. But I know O.

"The Bee Gees are so uncool, they're cool. Like Perry Como. 'How Deep Is Your Love' is very cool."

Marcy and O. know what they're talking about, even if they don't agree with each other. You have to have grown up in this country to know, and Gladys and I grew up in Vietnam. Gladys doesn't care that she doesn't know, which is its own kind of cool, actually.

"You could get kidnap!" Gladys says to Marcy, circling back to the subject she does care about—Marcy's threat to get a job at the Gap.

"You can't get kidnapped from the Gap, Ma!" Marcy grabs a broom and marches back toward the coolers. Her mother follows.

I pick my lunch, a bowl of *phở,* off the counter and balance it on my knees. Turning the rice noodles gently with my chopsticks, I examine the strands of scallion, flecks of chili and mint, the few tender pieces of chicken caught like fish in a net. The scent of the broth forms a warm, rich cloud around my face. I can smell cinnamon, lemon, the slightest bite of salt. The ingredients of a *phở* would seem so obvious to someone who doesn't cook: noodles, shredded meat, broth, and herbs. But that simple word "broth" contains a whole universe of flavors. Really, it only looks simple.

Even on the other side of the store, Marcy and Gladys make so much noise arguing with each other that I lose my appetite. Marcy opens a crate and starts to shove packages of frozen fish into one of my freezers. Gladys stands next to her, miserable, her arms knotted across her chest. Marcy works hard, which explains why I keep her around, but I get tired of hearing them fight all the time.

"You're invading my space," Marcy says, flicking her hand into the air as if her mother were an insect.

"You going to have problem," Gladys whines in her onion-paper voice. Gladys is hardly fifty, but she already stoops like an old lady and has begun to lose her hair. She grew up in the central highlands, near Kon Tum, I think, and she speaks Vietnamese with such a thick central accent that I can barely understand her. Her English is even worse, but her daughter refuses to communicate in Vietnamese, so she has no choice but to use English. "Gap no good," Gladys says. "Not good people." The final word sounds like a shriek: Peeeeeeeeee-pul. Hearing her accent makes me feel better about mine.

Marcy slides the last package of fish into the freezer, then stops for a moment, pulling at her cold fingers. She looks at her mother. Sometimes she pretends that she doesn't understand what Gladys is saying. Now she says, "Just give me a break."

Gladys yells across the store in Vietnamese. "Mai, you tell Marcy."

I don't get involved. Marcy's worked for me for three years already and tells me, when Gladys isn't around, that she won't leave. She just likes to taunt her mother.

Gladys glares at Marcy. "Honestly!" It's her favorite word. She will insert it, in English, into even the most monolingual Vietnamese conversations. Out of her mouth, in fact, it sounds Vietnamese: *On ech ly!* Then she stomps out of the store, her maneuver of last resort.

Finally, some quiet. I touch the tip of my pinkie to the broth, but it's lukewarm now. Somehow, I force down a few bites. I often feel like a parent, coaxing myself to eat. After all these years, you can see it in my face, which has become pasty and loose, like the skin of a grape that's sat too long in the sun. Everyone used to say I looked like my mother, but up until the year she died my mother still had smooth, healthy skin. Even during the war, when we had nothing to eat but potatoes, my mother's cheeks were full and rosy. And here I am, in America, and rich, looking older than she looked during the worst years of the war.

The front door jingles and I look up just as the funeral director pushes her way inside. You recognize her first by the hair, wild and red, thick with curls, as unusual as a talent the rest of us lack. "Hey, Mai. How are you?" she asks, as if we're the best of friends. Her gaze settles on me, waiting for an answer. Her fingers rest on the edge of my counter.

"Okay," I tell her. Might as well forget about eating. The woman will stay for ages, as if it's the most natural thing in the world to hang around my grocery and pester me. Maybe she's losing her mind. She's shopped here for years, coming by every couple of weeks to stock up on her supplies of ginger tea, or chutney, or whatever it is she usually buys. I never had a problem with her before. Once, when the Vietnamese manager of Hardee's died in a car wreck, I helped her out by setting up a prayer altar for the funeral. She seemed completely normal then. She never got chatty. In the past couple of weeks, though, she has rematerialized as a kook. She appears every couple of days, asking questions. Not normal questions, like, "How long do you cook this fish?" Or, "Is chicken good with Hoisin sauce?" She asks bizarre questions, like, "Do people eat ramen noodles in Hanoi?" And, "What do Vietnamese cook for New Year's?" I end up spending fifteen, even twenty minutes responding. The conversations grow like weeds, distracting me.

Several times, I've managed to avoid these sessions by pretending I'm busy. But still, she lurks. Her voice sounds discreet, but it is actually focused and prodding, and it carries across the aisles from where she hovers near Gladys or Marcy, pressing them for answers, too. They love the attention. She has the kind of hair that you see on the heroines of soap operas, and a look on her face that says you're the most fascinating thing on the planet. Gladys has rarely conversed with an American, and she responds to the woman Shelley's notice with giddy gratitude, as she would a proclamation from the government that she has succeeded here. Marcy, who can be careless and moody, swells with maturity at the idea that someone older, and attractive, has turned to her for information. As soon as the woman approaches, they stop whatever they're doing and address her questions with the concentration they normally reserve for their own conflicts. But their answers meander. Once, when she asked Gladys, "Who is the most talented Vietnamese composer?" Gladys explained that she had to quit school and go to work at the age of eleven. Another time, she asked Marcy, "Why is red considered such a lucky color?" Marcy ended up describing an elegant Chinese wedding she attended in Charlotte last year. What are they thinking? If a customer asks for tofu, would you give them cheese? The truth is, the woman wants to know about Vietnam and Marcy barely remembers it. And Gladys? Well, Gladys grew up in a village a three-hour walk from the nearest town. Try asking a redneck from Castle Hayne to name the most talented *American* composer. They'd probably say the Beatles.

"Van Cao," I told her, but I did not offer to loan her a CD.

This afternoon, the funeral director sets her purse on my counter and makes to fan herself with her hand. "What do you make of this weather?" she asks, feigning exasperation. "Freezing one day, a scorcher the next."

"Yeah," I say.

"Did you get weeks like this in Vietnam? Where it changes back and forth so often?"

Could the woman be more annoying? I force myself to recollect summer afternoons of blinding sunshine followed by driving rain, then sunshine and rainbows later. "Days," I say.

She lets out an extravagant gasp. "How dramatic! I really can't imagine."

"It not that different here," I remind her. Wilmington has moments when the fertile smell of the summer air reminds me exactly of home. But I am really only interested in putting her off. I push my *phở* aside, pick up a pile of order forms, and start to fill them out.

"Um. Here," she says suddenly, unzipping her bag and reaching inside. "I brought you these." She pulls out five faded *National Geographic* magazines and sets them on the counter. When I glance up at her, she shrugs and says, "My husband's a subscriber. We've got, like, a zillion of them." She looks kind of embarrassed, but also curious to see how I respond. Despite myself, I look through the covers. Each bears a photograph of Vietnam. Four come from the 1960s and early 1970s. The most recent, published thirteen years ago in 1989, bears the headline "Vietnam: Hard Road to Peace" and promises articles on Hanoi, Hue, and Saigon. Hanoi in 1989, ten years after I left it. I feel as if I've been offered an invitation to peek at what would have been my future.

I look up at Shelley. Actually, I'm touched by her thoughtfulness, but I'm also uncomfortable with interactions that have no commercial purpose. "Thanks," I say.

She busies herself by zipping closed her bag. "It's nice to have a use for them," she tells me and then, after an awkward silence, she mumbles, "I should be heading home anyway." She lets her fingers tap the air in a little wave, and then she's gone.

For a while, I just eye the magazines on the counter. Part of me would like to ignore them altogether, but I'm tempted to look. Warily, I pull them closer, run my finger across the covers. Then I open an early issue, just to check. It contains familiar images—water buffalo, women wearing *áo dài,* children spooning out their morning bowls of rice—and images like the ones I remember from North Vietnamese newspapers depicting the war in the South—sick babies, anguished parents, a U.S. Navy flotilla steaming down the Mekong. Though the photos interest me, I find myself happily unaffected. I'm an American now and I experience the same feelings of curiosity and pity that any American would feel viewing photos of an exotic country, a long-ago war. I've endured many emotions over the past twenty-three years, almost all of which I'd rather have avoided, so it comes as a pleasant surprise to look at pictures of Vietnam and feel, well, nothing.

Marcy ambles over. "Cool," she says, pushing the magazines around on the counter. But Vietnam doesn't really interest her. After a couple of minutes, she wanders off.

I look at every picture. Then, braced, I push the other magazines aside, ready to peruse the most daunting one, the one that features photos of Hanoi. I am primed and ready, immune. But it takes only a moment to discover that I am not invulnerable after all. There, on page 558, my city lies before me in all its dingy grandeur, a lost treasure that I'd convinced myself I no longer missed. In the ten years between the day I left and the period during which these photographs were taken, my city hardly changed. In one picture, a bride, posing in front of a gauzy mosquito net, reminds me of my cousin. In another, a man rides a bicycle exactly like the one my family used to own. Every detail in every photograph feels personal. Worn rubber shoes. Wooden doorways covered in peeling paint. The gritty, uneven slabs of city sidewalks. A woman scrubbing a baby in a basin of water, gripping its leg to keep it from slipping. I miss my mother, my father, my sister, my niece. Vietnam.

A few days later, Shelley appears again. This time, Marcy's at the register, while I perch on a stool back in produce, dividing a crate of basil into four-ounce plastic bags.

"Everybody on campus knows me," I hear Marcy say. "Even people I don't know, they know me." The girl's body is slender but curvy, and her clothes fit as tightly as the skin on a ripe tomato. It isn't hard to see why she's famous at UNCW. Even in worn jeans and a dirty T-shirt, she looks like one of those "Talk to a Sexy Lady" girls in the phone number ads on cable.

"Try studying for a chemistry exam when guys keep wandering by asking for your number," she complains.

"It must be kind of rough on you." Shelley's voice sounds both sympathetic and amused.

Eventually, she wanders back to where I'm working. "Hey," she says. She pauses, tugging at a curl.

I smile. "How you?" I ask. I don't want to admit that I've been staying up past one A.M. reading and rereading her magazines, but I do want to convey that I remember that she brought them.

"Okay, I guess," she says, wavering a little. I imagine that, with a job like hers, she's always depressed, at least a little. In Vietnam, we didn't mix with funeral people. They kept to themselves, which seemed like the price they paid for earning their livelihood off burying our dead.

Her eyes skim the contents of my shelves as if she's glancing through the headlines in the morning paper. "I need something good to cook for dinner," she muses. She's tall and sturdy, pretty in a healthy, thoughtless way. Today, she wears a silky peacock-colored dress, the kind of thing another woman might flounce in, but she seems indifferent to it. The truth is, a stranger wouldn't notice the dress. Not when she's got that hair. Would she need a mirror, often, just to marvel at it? Would she consider it an asset or a burden, or both? I can't even imagine how you'd comb it. My father used to say that the heavens give each person one spectacular gift. Marcy has the body. My mother got her fine gray eyes. My father got his voice. Shelley has that hair. And me? I don't know yet.

She picks up a bright yellow packet of Knorr tamarind soup base, looks at the picture on the front. "Do people eat this in Vietnam?"

"Tamarind, yeah. But I don't know they have that soup base. You can use it for *canh chua*. Sour soup."

"Sour soup?" She grimaces.

I nod my head encouragingly. "It's good. When I'm little, my mother make it for me like a special treat." Somehow, it seems important that she believe me. It's *good*.

She laughs. She seems so at ease. "My mother used to make me TV dinners," she says. "You probably don't even know about TV dinners."

"I learn a lot on cable," I tell her. I want her to know that I am fully integrated into American society.

She leans against the shelf, watching me stuff another bag of basil. "Swanson's did an entire turkey dinner. It was gross and gooey but my sister and I loved it. If my mother was going out, we got to eat Swanson's and watch horse racing on TV."

She talks as if we're exchanging vital information here. Then her face turns serious. "I don't want you to think that's all my mother fed us."

I look at her, surprised that she would care. "I don't," I mumble.

This response seems to satisfy her. "She makes an unimaginably delicious quiche, but I wouldn't rave about her pies."

I can't help myself. I laugh. She says, "I'll give you the recipe for the quiche. And you tell me how to make sour soup." Now we're back to sour soup?

I look down at my basil, stuff another bag. "Okay," I tell her, with

a sense that I'm trying something different here. It doesn't feel danger-
ous, though. It feels more interesting than normal. What could it mean to
exchange recipes with a stranger?

Shelley pulls over Marcy's little stool and perches on it, then slaps her
hands against her knees to signal that she's ready. "Let me tie the knots,"
she suggests. I can always use an extra hand. I give her a bag. She holds
it open for a moment, inhales the scent of the herb, and then, apparently
satisfied, expertly knots it. "Okay," she says. "Sour soup."

It takes me a moment to start. The truth is, I'm embarrassed about
my English. I can understand every word I hear on TV, and I can read
anything I want, but I don't converse much, and I know that when I do,
I sound like an idiot. Now I feel a sudden urge to say to Shelley, "I'm
smarter than you think." But that just sounds more stupid.

Sour soup. I pull a handful of basil from the box. "You eat it when
the weather get hot," I begin. "It make you sweat, keep you cool inside."
I look at the packet of Knorr on the floor next to Shelley's purse. It's a
simple dish, really. "I can write it down. You need lot of garlic, sugar, ripe
pineapple to balance sour ingredients—tamarind, lemon grass, tomato,"
I tell her. And then, because the talking feels easier than I expected, I tell
her more. I explain the things she doesn't need to know, the things that
suddenly seem important. I tell her that, when you make it right, it tastes
just like summer: earthy, sweaty, fresh. I tell her that, during those hot
months of my childhood, with the food rationing and the war, we rarely
had fish, but we could get tamarind, a fist-size pineapple, a few tomatoes.
If we had no sugar, my mother used sugarcane juice instead. On summer
evenings, the whole family squatted on the sidewalk in front of our house,
holding steaming bowls of soup balanced on our knees. The smell could
make your eyes water, but the broth slid easily down the throat, a perfect
blend of sweet and sour. All of Hanoi would be out on such nights, eating soup, drinking hot tea, nibbling on chilies in hopes that the sweat on
our faces would catch some slight breeze floating in off the river. I was
just a kid then, I explain. More than thirty years have passed, but I can
still see the tower of empty soup bowls left forgotten on the sidewalk, and
hear my father, squatting in the doorway, telling stories to the neighbor-

hood kids. During those summers, my father drew crowds. They used to call him Ông Ngàn Tiếng, Mr. Thousand Voices. With the most imperceptible shifts of tone, he would become a ferocious dog, a cranky old woman, a cunning thief. The older children vied for position around his knees. The little ones watched from a few feet away, peeking out at him from behind the shoulders of their parents. I, too, felt frightened by my father's voice. My earliest memories revolve around listening to his stories while staring intently at the strands of hair that curled like elegant writing against the damp skin of my mother's neck.

Shelley listens, sealing my Baggies with firm little knots. Every time she glances up, her eyes fix on me. I'm surprised that an American would listen so closely, or care about such unimportant things. After a while, she says, "That's not the Vietnam I ever heard about."

"No," I say. The Americans hadn't even dropped their bombs. We had only four in my family then: my father, my mother, my sister, Lan, and me. It was before Lan married Tan and lost him. Before she gave birth to My Hoa. Before I fell in love with Khoi. Before the cancer came and took my mother. "It was nice then," I tell her.

Shelley has stopped what she's doing. "My husband was in Vietnam," she says. "He worked as a military mortician in Danang."

I look at her. "He describe the place different?" The box of basil sits empty. I toss in the knotted bags that lie scattered like herb-filled balloons across the floor.

She says, "He never told me anything."

"Can't blame him for that."

Often, my words come out sounding harsher than I intended. Now Shelley blinks and I can see that I've hurt her. I stare at her, unsure of what to say. Then, quite suddenly, she smiles, almost as if to reassure me. "No," she says. "I don't."

From the register, I hear Marcy calling, "Hey, Mai." A moment later she appears in front of us, not even registering the oddness of the fact that I am perched on the floor with a customer, bagging basil. "This afternoon can I use the kitchen to bake a cake for Travis's birthday?" She stands above us, hand on her hip, a beautiful Vietnamese all-American girl.

"Cake?"

She nods. Marcy and her boyfriend enjoy hobbies. They believe there's a value in making things from "scratch," even if the cake would taste better and look prettier if you bought it at Food Lion. They will use up a whole good Saturday making hand-stamped wrapping paper, and then they'll spend Saturday night downtown at Marz, where Travis plays drums with a band called Maximum Go-Go and Marcy dances in some cage, like a Saigon call girl.

"Fine," I say.

She bounces from her heels to her toes. "After work, I'll just run out and get some eggs." She makes it sound like a statement, but it's really a request.

"Just use mine," I tell her, waving her away. I find Marcy's manipulations kind of endearing. She offers me one of her blithe, grateful smiles and dashes back to the register. I don't envy Marcy her youth or her beauty, but I would like to remember how it feels to care so much about wrapping paper, or surprises, or cake.

Shelley grins. "Must be nice," she whispers, exactly what I'm thinking.

3

Shelley

Here's one more indication of the arbitrary nature of the adoption business: Carolyn Burns, who could wait only five days for us to accept our referral for Sonya, has now given me a month to decide about this child from Vietnam. She calls the sudden change in policy "an understanding of the situation," but, of course, it's guilt.

I appreciate the extra time, though. This referral, for a twenty-month-old boy from somewhere near Hanoi, not only represents a sudden shift in age, gender, nationality, and ethnicity, but also presents a new problem particular to us. Years ago, I tried asking Martin about his experience in Vietnam, but he would only tell me, "I don't have any interesting stories," and leave it at that. In the past few weeks, I've heard more about that country from Mai Pham at the Asian grocery than I've heard from Martin in twenty years. I expect that Martin will say no when I finally approach him with this news, but I'm not certain enough to reject it out of hand. You never know. Maybe he'll see the child as an opportunity to replace his bad memories of Vietnam with something joyful. But maybe not.

I'm so reluctant to hear his response that I've waited nearly two weeks to bring it up. Things haven't exactly been quiet lately, anyway. In fact, we've had to deal with one catastrophe after another. A pipe burst in the funeral home's upstairs bathroom and caused a hideous leak in the front-hall ceiling. A member of the city council collapsed from a heart attack, prompting a standing-room-only service and three days of nearly constant interaction with the press. A day later, Rita's sister Helen passed away at hospice. Then Martin's son Abe broke his arm in a bike wreck and Martin had to race up to Chapel Hill. Everyone's felt the strain of recent weeks and so, as a sort of bonus for the staff's hard work, Martin gave them all the day off. When he's done that in the past, some employees have come to work anyway, banking the time to use later for vacation, but today, with no cases on the schedule and beautiful weather, everybody stayed home.

I'd like to go to the beach myself. We haven't been once this spring, not even for a walk. I could go alone, I guess, but I'd feel too guilty leaving Martin at the office. He refuses to take a break. Apparently, when he told me that he would pull himself together, he took himself more seriously than I did. Over the past few weeks, he has shown more commitment to our business than I've seen from him in months. In addition to the unusually heavy workload, he dealt with fixing the plumbing, took out a lease on a new Town Car, and visited two church groups to talk about end-of-life issues. Today, with no one in the building, he's done everything from filling out Rita's phone logs to changing lightbulbs in the bathrooms. He hasn't said anything about the way he faltered over the Rivenbark boy, but his behavior serves as a constant reminder: "Look at me. I'm better now!"

I spend the morning in my office. Around noon, I go downstairs and, following the noise, find him in the main chapel, vacuuming.

"Mauricio did that yesterday." I have to yell for him to hear me.

He turns the vacuum off and looks uncertainly around the room, apparently unwilling to accept that the carpet is clean enough. His face looks haggard and thin.

"Can I talk to you for a minute?" I ask.

He looks down at the vacuum.

I take his hand. "Leave it."

We walk out into the meditation garden that lies in the courtyard between the reception rooms and the chapel. When Martin and I first got married, the courtyard contained nothing but a patch of lawn and a couple of forlorn-looking benches. No one ever came out here and its only value lay in the fact that it offered a swath of dull green as a view outside the windows. Within a year, I had constructed deep beds around the edges and filled them with so many plants that we get blooms all year long now. Today, the Carolina jasmine blossoms cover the trellis and magenta tulips crowd beneath the chapel windows. At the end of the summer, when the lantana grows huge and the swamp sunflowers begin to bloom, the garden becomes a reminder of the lushness of life. Occasionally, I even grow tomatoes. People don't expect to see anything so wild in the courtyard of a funeral home, but they wander outside anyway. Some mourners will spend hours here.

Within these walls, the traffic on Market Street becomes a distant hum. I lift my face to the sun and close my eyes, pretending that we have, in fact, ended up at the beach. "What is it?" Martin asks.

I open my eyes. He looks impatient. Despite yesterday's rain, the patch of grass is dry and inviting, so I take his hand and make him sit down with me. I keep his hand in mine. "We have a new referral," I tell him.

He looks more pleased than I expected, but I haven't told him everything. "It's a boy. From Vietnam."

The range of expressions that cross his face is brief but vivid: surprise, anxiety, and, then, resolve. "That's great," he says.

"If you can't do it," I tell him, "we'll wait for another one."

His tone turns irritable. "Why should it matter where the baby comes from?"

"It might matter."

Martin says, "I don't have anything against Vietnamese people."

I would like to believe him. I've read and reread the information that came with this referral. The boy's name is Nguyen Hai Au. The staff of the Ha Dong Children's Center outside Hanoi found him in a box near the orphanage entrance when he was a few days old. He's nearly two now and he's suffered more bad luck in his adoption saga than I have in mine. First, when he was still a tiny baby, a Vietnamese family filled out the paperwork for him and then decided to adopt a girl instead. Six months ago, an American family chose to adopt him, then got pregnant themselves and changed their minds. Most adoptive families want newborns and babies, not a child who has lived long enough to develop fears, and opinions, and memories. Nguyen Hai Au has reached the threshold of the age at which it will become ever more likely that he will spend his entire childhood in an orphanage. He needs a home now. I want Martin to be able to love this child. I say, "I talked about Vietnam with Mai at the Asian grocery. I bought some guidebooks."

Martin's face looks strained, but he's trying. "The food is delicious there," he asserts.

"How about I learn to cook it?"

"Fantastic." He lies back against the grass, his eyes closed now. I'm pleased to see him rest, but he doesn't look relaxed. He looks like someone brooking no distractions.

I slide my hand beneath his shirt and let it rest on his warm belly. I can remember, early in our marriage, when I found this part of his body so attractive that I would have to put my mouth to it. At moments, I felt like an animal operating on nothing but instinct. Now, though, his body just looks delicate and sad. What are bodies, really, but sadness, bone, and tissue?

"Well, I guess I'll tell them yes, then," I say, offering one last invitation for him to change his mind.

Martin sets his hand on top of mine. "Say yes," he tells me.

"I was about to give up hope," I whisper.

Martin's voice is almost inaudible. He says, "Me, too."

4

Xuan Mai

One Tuesday, after I finish selling the lunches, I get Marcy to watch the register. "I gotta make a phone call."

"Take your time." She goes to the counter and pulls out a heap of diagrams she has stashed in a drawer for moments such as this one. She's taking a class in quilting.

My purse hangs on a hook behind the kitchen door. I unzip the change pocket and pull out a business card from among the coins. Yesterday, one of my lunch customers, Captain Weatherbee of the Wilmington Police Department, scrawled a name on the back of his card. Hannah Ellis. And her phone number.

For a moment, I hold the card, looking at the rough handwriting, the scuff of the pencil marks on the ivory paper. Then I pick up the phone and dial.

"Hello?" The voice sounds old and feeble.

"Hello. Yes. Uh, I'm looking for Hannah Ellis. You Hannah Ellis?"

"That's me, duckie."

Who's duckie? "My name Mai Pham. Captain Mark Weatherbee give me your name."

"You need a picture?"

"That's right."

"Come on over this afternoon. Say, about three o'clock. I'm at 417 Nun Street, downtown. I can't hear too well on the phone, so come on over and we'll talk. 'Bye."

She hangs up before I can say another word. "Marcy," I call out, walking to the front of the store. "I got errands. I'll be back in a couple hours."

Marcy's abandoned her quilt and now sits paging through a *Real Simple* magazine, the cover of which shows a scratched metal bucket with azaleas stuck in it. People live in America for this? "Okay," she says. She doesn't look up.

Gladys appears from down one of the aisles. "Mai, tell her she's making me miserable," she says in Vietnamese.

"You tell her, Gladys," I pull my keys out of my purse and step out into the heat.

Hannah Ellis's house is a pale green cottage set between two larger homes. The tiny front yard consists of two flower beds, divided by a path down the middle. Spring roses fill the beds, their blossoms in shades of pink and yellow. An elderly woman, not much bigger than some ten-year-olds, sits in a flowery housedress on a rocker on the porch. I stand on the sidewalk looking up at her.

"You my three o'clock?" Her voice sounds stronger than it did on the phone.

I nod.

Hannah Ellis gestures with her hand for me to come up. "Can't even see you down there, duckie." I walk up the path. "Where you from? You Chinese?"

It isn't a very promising question from a person I plan to commission to draw two portraits, but I push myself up the stairs anyway. Hannah Ellis lifts her hand to shake. Her fingers feel like brittle sticks in mine. "Vietnamese," I tell her. "Vietnam. My name Mai Pham."

She chuckles, rocking her chair back and forth as if it were exercise, then motions for me to sit in an armchair beside her. "Well, welcome to America, I guess." I perch on the edge of the chair while Hannah Ellis reaches over to a TV table on the other side of her rocker, pours two glasses of iced tea, and hands one to me. "Now, why are you here?" she asks.

Because I have nothing, and if I lose my belief in the spirits, I'll have even less. "I need pictures," I say.

"What kind of pictures?"

I take a sip of the tea. "Captain Weatherbee say you can make pictures. Like in court. I just tell you about the person and you make picture."

Hannah Ellis runs her hand around the wet sides of her glass, then dabs her forehead with the moisture. "It's damn hot, but I feel sick if I stay in the house too long," she says. "Besides, sometimes a breeze comes up and I can smell my roses." She glances at me. "I imagine it gets pretty hot over there in Vietnam."

"Real hot."

"I like the way you say that, 'make pictures,' " she says. She rubs more water on her forehead. "Hey, smell them? You smell my roses?"

A faint breeze wafts through the bushes. I do smell the roses.

Hannah Ellis rocks. "Are these crime pictures?"

"No."

"How you know Weatherbee, then?"

"I do a lunch business. He's my customer."

"I spent fifty years drawing crime pictures. I don't want to think about another criminal for the rest of my life."

"These aren't criminals."

She sets her tea down on the TV table and starts rocking again. After a while, she asks, "Who you need pictures of?"

"My mother," I say. "And a little girl. My niece."

"You don't have photos, I assume?"

"No."

"Well, that's why people come to me." She rocks for a while longer. "Are they dead?"

"Yes," and then, because the word sounds abandoned in the empty air, I tell her, "I'm Buddhist. We use pictures to honor our love ones."

She nods. "Nothing wrong with that."

The rocking slows. Hannah Ellis leans over and picks a black canvas bag off the floor, pulls out a drawing pad, a charcoal pencil, and a tattered copy of a book titled *Law Enforcement Facial Classification Catalogue.* "You've got to describe them to me in detail. I'm going to ask you a bunch of questions about both of your people, starting with your mother. We'll work on these pictures for as long as you like and then you'll have to wait a few days, or even a week, before I'll have anything to show you. Even if you're never satisfied, I still gotta be paid. So let me ask you: You sure that you got their pictures in your head?"

I nod. I may not be as pretty as my mother, but all I have to do is look in the mirror to see her. And as for My Hoa, well, sometimes I wish I didn't see her so clearly.

Hannah Ellis hands me the book. Its textured cover feels weighty and damp, worn smooth from years of use. "Page forty-one, female bone structure. We'll start there."

It happened in 1979, on the third anniversary of my mother's death. On that morning, My Hoa drank four cups of *nước gạo rang,* the roasted rice water that, because of her sensitive stomach, we often made for her. My sister, Lan, had gotten up first, grilled the dry rice, eaten a bowl of left-over rice herself, then hurried off to work. Our father, Bo, left soon after, anxious to secure a spot at the veterans' center for his morning game of Chinese chess. By the time My Hoa woke at seven, I'd already poured hot water over the grilled rice and let it steep in a glass. I dressed my niece in the same yellow shirt and shorts that she wore most summer days, the outfit Lan washed at night and hung to dry. Then I poured the *nước gạo rang* into an old teacup and handed it to her. She knew that she and Khoi and I would spend the day in Unification Park, and as she perched on her stool in the middle of the room, she beat her feet against the concrete floor impatiently.

My Hoa wanted the time to pass faster, but I wanted it to slow down. Khoi had found a boat to take him away from here, and this evening, with nothing but a small book bag over his shoulder, he would take a bus to a village near Hai Phong, climb on a fishing boat, and sail away. He had a rich uncle in Los Angeles or California—I didn't know the difference then—a man who owned two Fords and a house with an entire empty room that Khoi could sleep in. For months, we had planned to make our escape together, but over the past few days I'd changed my mind. As much as I hated life in Hanoi, I couldn't leave my family here, and neither my father nor my sister showed the slightest inclination to leave Vietnam. Bo had abandoned his belief in Communism, but he remained loyal to a government that had given a semiliterate veteran a good education. Besides, he planned to reunite with my mother in the afterlife and he didn't know how they'd find each other if he died overseas. As for my sister, she had rejected a prestigious scholarship to study in Moscow. Why would she leave the country in a leaky boat? Khoi didn't argue with them, or with me, but he didn't cancel my place on the boat, either. Just in case. Still, expecting that I wouldn't change my mind, he promised that in five or ten years, after he made thousands of dollars, he would entice my entire family away, and when we got to America, he would marry me. I smiled as if I believed him, but we were only nineteen. Five or ten years seemed impossibly long, and I'd heard about the girls in America.

I dressed while My Hoa gulped down the liquid in her cup. I filled it again, and she finished it again, laughing. She was small for her age, and looked exactly like her father, Tan, a slight and clever man who had made it home from war only to die of his wounds a few years later. None of us ever discussed the resemblance, but I always remembered it when, late at night, I saw my sister staring down at her sleeping daughter. I had never lost a man I loved and so I came to imagine that this ability to see him and not see him simultaneously would constitute both the best and the worst of it.

With My Hoa's eyes following me around the room, I put on my only good shirt, a white cotton button-down on which I'd embroidered lavender flowers. Standing in front of the mirror, I pulled my hair back with a

Bulgarian barrette, then let it down, then pulled it back again, considering how this skinny face and skeleton body would be the last thing that Khoi would see of me. At that moment, I wanted nothing more than to be beautiful. I wanted the delicate features of my friend Thuy, the rounded breasts of my neighbor Hang. I wanted hair like my sister's, which was full of body and always shone. I went to Lan's drawer and fished a tiny secret bottle of perfume from underneath her clothes. Not knowing what else to do with it, I rubbed some on my cheeks. My Hoa, wide-eyed and serious, stuck her hand in her teacup and splashed *nước gạo rang* all over her face.

"Auntie!" she called. "More tea." I looked at the clock. We would be late to meet Khoi, but I couldn't turn her down. In our household, the task of getting nutrients into My Hoa had become an obsession. The three of us—Lan, Bo, and I—had developed a dozen tricks to get her to eat and drink. Late at night, while she lay sleeping in Lan's bed, we would recount our successes like pickpockets after a day of thieving. Lan could get her to take a few bites of porridge by distracting her with stories. Bo slipped pieces of bread into her mouth while getting her dressed. I plied her with cups of *nước gạo rang,* making her feel grown up by calling it "tea." Surreptitious feeding. It was both our entertainment and our central task in life. Now My Hoa had asked for more. I put a few spoonfuls of grilled rice into the glass, poured more hot water over it, then blew on it. As the liquid cooled, My Hoa walked over and squatted down beside me, peering into the glass. "Pretty tea," she murmured.

While My Hoa waited to drink the *nước gạo rang,* I picked up Bo's metal toolbox and sorted through the family's food ration coupons. In anticipation of my mother's death anniversary, we had been saving our meat ration coupons all month so that we could eat beef tonight for dinner. The government called religion reactionary, but my mother had always insisted that the family commemorate its death anniversaries by making offerings and lighting incense before an altar to the ancestors. After my mother died, we lost our momentum. Incense was hard to come by in a city of professed atheists, and so, as each anniversary approached, we simply saved up our coupons to have a big meal. Being the cook in the family, I would ride my bike to the market, stand in line for hours, and buy what we needed. Tonight, as Khoi was boarding a boat to leave Vietnam forever, my family and I would sit on the floor in our house in Hanoi, eating beef for dinner.

By a few minutes before nine, My Hoa was ready. I stuffed some rice wrapped in a banana leaf into my bag and set her into the rattan child's seat on the back of the bicycle. I tied a piece of pink mosquito netting over her face to keep the dust out of her eyes, then walked the bike through our courtyard, out the front door, and down the alley to the street. The sun had not even appeared above the roofs of the houses to the east and my clean shirt already stuck in patches to my back. We rode down past Hoan Kiem Lake, then out Ba Trieu Street. At the gates of Unification Park, I heard my name, turned, and saw Khoi. He was perched on his bicycle, with one foot on a peddle and the other foot touching the ground to keep himself balanced. Hanoi boys always sat that way, leaning their elbows on the handlebars while they waited for a train to pass or for a mother or sister to finish bargaining for a piece of fish. Khoi, though, had a grace that made even a pause on a bicycle look beautiful. That one toe seemed to hold him to the earth. At that moment, he was nothing but light and air to me. I felt that if I reached out to touch him, he would disappear.

My Hoa, who was not a little girl to wait for anything, marched through the front gates of the park, assuming Khoi and I would follow, which we did. She was still young enough to believe the world belonged to her and, in recent weeks, had become more and more able to express it. At home, she appropriated everything. She had an old burlap rice sack in which she kept a collection of different colored bits of string, a tattered book of poetry, three of her grandfather's socks, my comb, a pencil, seven chopsticks, and a neatly folded piece of newspaper containing a lock of her mother's hair. Khoi, who called her "little princess," made dolls for her out of kindling sticks, fabric scraps, and wire. Every evening before going to bed, My Hoa would lean all the dolls against the wall, sit down on the floor, and stare at them. She called them "my people."

The three of us walked down the shady main path of the park and headed toward the swings. Every few seconds, I glanced at Khoi, wanting to memorize how he held his hands in his pockets and the way his rubber sandals kicked up dust from the path. Today, he walked along beside me in the park. Tomorrow, he would be no more real to me than a ghost, than someone dead. Letters did not arrive from America, so what was the difference, really, between going to America and being dead? The thought of it made my mouth go dry. I had to turn, then, and look at My Hoa, telling myself that, even without Khoi, I would still have my niece. I would still have something precious left.

My parents worshipped learning. Throughout my childhood, my father memorized poetry, and my mother, who could never hope to travel, continued to work on her French. On her side, those values made sense, because she came from an educated family. But my father was the son of farmers; he claimed he could trace his proletarian lineage back to the time of the apes. My mother's ideals had rubbed off on him, though, and he believed in them as avidly as any convert. That's why I don't imagine that either of them would be impressed by the fact that I own a little grocery in Wilmington, North Carolina. How does that elevate me? they would want to know. How does that help to improve the world?

Well, I would just say that this business suits me. I appreciate the clarity of my responsibilities. I appreciate the limits, too. And I like the way my position entitles me to observe the little dramas of society—my customers, Gladys and Marcy, the guests on *Oprah*—without having to get involved in any of them. Lately, it's become a little harder to keep a distance, though.

One afternoon, about a week after my first visit to Hannah Ellis, Shelley walks through the door and says, without any other introduction, "I should tell you. I'm going to adopt a baby from Vietnam. I've been trying to find out about his homeland."

Her face is bright, vulnerable, anxious for my response. I look away. Out in the parking lot, the glare of noon has begun to soften. Later in the day, I will get a rush of customers dashing in for bags of rice, or frozen catfish, or chilies. Each time the door opens, it will sweep in some fresh scent of spring. But at this hour, the door stays mostly closed and the air inside remains processed and artificial. Is adoption, then, her reason for coming to my store? Am I, after all, merely a mine for information that some prospective mommy seeks about my homeland? A strange emotion washes over me, one I can only compare to the feeling I experienced, long ago, when I realized a favorite classmate visited my house only because she loved my mother's cooking. I haven't felt hurt in many years, but I recognize the emotion quite easily now.

And so I don't respond as kindly as I could. "Why?" I ask.

The sarcasm in my voice is clear, perhaps even more pronounced than I intended. Her face colors. Her lips purse. She looks away, then back at me, her gaze steady. "I've always wanted a child," she says simply. "And there's a boy in Vietnam who needs a home."

Now I experience a little bit of embarrassment, which I also haven't felt in years.

We talk. I have heard about infertility, of course. You see it every few months on *Oprah,* but like the shows on alcoholism or Alzheimer's, I watch for ten, twenty minutes, then switch it off. In my experience, we worried about getting pregnant, not about *not* getting pregnant. Of course, people failed to have children in Hanoi as well as here. I had a barren aunt, but no one talked about it. My father's cousin left his wife because she couldn't bear a child, and a lot of people considered his actions to be perfectly natural and just. I remember, too, the couple from Lao Cai who lived up the alley. We neighborhood kids solved the mystery of their childlessness by constructing a story even more bizarre: the *husband* and *wife* were actually *brother* and *sister.* I never considered the failure to have a child as anything resembling a tragedy. Love and death and war created tragedy. How could you mourn something that never even existed?

Shelley doesn't use the word *tragedy,* either. She doesn't present herself as a victim, or even as someone deserving of pity. She recites the litany of her experience with a straightforward, almost amused detachment. But the numbers pile on top of each other in what amounts to an avalanche of suffering and bad luck. Five years of trying. Six pregnancies. Six mis-carriages. Two failed surgical procedures. Four doctors. Three fertility clinics. Six rounds of hormones. Hundreds of injections. Thousands of dollars in medical bills for services not covered by insurance. A year spent begging her husband to adopt. A third successful pregnancy for her sis-ter, an event that precipitated her husband's sudden, much appreciated, change of heart. And then, three months of wrangling with adoption agencies, ten hours of interviews with social workers, hundreds of pages of paperwork, eight months of waiting, five drives to Raleigh, three drives to Charlotte, two lost birth certificates, thousands of dollars in fees, and one failed adoption, only weeks before they hoped to leave to pick up a little girl from Europe.

"And then they told me about this little boy in Vietnam," she says in a little sigh of exasperation, as if it's the latest not-so-funny punch line in a never-ending set of pranks designed to keep her from actually having a child. I start to laugh, but the expression in her eyes surprises me. She doesn't look defeated. She looks kind of hopeful. Hopeful without any kind of conviction, but hopeful nonetheless.

"I think you'll get this boy," I stammer. Even as I say it, I'm question-ing myself. How could I know? Why should I care? I can't know. But I do care. I do.

Shelley begins to smile and then she turns away. Her hand goes to her eye and rubs at it. If she's crying, she doesn't want me to know. Then she says, "I brought you something. Hold on." She steps out the door and into the parking lot, then returns a minute later with an armful of books.

I clear some inventory sheets off the counter and she lets the books slide onto the glass. They're all guides to Vietnam. Together, we gaze down at them. "I've been trying to find out about his homeland," she explains, then she motions with her chin. "Take a look." Together, we page through the volumes. With this mountain of factual information to draw our attention, the mood between us lightens. I point at various famous sites. We joke. Shelley has a question for every picture, every page. "Have you been here?" "How far is that?" She pauses often to scrawl notes in the margins or look something up. While she writes, I look at photos of Hanoi, more recent than the ones in *National Geographic*. I feel braver than I did when I looked at the old magazines, and I discover that I enjoy this. One guidebook, *Lonely Planet,* has a whole section of photographs of "the Old Quarter," the streets surrounding my house. We never called our neighborhood "the Old Quarter." The whole city was old, rundown, cramped, and rusty. There's a hazy dawn shot of Hoan Kiem Lake—they call it "the Lake of the Restored Sword"—where my mother did her calisthenics, and one of a woman selling *bún chả,* rice noodles with grilled pork, the fragrance of which I can remember so distinctly that the sterile air in my market seems suddenly quite filled with it. Then I spot a picture of the Dong Xuan Market, forget myself, and laugh.

Shelley looks up. "What?" she asks, as if she fully expects an explanation. I remember the casual interrogations that used to take place between myself and my sister. We felt entitled to information. Thoughts only existed to be shared.

I point my finger at the photo—a line of market women offering their wares—and try to explain. "These ladies," I begin, "they're very rude. Uneducated. When I'm a girl, my mom give me money to go buy bamboo shoots. But when I get there, they hold up their vegetable—it's long, skinny, like a man's you-know-what—and they say, 'Hey, girl! Get some practice on this guy before you meet your husband.' "

Does she have any idea what I'm saying? Apparently so. Shelley grins. "Yeesh. What did you do?"

"I ran away. I know my mom get mad that I don't bring home bamboo shoots for dinner, but I'm too afraid to buy it."

"By that point, you probably weren't in the mood to eat them anyway," Shelley remarks. She looks back down at the picture. "Was it at this market in Hanoi?"

Of course it was, and I'm about to say so, too, but then I remember that I have an old lie to sustain. Most Vietnamese Americans equate northerners with Ho Chi Minh, so for over twenty years I've called myself a southerner. "Saigon," I say. "Wait. I show you." I go back to my refrig-

erators and fill a bag with whole bamboo shoots, then take them back to
Shelley. "Bamboo shoots actually delicious. Forget what I tell you about
those ladies."

She looks at the pale yellow vegetables, long and limp. "I see what you
mean," she says uncertainly. "They're not like those little strips you get in
Chinese food."

"Completely different. Slice them longwise, stir-fry with lots of garlic,
little bit fish sauce. Cook for a long time to make tender. Then add little
bit green onion at the last minute, to make pretty and smell good."

She holds the bag carefully, like a child clutching pet store goldfish.
"I'll cook it tonight," she says firmly, as if she's making a promise.

I'm about to suggest that she add a bit of pork, too, but a phone
rings, muffled somewhere. Shelley sifts through her purse until she finds
it. "Hello? This is Shelley?" She sucks in her breath. "Damn. I forgot.
Okay." She shoves the phone back into her purse, then pulls out her keys.
"My husband's going to be so mad at me," she mumbles, then, becoming
a customer again, asks, "What do I owe you for the bamboo shoots?"

I wave her away. "Don't worry about it."

She smiles and starts to collect her books, then stops. "You know what?
I've got so much work the next few days. You keep them for a while." She
races out the door before I have a chance to say another word.

I walk over to my steam table, pick a Brillo pad out of a bucket of
sudsy water, and begin to scrub at the caked-on grit from the caramelized
catfish I served for lunch. Within moments, a swath of blue-gray foam
spreads across the stainless-steel surface. The table is filthy, but today
I'm impatient. I leave the Brillo on the table, then dunk my hand in the
water and wipe it on my pants. In an envelope in my purse, I find Hannah
Ellis's drawing of my mother. She said she spent five hours completing it.
So much time, and she came up with a mouth that looks too smug. Still,
some mixture of my memory and Hannah Ellis's talent did combine to
create an image that is clearly my mother. When people described her,
they always said she was *xinh,* pretty, not *đẹp,* beautiful. The difference is
not one of degree, as it would be here in America, but of quality. I think
of "beautiful" as smooth and lush, rich, like cream or velvet. My mother,

on the other hand, had a freshness, a lightness to her, a glow that reflected back at you, like sunlight bouncing off water. Somehow, in the shape of the face, the gaze of the eyes, Hannah Ellis managed to capture that.

But, even after three interviews, she hasn't produced a single sketch that looks like My Hoa. Somehow, none of the drawings approaches the quality of single-mindedness that served, in her face, as a clear revelation of personality: the hard set of her mouth, the seriousness of her brow, the concentration in her eyes that, even in the giddiness of play, seemed bent on accomplishment. I know that Hannah Ellis was frustrated, worried that, after all this time, she's lost her gift. Perhaps. Or maybe it's My Hoa's spirit, not wanting me to find her.

She would be twenty-five now, only a few years older than Marcy, which is both interesting and unbearable. We all knew what kind of girl she was, but what kind of woman would she have become? What kind of lover? What kind of mother? So many questions you can ask, but never answer.

5

Shelley

When I reach the office, I pull in next to Martin's car and immediately see that he's in it. We look at each other, not happily, then roll down our windows. "Where are you going?" I ask, my voice all friendly and light, hoping he doesn't know that I've forgotten an appointment with a client. At this moment, I see my boss, not my husband.

"I have a meeting at the registrar of deeds," he says. His face has a look of annoyed resignation, not just that I have let him down, but that I have always let him down. Something has shifted between us lately and, much as I'd like to locate some other cause, I have to mark its beginnings in the morning he agreed to adopt the little boy. These days, we're tense with each other. He complains that I'm slacking off at the job, that the adoption has distracted me. He's right that I'd rather bag basil at the Good Luck Asian Grocery than counsel the bereaved, but I don't agree that I've given him any cause for anger. I could have flown to Europe and tried to win back our little girl, but I didn't. Doesn't that demonstrate the deepest sense of commitment to Martin and our business? But I can't say that.

"I'm not that late," I insist.

Behind his glasses, an eyebrow goes up. His focus on work has become so consuming that he hasn't even taken the time to go through our adoption referral packet. "I'll look at it later," he tells me, but he doesn't. Meanwhile, he has ample time to deal with the funeral home driveways, which, though they've been cracked for three years, he insists on repaving this week. Even at home, he has become businesslike and distant, staying up late at night to go over our accounts and leaving for the office early in the morning. Sometimes, he hardly notices me, and acts as if we're bound only by the tattered professional connection we have at the office. I know we have a problem here, but I'm scared to bring it up. I don't want to make things worse.

"I'm sorry," I mumble.

"Can you try," he says, "to get things right in the future?" I'm too surprised by his tone to answer. And then, before I can say anything at all, he rolls up his window, pulls out, and drives away.

I should rush inside, but I can't move. My head falls back against the headrest. When I feel hurt, it starts in my shoulders, then moves up my neck to my head and settles, hot and throbbing, just behind my ears. Does the person in pain inside the building mean more to Martin than the person in pain inside this car? I remember the night, not long after we got married, when the phone rang while we were making love. It was my mother. We paused, staring at each other like teenagers caught on the couch.

"Shelley?" Answering machines were fairly new then. I felt a momentary panic at the sound of her voice, suddenly soaring, unannounced, across our bedroom.

Martin burrowed his face in my curls, the weight of his body keeping me from leaping out of bed. His voice was quiet, steady, speaking to my mother in the air. "We're not home right now, Margot."

"I thought you'd be home by now."

"We're not," he insisted.

"Where could you be?" my mother continued, thinking aloud.

"We're at the beach. At the mall. We flew to the moon. We're in

Africa . . ." Martin's voice was soft and ticklish, a murmur in my ear. I felt his hand move down, firm and persistent, between my legs. "Scaling Mount Everest. We have a meeting with the president. Shelley's hosting *Saturday Night Live*. She's become a matador."

"Maybe you're at the mall," my mother mused.

"Please hang up." I was fairly begging now.

She seemed to ponder the possibilities for a while. "Well, call me later," she finally said. I heard the phone click off, the brief buzz of the dial tone, then silence. Martin pushed inside me. I laughed and moaned at the same time. I felt Martin's lips against my neck. His hand skimmed beneath the covers, searching for mine. We kept making love. And then, afterward, our skin damp with sweat, he whispered, "I don't want to miss a single day with you."

I had been in the funeral business only a year or so. I had a lot to learn still, but I had learned the most important thing already. This business makes you grateful for the things you have, and grateful to be grateful, too, as if it's some proprietary knowledge that only those of us who see death daily share. How can Martin and I, of all people, have forgotten about that?

It's two-thirty when I get inside the building. Rita hands me a couple of message slips. "York called again for the urn order. Your sister wants you to pick up Keely from school tomorrow so she can get ready for the birthday party. Mr. Sloane's waiting for you in the front receiving room."

"Can you stick this in the fridge?" I set the bamboo shoots on her desk.

"What is that?" she asks. We eye the bag together. I think of Mai, standing in front of the Vietnamese market women, getting an early and utterly baffling lesson in sex.

"Penises," I want to tell her. Instead, I say, "Dinner," then head down the hall.

At this hour, the reception rooms look like yards of empty carpet, devoid of any practical function. We finish all our other business appointments by noon most days and the afternoon events won't begin until five o'clock. Empty, the place looks so forlorn that I have to remind myself that people call ours the prettiest funeral home in Wilmington. That's probably because, unlike some of the newer mortuaries, designed to look like corporate conference centers, our building started out as a private home. In 1912, a Wilmington banker named Thomas Lask constructed it for himself and his family of seven. Martin's grandfather Paolo bought it from the Lask family and converted it into a funeral home in the 1930s, building for himself a smaller private home next door, where Martin and I now live. Except for the Marino and Sons sign, and our oversize parking lot, the building still resembles a private home, antebellum in style with its stately white columns and forest green trim. We get a lot of trick-or-treaters at Halloween. Some kids mistake it for a real house. Some approach on a dare. Most come for the ice-cream cups, which Martin offers to anyone in a costume.

The building hasn't changed much since Paolo bought it. Traditionally, wakes and viewings took place in the living rooms of the families of the deceased, so it made sense to keep the spacious entry hall, grand staircase, and elegant receiving rooms. A few years ago, Martin and I changed the color scheme from reds and golds to more muted blues and mauves, but we considered it an update, not a redesign. We kept the chandeliers, the mahogany furniture, Paolo's portrait over the mantel. I appreciate Paolo, who looks solemn but also faintly confused. The idea that he might have struggled in this profession gives me confidence because it took me a while to feel comfortable here myself.

I step into the front receiving room, which resembles a living room, only more professional, like the waiting area in a bank. We keep the tables empty except for boxes of Kleenex and small stacks of business cards announcing the services of grief counselors and therapists. Mr. Sloane sits in an armchair by the window. In his blue nylon sweat suit, he seems quite virile for a man in his sixties, except that he's hunched over, staring into the space between his legs like someone leaning over the railing of a bridge, contemplating a jump.

"Mr. Sloane," I say. "I have to apologize to you. I'm so sorry." I hold out my hand.

I seem to have startled him and it takes him a moment to reconnect with his surroundings. "No problem," he says. His handshake is firm enough, but automatic.

I take the chair next to his. "How are you doing?" I ask. In our line of work, this is not an idle question.

Mr. Sloane pats his hands forcefully against his legs. "Mrs. Marino, I've made a decision about Sylvia and I need your help."

"I'll help you in any way that I can." I hold my hands in my lap and wait for him to continue. His wife, knowing she had only a few months to live, dictated a fairly detailed set of instructions, including seating arrangements for the funeral and the directive that the organist should play "Be Thou My Vision" just before the service.

Mr. Sloane leans back in the armchair, sighs, smooths a few displaced strands of hair against his head. "You're going to think I'm crazy," he chuckles.

"I doubt that." I've seen it all.

He glances over at me, gauging my possible reaction, then says, "I've decided to bury Sylvia on her stomach."

I nod. Well, it's a new one.

"Do you have a problem with that?"

"I don't suppose so. I'll need to talk with Bennet, who did service on her. He's probably already positioned her on her back." I stand up and glance at my watch. I know very well what time it is, but I want to underline the fact that we have only a few hours until the viewing.

Mr. Sloane looks surprised to see me move so quickly. "No, no. Sit down, Mrs. Marino. We don't have to do it for the viewing. I'm not insane." He pulls my chair a bit closer to his, then motions for me to sit back down. I sit, but on the edge of the chair, folding the pink message slips between my fingers.

Mr. Sloane leans back and repositions his leg, a dusty Nike resting on his knee. There's a stain of sweat around his white undershirt. I think he may have jogged here.

"Do you have kids, Mrs. Marino?"

"Well, no."

His eyes narrow. "That's funny. I thought you had kids. My youngest son went to school with a Marino."

"Martin has two boys from a previous marriage. Abe and Theo."

Mr. Sloane nods. "That's right. Theo Marino."

"Right," I say.

He rubs the tips of his fingers against his stubble-shadowed face. "The thing is, Mrs. Marino, we had three kids. You'll meet them this evening. And you know what was the hardest thing about pregnancy for Sylvia? Sleeping on her side. She simply couldn't do it. I don't know how she made it through those last months, tossing and turning like she did. Miserable. Once the babies were born, she didn't care how much sleep she got, as long as she could sleep on her stomach. I felt so guilty each time I got her pregnant, putting her through that. Poor thing. Can you believe it?"

I shake my head.

Mr. Sloane sets his feet on the ground, leans back in his chair, stares out the window. "Then she got cancer last year. She was a saint. With bone cancer, they say it's like experiencing the agony of childbirth, but for months and months. The doctors gave her painkillers, but she refused them, said they knocked her out." He stops and stares at me. "That's heroic, don't you think?"

"Absolutely."

He nods. "Sylvia didn't complain about anything," he continues, then turns to me and raises a finger. "Except one thing. Guess what?"

"Sleeping?"

He smiles. "Right. In the hospital they made her sleep on her back. Last week, she finally agreed to the painkillers. She knew it was the end. She said, 'Richard, I'm ready.' That was how she said good-bye: 'I'm ready.'" He leans over again, looking down at the floor. His voice grows softer. "She kept talking, though. That was the surprise. She said, 'My stomach. My stomach.' And she moved around this way and that." He shakes his shoulders, a patient imprisoned in bed.

"She didn't want to be on her back," I say.

He nods. "Even when she didn't know anything else, she knew that."

Mr. Sloane turns to me, his eyes expectant.

"Then we'll have to bury her on her stomach," I tell him.

He smiles, his face flushes, then he drops his head and his hands go up to his face. I reach over to the table between us and slide the box of Kleenex closer to him. I don't like to leave a person crying, so I just sit there, gazing at Mr. Sloane's profile. I'm thinking that I have to tell Bennet to turn the body over. I'm thinking about how much this man loved his wife. And I'm thinking about what I'd do, if I had the choice to have children but die at sixty, or to live a long and healthy life, but never have a child. It's silly to even think this way. Martin would say I'm crazy. But I know what I'd choose.

After Mr. Sloane leaves, I run up the stairs to my office. The computer still hums, but the screen's gone blank and a loose ring of cream has settled on the surface of my coffee. On my desk sit two binders, one from York that I use to order register books, urns, and prayer cards. The other gives details on a line of metal caskets we're considering from Messenger. The cremation business has taken off and I'm behind on my urn inventory. The vendors have been e-mailing daily for a decision, so I open the York binder and begin to consider it. I need two new models of urns for pets, an urn for veterans, one for children, and a couple embossed with sprays of flowers, which widowers invariably choose for their wives.

I can't seem to focus on any of it, so I'm relieved by the distraction of Rita buzzing. "Shelley? It's a lady with an accent, says her name is Mai."

I pick up the phone. "Mai?" Did I forget my wallet?

"Hey," she says. "Seems like you like to cook."

"Well, yeah."

I hear the *ching-ching-ching* of a cash register. "Cash or credit?" she asks. Then, "How about you help me cook sometime, I teach you make Vietnamese food for your kid."

For *my* kid? No one has ever called him *my* kid. The adoption agency calls him my "referral." My mother and sister call him "the Vietnamese baby." Martin doesn't call him anything. So, *my kid*? These words, coming from a woman I hardly know, feel like my first confirmation that I could really be his mother.

"Sure," I say. A wave of happiness rushes through me, as powerful and unreliable as a chemical high. "When?" I want to sustain it.

"Tomorrow too soon? Fridays I make dish called *bún thang*. Noodle with all kind meat and vegetable. Real lot of work. You free?"

"What time?" My calendar sits on my desk, but I don't check it.

"Gotta start by seven in the morning. Maybe too early for you."

"No. Seven A.M. It's okay."

After we hang up, I open the calendar, already plotting how to get out of any appointments on Friday morning. But I'm lucky. I'm free. Then, before I forget completely, I make a note to pick up my niece. And then I phone down to Bennet to tell him to turn the body over.

At twenty to five, I'm pulling on my jacket for the Sloane viewing when someone knocks. "Shelley?" Martin opens the door tentatively, poking his head in. In the old days—last week—he would have walked right in.

"Hey," I say. I button my jacket and, somewhat self-consciously, shake up my hair, which has gone limp in the heat. Our marriage is contracting. We learn less about each other every day. The brief joy I felt in my conversation with Mai has faded, predictably, to the tense uncertainty that colors my life these days. I walk over and pull the door open for him.

Martin stands there, chin lowered, eyes gazing toward mine. The expression on his face is cool, but not unfriendly. "Mr. Sloane said you got him through a bad spell this afternoon."

I wave it off. "I just listened." Still, I'm pleased to be an ace funeral director again. Martin smiles at me. Despite all that's passed, I never forget that he is, essentially, a generous man. On the day I found out that my sister, Lindi, was pregnant with her third child, Martin found me in the garden, trying to shove eight dozen bulbs into a tulip bed the size of a bathtub.

"Hey," he said. Lindi had called to tell him that I knew.

I stabbed at the dirt with my trowel. "I am so sick of feeling sorry for myself."

Martin took my hand, gardening glove and all, and pulled me up, then held me. "It's okay," he whispered, smoothing down my hair.

"It is not okay." I stepped away from him. Would I always feel so desolate? "It is not okay!" I screamed. "At least admit it."

Martin winced. His hands dropped to his side and his gaze settled on me with the desperate expression of a person watching a loved one drowning. Then he closed his eyes, and when he opened them again, he said the one thing I'd least expected. "Shelley." He sighed. "Let's just adopt."

Husbands can surprise you, even after many years. And you can surprise yourself, too, by the depth of your love for them. Now, without thinking, I slide my hand around his neck and pull him inside my office, pushing against him until his body shuts the door, reminding him that I'm his wife. We haven't touched for days. He smells of Dial and sweat. He holds me, tight. And then, suddenly awkward with each other, we let go. He walks to the window and looks down at the cars filling our lot for the viewing. I pull a lipstick and compact out of my desk and check my makeup. I think we're both embarrassed, but I feel warmth between us, too.

"I want to ask you for something," I say.

He turns around to look at me. "What?"

Actually, I could ask for many things right now. Attention. Kindness. Camaraderie. And, how long has it been since we made love? But I will only ask for this. "Tonight," I say, "can you look at the baby's pictures?"

I'm surprised to see how long it takes for him to connect "baby's pictures" with *that* baby and, once he does, his body sags. He lifts his hands to his face and rubs hard, like someone trying to warm himself. Then, he sighs. "How about after dinner? Would that be okay?"

I nod, probably too enthusiastically. We are two people, each on our own deserted island. But, for the first time in so many days, we are signaling to each other. "Tonight's great," I tell him.

He grins, but his eyes look pitiful. Then, giving me this casual wave, as if we've just been discussing vacation plans or something, he disappears out the door.

I walk to the window. Down in the parking lot, cars have begun to pull in for the viewing. Rita stands at the bottom of the stairs, greeting the mourners. After a moment, Martin appears beside her, then reaches out to shake somebody's hand.

After dinner, we clear the remains of our sautéed bamboo shoots and prepare to talk at the kitchen table. I try to be hopeful. This table offers happy memories of our life together. We found it in an antiques store near Asheville a few months after we got married. It's a yellow Formica, with a scrabbly white design running across the top and four dented yellow chairs. At the same store, Martin discovered a 1962 edition of *The Joy of Cooking* and on the drive home we decided to bake every cake in the book. It took us a year, but we baked the lot of them. Forty-seven cakes. Sunshine cake. Tutti-frutti cake. Burnt sugar cake. Fig spice cake. When I look at this table, I think, So many cakes! That's part of the reason I've put on fifteen pounds since my wedding. When you're first in love, you don't care. After that? Well, there are moments when cake offers consolations a husband cannot.

Martin has brewed a pot of tea and poured us each a mug. I push the pot and the mugs to the edge of the table, away from my fat folder of documents. I don't want a drop of anything touching my pictures of my boy.

Martin's agreement to look at the referral signifies some openness, however slight. He runs a finger across the top of the folder and this simple willingness to touch it gives me hope that he could one day become enthusiastic. "When did it arrive?" he asks. He's just making conversation, but I'm reluctant to let him know how long I've waited to show him.

"A few days ago." Nine. What's the difference, really?

I page through the documents: immunization forms, medical forms, documentation of abandonment. I have both the photocopies of the Vietnamese originals and translations of each page into English. The baby's pictures sit in a small manila envelope. Someone wrote "Photograph: Nguyen Hai Au" in block letters on the outside. I touch my finger to the script, hold it up for Martin to see. "That's his name," I tell him. Whoever abandoned the baby tucked a slip of paper into his clothes with the name "Hai Au" on it. "Nguyen," according to Carolyn Burns, is so common in that country that it's just a Vietnamese way of saying "John Doe."

Martin raises his eyebrows, nods with interest, as if I've just shown him some impressive calligraphic rendering in the latest issue of *Discover*.

I add, "I don't know how to pronounce it yet."

"Let's see the pictures." He gestures with his chin toward the envelope.

It's harder than I expected to pull out the photographs and hand them over. There are only two, one of him as an infant and one, taken a year later, when he is pulling himself up the side of a crib. I've only looked at them maybe three or four times myself, anxious to keep the experience fresh, afraid that, as with the photos of Sonya, too much viewing might jinx things. Martin takes the first photo by the corner, sets his fingers to his glasses, as if that will help him see it. I can't read the expression on his face. I cried the first time I saw it. That's too much to hope for now, so I just watch him. Martin gazes at my little one lying on the mat. The baby's arms spread slightly away from his body. His head rests against a small blue pillow. He looks dazed, but interested. He's only a few weeks old, so close, still, to the womb, but cut off from it twice already—once during birth and once when she, whoever she was, let him go. Even after so few glimpses, I've come to know the fluff of his hair, the curve of his chin, his eyes, dark as blueberries, staring out at me. I would like to be the air blowing softly against his cheek.

Martin looks down at the picture. "He's cute," he says. "Very cute."

After he's gone through the pictures, the official forms, and the documents that need filling out and signing, we linger at the kitchen table, the contents of the referral packet spread out in front of us like the map for an adventure he hesitates to go on. Martin idly pages through the adoption agency information manual. I stand above him, digging through the medical document envelope, searching for the page that discloses how the baby tested positive for anemia, but not for hepatitis or HIV.

Our business phone rings and Martin, who's on call tonight, goes to the counter and answers it. "Marino and Sons." Then, "Hey, Mill." It's Millicent Tweedy, the head nurse at New Hanover's ICU. "Okay. I'll be there in a little while."

"Who?" I ask when he hangs up. It's a conditioned response after all these years. I find the baby's medical report and pull it out to give to Martin.

He stands at the counter, one hand on the back of his neck, the other making notes. From behind, his body looks thin and less substantial. He says, "A woman named Myra Kapner. She belongs to the synagogue. Heart attack. I need to let the rabbi know."

He leaves messages on the office phones for Bennet and Albert, asking them to add this case to tomorrow's schedule. He calls Rabbi Solomon at home. Tomorrow's Friday, so we'll have to hurry to have the burial before their Sabbath starts at dusk.

Even when he's finished, Martin doesn't come back to the table. He stands by the telephone, folding and unfolding the piece of paper.

I lay the document in front of his chair at the table, then sit back down across from it. "What?" I want to know.

Martin sighs. I see it in his shoulders. "I know this has to be hard on you." It's the kind of thing that someone says when they're about to make it harder.

"What?"

He turns around and walks back to the table. The look of pain on his face is something I've never even seen before. "I don't have enough love left to give to another person."

I try to laugh. "Love makes love," I say.

He shakes his head. "Okay, not love. Worry. What is parenthood besides love and worry?"

I feel like some huge metal crate has crashed into my skull. "Are you telling me something new here?"

His fingers drift across the papers on the table. "I just don't think I can handle a baby, Shelley," he says. "I've given it a lot of thought."

"Are you saying you don't want any kid at all?"

He stares down at his hand. "I know how much this means to you," he says. "I was really trying, you know."

"What is *trying?*" I demand, forcing him to look up at me. "What is *trying* about jerking your wife around?"

Martin at this moment looks the way our clients sometimes look if they have lost loved ones in the past few hours. Their eyes are wild, disoriented, jerking here and there as if they might find some better truth up there on the wall, or through that doorway, or in the empty shadows of their hands. Myra Kapner's family probably look like that as they make their lonely trek from the ICU to the parking garage. It's one thing to know, intellectually, that someone has died. It's something else entirely to believe it.

I leave Martin in the kitchen, eyes on the table, searching for what *he's* lost: our old and comfortable childless life, unchanged and unchanging. My husband has grown brittle. What would I have done, all those weeks ago when I gave up Sonya, if I had known that Martin's flailing would lead to this? Would I have gotten on that plane and left him here to fend for himself? I walk upstairs and get in bed, curl under the covers and stare out the window into the magnolia I planted the year that I moved in here. In the darkness, the stiff wide leaves stand out against the sky like the hulls of little boats. I imagine I'm underwater, looking up at a whole crowded regatta sailing over my head, swimmers and revelers and sailors with muscles and coppery tans. Do all of us feel this way, that life must be happier for everyone else?

Someone once told me that people reveal everything essential about themselves when you first meet them. The problem, of course, is that you can't easily distinguish the important details from the insignificant ones. Martin, too, revealed everything, but it's taken me all these years to figure out which details mattered.

I was a counselor at Camp Merry Acres and Martin's two boys were my campers. Every Tuesday and Thursday afternoon, the whole camp went to the beach. On those days, Martin would show up around two, then spend the next couple of hours watching his boys out in the water. At first, I thought he was old (he was thirty-two and I was only twenty), lonely, and goofy looking in his business shirt and shiny shoes. Why would he spend his afternoons at such a hot and aimless occupation? He looked so awkward, shuffling over the dunes, settling himself on what looked like a guest towel. Often, he wore a tattered green baseball cap and used it to fan himself. At other times, he held a section of newspaper over his head, which made him look like a very big camper sitting under a very small tent. Sometimes, in the heat, his glasses would begin to slide down his face and he would take them off and squint down toward the bright water like someone unsure of what he was seeing. He looked uncomfortable but determined to stay. I'd grown tired of the other counselors, so I walked over one day to talk to him.

Abe and Theo were seven and six then. They stood in waist-high water, singing loudly and performing some kind of frenetic dance. The water was calm as a bathtub. Abe stepped out a little deeper and did a neat somersault. Theo held his fingers to his nose, bent over, and pushed his head beneath the surface. He disappeared for a second, then one foot shot straight up from the water and the other came out, kicking sideways. Finally, his head emerged, sputtering. "Not bad," Martin called out to him. "Give it another shot."

Theo tried again, with only marginal success.

"You've got great kids," I remarked. I had heard that he was divorced and I felt sorry for him, being a single dad and all. His ex-wife had moved to Florida, so he was pretty much on his own as a parent. His kids were terrific, though, and I thought he should know.

Martin turned toward me. The expression on his face told me he knew already. "Aren't they?" he asked, not appearing to feel sorry for himself at all. Close up, he looked amused and fairly content. He had skin that was boyishly soft for a dad, and large, coffee-colored eyes that now settled on me. I'd just come back from spending my junior year in Scotland, and one of the things I'd decided over there was that I wouldn't hate my body anymore. It's awkward, though, to stand in front of a strange man in nothing but a Speedo. I dug my toes through the hot sand and brought my hand up to my ear, which served to cover one breast. Abe yelled, "Dad!" and Martin turned his eyes away.

I followed his gaze out to the water and watched the boys. It would have been a good moment to walk away, but I didn't. I wanted him to look at me again.

Martin leaned back, resting his body on his elbows. His eyes remained on the boys, but he asked, "Which beaches have you been to?"

· As a conversation starter, it was kind of weird, but I wanted to answer. I sat down a few feet away from him. For several seconds, the sand stung the backs of my legs, then it eased. I said, "Myrtle Beach, of course. I've been to the Outer Banks. Biloxi. Those are the ones in this country. Then, I was in Scotland for my junior year last year. I went to this town called Arbroath. On the coast."

He looked at me with more interest now. "So, you're an adventurer," he said, a touch of admiration in his voice.

"I don't know about that," I said, but I was secretly delighted.

"Which beach was your favorite?"

I gazed down the slope of golden sand to the water. The beach had the soft curves of a body lying languidly in the sun. "This place is as beautiful as any of them," I told him. "It's so wide, and the sand is so fine. I love the colors of the ocean here."

Out in the water, the boys chased each other in circles, drifting farther from the shore. "Theo. Abe! Come back in toward me," their father called, his voice casual but slightly urgent. It occurred to me that he had come here to lifeguard and, though I felt the slightest tinge of annoyance—that was my job, wasn't it?—his nervousness about his kids struck me as sweet. Abe started an awkward crawl back toward the beach. Theo followed with a dog paddle. When they'd reached a safer distance from the shore, he looked at me again. "So, Wrightsville Beach is your favorite?"

He didn't sound surprised or disparaging, just curious to know. I took a handful of sand and salted my leg. Somehow, talking to this dad about it, my months in Scotland suddenly felt like an adventure. His interest in me made me interested in myself. "I wouldn't say that," I told him. "My favorite would be that beach in Scotland. Arbroath." One weekend, near the end of my time in Edinburgh, I took the bus to Arbroath and rented a room in a little bed and breakfast on the North Sea. The room didn't even have a window. A storm came up just after I got there and I spent the afternoon curled up in bed reading *Fat Is a Feminist Issue,* the book that changed my life that year. Later, I ran through the rain and got myself a take-out dinner from the fish and chips shop across the street. For two whole days, I felt shaky with nervousness and intoxicated by the thrill of being alone. Although I'd lived in Scotland for nearly seven months, my junior year abroad had been heavily managed by a team of administrators from the States. That weekend marked my first hesitant attempt at solo travel. I'd gotten the idea from Simon, a guy in my Russian literature class who had journeyed through Africa and Europe carrying nothing but his passport, a few hundred British pounds, and a knapsack no bigger than a pillow. Simon and I had endured the most relentless days of March together, lying naked beneath his Indian-print bedspread, smoking pot. With the rhythmic chanting of Sufi music in the background, Simon told me about the hash in Marrakech, the hash in Athens, the hash in Nice. Simon's stories, combined with the pot, the Sufi music, and his little goatee, had made that dorm room feel like the most exotic place I'd ever visited.

By the end of March, when the tips of purple crocuses finally started popping up in the muddy gardens around Charlotte Square, I'd grown sick of Simon. For such a worldly guy, he was surprisingly provincial about sex, and I discovered that my capacity to listen to drug tales could only last a month. I dumped him then, but I couldn't stop imagining Cairo and Calcutta and Nice. By the time I went to Arbroath, I considered it a trial run for my real adventure. After graduation, I would work and save my money, then I'd go. Anywhere I wanted, for as long as the money held out, with only a knapsack the size of a pillow. This trip would divide my youth from the rest of my life.

Martin took off his hat and fanned himself. His dark, thick hair lay flat against his head and formed little sweaty ringlets around his ears. He didn't look old at all, actually, for a dad. "Arbroath," he said, testing the word on his tongue. "Tell me about it."

I first saw the Arbroath beach the morning after the storm. "It wasn't beautiful," I remembered. "It was rocky and narrow and so cold that no one ever swam there. But the ocean looked like something out of a movie. Big, crashing waves. That was water you could drown in."

His eyes were on his boys and, though I wanted him to look at me, I didn't doubt that he was listening. He squinted out at the ocean, using the hat to shield his eyes. "You liked that?"

"Well, yeah, I did. I like drama. But there was something else." I hadn't told anyone. Whom would I have told? My mother had shown her interest in Scotland by sitting on the couch one evening and paging through my photo album, asking questions like, "Was it great?" and "Did you just love it?" My sister, Lindi, who'd spent her own junior year in Spain, responded to everything I described by saying, "Oh, yeah, that happened to me, too." After my first week or so back, I'd stopped talking about Scotland altogether.

It's odd how you can tell things to strangers you'd never think to tell the ones you love. With this dad listening to me, I kept talking. "Between the road and the beach was a concrete seawall covered with graffiti. I felt like I was reading someone's diary. One spot said, 'Poor Misty died here. Lord, bless her up in puppy heaven.' "

The words sounded so stupid that I stopped, but he had a grin on his face, as if he found Misty interesting, too. I continued. "It was all so intimate. A whole chunk of writing looked like Arabic. Another chunk said, 'Where's the jobs? Where's the jobs?' And one said, 'Julia, please forgive me!' I must have walked for miles, just reading this stuff. It was crazy. I'd taken a four-hour bus ride to get to that beach, and most of the time I was there, I had my back to the ocean."

Martin said, "There's a whole story there."

"What?"

" 'Julia, please forgive me.' "

I nodded, suddenly exhilarated. His curiosity about my life felt almost unbearably alluring.

At that moment, out in the shallows, Theo yelled, "Dad, watch me!" Martin glanced at me, almost as if to make sure I wouldn't disappear, and then, returning to his son, his face opened into the most radiant smile. Over all these years, I've remembered that smile as a marker of the moment I first began to love him. I believed I had taken in all the most salient facts about him—that he was attractive, curious, interesting, kind, and a devoted father, too. But I failed to focus on a fact that was just as revealing: No other parent had felt it necessary to sit on the beach and keep an eye on their kids. The sense of anxiety he revealed that day has grown over the years, and now it's breaking him.

6

Xuan Mai

Cooking is violent. I slice through the flesh of chickens, crack open eggs, chop beautiful vegetables into tiny pieces. Destruction, then re-creation. Again and again. It's the most valuable thing that I do with my life, this nourishing of people. I imagine my sister, my relatives, and my childhood friends alone in their kitchens on the other side of the world, slicing and chopping and whisking and frying, making food for other people, just like I do. If only in my own mind, cooking gives me a bond with them. It's a solitary and precious thing in my life, so I'm rather surprised by myself for inviting someone else to join me. But after all these years, I guess I'm ready for something new.

At a few minutes before seven A.M., I pull my van in right by my door. The rain is coming down in dense sheets of water, so even the dash from the van leaves me drenched. Inside, I shake off my wet raincoat, switch on the lights, then the fan. On a day like today, it's all I can do to keep the mildew from racing up the walls. My watch says 6:54. The clock over the noodle aisle says 6:59. Other than my van outside, there's only a single green car parked on the far side of the lot. Maybe she won't show after all, which would come as a relief. I don't know if we have anything else to talk about. Those few conversations may have been flukes, actually. I haven't really talked with anyone since I came to this country. Even when I lived with Khoi in San Francisco, we didn't talk much, or we tried to talk and found ourselves going in circles, then finally gave up on it. Here in Wilmington, I don't talk, either. I interact, of course, with Marcy, Gladys, my customers, and delivery drivers, but that's just exchanging information, entirely different from what I used to do in Hanoi with my sister, Lan, my parents, my friends. On winter evenings, Lan and I would lie together under the blankets, feeling too cold to sit up and read but too awake to go to sleep. We would talk then, earnestly, but heedlessly, too, sometimes listening and sometimes not. The topics didn't matter; lying there whispering in the dark gave comforts that I didn't even know I needed. In fact, it wasn't until years later, observing Gladys and Marcy on their good days, that I realized how much I missed that kind of aimless conversation.

A tapping at the glass makes me turn around. Shelley, in a yellow rain jacket, stands outside, peering through the door. With all that hair hidden beneath the folds of her hood, her face looks scared and lonely. She gives a sad little wave.

"Where you park?" I ask as I let her in. I can only see my van and that one green car on the far side of the lot.

She pulls off her jacket, freeing her hair amid a shower of raindrops. "That's my Honda," she says, gesturing toward the green car. She pushes a few wet curls off her face, then holds the dripping jacket in her hand, unsure of what to do with it.

I take the jacket and hang it on the hook next to my own wet raincoat. "Why you park so far away?"

She smooths down her shirt. "I was just watching the sky," she says.

Outside the window, the sky is gray. Like the sidewalk. Gray. She looks like she might cry. "You sure you want to do this today?" I ask.

"Of course," she says.

In the kitchen, I fill the electric kettle and plug it in while Shelley wanders around, looking at everything. There's not much to see. The room is an attachment to the original building, a shed with a metal roof. Before heading home every night, I spend nearly an hour scouring dried food off the pots and pans, wiping grease from the counters, sweeping bits of raw broccoli and onion skin off the floor. The health department gave me a 99.5 percent rating. I should have gotten 100, but the overhead light is too far from the stove and the landlord won't move it. Here's another thing the landlord won't do: replace the roof. On days like today, the rain comes down like rocks crashing over your head. I almost have to yell. "I only got Vietnamese coffee," I tell her, pulling from a drawer two metal coffee filters that fit over the tops of glasses. "I don't got no Mr. Coffee coffee or anything like that."

"That's fine." Shelley rubs her hands together as if she's cold.

It's 7:06. We wash our hands and put on plastic caps. Shelley's hair fills her cap like the foam in a cushion. I open the door of the refrigerator and pull out a steamed pork sausage. It's big as a loaf of bread, made in Westminster, California, but produced in the Vietnamese style, with a thin layer of banana leaf around it to keep it moist and fresh. I unwrap the leaves, letting loose the fragrance of banana and exposing the pale pink meat within. "You got to cut this very thin," I tell her. I pull a knife from a drawer and demonstrate on a cutting board, slicing a few discs of the sausage, then laying those on top of each other and cutting down through the middle of them, again and again, until I have a pile of tiny matchstick pieces.

She picks up the knife and goes to work. I pull a bag of bean sprouts out of the refrigerator and carry them to the sink to wash. Shelley and I stand only a few feet apart at different ends of the counter. She asks, "Who taught you to cook?"

"My mother," I say, feeling vaguely sheepish. I will never be the cook my mother was, able to know, intuitively, that roasting a chili over flames will give your broth a smoky flavor, or that searing a chicken will hold in the juices. I never make up anything new, like she did. I just try to follow her technique and remember her recipes. "She could really teach you how cook for your kid."

I glance at Shelley. She's stopped cutting.

"What's funny?" I ask.

" 'My kid.' " But her words come out unevenly. They sound cracked and forced, which is how I realize that she's crying. I keep my eyes on my bean sprouts, trying to figure out what to do. In my life, I've witnessed people crying of course, but I can't remember what I did about it. You get out of practice. Who cried? My mother never cried. My father cried when my mother died, and I held his hand, but I can't do that with Shelley. Khoi never cried (I cried, and he did what he could—which wasn't much—to soothe me). My sister cried when her husband Tan went off to war, but she tried to be stoic about that. Later, when he died, she wouldn't let us near her. I'm sure I had friends cry over broken hearts, or failed exams, but my mind goes blank as I try to recall what I did, if anything, to help them.

For a long time, we say nothing. Shelley pulls some tissues out of her purse and cries into them, the sausage forgotten. I shake the bean sprouts in the colander and let them drain, then start on the egg pancakes. The sound she makes—a faint, rhythmic gulping—reminds me of the last time I cried around Bo. It was only days before Khoi planned to leave Vietnam and I had decided against going with him. My father had insisted that, at nineteen, I was old enough to make my own decision and, after vacillating for weeks, I felt surprisingly confident that I'd made the right choice. Still, I cried. Bo didn't try to comfort me directly, but he refused to abandon me, either. While I lay on my bed and wept, he sat at the table, taking apart a broken clock, and talking. Nothing that he said related to my decision, and I remember understanding, even through my tears, exactly what he was doing. He talked about his boyhood, his parents, my mother, a man at the veterans' center who made toys out of old tin cans. None of it mattered, but it helped.

I shake some fish sauce into the eggs and whisk the mixture until yoke and white meld together. Then I pour my first thin pancake into the pan and begin to talk. "Vietnamese cooking, you got think about everything. Not just taste. You got think about how the food look together on the plate. How it smell. You got mix texture. Like, soft eggs with crunchy bean sprouts. The color red with the color green. Salty and sweet. You need contrast."

I wish I didn't sound like such an idiot in English but, once I've started, I find it fairly easy to keep going. I talk. I fry pancakes. When bubbles form across the yellow skin, I prick them with a fork. A rich and mellow fragrance begins to fill the room. I talk about seasoning, cooking times, sugar. I talk about soaking noodles, boiling noodles, heating wet noodles in the microwave to soften them. I finish the pancakes and peel three pounds of shrimp. I discuss different ways you can cut an onion, depending on the dish it will go in. I talk and talk. I fill the air with every-thing I've ever known or imagined about food. And my father's method seems to work. Shelley cries until she's had enough, and then she stops. Without saying anything, she gets up, washes her hands, and goes back to her task. She cuts, turning the entire sausage into tiny pieces. Her sau-sage sticks are more perfectly regular than mine have ever been, a pink haystack of meat at the edge of her cutting board. I pause to say, "You do good," because I really do admire her skill.

She lifts a hand and uses it to push her cap up her forehead. Her eyes are red and puffy but clear now. She smiles at me. "I never knew that microwave trick with the noodles."

I shrug. "I learn it on *Iron Chef*."

At the other end of the counter, the coffee has finished dripping through the filters. I've already poured the sweetened condensed milk into the bottom of the glasses and now I stir it to mix it in. "Here," I say gently, handing her a glass. She looks calm now, but no more cheerful. "You okay?" I ask.

She nods, stretches her long legs. Her face is grim. "My husband's backing out of the adoption."

"Completely?"

"Completely."

"Why?"

She takes a sip of coffee, then says, "He's been having a hard time lately. I guess he thinks a child would just push him over the edge."

I say, "He got a hard job."

She looks at me impatiently. "People manage," she says. Then, rub-bing the back of her wrist against her swollen eyes, she adds, "I don't have any more sympathy. I'm so angry. I just keep thinking that I'm too young to give up on being happy." The words come out frankly and without hesitation, as if the two of us have confided in each other for years.

I stare down at my coffee, unsure of how to respond. How can I talk about happiness and grief? Would she expect that of anyone? Or does she just expect it of me?

Shelley lifts her glass to take another sip, then asks, "What matters in life, really? In my business, we end up wondering about that. I want to value the things I can appreciate at the end of my life. Money doesn't matter, ultimately. Status means very little. The most basic things matter. Love matters. Family matters. Happiness matters. Mai, don't you think we're entitled to that?"

I look up. She holds my gaze. Is happiness a right? Did my mother think about happiness when she ran from her village, afraid for her life? Did my father think about happiness when he became a soldier for the revolution? Actually, they did. My father always said that they fought the war for selfish reasons—food on the table, a better life for themselves and their children. The Communist Party used the words *freedom* and *independence,* but it also used the word *hạnh phúc.* Happiness. People fought the war for happiness, too. In all these years, I've forgotten that. I say to Shelley, "We are," and then, to my surprise, I add one minor but revealing truth about myself. "For long time," I tell her, "I don't think about happiness much."

Shelley smiles at me. Despite all the tears, her face is radiant. "Here," she says, standing up. "Let me show you something." She lifts her purse, which has been hanging on the back of her chair, and pulls an envelope out of the side pocket. From inside, she takes out a photo and shows it to me. "This is my son," she says.

I'm not sure what she means. She looks calm, though, holding the photo in her hand and waiting for me to take it. I wipe my hands against my pants, then lift the photo by the edges. We look at it together. A baby lies on a rattan mat on the floor. The mat has a red design running through it, and there, behind the child's shoulder, I see part of the character for "double happiness" in old Chinese. I can't read Chinese, but any

Vietnamese will recognize that word. Every Vietnamese has sat on a mat like that one, with the very same inscription, the fibers brown and pliable, retaining the vaguest smell of the fields. Every Vietnamese baby has lain on a mat like that, swaddled in quilts, staring up at mother, brother, family, ceiling, sky. Happiness, it says. *Double* happiness.

"What his name?" I ask. He's a pretty little boy. Pale skin. Plenty of hair.

"I can't pronounce it." She turns the picture over to show me the name written on the back. Nguyen Hai Au.

"Hai Au," I tell her, carefully splitting the syllables: Hi-Oh. "It's a nice name. Unusual. It's a seabird."

Shelley stares down at the picture. "Hai Au," she says, trying out the sounds on her tongue.

We finish cooking. Shelley cuts the green onions and shreds the boiled chicken while I heat several gallons of broth and arrange the ingredients for the steam table. I prepare a couple of servings of *bún thang* for Shelley to take home, then walk her out to the front door. She seems relaxed now, almost content. I'd forgotten this feeling of camaraderie with another person.

When we come within sight of the window at the front of the store, Shelley stops. A man in a blue raincoat is sitting on the sidewalk, leaning against the window. His knees press against his chest, and his head has fallen to the side, as if he's passed out. Shelley goes to the window and looks down at him. I've only met him once, years ago at a funeral, but I suspect it's her husband.

"You think he want to eat some noodles?" I ask.

Shelley holds her hand against the glass. "I don't think so," she tells me. For a long time, she just stands there, unwilling to step outside.

7

Shelley

Martin walked to the market from our house, which is two miles, at least. I wouldn't mind, on a nice day, walking there past the sweeping lawns of Forest Hills, but on a rainy day it's ridiculous. Martin's dust-colored jeans have turned a muddy brown, his sneakers leak puddles, and water runs in streams down his rain jacket and into the cushions of the car. A rolled-up and water-soaked magazine sticks out of his jacket pocket like some kind of talisman that has shown no effect. I can hear him shivering and I reach over to turn off the fan so he doesn't get sick. The air in the car feels close, heavy with moisture, like the inside of a cloud. Out on Oleander, the rain has picked up again. The storm gutters are overflowing and the car slides through the patches of high water with a *whoooosh*. I turn down Country Club Drive, keeping my eyes on the road. Hanoi in the summer often gets sudden, torrential rains. Does it ever look like this?

"Why did you walk?" I ask, as if I'm merely curious.

"I'm trying to hold things together," he tells me, as if that explains it. He leans his elbows against his knees, rubbing his face with his hands. At some point last night, I heard him drive off in the Lincoln to make the retrieval at the hospital. He never came to bed, so I suppose he stayed up all night. That would explain why he hasn't gone in to work, but why the walk in the rain? And where are his glasses? I imagine them bobbing forlornly down some storm drain on Forest Hills Drive, but they could, of course, be lying forgotten on the kitchen table.

"I just want to explain what I meant last night." His voice sounds shaky, like something held together with spit and Scotch tape.

"Will 'explaining' still come down to you refusing to adopt this baby?" I ask.

"There are things I've never told you. Things that might help you understand."

"Will you still refuse to adopt?"

"Well, yes."

"Don't worry about it," I say. Really, I've heard enough already. I reach my hand over and pat his knee. I have rarely seen Martin so rattled, and never so rattled over me. Once, not that many years ago, he told me that I make his life happier, less heavy, easier to bear. I don't know exactly how he's feeling now, but I know that I'm not making anything any easier. As for me, I feel only a kind of distant concern, the way I would feel toward anyone who had just trudged two miles through a storm with bad footgear and no umbrella. Otherwise, I'm detached. Martin's decision pushed me toward mine. And watching Mai cook and manage her store, all alone—and in a foreign country, too—helped me to see the kinds of challenges that people overcome. If Mai could build an entirely new life for herself, maybe I could, too.

"His name is Hai Au," I say, trying to pronounce it exactly like Mai did. "The baby. Hai Au. It's a seabird."

Martin doesn't seem to have heard me. Out of the corner of my eye, I see him run his hands through his wet hair. Flecks of water spray against my cheek. "I'm burned out," he says. "I can't start all over again. I can't take any more grief. I can't even take the possibility of grief."

He seems to hope that once I understand his feelings, I will come around, but he should never ask for that. There is something immoral about asking a person to give up anything as essential as having a child.

Would you ask someone to give up their health? Their vision? The possibility of joy?

"Shelley? You don't really care, do you?"

If this is the time to reveal information, then I'll do that. "I could have flown to Bratislava. For Sonya. The mother was willing to meet with me."

He looks at me. "What do you mean?"

"I didn't go because you needed me here," I tell him. And then, because I can't resist, I add, "I gave up that baby for you." In a sense, it doesn't matter now. He doesn't want a child in any case. But, still, I want him to know.

The air feels so moist that I could almost believe the walls of the car were porous. Martin says, "I'm sorry." His voice is quiet and gentle. I believe him, too, but I need more now. My thoughts return to Hai Au, the little seabird. I hope that he is dry and warm over there in Vietnam. For the first time in so long, I feel light, almost weightless, relieved of the burden of convincing Martin to come along with me. How silly, I think, that I took so long to figure it out. "The choice is yours," I tell him. "I'm adopting this baby. You can either adopt him with me or not."

Martin says nothing. We reach the corner of Market Street and I stop at a red light. In front of us, the cars passing through the intersection are only hazy shadows in the rain. Without their headlights, they'd disappear altogether. Next to me, Martin shifts in his seat, causing his raincoat to squeak as it rubs against the wet upholstery. His prunish hands, pale and bloated, rest motionless on his knees. I almost feel sorry for him.

"You talk like you're adopting a puppy," he says. "You promise that you'll be the one to feed it and take it out for walks. But a baby doesn't work that way, Shelley."

This reminder that he's a parent and I am not wipes out any potential for sympathy I might have had. Perhaps he's purposefully trying to hurt me. If so, it would be a first. In our years together, there are lines we've never crossed. But that was long ago, before this.

Lightning flashes across the tops of the trees and, a moment later, I hear the thunder break. My voice brims with a confidence I don't yet feel. I say, "I know how a baby works." And then I jump. "What I mean is, if you don't adopt this baby with me, I'm leaving you."

We drive the rest of the way home without speaking. The damp air feels steamy. Now that I've said it, I don't feel angry anymore. Instead, I feel relieved, and exhausted, too, as if I've accomplished some despicable but necessary task. I pull into our driveway, bringing the car as close to the kitchen door as I can get. "Put your wet clothes in the sink and I'll stick them in the wash," I say, needing to hang on to some reminder of our domestic life together.

Martin stares straight ahead, toward the line of live oaks that stand like guards along the back of our property. When he finally speaks, his voice strains from the effort of trying to control himself. "When did you stop seeing me as the man you loved and start seeing me as some tool you needed to get a baby?"

I tell him the truth: "I never did." He turns to look at me, anger and despair mottling that precious face. "Why can't you believe that I could love you and need a baby, too?" I ask.

Now he's crying, which is the worst thing I've witnessed, maybe ever. And the sorrow spreads through the close car like some airborne disease. Until this morning, my desire to have a child has consumed me. Now that I've made my decision, however, I feel nothing but pain, and I realize that this single moment will affect our lives forever.

I reach out my hand to him, but he pulls away. This is not a grief that we can share.

"I just want to make sure everything's in order," I tell Carolyn Burns on the phone. Somehow, sensing Martin's hesitation, I haven't been pestering my agency as much as I used to. Now, though, I have no reason to hold back.

"Terrific," she says. It's a professional response, not an emotional one, but at least it's something positive for a change. Over the next twenty minutes, we go through everything: plane tickets, hotel reservations, how many forms I'll have to have notarized before my departure. "And your husband won't be joining you, will he?"

"Right," I tell her, which is true. "We've decided that I'll travel on my own." I have to be careful in what I say about Martin. There are two phases of the formal adoption, the first in Vietnam and then the second, a readoption, here in the States. As I see it, Martin's name can stay on the documents for Vietnam. Then, he can simply fail to readopt when I get home. "There won't be any problem with that, will there?"

"Not at all. You can expect to travel in about a month."

"A month?" It almost seems too soon.

After hanging up with Carolyn Burns, I'm putting Martin's wet clothes in the wash when the phone rings. It's my sister, Lindi. "You have to be there at noon exactly," she tells me.

"Where?"

"I knew you'd forget. You have to pick up Keely at day care! I'm at the end of my rope here, Shelley. Keely's birthday party? Remember?"

"I remembered," I lie. "We have a Jewish funeral this afternoon," I tell her. "I'm just really busy." During my first few years in the profession, I got away with such excuses, but no one buys them now.

Lindi runs her life like a general conducting a military campaign, and she considers my obligation to her daughter's birthday party to be similar to a government's commitment to a multilateral operation. "I will be so disappointed in you, Shelley."

"I'll take care of it," I promise.

I hang up with Lindi and glance at my watch. It's nearly noon. My stepson Abe is coming down from Chapel Hill for the party. If I pick Keely up at day care, he will watch her for me this afternoon. Still, if Lindi hadn't called, I would have forgotten Keely completely. And here I am, planning to take ultimate responsibility for a child.

The rain has slowed to a drizzle by the time Keely and I get home. Abe, thank God, is already standing at the kitchen counter. The sling on his arm from his bike accident doesn't keep him from digging his fork into the Tupperware containing Mai's *bún thang*. In his teens, Abe had trouble with acne and hated himself. Now, the faint scars and his lean build make him look like a world-weary rock star, though he's shy and hasn't figured out that he's handsome yet. He grins when he sees I've brought along the birthday girl, who lunges at his legs.

"Did you see your dad?" I ask, kissing his cheek. I set Keely in a high chair.

Abe leans over the noodles like an ardent lover. "He's upstairs. He looks awful." I can't tell what Martin's told him.

I pull some bowls out of the cabinet and set them on the table, pour Mai's broth into a saucepan to heat, then put some noodles on Keely's tray. "Abe, do you have to eat out of the container? Isn't your dissertation on bacteria?"

"Not that kind."

I grimace at him. "It doesn't even have the broth in it yet." In truth, I find this mundane interaction consoling. Life can go on, apparently, even if you're getting a divorce.

Keely strings her noodles across her nose. "Muk," she yells. I pour her some milk.

The three of us sit at the table, eating *bún thang,* discussing the bullfrog tadpole that Keely is raising at day care. I can hear Martin moving around upstairs, but he doesn't appear until I'm up at the sink washing dishes. With a shower and a shave, he's managed to turn himself back into the conscientious undertaker.

"Hey, birthday girl!" Clearly, he has more presence of mind than I have. He has not forgotten.

"I two!" Keely reaches her arms into the air, signaling that she's willing to hug him. A glaze of milk forms a five o'clock shadow on her upper lip.

"Wait a minute," he says. He gingerly lifts her out of the high chair and carries her to the sink, where he rinses her face and hands with a wet rag. "Okay, now. Happy birthday!" he tells her. Then he tosses her into the air. Keely shrieks.

Abe and I lean against the counter, watching them. Moments like this one used to make me sick for a child. Now I feel sick for Martin as well. "Tonight's Keely's party," I tell him.

His face registers surprise. "Is that so?" he asks Keely. "What time?"

"Bedtime," she says somberly.

"Six," I say. Maybe he can find a way to get out of it.

"We've got the Kapner funeral at four. I'll come at six-thirty." He gives Keely a magnificent smile. I never imagined he'd be such a good actor.

Martin kisses Keely on the nose, squeezes Abe's shoulder, then disappears out the door. He hasn't looked at me once. I glance over to Abe. He's noticed.

Hay covers the back lawn of Lindi and Richard's house, simultaneously sopping up the mud and adding to the "barnyard" motif. Now that the clouds have cleared, rays of sunshine sift down through the trees and a fresh breeze blows in from the beach, offering what might be the last cool evening before summer. Keely's guests race here and there, offering carrots to lambs, petting the calf, riding the pony. Besides picking up the birthday girl at school, my job centered on getting her to the party by five-forty-five. That accomplished, I stand by the hors d'oeuvres table with Abe, Theo, and Theo's girlfriend, Anna-Sophie, sipping martinis out of jelly jars. All around us, children hurl themselves after chickens, their parents trailing at a distance like cowboys trying not to spook the stock. We discuss vodka.

Anna-Sophie says, "I don't choose my liquor based on the shape of a damn bottle."

Theo, who divides his time between struggling as a painter and struggling as a musician, considers Anna-Sophie, who is Dutch, to be enormously sophisticated. Sometimes her condescension makes him petulant, though. He whines, "Well, I *like* Absolut."

Abe grins. He says, "And I *like* that bottle," but he's just making trouble.

From across the lawn, I spot Martin. He has changed out of his suit and put on a blue work shirt, the faded blue jeans he wears hiking, and a cowboy hat from some Halloween. He heads up the lawn in the direction of Keely, who is bobbing on a dappled pony. If he's seen me, he hasn't shown it.

The sight of Martin in his cowboy gear serves to shift the conversation. "There's Tex," says Theo. Martin lifts Keely from her pony and holds her in his arms while talking to a couple of cowboys I don't know. Keely has slung her arm around Martin's neck and wears a look on her face that says, "This is mine." I used to feel that way, too.

Lindi motions to me from the open front door of the house. In blatant disregard of her barnyard theme, she's wearing a pink and green Lily Pulitzer pantsuit underneath an apron that says "If Mom's Not Happy, Nobody's Happy!" I excuse myself and hurry over. "Can you get people to eat?" She sounds huffy.

"Sure."

Lindi rubs her hands against her apron, glancing out across the lawn. "I've been telling Richard for fifteen minutes," she says, scowling, tipping her head toward her husband, who, though usually mild-mannered, now stands by the pony ride braying like a donkey.

I walk from group to group, summoning people to eat. I'm good with crowds, discreet and direct at the same time. It's a skill you master in my business. Eventually, I come upon Martin, who has left Keely with her father by the ponies. Martin's talking to our accountant, Jim Daltry, and Jim's wife, Mave. He looks so amiable and thoughtful. He's a good man, a man anyone could love. A wave of feeling for him sweeps over me. I think: We can find a solution, he and I. I say, "Hi, guys. Y'all go on over and get something to eat." My eyes rest on Martin.

The Daltrys smile and nod. Martin, without even glancing in my direction, turns and walks off. I feel so cold. I want to take a hot bath, be anywhere but here. Mave and Jim stare at me. They'd have to be idiots not to wonder. I squat down, gazing out at the children scattered on picnic blankets, already taking bites out of honey-slathered biscuits. "I just can't get over these children," I say, and, inside, I tell myself that this time next year, my boy will be here, too.

By eight-thirty, most of the guests have departed. Keely, with smears of icing on her chin, crouches under a picnic table with her brother Sauly, an open box of Legos lying on the ground between them. Their father sits on the front porch, strumming a guitar and singing "Sugar Magnolia" with Nathan, his blue-haired eighth-grader. My mother has gotten a ride home with a friend who lives in Landfall. Abe, Theo, and Anna-Sophie have taken off in Theo's beat-up van. While the farmer from Scotts Hill leads the lamb into its pen, my sister directs one of the waiters on where behind the house to put the hay bales. I'm sweeping hay into piles with a rake. I didn't see Martin leave.

Lindi wanders over to me. "You know what bugs me?" she asks, reaching down to scrape at the mud that's splattered the pink embroidery at the bottom of her slacks.

I shake my head, pushing the hay here and there. I'm wondering where Martin's gone, what we'll say to each other later.

"Childocentricity."

"What?"

"Parents who don't notice any kid but their own. I say, 'Your Alexandra is so adorable, the way she grips that saddle when she rides the pony.' And they're supposed to say, 'Oh, well, Keely is just the cutest thing running after those chickens.' But, instead, they say. 'Yeah, Alex seems like a natural on a horse.' Like Keely doesn't even exist."

"Keely is so cute the way she runs after those chickens."

"Thank you. That's convincing."

I swat at the hay with the rake, unable to look at Lindi. After a moment, I feel her arm go around my shoulders. "What is it?"

I hate to ruin her evening, but I can't lie to her, either. I tell her what's happened. When I finish, I say, "I need this baby."

Lindi looks like I've just disclosed a plan to amputate my arm. "You don't even know this baby," she reminds me. "You'd give up Martin for a kid you've never even met?"

"I want to be a mother," I say. "You should be able to understand that."

Lindi looks down and kicks at a clod of dirt with her sandal. "That man is so selfish," she says, suddenly bitter, as if Martin's character has caused problems for years.

"He's not selfish," I remind her. I can be honest on this point: He is a good man. But recognizing that fact makes the situation worse. The self-pity wells up through my body like the soft mud pushing through the scattered remnants of hay. "He's got his sons. He doesn't want more. I'm just a stepmother." I start to cry. Lindi guides me down the driveway. We stand by the mailbox. I keep my head down, embarrassed by the thought that the waiters will see me. "I'm like a hungry person," I say. "I can't wait anymore. This little boy needs me. And I need him more than I need Martin, Lindi. I do."

Lindi puts her arms around me. "I know," she whispers in my ear.

She holds me. I could stay in her arms for about a year. After a while, I say, "Do you remember all those times I called you? First, when I was so frustrated because Martin wasn't ready to try, and then, later, after he agreed, and I kept miscarrying?"

Lindi's hand smooths down my hair. "Once you called from the bathroom. You had the bloody toilet paper in your hand. You were crying so hard, I couldn't understand anything but 'I'm bleeding!' I thought you'd been attacked."

My laughter slows the weeping. "You never told me that," I say into her shoulder, which is wet from my tears.

Keely screams. Lindi jerks away, leans over to look beneath the picnic table, then sees that Keely and Sauly are fighting over the Legos. "Meltdown," she says.

"I'll go on home." I wipe my nose with a wadded-up napkin I've found in my pocket. "Tell those guys good-bye for me. I'll see you tomorrow."

She takes my hand. "You going to be okay?"

I nod. Lindi squeezes my hand, turns, and walks back up the lawn.

The roads are empty as I drive home. I feel dazed, woozy, and remember I didn't sleep last night. It's hard to believe that I cooked with Mai this morning. It's hard to believe that so much could happen in one bad day. The night is clear. A few stars twinkle in the dark patches between streetlights, sending signals that none of us can understand. Then I pull into the driveway. Martin's car isn't there.

After my bath, I phone Theo's and Anna-Sophie answers the phone. "Are you looking for Martin?" she asks. She always sounds suspicious.

"Um. Yeah."

A hand goes over the phone and I hear the inaudible rhythms of people talking. Then Theo comes on. "Hey, Shelley."

"Theo, can I talk to your dad?"

"What's going on with you two?" I've rarely heard him so agitated. He's the goofy, easygoing little brother, the one who forgot to go to his own high school graduation. But he's clearly annoyed by this news, or by the fact that our troubles slipped past him.

"What did he tell you?"

"He asked to spend the night here." Theo sounds accusatory, as if his father has broken the rules. Theo, not Martin, is the one who has girl trouble. "Tell me what happened," he demands.

"Nothing happened. Can you put him on the phone, please?"

"No. He doesn't want to talk to you. Shelley, are you having an affair?"

I have to laugh. Ours are not such ordinary betrayals. And it's kind of cute, Theo acting like a concerned adult. "Of course not," I tell him. I feel resentful, too. I don't want Theo talking to me like I'm the child. He can't go six months without breaking another poor girl's heart. Don't talk to me, I want to say, about affairs. "Look, we had a fight. It has to do with the adoption. It's no big deal. Let your dad tell you so himself."

"He says you're getting divorced."

"He said that? When did he say that?"

"Just now. He says you want it. There's another guy, right?"

"No!" I try to sound firm, but I can hear my voice failing me. "I told you, it's about the adoption." He doesn't answer. "Will you tell him I want him to call?" He still doesn't answer. "Theo! This is not your problem, okay?"

"Okay."

"Tell him to call."

Next, I phone my mother. Martin and I are supposed to have brunch at her house tomorrow with Lindi and Richard and their kids.

"Hello?" Her voice sounds like something buried under a blanket. Sometimes, my mom's up till all hours watching reruns on Turner Classics. Other times, she's in bed by nine-thirty.

"Mom, I'm sorry I woke you. I'll call back in the morning."

"No, I'm not awake," she says, and then, "Asleep."

"Martin can't make it for brunch. I just wanted to let you know."

This information fully wakes her. "Did someone die or something?" It's an old joke, and not even funny anymore, but I appreciate it. It took her years to accept that her daughter had married a funeral director. If someone asked her about Martin's profession, she used to say, "He runs a small business," and hope they'd drop the subject. Then her husband, Cal, got sick and Martin became the one my mother turned to with her grief. Her anger, really, though she would never call it that. She and Cal had been married for only two years. He'd just turned sixty and she was fifty-four. They went to the theater together, gave parties, played golf. And then he had his stroke. Just slid to the kitchen floor one day before they'd even finished breakfast. After that, he couldn't feed himself, couldn't use the toilet, couldn't say a single word. He lingered for ten years. I felt bad for Cal. I wouldn't wish a death like his on anybody. But I felt worse for my mom.

"Nobody died," I say. "It's just Martin and me. We're separating or something."

"What are you talking about?"

Of course, it's a shock. People expect some preparation for marital disaster, something more like a hurricane than an earthquake. My mother did not see it coming. We didn't even see it coming. People say that having children can bring a fragile marriage to the brink. In my experience, not having children can tear apart even a strong one.

"Martin's staying at Theo's." I'm only capable of providing facts.

"Oh," she says. My mother can say more with one syllable than most people can say with a thousand words. Why don't we have lids on our ears? Why can't I block the sound of the pain in my mother's voice?

"Shelley?"

"I'm still adopting this baby. I could leave for Hanoi as early as next month."

"Can't you just—"

"Mom, I can't." I have to get off the phone.

"Shelley—"

"Please!"

When my mother married Cal, she moved into his place in Landfall, an exclusive gated community on the intracoastal waterway. You can't get a house in Landfall for less than a quarter of a million dollars. Cal's place cost a lot more than that, but he'd retired from Procter & Gamble with something like $7 million, so it didn't matter. He bought this hideous Italianate thing overlooking the waterway, spent a year converting it to a less ostentatious Cape Cod, then met my mother on the golf course and married her. They had a couple of catered affairs with cocktails on the slate patio and a buffet by the pool, then Cal had his stroke.

I find my family already congregated on the patio, sitting on lawn chairs under the shade of the big dogwood. Lindi and Richard, decked out in starchy tennis clothes but looking worn from last night, sit drinking screwdrivers out of tall glasses with little orange wedges stuck on their rims. Keely sits with her knees drawn up to her chest, her face in a picture book. Nathan, with his blue hair, slouches in a chair facing the pier and the little rowboat that he and his brother used to take clamming. Sauly, the middle child, is stretched out on the ground, arranging things in little bags. My mother fiddles with the flowers on the table. She sees me first when I appear around the side of the house. "Sweetie! Hello! I need you to help with things."

My mother always moves fast. When she was thirty years old, she found out my dad had cheated on her and she filed for divorce the next day. When she was fifty-four, after dating and dumping God knows how many men, she met Cal and married him a month later. She's so impatient that, at sixty-seven, she still takes the stairs two at a time. Now, she hustles me up to the house and inside the kitchen door before I even have a chance to wave.

"I haven't said a word," she says, pressing me onto a bar stool. "I called Martin this morning."

"That's a word, Mom."

She blinks. "I mean to them," she says, vaguely pointing out the door. "Lindi knows."

My mother starts spooning fruit salad from a Tupperware container into a big glass bowl. "I had to talk to Martin."

"What did he say?"

"He says you're the one who made the decision."

We stare at each other across the top of the coffeemaker. "We both made decisions," I tell her.

She takes in this information in the same way that she inhales when a friend decides to smoke. She doesn't like it, but she's eager to let you know that she's determined to make the best of it. "There's got to be a solution here," she announces.

"I don't know what it would be."

"Shelley?"

"His name is Hai Au," I say. "The baby."

"Shelley?"

"Say it. Hai Au." Pronouncing his name means making a commitment to him. "Say it, Mom."

She sighs as if I've asked her to do something extremely silly. "Hi-Ho."

"It's really beautiful, if you just listen to the sound. And it's perfect because it's the name of a kind of seabird and he'll grow up here near the beach." I have to admit, to myself at least, that he would have an easier time with a simpler name, like "Mai," but he and I will manage.

"Shelley!" she says. "Listen to me."

The floor of my mother's kitchen is white-and-black-checkerboard linoleum. Every inch of it scuffs. But I've never seen a grain of dirt on my mother's floor. Or a scuff. "What?"

"You should adopt another baby."

"No."

She says, "It's probably just the stress about Vietnam. I'm sure he'd take another baby."

I look at her. "He doesn't want a baby, Mom."

Her expression shifts slightly, and I can see that, despite herself, she believes me. Before she can say anything, however, Sauly pulls open the screen door and races in. "Aunt Shelley!" he yells, although we're only a few feet apart. "We're all going to make these bees together."

"Bees? Give me a kiss."

The kiss is automatic, and then he pushes two bags of pipe cleaners, one black and one yellow, into my lap. "It's for the nature fair. I need it by Monday. A whole beehive. We're talking, like, thousands of bees." Sauly is a ten-year-old version of my mother.

"Thousands?"

"Maybe a million."

My mother puts her hands on Sauly's shoulders. "Let Aunt Shelley finish helping me in here, then we'll come out and you can show her the hive."

I grab the bowl of fruit salad. "Mom, I'll take this on out," I say. My mother's face is taut and anxious. I follow Sauly out the door.

At brunch, we talk about bees. And how to attach a million knotted pipe cleaners to a hunk of Styrofoam sprayed yellow to look like a hive. Sauly has one prototype for a bee. His father has another. Nathan has made some weird Sid Vicious punk sculpture that he insists will play the role of queen.

"Mom, tell him to stop bothering me," Sauly complains.

"You mean 'bugging' you," says Nathan, finally yielding a smile.

Lindi cuts a piece of quiche. She says, "Nathan, leave your brother alone."

Richard serves himself some fruit salad. He seldom gets involved in family squabbles, perhaps because of some privately negotiated division of labor. "Where's Martin?" he asks, taking a bite out of a strawberry.

My mother shoots Richard a look, and a little shake of the head, that shuts him up. I love Lindi for the fact that she hasn't told him, but now Richard stares at me. I glare at my mother.

Nathan looks up from his muffin. "Who died?" he wants to know. He loves the macabre.

"No one died."

"So why didn't he come?"

I lie. "He had a lot of work to do."

"Yes," says my mother, jabbing at her quiche. "Poor dear. I talked to him this morning." When my mother lies, each word announces: "Don't believe this."

Luckily, the kids are distracted. Sauly says, "Aunt Shelley, do you know about the bee dance?"

I shake my head. I can think of nothing better than hearing about the bee dance.

Sauly jumps out of his chair and stands beside the table. "It's how bees tell each other where the flowers are. There's two main dances. The round dance and the tail-wagging dance."

"Do the tail-wagging dance," says Nathan. "I just love the tail-wagging dance."

Sauly looks at his brother contemptuously, then resumes speaking. "The round dance says, 'We found flowers and they're close by!' " He takes a few steps away from the table, then starts walking in this slow circle, jiggling his entire body in a way that's apparently meant to resemble a bee. "Then, see, I turn around like this and go the other way. That means, 'Hey, guys, the flowers aren't even a hundred yards away.' "

Keely stands up. "Tail-wag dance!" she screams. Lindi whispers something to my mother, and they both look at me. Richard's eyes move back and forth, trying to figure out what's going on.

"Follow me, then," Sauly says to his sister. He jogs in a half circle, Keely right behind him, then turns and runs straight across the patio. They both wiggle their rear ends. "Each time we wag our tails, that's a waggle run. If we go ten waggle runs in fifteen seconds, that means the flowers are a hundred yards away. Seven waggle runs means six hundred yards. Four waggle runs means a thousand yards."

At this point, all of us just watch the children silently racing back and forth across the patio. After about a dozen waggle runs, Sauly says, "And if we go to the right, it means the flowers are to the right of the sun. And if we go to the left, it means the flowers are to the left of the sun."

I say, "I had no idea that bees were so smart."

Sauly stops. He's already breathing heavily. "Bees might be even smarter than dolphins."

"I have an announcement to make," says my mother.

"What's that?" asks Sauly, who thinks he still holds the floor.

"Aunt Shelley will need help with little Hi-Ho," she says. "I'm going to go with her to Vietnam."

Lindi, Richard, Nathan, and I stare at her as if she's crazy. She takes a bite of her quiche and looks out toward the waterway. Keely and Sauly yell, "Hooray," and take off again across the patio, relaying to their invisible bee colleagues that the flowers are out there, somewhere just to the left of the sun, sweet and pure, brimming with nectar.

8

Xuan Mai

Gladys wants to play Scrabble, which is silly because she speaks terrible English. But Marcy and her friends play Scrabble, so Gladys insists that we play, too. Because it's a slow afternoon and I'm bored, we set up a card table by the front counter and lay the game out there. I have to admit, I kind of like Scrabble. I like the feel of the tiles and the little wooden stands. It's just a game, but each piece is smoothly polished, free of splinters and cracks. After all these years, I still can't get over the quality of goods in America.

"Who's that picture of?" Gladys wants to know. She puts "R-A-T" down on the board.

"What picture?" I ask, though I know which one she means. I make "T-O-P" with an *O* and a *P,* then pull two more tiles and set them on my stand.

"The one you've been looking at so often lately. You keep it in your purse."

No wonder Marcy never wants Gladys around. "That's my mother," I tell her. Then, just to avoid more questions, I say, "Captain Weatherbee, the policeman, told me about a lady who can draw portraits from memory. I didn't have a picture of my mother, so I asked her to draw one."

Gladys makes this kind of ticking sound with her mouth. She leans forward in her chair. "Let's see."

It's too much trouble to argue. I go get my purse and pull it out.

Gladys holds the picture in one hand, glancing back and forth between me and the image of my mother. "*Xinh,*" says Gladys. Pretty.

I don't like her staring at it. "Will you take your turn?"

Barely lifting her eyes from the picture, she grabs a *C* and an *A,* then puts them down on top of the *R* in "R-A-T." Now we've got "C-A-R."

"Finished?" I ask, reaching for the picture.

She returns it grudgingly. "I wish I had a picture of my mother."

"I'll give you the woman's phone number," I tell her. "Now can we play the game?"

Gladys fingers a tile, tapping it idly against the table. "Marcy always had a picture of me. You know what I did when I sent her off on the boat?"

I don't move. I don't look up. I don't want to hear any stories about Marcy or Gladys or boats. I stare at our Scrabble game. I concentrate on finding a word.

Gladys says, "I sewed a little purse out of plastic sheeting. Inside, I put a photo of me and Marcy in it, a letter for her to read when she got older, and a twenty-dollar bill. That was all the money I had left after buying her place on the boat. Then I strapped the purse around her belly, underneath her clothes, and told her not to take her shirt off for anything."

I have *A, R, P, Z, N, T,* and *V.* It bothers me that Gladys can beat me at Scrabble.

"She was only five years old, but she said, 'Mommy, I promise.' That just about killed me. An hour later, she was gone."

I put an *A* and an *N* after the *P.* "P-A-N."

"And you know what? When I finally saw her again, in Charlotte ten years later, she still had that picture. It was sitting in a frame on her dresser in my cousin's house. She'd held on to it all that time."

I look up to let her know that I have heard her. "Your turn," I say.

Gladys rests her chin in the palm of her hand and looks down at the table. I can't see her eyes, but it occurs to me that she's crying. Suddenly, everybody starts to cry when I'm around. I stare at the Scrabble board and wait, but she doesn't stop. And so I do the thing I would least expect myself to do. I put my hand on her hand, her leathery country hand that I have never touched in all these years, and I leave it there until she's finished. When, finally, she sniffles and lifts her hand to wipe her eyes, we both pretend that nothing's happened. Gladys fingers some tiles, then lays a G and an N on either side of the E. "G-E-N."

"Gen?"

"Gen. Like the drink. Gen."

"That's 'G-I-N.' "

She nods, not surprised, and pulls the pieces off the board.

"Try again," I encourage her.

She looks down at her tiles, then picks up a handful. Around the N, she builds the word "E-N-G-A-G-E-D." "Engache," she says in her appalling accent. There it is, on the table. She's used up six letters on that word, and gotten double points as well. Engaged.

"Your turn," she says.

At four o'clock, Marcy and her boyfriend Travis come by the store to pick up Gladys. Because Marcy dances in that cage at the bar downtown, Gladys calls her daughter a GI slut, which is funny because Gladys really was a GI slut. Now Marcy looks down at the two of us, the Scrabble game, our little pot of tea, and she scowls distinctly. "Sorry, Mai," she says in English, then continues, "Jesus, Ma. I'm the one who works here. Can't you get a life or something?"

Gladys looks at her daughter and the smile on her face is both proud and insecure, as if she's amazed to have produced something so lovely and worries that she'll lose it. "What does she mean, 'Get a life'?" she mutters to me in Vietnamese, but before I can answer, she has grabbed her purse and shuffled after Marcy, out the door.

I put the Scrabble board away, then take the tray with the teapot and cups on it back to the kitchen. I rinse the cups, letting the warm water rush over my hands. I never knew that Gladys and Marcy had been separated for so long. I guess I never asked. All Vietnamese have an ugly boat story, and mine has always felt depressing enough that I didn't want to hear any others. I have spent so many years trying not to hear anything new, trying not to know.

Water. People would have given anything—the taels of gold hidden in the hems of their shirts, the jewelry stashed in the hollow heels of their shoes—anything to have water like this, clean and fresh, ready to drink. Once you've experienced thirst like that, it stays with you. At any moment of any day I can still recall that stickiness in the back of my throat, that ache to drink.

Khoi and I spent six days in the clammy, stinking belly of that boat. We were two out of forty-two human beings packed into the hull. In our previous lives, we might have been teachers, mechanics, doctors, students. We might have been clean, polite, good cooks. Here, we lived like animals. We peed and vomited and shit right there in front of each other, in buckets when we had the chance, on the floor when we didn't. When we slept at all we curled up fetuslike, wrapping our bodies around our meager possessions. We didn't trust each other. We didn't talk.

A storm made the waves crash against the boat, causing people to scream in terror, to throw up until there was nothing left inside. I don't remember feeling fear myself. I had only one thought on my mind: I had to have Khoi. Most minutes of most days, I was completely absorbed by the effort of getting on top of him. My hand was a scavenger, a rat racing down his pants to grab him. At two or three in the morning, he would finally give in. Then, for as long as he would let me, I pushed myself onto him, up and down, up and down. His body sustained me. When he eventually pushed me away, I screamed that I would die without it. The old ladies on the boat called me "whore." The men called me "cunt." The younger women turned their eyes away.

Once, when the storm passed, Khoi led me up the ladder to the deck. "You always wanted to see the ocean," he said. "Come up. It's so beautiful." But the bright sun assaulted me. I held my hands over my eyes and screamed that I couldn't breathe. Finally, the captain told Khoi to either take me down or toss me over. Back inside the dark bowels of the ship,

I took great deep gulps of the rancid air, sucking it down like a nursing baby.

The storm had blown the boat off course, and after we ran out of fuel we drifted. The first mate measured rations with an empty can of condensed milk: Each person got one can of rice per day, and double that in water. Khoi mixed two cans of fresh water with an equal amount of seawater and used that to cook our rice. He fed it to me with his fingers, and when I gagged and spit it out, he picked the grains of rice off my chest and fed them to me again. He joked that he'd discovered a new recipe for fish sauce and that when we got to America he'd sell it and make us thousands of dollars. He didn't know that people in America don't eat fish sauce.

After six days, a Swedish tanker spotted the boat and towed it to Hong Kong. A bus carried us from the port to the refugee camp, where I lay on a bed in a Red Cross hospital, a needle stuck in each arm. The nurses were foreigners. None of them could speak Vietnamese and, whenever the translator, a guy from Saigon, came through, I asked him to strangle me. Everyone thought I was crazy, and they became even more convinced of it when stories of my behavior on the boat began to circulate. My craziness must have appealed to the foreign nurses, though. They brought me treats—pink ribbons, a shirt with a drawing of the Eiffel Tower on it, chocolates I refused to eat. Sometimes, the small blond nurse from Belgium would sit by my bed and play international pop songs on a handheld tape recorder. The music soothed me. One morning I found myself gripping the Belgian nurse's hand. Another afternoon, while the Belgian nurse was rewinding the cassette, I wept. She must have held me in her arms until I fell asleep. Later, when dinner arrived, I tried to eat it.

The day that the needles came out of my arms, I slept the whole afternoon. When I woke, I lay with my eyes closed. I could hear the voice of the translator.

"It's a tragedy," he said. His words were kind and hesitant, lacking the brusque efficiency he usually used in his job. "And she was an only child?"

I heard Khoi's voice. "Yes," he said. "Only that one perfect little girl."

The truth, even from Khoi, made me shudder, but hearing it relieved me in the way that vomiting relieved my nausea. Then I thought: The Belgian nurse must know. And the Belgian nurse had hugged me. For one fine moment, I was able to breathe again.

The translator asked another question. "Do you two plan to have another child?"

I stopped breathing. "We don't know," Khoi said. His voice sounded sad, convincing. "The medical system killed her. We knew we'd never have another baby if we stayed in Vietnam."

In my mind I saw My Hoa then, her face full of joy and anticipation. What did she want from me? A piece of cake? A silly song? A story? I screamed. The air flooded in through my nostrils and down my throat, causing me to choke and flail in the bed. Someone held me, and when I opened my eyes, I saw Khoi.

"You piece of trash," I whispered. "Dirty dog. Liar. Murderer."

He winced, but his voice was steady when he answered. "I may be wrong," he said. "But I'm doing my best. Please. Just try to understand."

I stopped struggling and we stared at each other for a long time. When he finally loosened his grip, I pulled myself up and spat at him.

Somehow, Khoi and I managed to make something resembling a life in San Francisco. It so closely resembled a life, in fact, that after some years I had to leave it. That's when I moved to Wilmington. For a while, Khoi used to send me packages every month or so, gifts that he hoped would entice me to return: postcards of the Golden Gate Bridge, Ghirardelli chocolates, cable car key chains. These were not the things he loved about the place. They were the things that he, as an immigrant, knew had made the city famous. But I never cared about San Francisco as a city, and so, after a few months, he shifted his strategy and started sending items I couldn't get in North Carolina: candied ginger, water rose apple tea, nostalgic poetry by expatriate writers. None of it tempted me because those were the very things that had driven me away. I didn't want those reminders of my previous existence. I didn't want to be part of a Vietnamese community. I wanted the sparkly anonymity of America. If I could have separated myself from Vietnam completely, I might have done so, but I had to make some kind of living, and running a market is the only thing I know how to do here. I said as much once to Khoi on the phone, and not so long ago, either. He continues to get upset over the idea that all I do is work to earn money. He reminds me that I had planned to study litera- ture. One night, he said, "You had such great hopes for yourself."

Had he completely forgotten that he once expected to become a famous architect? "Well," I retorted, "so did you."

Whenever we hit a standoff like that one, we get off the phone as quickly as possible. That's the problem that Khoi and I always have with each other, even though I haven't seen him in years. No matter what we're talking about, we always hit a point of despair. We end up talking about things we don't want to talk about anymore, so we hang up the phone just to keep ourselves from upsetting each other.

But, a month or two later, one of us will try again.

A couple of days after Shelley and I cook *bún thang,* Khoi calls. "How are you?" he asks, without even a hello. His voice is affectionate. He never identifies himself, never has to.

"I'm okay," I tell him. "How are you?" I'm under the covers, watching German ballet on PBS. I switch the TV off and ease my head back into the pillow.

Khoi and I never make small talk, but it always takes a while, when months have passed, to figure out where to start. After a moment, he sighs, "I'm so tired all the time."

"Did you open the new store?"

"Yeah. I can't even keep the stuff on the shelves," he says, without enthusiasm. Khoi is rich. Two decades ago, back in Vietnam, our fami- lies would have been shocked to hear that this sweet, shy architecture student would found a chain of Asian supermarkets and become one of the wealthiest Vietnamese in America. But, from the moment we arrived in this country, he has sweated and saved to make it here. For six years, I sweated and saved along with him. Then, the day we opened our first Lotus Superstore in the Richmond district of San Francisco, I decided to leave. Khoi tried to convince me to change my mind, but he knew that I was stubborn. "Where will you go?" he asked. In one of the local Vietnamese papers I'd seen an ad for an Asian grocery for sale in Wilmington, North Carolina. I showed it to Khoi. "There," I said.

Now, fifteen years later, he still complains that I abandoned him. "If you were here, it would be better," he says.

I don't really take him seriously, though. Such musings are just his way of saying that he misses me. I understand, because I miss him, too. It's not love, exactly. No, maybe it is love, but it's not romantic. Many years ago, I left my ability to be romantic beneath a tree in Unification Park in Hanoi. Khoi retained a bit—he got married, didn't he?—but, even when he talks about Thuy, his wife, I can sense his emptiness.

"I'm better off where I am," I tell him, as always. "You're better off, too." Then I change the subject. "How's Gordon?"

His voice becomes lighter at the mention of his son. "He's in the San Francisco Boys' Chorus. He's only the second Vietnamese ever admitted."

I calculate in my head. "He's seven now?"

"Right. Our only problem is that he refuses to speak Vietnamese. Sometimes we ignore him when he uses English, but he stomps out of the room, yelling that he's not going to talk in our fake language anymore."

"Well, he's American. Don't push him."

"I have to." I can hear the resignation in his voice. "It's his culture."

"I guess." My gaze settles on Hannah Ellis's portrait of my mother. I've set up an altar on my dresser, and I light incense for her every morning now. But I have nothing for My Hoa, still.

He says, "I have to tell you something."

I wish I could remember my mother's last words. "What?"

"I'm taking Gordon to Hanoi."

I close my eyes, push myself under the covers. A dark cocoon.

"Did you hear me? Hanoi?"

I should have expected it. I've always considered my departure from my homeland to be a permanent break, like cutting the flower before it wilts on the stem. But now people keep returning. Even Gladys—who calls the Communists "red devils"—is talking about starting an import/export trade in cheap shoes. She can go back and stay there if she likes. I don't care. But with Khoi, I care. Khoi knows where my house is.

"Don't worry," he tells me. "I won't do anything to hurt you."

I imagine Khoi and his son, sitting on those creaky wooden chairs in his parents' home on Tran Hung Dao Street. The whole family will squeeze together around the tiny table, drinking tea, admiring the little American prince. And friends and neighbors will file through in packs, wanting to hear what happened. For years they've thought that Khoi and I were dead.

"Everyone will hear you're home, Khoi," I say. You could never keep a secret in Hanoi. People always joked that this crowded city was really just a tiny village. "People will ask."

He admits it. "It's true. I have to do it, though. For Gordon."

"I know." My voice is a quiet murmur. I don't even have to speak. Khoi would have gone back to Vietnam years ago, if not for me. But still, I'd give anything to keep him away forever.

"I've been thinking about something."

"Don't even say it."

"Just let me go and talk to them. You never know. It's been over twenty years. People forgive."

"Stay away from them."

"I leave on May twenty-fifth. At noon. Call me if you change your mind."

"Right." I have to get off the phone. "It's late, Khoi. I get up at six."

"Think about it. The twenty-fifth, okay? All you need to do is call."

"Okay," I tell him, but I won't, and he knows it.

My mother believed that destiny affected everything—war, death, illness, fortune, even the choice of tomatoes at the market. When I got sick and missed the Communist Youth outing to Do Son Beach, she had no sympathy for my misfortune. "It's fate," she told me. "Don't go moaning about something you were never meant to do." Her lack of sympathy pained me, but her logic upset me even more. It was the summer of 1975. Vietnam had driven out the American imperialist aggressors and become the envy of the world. My teachers told us that a modern country had no place for superstition. We needed to have clear minds, like Uncle Ho's. But my mother acted like someone living in the stone age. She said, "It's your destiny, child. Don't go near water."

I didn't believe her then. I believe her now.

You can't avoid your destiny. I learned, in the worst possible way, that I should stay away from water. And I've learned, since then, to notice signs. Like noticing the ad in the paper for the Good Luck Asian Grocery on the very day we opened Lotus Superstore in San Francisco. And Shelley. She's a sign. These days, she comes to cook with me two, sometimes three days a week. She brings books, lists of questions, photographs of Hanoi, and while we stand there making my lunches, we talk. In my mind, I call these mornings *về quê,* going home. Khoi has his way, I have mine.

I haven't figured out how Shelley is mixed in with my destiny. But here's a sign: She shows up unexpectedly at the very hour that Khoi flies out of San Francisco, on his way to Vietnam.

I'm standing in the back of my store with two old-lady customers. One of them, with dyed blond hair and heavy gold jewelry, scowls at the nutritional information on a bag of preserved turnip. "Is it meat?" she asks me.

Her friend, a leathery-faced woman with a little pixie haircut, jumps in. "Connie, it's a vegetable. Remember? *Turnip.* Like, turnip greens?"

Connie eyes it suspiciously. "Looks like meat to me."

I lean against the refrigerator. Connie and her friend are having a "Thai" dinner party and have asked me for help. They think I'm Thai. Fine. They can think I'm from Kenya if they like.

"This turnip real good in the pad thai," I offer. They page through their *Delights of the Orient* cookbook.

The bell at the front of the store jingles. I have a glimpse of Shelley's red head at the front door, then she disappears down an aisle before bursting around a corner to reappear in produce. It's three o'clock in the afternoon. Out in California, Khoi's plane is taking off.

"Mai!" Shelley gasps before the sight of my customers stops her. When they fail to notice her, she points to herself, then to me, then holds up an envelope. "I need to talk to you," she mouths the words. I nod and tip my head toward the kitchen. Looking grateful to have a task, she turns and strides away, her hair like a flame tearing down an empty road.

Fifteen minutes later, after dispatching the Thai dinner, I duck into my kitchen. Shelley already has the tea ready. She hands me a mug and says, "There's another delay." Then she unfolds two pieces of paper and spreads them on the counter. "I made them fax me the original so I could show you."

Somehow, I've adjusted to her speed in conversation, the way she jumps into a subject as if we've been discussing it for hours already. I pick up the papers. The first is on Southeastern Adoptions stationery. "Dear Mr. and Mrs. Marino," it says:

As I stated to you on the phone, I'm sorry about this new postponement of your adoption. In cases such as this one, I don't anticipate the problem delaying your trip to Hanoi by more than a month or two. However, as you know, it's impossible to speculate on such matters, particularly when it pertains to the rules and regulations of a foreign government. At your request, I'm faxing a copy of the embassy letter. Please understand that our staff is doing its best to facilitate this matter. Feel free to contact me if you have any questions. I appreciate your continued patience.

Yours sincerely,
Carolyn Burns
Parent Liaison Officer
Southeastern Adoptions

The second page, which bears the insignia of the embassy of Vietnam, is even shorter:

Re: International Adoption Case #20166
Child's Name: Nguyen Hai Au
Location: Ha Dong Children's Center, Ha Noi

To Whom It May Concern:

Due to administrative backlog, we must postpone the finalization of the adoption of Nguyen Hai Au until further notice.

> Sincerely,
> Mr. Phung Van Luan
> Political Counselor
> Embassy of Vietnam

Shelley watches me, eyes crinkled with worry. "What does 'administrative backlog' mean?" she asks.

"It's embassy talk, I guess."

Her lips begin to tremble. "I don't even know when to buy plane tickets!" she cries. These days, she's plagued not merely by her own anxiety and the breakup of her marriage, but also by the tension between bureaucratic vagueness and her mother's need to travel to a third world country with a definite itinerary and firm reservations.

I read the letter again and try to interpret it. I can remember standing in line for hours every month just to pick up my family's ration tickets. As far as I'm concerned, "administrative backlog" just means "business as usual" in Vietnamese. I hand Shelley the letter and try to look confident. "You don't worry. This just normal slow, that's all."

Shelley throws herself down on a stool. She reaches toward her mug of tea, then lets her hand fall back to her knee. "I can't take this," she says, staring at the smiling cat on my Happy Time Korean Wholesale calendar.

I fold the papers and put them back in the envelope. I could remind her that she wanted to understand Vietnam and, well, bureaucracy is Vietnam. That would be cruel, though. "You'll get your boy," I tell her, trying to sound confident. But what do I know, really?

Shelley's eyes alight on me. She twists a strand of hair around her finger. "When are you heading to D.C. next time?"

I shake my head. "I can't."

But her eyes already shine with the plan. "Please go by the embassy with me."

I can make it to Charlotte and back in a single day. But with D.C. I have to drive up on Sunday night, shop Monday morning, then turn around and drive back that afternoon. It's six hours each way. I always feel sick on Tuesdays. "Won't do you no good," I tell her, trying to squirm out of it. "I'm just *Việt Kiều,* not even real Vietnamese no more. They hate people like me."

Shelley just looks at me. "Don't say no," she pleads.

Shelley's mother brings her over to the store at seven on Sunday night, just as I'm closing. The trunk of their car contains an Igloo cooler, a thermos, a case full of CDs and cassettes, a portable stereo, and a small suitcase on wheels. They start hauling everything to the back of my van.

When I go to D.C., I stick a toothbrush, toothpaste, hairbrush, and change of underwear in my purse. "Why so much stuff?" I ask. "We back tomorrow."

"It's twelve hours on the road, at least," Shelley says, plaintively, as if I'm complaining that she even brought a pair of shoes. She pulls a gallon jug of water out of the trunk. "I guarantee you. We will need this."

Shelley's mother walks over to me. She's small and stylish and wears her hair in a shade of blond that, on a woman her age, has got to come from a bottle. Still, she looks surprisingly pretty and youthful. I imagine she's the sort of person who, confronted with the fact that nature hadn't given her hair that color, decided that nature was wrong.

"I hear you going to Vietnam, too," I say.

"I made her promise that we take one suitcase each. No exceptions," she tells me, watching Shelley crawl around in the van, shoving parcels into corners. "By the way, you're lovely to indulge her like this."

I shrug. "It a long drive. She good company."

The mother folds her arms against her chest and sighs. "Actually, I'm proud of her," she says, as much to herself as me.

I smile. "I hope she understand this trip to embassy won't do no good."

We can only see Shelley from the back, squatting in her khakis, sorting through plastic bags of food. Her mother laughs. "That doesn't matter. I mean, it would be delightful if you two could push things forward. But, really, she just needs to feel like she's doing something. She's already painted the baby's room twice, and, as you know, she doesn't even plan to stay in that house."

Shelley has now squeezed herself between the two front seats. She holds the stereo plug in her fingers, then turns her head and yells, "I'm putting the cigarette lighter in the glove compartment, Mai, so I can plug this in. I'm putting my maps in there, too."

"I got my own maps," I tell her. "And I know how to get to D.C."

Shelley's mother puts her hand on my shoulder. "Don't even bother, dear," she tells me.

I'm worried about my transmission, so, even though Shelley offers to take a turn, I plan to drive the whole way. We're twenty miles out of Wilmington before she feels organized enough to settle down. Some singer I've never heard of—Willie, Billie, a black lady with a boy's name—is on the stereo. Shelley has filled the thermos with coffee, and brought two special mugs with tiny holes in the top, good for holding drinks without spilling. Maybe I'll get myself one of these.

Outside, the sky has turned a steely black. When I first arrived here, the smooth, unblemished highways of this country impressed me. In Vietnam, it would have taken me more than a day to go the distance I'll drive tonight in just a few hours. But I miss the life on the roads back home: the farmers in the fields, the villagers hauling goods to market.

In comparison, these I's I drive—I-40, I-95—are barren, endless, lonely. Sometimes, driving by myself on these roads in the middle of the night, I half-believe I'm lost in space. I'm an astronaut cut loose from my rocket, condemned to drift forever.

"You hungry?" Shelley asks, pulling me back in. She reaches over the seat and drags a plastic bag onto her lap. "I made us some dinner."

I start to shake my head and tell her that I don't have a big appetite. Normally, I can make it to D.C. on a couple of apples. But then I realize that, actually, I'm starving. She has lugged a huge amount of food into this van, and I want it. "Sure," I say, taking a sip of coffee. Over the past few days, the temperature has settled into summer, but here in the cool car, the hot liquid tastes good.

Shelley pulls a plastic Tupperware container out of the bag. I hear the sucking sound of the top coming off, then she holds some kind of hard-boiled egg between her fingers. "Just try this. For a snack."

"What is it?"

"A deviled egg. Haven't you ever been to a picnic?"

"I been to picnics." Not in the States, though.

"Just try it."

I hold the egg between my fingers and take a bite, keeping my eyes on the road. It's creamier than a hard-boiled egg, and less bland, too. Somebody had a good idea.

"Well?"

"It's cute."

She watches me chewing. "But do you like it?"

I nod. "Cute."

"My mother used to take me and my sister on car trips when we were little and she'd bring, like, a stick of gum for each of us. She'd be pointing out the sites along the road, ordering, 'Look at the scenery, girls! Absorb! Absorb!' and I couldn't do a thing but fantasize about McDonald's. Now I always make sure to have a lot of food with me when I travel."

"What you bring on the plane with you to Vietnam?"

She throws back her head and stares up at the ceiling. It's an issue she's clearly considered. "I'm thinking granola bars, Planters peanuts, apples—they don't spoil too fast. My mother bought a supersize box of cheese crackers at Target. She's gotten more liberal about food, maybe because she's got money now." Shelley pops another egg into her mouth, chews for a while. "She's going to drive me crazy over there. She wants to be a help, but everything has to be perfect. Where's our hotel? Does it have an iron in the room? Does it have a blow dryer? Can she get coffee in bed in the morning? I can't worry about that stuff. I'm going to have a baby to deal with."

We eat more eggs, letting Willie's voice drift around us. Shelley has taken her shoes off and planted her bare feet against the dashboard in front of her. She sips her coffee and sighs. "I've died and gone to heaven."

I smile, move into the inside lane, pass a sputtering truck. "You want to hear about first time I ever taste coffee?"

Shelley looks at me as if my kindness knows no bounds. I could describe the sound of boiling rice and, if that rice was boiling in Vietnam, she'd listen.

Interstate 40 spreads out in front of us, a plain brown ribbon stretched across the dark farmland. In my mind I see Hanoi. "It was the middle of summer, so hot. I had to take my daddy's bike to be fixed." I remember the morning perfectly, even though I haven't thought of it in years. How old was I then? My mother died that summer, so it was 1976. "I was sixteen."

That morning, the sidewalks were scattered with the blossoms of the flame tree, bright orange and shaped like fans. The toothless old mechanic sat at the corner of Hang Dao and Cau Go streets, not far from my house. He spent hours working on the bike, pulling off the rusty broken chain, cleaning the gears, submerging the tire tubes in a basin of water to search for holes. He probably could have done the job in less than an hour, but he took his time with it, talking to me, telling stories, scouring the grungy spokes with the bristles of a worn toothbrush. I didn't care how long he took. "My life so different then," I tell Shelley. "Now I got no time. Back then, I got nothing but time. Americans say, 'Time's money.' I'm rich back then."

I glance at Shelley and she grins. I don't mention the relief I felt that afternoon, which is probably the reason I remember it at all. My mother had been screaming for weeks, crazed from the pain. She wasn't even strong enough to lift her head from the pillow, and she'd begged us all to kill her. She was headed for the next life anyway, she argued, making beautiful promises to the person brave enough to do it. To me, she promised good marks in school. To Lan, she promised brilliant children. She promised my father robust health. She didn't care how we did it. Strangle her. Stick a knife through her heart. Just do it, fast. Lan, my father, and I took turns in the hospital, wiping her face with cool rags, trying to soothe her. It was strange to see a woman who'd gone through so much sorrow in her life suddenly refuse to put up with one more minute of it. During those brief intervals when she finally screamed herself to sleep, we'd cluster together, whispering, as if we might be able to find a solution. We'd heard of drugs that made people numb, but we didn't know how to get them. It was 1976, just one year after the end of the war, and that barren hospital had nothing that would ease her pain. Some days, I was so frantic to make the misery stop that I worried I'd actually take a knife and stab her. But then, as suddenly as the pain had started, it went away. One afternoon, in the middle of a wail, my mother closed her mouth. After that, she lay there silent, staring at the ceiling, faintly smiling. When we took her hand, she squeezed it.

The morning after the screaming stopped, sitting by the old bicycle mechanic, I felt a relief that colored everything around me. Even the glint of the sunlight on the asphalt seemed cheerful. Up until my mother's illness, my life had not been particularly sad—no more so, that is, than the life of anyone else in Hanoi at that time. But because I'd never felt deep sadness, I'd never felt such relief from it, either. The knowledge that my mother wasn't suffering gave me a sense of joy that was as powerful an emotion as I had known.

We reach the junction of I-95 and head north toward Washington. Outside, the sky has grown perfectly dark and all I can see is the triangle of pavement in my headlights and the two red dots that represent the car ahead of us. "I wish I could describe that day," I tell Shelley. "It was something beautiful. Seems like everybody smiling. And when the old man finished his work, I try to give him his money, but he won't let me. He say I should buy him a coffee instead."

I pause to let a small car speed past in the fast lane, then I continue. "Now, that's funny in Vietnam. Nobody ever hear of a sixteen-year-old girl buying an old man coffee. But, like I say, I got the time, and I'm happy that day. So we walk my bike down to a café by the lake and we drink coffee."

"Did you like it?" Shelley asks.

I shake my head. "It's real bitter. Like tree bark. Sweet tree bark. But I drink the whole thing."

We travel on, listening to the sorrowful tunes of Willie. "Then the old man did something I couldn't believe." I can remember it perfectly, how I'd gotten on my bike to ride home and the old man bowed to me. "Who would ever imagine this! A grandfather bowing down to a young girl. But he did, like I was a princess. And then he said, '*Làn thu-thủy nét xuân-sơn, hoa ghen thua thắm liễu hờn kém xanh.*' To me, nobody ever said anything better."

Shelley looks at me, waiting for a translation.

"That sentence real famous to Vietnamese, because it comes from *Truyện Kiều,* The Tale of Kieu, our most beautiful poem. It long as a book. It about a girl, Kieu, whose life is real sad, but she's a good girl. Lovely girl." I consider the words for a moment, then say, "It mean something like, 'Her eyes like autumn rivers, her eyebrows like the hills in spring. She makes the flowers jealous because her beauty, and the willow trees jealous because her skin so fine.' "

Shelley says, "It sounds like something from Shakespeare. 'Her eyes like autumn rivers.' "

"Yeah. 'Compare you to a summer day.' Like that."

"You know the sonnets?"

I shrug. "A little." I don't want to sound too pleased with myself. "I studied literature at Hanoi University. We read Shakespeare, but I didn't know English then. We only read Vietnamese translations." My father used to complain that the family would have to go without fuel on the death anniversaries of our ancestors because I kept the lamp lit so late at night. He never made me turn it off, though. He was proud of my diligence, proud that he, a poor boy from the countryside, would have a daughter at the country's finest university. And he refused to believe that our family was so desperate we couldn't waste a bit of kerosene in the interest of my education. My father, who had memorized the entire *Truyện Kiều* as a way of testing his own intelligence, used to recite it to me and Lan when we were children. Those were the words to which we drifted off to sleep.

Shelley says, "You seem to know the English pretty well now."

"I just memorize the words, like we do in Vietnam. Shakespeare too hard. I don't really get him." Still, I've learned most of the sonnets. That's one thing I can say about a Vietnamese education. If I read the words often enough, I will learn them. And what else do I have to do late at night in Wilmington? It's one option if you can't sleep.

Outside, above the jagged line of pine trees, I can see the moon rising in the blue-black sky. I still remember the face of that old bicycle mechanic, that old gentleman. "If someone tell you you're pretty like Miss Kieu, it's a fine day for you."

"You're prettier than you think you are," says Shelley.

I grin at the road. "Thanks," I say.

The Willie lady finishes on the CD and Shelley puts in one she calls "Blues Grass," which sounds just like more people singing. "Let's eat more," she says, digging around again in her bag.

We eat cold fried chicken, more deviled eggs, and pickles. Shelley made cheese sandwiches, too, but I've had enough by now. She opens a package of Oreos and puts them on the armrest between us. We cross the Virginia border. I lift my coffee out of the cup holder and take a sip. I can't believe it stays hot this long. When we get back, I'm going to Target.

"I want to ask you something," Shelley says. "You say you're from Saigon, but you only tell stories about Hanoi."

Somewhere, in the back of my mind, I guess I've expected her to arrive at this conclusion. No one in Wilmington knows the truth. What would

Gladys do if she learned that both my parents fought with Ho Chi Minh? Now, my secret slips out like a bird from a cage and I make no effort to restrain it.

"Vietnamese in America, they don't like Hanoi people," I explain. "So I tell them I from Saigon, my family northerners who come down to the south in 1954 to get away from the Communists. It's better for my business."

"Would they stop shopping at your store?" Shelley asks.

"Before, yeah. Now? Maybe they don't care so much. But I been lying for so long, you can't go backward and tell the truth."

The Blues Grass has a twang that reminds me of the music of minority people, up in the mountains on the border with China. I like it. When the CD ends, Shelley switches off the stereo and turns to me. "You say your father used to recite that poem to you. Can you recite it to me?"

I nod. "But it's been long time. The whole thing take hours."

"I've got hours," Shelley says.

For some reason, I don't feel self-conscious and, to be honest, my voice sounds quite lovely in Vietnamese. I think for a moment, take a deep breath, then speak the first few lines. " '*Trăm năm trong cõi người ta, chữ tài chữ mệnh khéo là ghét nhau.*' " The sound is soft and rhythmic, soothing as rain. I think of my father, sitting beside me on the bed, holding his palm against my cheek. I recite the next line, then the next.

It surprises me, after all these years, how the words gush from memory, like water from a spring. I continue for an hour, then two. At first, I glance over at Shelley every now and then, to make sure I should keep going. But Shelley's head eases back against the seat of the car. Later, her eyes are closed. Still later, I can hear her breathing.

My father. Bo. Are you still alive? Do you ever think about your little one?

I come from the union of an impersonator and an impostor, which is how, I suppose, I learned the skills of deception. My father was born in a coal-mining village near Cam Pha. The eighth son in a family of twelve, he left home in 1950 for the simple reason that his parents couldn't feed him. He was fourteen years old and hoped to get work in a factory in Hai Phong. Instead, he joined the Viet Minh forces because the prospects for food seemed better. At that point, my father's political beliefs resembled those of many people in the country at that time: He followed the demands of his stomach. Although such an ideology (if you could call it that) seems, in retrospect, ridiculously simple, it had an obvious soundness that contributed to the swelling numbers of people who joined the ranks of the Viet Minh. My father dreamed of rice—not those scant and bitter brown grains that failed to adequately fill his belly, but white rice, fat and succulent bowls of it, fragrant, warm, satisfying. If you were hungry, it didn't seem so silly to put your life on the line for food.

During his first few years in the army, my father's battalion massed itself in the northern mountains, along the Chinese border, a cold and spooky place for a boy from the coast and, though he suffered continuously from malaria, he grew strong and agile and somehow survived. The soldiers spent most of their time hiding in the jungle, ducking into villages only occasionally, to resupply, or recruit, or commit sabotage, or, sometimes, murder. The political indoctrination was convincing and basic: Drive out the French imperialists and their Vietnamese lackeys; bring independence to Vietnam. Over the years, my father came to understand and cherish those goals in a more subtle and profound way, and he became very good at convincing others of their merit. Though his skills as a fighter didn't impress anyone, he possessed a talent that did. Even at that young age, he had a booming voice, and an easy way with it. The officers gave him the bullhorn and he spent his days walking up and down the lines of troops, singing of patriotism, telling jokes, spurring the company forward. He didn't feel like a leader, but he became excellent at acting like one.

My father met my mother in late 1953, during a forty-five-day trek west from Thai Binh, as General Vo Nguyen Giap gathered his troops for the battle that would eventually take place at Dien Bien Phu. My father had lived in the jungle nearly four years already. He had grown solid and tough, if not exactly brawny, and he thought little of traveling through the mountains with nothing but his rifle and bullhorn, an extra set of clothes, a blanket, a mosquito net, and enough rice to last a week. My mother, a member of a supply brigade that converged with his battalion at a crossing on the Da River, had only joined up a month before. Her delicate skin, which she had always shielded from the sun, had become cracked and burned. Blisters covered her hands and feet. Her muscles ached. To him, she looked lovely and exhausted, and he had never seen such fine gray eyes, which were both sorrowful and expectant, a quality that so perfectly matched the mood of those years that he took it for wisdom (as it turned out, she was, in fact, wise, but she never agreed that the look in someone's eyes could prove it). At that time, she barely spoke, certainly never complained, but he wanted to help her. For five days, the troops marched in tandem, and, taking advantage of the flexibility of his position, my father spent much of that time marching beside her, doing what he could to lift her spirits. She cried regularly. He wooed her with the wild vegetables he collected in the forest. He cooked for her, sang for her, teased her to make her laugh. When he asked her about her childhood, she told him she'd grown up in a rice-farming village near Hai Phong.

He shook his head in disbelief. "I grew up near Hai Phong myself. I know the accent."

The troops were camping above a narrow valley, and my father had found a rock that served as an overlook. From here, they could see a dozen Thai minority villages spread out below them. Birds fluttered through the trees before settling down for the night. In the distance, a band of monkeys whooped like ghosts. In another era, this spot would only have seemed beautiful and eerie. Now it seemed beautiful, eerie, and tragic, too. My mother looked away. When she was younger, she had found tragedy terribly romantic. Now she merely found it tragic. She was only sixteen.

"You might as well tell me what happened," my father said.

On that evening, on that particular outcropping of rocks, a half dozen couples giggled and flirted, and their presence nearby left my mother reluctant to tell the truth about herself. Paranoid and frightened, she believed that someone might overhear, that her own words might kill her. She thought of her parents, dead in the fields; her house, looted and

empty. Life could disappoint you in the most unexpected and heartbreaking ways. Somehow, in the course of a very few hours, her own existence
had exploded into tiny fragments, then reconfigured itself into this scene,
this evening, on this mountain. For days and days, one question had consumed her: What would happen tomorrow? The answer never changed:
Her life might explode again. But now, for the first time in weeks, that
answer failed to scare her. Why bother with fear? She could be brave or
fearful, she realized, and it wouldn't make any difference. She might die
tomorrow either way. My father, sitting next to her, had seen so many
friends killed that he knew this truth already. Most of the people on that
mountain, in fact, knew it absolutely. But my mother had been slow to
learn, perhaps because grief and confusion had made her mind so murky.

And so she told him everything. "My family owned most of the land in
Giang village, north of Hanoi," she said. As the Viet Minh's campaign for
independence grew increasingly daring and successful, her father, who
was loyal to the French, arranged for his daughter to go live with an aunt
in the city. But before she could leave for the capital, Viet Minh troops
entered the village. It was October 1953. A French newspaper would
later claim that, "An intense firefight left sixteen saboteurs dead and
twelve wounded, while loyalist troops suffered only minor casualties."
Perhaps it was so, but the French, without explanation, withdrew from
the district a few days later. Having lost the protection of the government
authorities, my mother's parents decided to travel with her to the city. But
on the morning they planned to leave, six Viet Minh cadres appeared at
their door. "Dogs of capitalism!" they shouted. "Get to work." With that,
they used the butts of their rifles to drive my mother and her parents into
the fields. For the next two days, the three of them worked their land like
primitive beasts, without tools, or food, or rest, or water. Along the edges
of the fields, the other inhabitants of the village silently watched them.

My grandmother had always been frail, but she lasted surprisingly long
before her heart gave out. When she finally did collapse, my grandfather
stumbled over to help her. The soldiers began to beat him. They recognized the poetry in using forced labor to kill the elite, but the process
had taken much longer than they had expected. Impatient, they finally

shot him in the neck, a gesture that wouldn't kill him instantly but would certainly hurry him along. My mother, terrified that they would shoot her, too, continued moving diligently through the fields. Once they'd dispatched both the adults, however, the soldiers grew bored and wandered off. My mother ran to her parents. Her mother was dead already. Her father lay on the ground, bleeding, dying, staring toward the sky. She felt a hand on her arm and turned to see one of her neighbors, a man who had often worked for her father. "Go to Hanoi," he told her. She didn't move. "They will kill you if you stay," he urged. "Go now." She pulled herself up, took one last look at her parents, and ran.

But somewhere on the road between Giang village and the city, my mother panicked. She convinced herself that the soldiers were chasing her, that they would track her down and kill her, just as they had killed her parents. If she had been reasonable then, she would have realized that she looked like any of the thousands of traumatized peasants clogging the roads during that chaotic autumn, that she could easily have made it to Hanoi. But she wasn't reasonable at all. For days, she lay in ditches, curled up behind haystacks, surviving on irrigation water and air. And then one morning, as she sat in a field by the side of the road, a farmer told her about a women's division moving through that village. At dusk, she saw them marching by in tight formation. There were fewer than a dozen soldiers, but they looked strong and spirited, and were singing loudly. She pulled herself out of the ditch and stepped into line. Camouflage, she thought, as she continued with them down the road, toward the hills and away from the city.

As my mother told her story, my father listened intently. His military life had been colored and energized by tales of French cruelty. Like most Vietnamese, he had witnessed such ruthlessness firsthand. As a child, he saw a French colonel nearly rip the arm off a village boy who had whistled mockingly during a military parade, and he had been among the crowd of children who discovered the body of that same boy when it washed onto the beach a few days later. Individual stories no longer served to anger him directly. Rather, they hardened his sense of resolve and, if anything, made him wonder why his people had, for so long, tolerated such oppression. Still, even though he had never heard that the nationalists, his own comrades, committed atrocities, the news of it didn't shock him so much as confirm a hunch. War made the spirit ugly.

Though my father felt no surprise about the details of her story, her means of describing it startled him. She didn't merely relay the facts of her experience. She took these facts and sifted through them like a hand through rice, meticulously, considering each grain of meaning. Her grief seemed so complicated. Of course, she mourned the loss of her parents, and her privileged life, and her dreams for her future. But she also berated herself for the way that she had failed to help her parents, as if such a thing had been possible. At the same time, she asserted a distinction between "then" and "now," describing her "then" self as both a child and a coward, and her "now" self as hopeless, but more astute. This new existence, she told him, offered a relief she would never have experienced had she fled to Hanoi, where life with her aunt would have been too terrible a reminder of her loss, like squatting in the empty shell of her childhood home. Perhaps most surprisingly, though she despised the soldiers who had killed her parents, she had no harsh words for their cause. "I haven't said much since I've been in these mountains," she told him. "But I've listened to what you say to the troops. The French should go."

The acknowledgment impressed him. "I'm surprised to hear a rich person say that." He'd never met a rich person, but he'd had his expectations.

She shrugged. "I'm not rich," she said. "I have nothing."

Somehow, the horror of her experience did nothing to diminish the fact that she charmed him. She had delicacy, beauty, and a complex intelligence, qualities that he might have believed existed, but didn't expect ever to encounter himself. In his mind, he refused even to compare her with other girls—not with the rowdy and fearless ones who filled the craters along the supply routes webbing these mountain passes, and certainly not with the farm girls he remembered from his village, hardworking and amiable enough, but inconsequential. He had chosen to believe the slogans of the revolution that he belted out of his bullhorn a hundred times a morning: "Nothing is more precious than freedom and independence!"

"All for the front!" "When the enemies come to the house, even the women fight back!" "United, united, greatly united; successful, successful, greatly successful!" But the grand depictions of a determined army and a just society never allowed for the kind of ambiguity that her mind not only recognized, but accepted. When he thought about the soldiers who had killed her parents, he wondered how there could be righteousness without compassion. Just as this girl began to believe in the justice of the cause, he began to doubt it.

Later, my parents always marked that conversation as the moment they fell in love. My father, the raconteur, described it to me a hundred times: the way the sun slid down beneath the distant mountains, the supernatural calls of the monkeys, the sadness in my mother's eyes. She remembered the details, too, but described them with less drama: sleeping on the ground made her stiff; he gave his rations to her; she liked the animation in his voice. What they never said, but what I came to understand as I grew older, was the fact that, in addition to their love, they had exchanged something else that evening, something that, in its effect on both their lives, would turn out to be just as important. He had given her a way to live in that world and, in knowing her, had lost some of that ability himself.

At exactly nine the next morning, I return to Vietnam. Or, at least, a little piece of Vietnam in downtown Washington, D.C. Unlike all the mansions Shelley pointed out on Embassy Row, the embassy of Vietnam is located on the fourth floor of an office building on Twentieth Street NW. I stop beside the door, looking at the words "Embassy of Vietnam" written in English and Vietnamese.

"You okay?" Shelley asks. Her hand pauses on the doorknob.

I nod, then follow her inside. I'm just a little disoriented, considering I haven't been on Vietnamese territory in twenty-three years. That's all.

The waiting room, simple and utilitarian, could pass for a doctor's office were it not for the "See Vietnam" travel posters hanging on the walls. Ha Long Bay. A Cham ruin. The Quan Su Pagoda. Shelley walks straight to the reception window. Because I'm trailing behind, she turns and waits for me to catch up. Her face looks uncertain. "Could you ask?" she whispers, moving aside.

I adjust the strap of my purse on my shoulder, smooth down my dress. It's Shelley's dress, actually, her gauzy peacock dress that she knows I love and which she pulled from the depths of her suitcase and handed to me this morning. "Please," she said. "You look real nice and all, but I think maybe we should try to seem more professional." I looked down at my worn yellow slacks and faded pink blouse. They are my work clothes; what could be more professional? Shelley refused to yield. I grumbled, but then I put it on. Actually, I felt curious to see how I would look. Standing in front of the motel mirror, I checked myself out. Not bad, really. I spread some of her lipstick over my lips. "Foxy," I said.

Shelley whistled like boys do when a good-looking girl walks by. "I don't want to sound like your mother or anything, but see how pretty you can look when you try?" I grinned at my reflection in the mirror.

Even though Shelley is nervous, being with her gives me a sense of security that might explain why I have managed to enter the embassy at all. I don't feel confident, exactly, but I do feel willing to try. A young woman sits behind the reception window, looking down at a sheaf of papers. Hearing the sound of my approach, she says, "Can I help you?" then lifts her head. As soon as she sees me, she repeats the question in Vietnamese. *"Cô cần gì?"*

Without even thinking about what I'm doing, I shift into some long forgotten mode of speech. It's not the laid-back Vietnamese that Gladys and I speak in Wilmington, but the Vietnamese of my youth—formal, appealing. I'm a Hanoi girl again, facing the stone gray face of the bureaucracy. "I'm sorry to trouble you, miss. I've come here to make a request of Mr. Phung Van Luan. Please. I'd like to meet with him if possible."

The receptionist's face grows hard. "What does this pertain to?"

I glance at Shelley. After much discussion, we decided against trying to make an appointment, because the political counselor might have merely refused to schedule it. Instead, we're counting on the possibility that two desperate women standing in his office would be difficult for Mr.

Phung Van Luan to ignore. "It's about an adoption, miss. My friend here is scheduled to adopt a baby from Hanoi. There's been a delay."

"A baby?" Sympathy seeps across the young woman's face. "I'll see what I can do."

A few minutes later, we're ushered into the office of Mr. Phung Van Luan, which looks out over a cluster of similar-looking office buildings. The man himself is middle-aged, tall and fit, wearing a green polo shirt and khakis. He walks around his desk as we come in, reaching out to shake our hands. "Good to see you, Ms. Marino. Ms.—" He pauses, jiggling change in his pocket.

"Mai," I say. "Pham Thi Xuan Mai."

He looks at me with interest. "Should I call you *cô* or *em,* Ms. Mai?" he asks. His English is perfect.

I look at Shelley, then down at the floor. "Whatever you like." I can feel my face turning red.

"You've got to excuse us, Mrs. Marino," Mr. Luan explains, motioning for us to sit down. "We Vietnamese are very proper."

I follow Shelley's lead and sit down on the couch. She perches on the edge of the cushion, like a rocket about to take off. "Mai's been teaching me some Vietnamese," she says, adding, with a stress in her voice, "in anticipation of the arrival of my son. I know that '*em*' is what you'd call a lady younger than yourself. And '*cô*' is what you'd call one who's older."

Mr. Luan nods, impressed. I'm impressed, too, that Shelley remembers her lessons, and relieved that she hasn't added the second part, the fact that "*cô*" is polite, and that "*em*" is also a term you would use for a lover.

"Now, ladies, how can I help you?" Mr. Luan pulls over an armchair and sits down beside us.

Shelley explains her situation, starting as far back as the lost child from Slovakia. She's clever. She gives just enough detail to make her story compelling, but not so much to risk boring the man. He listens attentively, nodding his head from time to time, occasionally looking at me. When Shelley has finished, he stands and walks to his desk, slides on a pair of glasses, then shuffles through some papers. "Here it is," he says, holding up a single page and reading it. "Yes, there's been a delay. A little boy at the Ha Dong Children's Center."

Shelley stiffens, nodding as if each gesture will have some bearing on her future.

Mr. Luan, carrying the paper, walks back to the armchair and takes a seat. He looks at me. "Tell me about yourself, Miss Mai," he says. Then, adds, "*Em sang Mỹ bao lâu rồi?*" How long have you been here, Em?

I stare at my hands on my knees. It's strange, after all this time, how official power can still intimidate me. And I'm an American citizen now. "Twenty-three years," I answer in Vietnamese.

"*Em quê ở đâu?*" Where are you from?

My old lie, the one I use with Gladys, won't work here. He's a Communist himself, so he won't be moved by a story about my parents heading south to flee Ho Chi Minh's regime. I tell the truth. "I grew up Hanoi," I tell him, in English, wishing for the millionth time that I could be prouder of the way I speak the language in this country.

The man turns out to be less interested in my political history or linguistic skills than in my personal one. "How old are you?" he asks.

"Forty-two."

"Are you married yet?"

I shake my head. In Vietnam, I'd feel mortified by this fact, as if I'm damaged goods or something. Here, though, it's just the question that bothers me. I wonder how long he has been in this country. He hasn't learned that, in America, we consider certain questions rude.

The political counselor shakes his head in mock dismay. "Forty-two years old and still single. That's late for such a pretty lady."

Despite myself, I blush. Back in Hanoi, I would resent this bureaucrat for abusing his post in such a way. I still resent it, but I'm flattered, too. A man hasn't spoken to me like this in years. Not in Vietnamese. Never in English. A warm feeling courses through my blood. I hate it, but I kind of like it.

Shelley watches.

Mr. Luan stares at me for longer than he should. Then, slapping his hands against his knees, he turns to Shelley. "So, Mrs. Marino," he begins.

"I've looked over your file and I don't see any reason why we can't move this thing forward. Your case should be completed in a month. Shall we say that?"

Shelley looks amazed. "Yes," she stammers. "Thank you so much."

Mr. Luan looks at me, his eyes moving up and down my body. "My pleasure, Mrs. Marino. My pleasure."

For the first hour, headed south on I-95, Shelley won't call me anything but Foxy. I swat the air every time, but I do look good. We drink Diet Cokes and eat Cheetos. Shelley's put the Rolling Stones in the CD player. I like the James Taylor better, but I don't mind.

We didn't leave D.C. until after five, then we got stalled in rush-hour traffic. It's dark by the time we reach Richmond, and just past eight. Other than a quick stop at McDonald's, we plan to drive straight through and make it home by one A.M. After all the joking about Mr. Luan, we're quiet, staring through the windshield into the black night.

Even with the music blaring, we both hear the pop. The van jogs to the side, then surges forward, then settles back down. Shelley looks at me. "You okay?" she asks.

I nod, keeping my eyes on the road.

"What was it?"

"I don't know." I don't think the transmission would make a pop. The van feels strange to the touch, hard to maneuver, cranky. "How far to the next exit?"

Shelley pulls out the map and begins to scour it. "We're somewhere near Petersburg. Maybe ten miles."

We drive in silence, but it's an attentive silence now. I can feel the van losing power, although it continues to move. We pass the first indication of an approaching exit. Three miles. One mile. A quarter mile. I pull off. It feels like I'm going to lose power, so I coast to the edge of the road.

"I've got my cell phone," Shelley says.

"I got mine, too."

"Let's call triple A." She pulls her phone and wallet from her purse, finds her little AAA card, punches in the number, and waits. She listens for a while, punches in a few more numbers, then waits again. I stare out the window. Now that we're off the interstate, the night seems even darker. "Yes, hello," says Shelley. "My car broke down. I need some help."

Shelley reads out her membership number to the operator at the other end of the line. I pull the lever for the hood of the van, get out, and go to take a look. The air is mild, breezy. I open the hood and stare down at the engine. Light wisps of steam rise toward the rusty hood. Shelley opens her door and gets out. "They say they'll be here within an hour." It's nearly nine.

We get back in the car, drink more Diet Coke. Thick stands of trees line both sides of the road. I consider the value of all the frozen food in the rear of my van. I have insurance coverage for the van breaking down, but not for the thousand dollars' worth of frozen food packed in ice inside it. And eight hours to get home before it spoils.

Lights appear on the road up ahead. "Maybe that's them," Shelley says.

Slowly, a car approaches. It's an old sedan, scuffed and wheezy looking, and it pauses beside us. A man with a cigarette in his mouth motions to us and I roll down the window. He takes a drag on his cigarette, then lets his arm dangle outside his car. "You girls need some help?" he asks, grinning and squinting at us.

Shelley leans over me and yells, "Thanks. Our husbands just called from a cell phone. They're behind us on the interstate and they'll be here in a few minutes."

He looks uncertain. "You sure?"

Shelley nods energetically. "Thanks anyway." She sits back in her seat, then, under her breath, says, "Roll up the window." I roll it up. "You never know," Shelley says. The car pulls away.

We sit a few more minutes. I wish I could see stars, at least.

Shelley says, "Good thing I'm here."

"If we get murdered, you'll wish you were somewhere else."

"True," she admits. Then she turns in her seat to face me and pats her hands against her knees. "Let's talk about scary things," she says. Her voice is light and optimistic, as if she's suggesting that the two of us throw a party. "Only things that are worse than this."

It's a weird idea. "You first," I say.

Shelley tells me about her senior class trip to the Grand Canyon. The chaperones had made the students promise not to wander off, but late that night, during a game of truth or dare, they came up with the idea that one of them should go off and sleep alone. None of her friends would do it, so Shelley, who felt the need to prove herself that night, volunteered. "There was no moon. I forgot to take a flashlight, and then I was too stubborn to go back for it." It took her about ten minutes to get lost. Finally, she threw her sleeping bag down on the ground and climbed in. "When I woke up in the morning, I was about five feet from the rim of the canyon," she says. "I'd never even seen it."

I wince. Shelley nods. "I still have nightmares about it."

I smile. "You stupid as a cow," I tell her.

"Maybe even stupider." We stare at the empty road, sipping our Cokes. After a while, Shelley says, "Okay, your turn. Tell me some stupid scary story."

I watch the outline of a tree moving gently in the wind. Once, I saw a pink moon over Virginia, but tonight the moon is just the vaguest glow behind a cloud. I take another sip of Coke. I don't hurry. I'm nervous, I guess, but not as nervous as I might have expected. After all these years, I will tell my story, and I will take my time with it. "This is the stupidest scary story I know," I begin. "It was in Hanoi one summer, 1979. Me and my boyfriend took my little niece to Unification Park."

I don't look at her. I don't pause. I don't skip. I speak carefully, leaving nothing out. I begin by explaining that, given a choice, I wouldn't have taken My Hoa along for those last few hours I had with Khoi. But once we arrived at the park I was grateful for the way she drew our attention from the painful matter of saying good-bye. Without My Hoa, Khoi and I would have been speechless, trying too hard to figure out the meaning of forever or five or ten years. And so we gladly followed as she tried out every swing, made a circuit of every tree, and traveled like a tightrope walker along every curb. That morning, we looked like ordinary parents, not a pair of lovers saying good-bye, and our ordinariness helped us pretend to forget the truth ourselves. Only once, sitting together on a bench while My Hoa conducted us through her repertoire of songs, did I feel Khoi's hand move closer to mine, and I took it.

My Hoa wouldn't stop to eat or even to take a sip of water. In anticipation of this trip to the park, she had hardly slept the night before. She considered any distraction from playing to be a waste of her time. When she finally began to sway from exhaustion, Khoi carried her on his shoulders and they walked along the lake pretending to be sailors. Finally, we spread a blanket near the shore and I convinced My Hoa to lie down. Within a few seconds, she was asleep. I looked up at Khoi and started to cry.

He pulled a handkerchief out of his pocket, but I pushed his hand away. "I don't need that," I said. I took a paper fan from my bag and began to fan my sleeping niece.

Khoi stood. For a moment, he looked uncertainly out at the lake and I thought that he might simply turn and walk away. Then he grabbed my hand and pulled me up beside him. He led me to the far side of a queen of myrtle tree, its branches heavy with lavender flowers, and he gently pushed me against it. "I'm not gone yet," he told me quietly. For the first time that morning, I was willing to kiss him. My arms moved up and around his neck and as soon as our lips touched something shifted inside me. I held him as if I were sinking, as if the grip of my arms might keep him from floating away, as if nothing else existed but blackness and sweat, his mouth, and mine. Over the course of our time together, Khoi and I had kissed in every secluded corner of Hanoi. We had become excellent at it, not merely in the way we touched, but also in our ability to protect ourselves from the world around us. Khoi could make himself disappear in an instant, melting into the shadows along the walls so that anyone passing would see me standing all alone, suspicious perhaps but not guilty. For my part, I became two girls when I kissed. One girl could carry on the most articulate dialogue with Khoi's lips. The other girl just listened. She could hear an approaching bicycle, or footsteps, or father, from an astonishing distance away. She kissed with her hands against

Khoi's chest, ready to push him back as soon as the tiniest leaf began to rustle. In two years, we had never been caught.

But this was a different kind of kiss, impermeable. I was only one girl then, and a deaf one.

When I finally pulled away, Khoi was smiling. "I didn't know you could kiss like that!" He laughed.

I laughed, too, and then I remembered My Hoa. Peering around the side of the tree, I saw the empty blanket. "The baby," I whispered, and ran. Somehow, I had forgotten her, and now I forgot everything except for her. I raced along the edge of the water, over the wooden bridge and down the other side, calling My Hoa's name. Khoi followed. Both of us were screaming. Then we saw the crowd farther down the shore of the lake. Two men stood in waist-deep water. One of them had a yellow bundle in his arms. Khoi and I ran up and stood at the edge of the crowd. The man with the bundle began to sob. I couldn't speak or move.

This is the way I've remembered it for all of these years. The empty blanket. The yellow bundle. That man, wailing.

Shelley takes my hand. She says nothing, but I can feel the question. "That all," I insist, as if she's pushed for more. "My Hoa died." I've never actually said those words: *My Hoa died.* Now the sentence flies through the air like something that just got loose.

"I'm sorry," she says. Her hand feels cool in mine. In the darkness, her face offers sympathy and hope. She doesn't prod. Still, I feel the question: What happened after that?

A wave of heat sweeps over me, as if summer has arrived in the last ten minutes. I say, "I need to go." I pull my hand away, open the door, and slip out onto the dark road. I walk around the van, then veer down the slope and into the trees, into the quiet and unpestering night. I move by feel, pushing myself from tree to tree, a ball bouncing off hard surfaces, rhythmic, purposeful in my attempt to lose myself. I want wilderness, but I've only found a few scattered trees. I pull up my dress, crouch down and pee, then stand and step out onto an empty parking lot, a dark building, a streetlight, a sign that reads CARLTON'S LUMBER: WE BUILD HOUSES. I sit down on the curb, dig my fingers into the dusty gravel, listen to my breath.

After. I have shied away from after. Parts of after, of course, remain clear—my days on the boat, during which time I became, conveniently, deranged. If I tell myself anything at all, I say that I saw the yellow bundle and then the world went black, like a curtain coming down on that one scene, then rising again to reveal the new setting on the boat. But what happened *right* after? I don't remember, I tell myself. I don't remember. I don't remember.

I remember.

After My Hoa died, I ran away. Khoi took my hand and pulled me from the crowd. We did not identify ourselves. We did not identify her. We left that unlucky fisherman, who meant no more to My Hoa than any passerby on the street, to hold her dead and sopping body. Khoi and I ran away.

Imagine. Yes, imagine that.

Imagine what might have happened had I stayed in Hanoi, carried My Hoa home, and faced my sister. Imagine the scene: a busload of relatives moving slowly out of Hanoi toward Cam Pha and my father's village burial ground. The aunts would be yelling curses at the heavens. "Enough already!" they'd wail. "Enough." The uncles would stare out the windows, speechless. In those days, funerals occurred with regularity, but My Hoa's funeral would be different. My mother passed away at forty-two after suffering horribly from cancer. Her death was early, but not unexpected. And my brother-in-law, Tan, took four years to die after the military ambulance brought him home from the hospital. His death had also come early, but in those years during and just after the war, the death of a young man seemed almost normal. I remember the evening of the day that we buried my mother, when my father finally cried. Holding me in his arms he said, "You'd think we'd have gotten used to it." No one we knew had gotten used to it.

Imagine me at My Hoa's funeral. Imagine the unimaginable: the face of my sister.

I did two terrible things that day. The first was the worst. The second was worse.

"Mai?" Shelley appears through the screen of trees. "The guy's here." Her voice is gentle. She takes my hand and pulls me up. I follow her back toward the yellow lights of the tow truck. "Did you just get a tune-up?" she asks.

I try to focus on the history of my van. "Yeah. I did."

"The spark plugs were loose. The mechanic didn't screw them back on properly."

The tow truck guy is old, gangly, toothy, wearing a jacket with a patch that says "Henderson" on it. Henderson mutters something that sounds like, "Get you some aggravation." Shelley communicates with him.

"So you think we can make it home now?" she asks.

I comprehend the nod, at least. It is nearly eleven. I may not lose my inventory after all. Henderson wipes his hands on his pants, pulls himself back up into the cab of his tow truck, and motions for us to go ahead of him. My van starts without even a cough. I turn it around, drive back to the entrance to 95, then pull right on. The tow truck follows for a couple of miles, then blinks its lights at us before taking an exit.

"A southern gentleman," Shelley sighs. "We were so lucky it wasn't worse." She reaches down into one of her bags and pulls out the Oreos.

"Shelley?"

She pushes the cookies toward me. "Let's binge," she says.

I eat a couple of cookies, then take a sip of my Coke. "I ran away," I tell her, because I have to finish with lying now. "I saw that she drowned and then Khoi and I ran away. I never even wrote to them."

Shelley says nothing. Her hand touches my shoulder, then drops to her lap. We drink our Cokes. We drive through a complete and glassy darkness. How much can you tell a new friend before she decides she doesn't want you after all? The headlights turn the asphalt of the road into something as smooth and slick as water. For an instant, I am a gull flying inches above the surface, skirting the waves. Or what else? A random breeze. Barren clouds. A moon, hovering.

Shelley says, "We all have things we aren't proud of."

It's a sweet thing to say, and so generous that I should disagree, but I am not so selfless and brave. Shelley pulls her knees to her chest, twists a finger through her hair. "Can I ask you something?"

"Go ahead." I have nothing left to hide.

"What do you want most in your life?"

I glance at her, but it's too dark to read the expression on her face. I look back at the road in front of me. "I cause too much damage in my life," I tell her.

Her voice is gentle. "I mean in the future. From now on."

From now on? I've asked myself a lot of questions over the years—How could it have happened? What was I thinking? How can I atone?—but not this one. I don't make choices based on my own desires anymore. But, still, she asked.

"I like to see my dad," I say.

"What's kept you from going back?"

I consider the question for a moment. "Fear, I guess. I afraid see my sister. But, also, I decide long time ago that this my punishment."

"This life in America?"

"I guess." This conversation forces me to admit a truth I haven't allowed myself to consider: In staying away from Vietnam, I've punished my father as well. "I selfish," I tell her.

Shelley says, "That's not what I was getting at."

I think of the Indian mystics I've seen on the Discovery Channel, flailing themselves with whips. Are they helping anybody? Can't you do penance and good deeds, too? Even convicts, whether they like it or not, clear trash by the side of the road. "I sort of waste my time here," I tell her.

Shelley says, "You should come to Vietnam with me."

I keep my eyes on the road. The proposal feels like the solution to a problem that, deep down and unheeded, has plagued me for years. Without any hesitation, I say, "Okay."

For a long time, neither of us says a word. Shelley puts in the Willie lady singer again. The highway is empty but for a single car in the distance up ahead. After a while, we whiz across the state line. The air in the van has turned almost nippy, so I reach over and turn off the AC. A few more hours and we'll be back in Wilmington. I can stop worrying and get my food into the freezer. "North Carolina," I announce, my voice nearly singing.

9

Shelley

The sound is muffled, soft, weak as the song of a sickly bird. It is a bird. No. It starts and stops in some familiar pattern. *Ring. Ring.* I shift beneath the covers, slide up for air, then finally reach across Martin's side of the bed to pick up the phone. "Hello? Marino and Sons."

"Oh, hey. This must be Shelley?"

"Right." It's 5:17. So dark. The universe seems hollow.

"This is Frank Deleon from the hospice."

"Hey, Frank." I've been taking Martin's off-hour calls for a month now. People are still surprised that they don't hear his voice, but neither of us has rushed to announce that the Marino marriage is foundering. I sit up, switch on the light, fumble in the drawer for a pen. I've gotten so disorganized. "What can I do for you?"

"We've got an MS patient just passed away. Marina Eleosoros. E-L-E-O-S-O-R-O-S."

I pull out an old issue of *Harper's* and see the familiar lump of a pen stuck inside it. I open it and write "Eleosoros" across the top of the page. "I'll have Albert there within the hour. Anything I need to know?"

"No family to speak of. She left a detailed plan for the memorial service and cremation. We'll send it over."

I scrawl the details around the margin of the magazine. "Albert'll see you in a little while. You take care, Frank."

I call Albert. He picks up on the first ring. "Hey, Shelley."

"Do you ever sleep?"

"Catnaps," he says.

"I need you out at the hospice. An MS named Marina Eleosoros. Cremation."

"Bennet will be glad for that."

He's right. For multiple sclerosis, cremation makes sense. The disease demands a lot from an embalmer. Sometimes, the limbs are so severely clenched that you have to break a bone to straighten them. Many families demand an open casket anyway. They don't want to remember their loved ones as they were in those last years, trapped inside a twisted body. They want all the limbs in the proper places. We can do that, but never easily. Usually, I'm all for open caskets, but in cases like these I'd like to say, "Could you rely on memories instead?"

When I get off the phone with Albert, I turn out the lamp and roll back over to my side of the bed. The yellow glow from Seventeenth Street throws dim light across the room and I can make out my clothes in a heap on the floor. I consider the previous evening, those hours stalled by the side of the road, the tone of Mai's voice while she told me her story, like someone slogging through mud, weary and miserable but persistent. And, then, her decision to come with me to Vietnam.

What would a soul look like, I wonder, if we had to embalm it? Would Mai's soul be clenched and disfigured? Would Bennet have to break one of her fragile limbs to straighten it? And what of mine?

I get to the office before seven, make some coffee, and carry a mug down to the preparation room for Bennet. Later this morning, I remind myself, I'll have to call my mother and tell her that she doesn't have to come with me to Vietnam.

"Good morning!" I say, trying my best to sound perky.

I find him sitting on a rolling stool, filling out paperwork. As always, the room is surgically clean, gleaming. People would imagine an embalming room smelling of formaldehyde or, worse, dead bodies, but we've got chemicals to mask decomposition and chemicals to mask the chemicals that mask decomposition. As a result, it doesn't smell like anything, really. That's why we call it mortuary *science*. Bennet looks up at me and grins. "You're here early," he says.

I glance at the preparation table. A form lies curled up fetuslike beneath a sheet. "Is that the MS?" I ask. She looks no bigger than a child. It's a wicked disease.

Bennet nods, making a couple of notes on his clipboard, then puts the pencil down and takes the mug. "Hey, go look in my office."

He follows me down the hall. Through the open door of his office, I see a long figure stretched out under a jacket on the couch. I take a couple of steps inside and lean over to get a closer look. "Abe? What are you doing here?" He should be in Chapel Hill.

He opens his eyes and grins at me. "Hey, Shelley." He sits up, massaging his arm.

"You're out of your sling," I say. "How does it feel?"

He yawns. "Just a little sore."

I bend over and give him a kiss, as much to hide my hurt as anything else. When Abe comes home, I'm the one who takes care of him. I'm the one who cooks the fettuccini Alfredo, buys the hazelnut French roast, calls his high school friends to tell them he's coming. In normal times, I would have discussed with him, three times at least, the plan for getting that sling off his arm. And now I don't even know when he's coming to Wilmington? "How long have you been in town?" I ask, trying to sound neutral about it.

He rubs his face with his hands, then looks at his watch. "God. I just went to sleep three hours ago."

Bennet laughs. "You're a sleep wimp. You shouldn't have stayed out so late." He's been teasing Abe on this point since high school. Bennet needs maybe three hours a night. Abe needs ten, plus naps, and the disparity between himself and his friend makes him crabby and phlegmatic.

I sit down next to Abe on the couch. "Why don't you go upstairs and go back to bed?" I'm talking about my house, our house, across the parking lot, and he knows it, but he shakes his head as if I'm an overzealous hostess offering too much to her guest.

"I'll be fine." We haven't seen each other since Keely's birthday party and now he scrutinizes my face like it's been years. "You want to go get coffee?" he asks.

I had planned to catch up, finally, on work I haven't done in weeks. "Sure," I tell him.

We decide to walk to the café a few blocks down Market Street. I usually cover this stretch of road by car, and the mansions, surrounded by high walls and lawns and oaks, seem larger and more forbidding from this angle. Twigs and old leaves crunch under our feet on the sidewalk, evidence that pedestrians rarely pass here. To our right, the cars flash by like missiles that might hit us.

"Theo won't talk to me," I tell Abe. "Your dad won't really talk to me, either." Martin has been staying in Jim and Mave Daltry's carriage house for nearly a month. Eventually, of course, I'll be the one to move out, but we haven't worked out the details yet.

"Have you tried to talk to him?" Abe asks.

"I guess there's not that much to say," I admit. Then I add, "It's my fault, but it's not entirely my fault."

Abe keeps his hands in his pockets. "It's nobody's fault."

I'm surprised, and grateful, that he would say such a thing. He's a very smart boy, and fair, but not always so perceptive. Once, after a girl jilted him in junior high, he said, "She really liked me. She let me do her math homework every day," as if that proved his point.

"What did your dad tell you?" I ask.

We pass the gates of the National Cemetery. A gardener wanders through the gravestones with a leaf blower, making little tornados fly between the bare white crosses. I'm anxious to hear which reasons Martin has offered to explain our crisis—my stubbornness, Vietnam, his refusal to have more children. Or maybe something less obvious: our sex life. Or some vague "moving in different directions."

We reach the café parking lot and thread through the cars that, even at this hour, already fill the spaces near the door. "Abe? What did he tell you?"

Abe stares at his shoes. "He said he doesn't think he loves you anymore."

I stop. He stops. I look at him, then turn and keep walking. "Oh."

He follows me, jogging to keep up. "Isn't that what we've been talking about?"

I reach the door to the café, but then I turn around, making a big loop back out toward the shrieking cars on Market Street. Abe calls, "Shelley? The coffee?"

"Go ahead." I walk back the way we came, then veer off the road again, up through the gates of the cemetery. The guy with the leaf blower glances up as I rush past. I head to the top of a hill, then down past a small circle of trees toward the back exit. I don't know what my body would do if it stopped moving. Isn't anything sacred? I still love him. This is a case of missed opportunities, unfortunate timing, bad luck. We can get divorced. Fine. But does he have to stop loving me?

The first time I asked Martin for a date, he pretended I hadn't. The campers had spent the day at the beach and he had shown up, as usual, to sit in the sand. The fact that his kids didn't go near the water that afternoon seemed to relax him and he focused on me in a way he never had before. We talked about the Trans-Siberian Railroad and how, when I went on my great adventure, I might have to spend twelve nights on a bench. That evening, I somehow got up the nerve to call him. "I was wondering if you wanted to go see a movie," I said. And then, "This is Shelley."

He didn't answer immediately.

I was so nervous. "From the beach. From camp. You know," I said. "Shelley."

"I know," he finally said and during the next long pause that followed, I told myself that I didn't care about him because I was leaving soon for Africa. "Is it a camp outing?" he asked.

The rushes of embarrassment that he produced in me had begun to feel familiar. "Well, no. I just thought it would be fun," I said. "Fun" sounded like it had six syllables.

Two nights later, Martin, Theo, Abe, and I went to see *Return of the*

Jedi at the College Road Cinemas. Martin paid for all of us. He bought each person popcorn and a Coke and we shared a supersize box of Junior Mints. The boys insisted that I sit between them and Martin treated me like a friend of his kids. Halfway through the movie, his pager went off and he went out into the lobby. Theo tugged at my arm and whispered, "Someone died."

After the movie, we found Martin waiting by the video games. Theo dragged me over to him. "Someone died, right, Dad?" he asked.

Martin smiled at me and nodded. "Sorry about that."

Theo looked up at me and said authoritatively. "See, I told you."

Abe said, "Who died, Dad?"

Martin said, "An old man died. You don't know him."

Theo looked up at me. "It was just an old man who died. You don't know him."

The boys sang camp songs all the way out to Wrightsville Beach. By the time they got to my house, they had reached seventy-seven bottles of beer on the wall, and, because I didn't want to interrupt them, I just got out of the car, waved, and closed the door. Martin gave me a friendly wave and drove away.

It took him so long to love me, and he throws it away over this? I stop beneath the trees. I feel a hand on my elbow, then Abe's arms go around me. I start to cry.

He leads me to a bench overlooking the World War I monument. For long minutes, he leaves me alone. I need a Kleenex. His hand rests gently on my knee. I'm not so distracted by heartbreak to miss the fact that he's grown up. If I wasn't sobbing, I would compliment him on it.

"I just never expected this," I finally say. "Are you sure?"

He shrugs. "I know this law student up at Duke. He brags about how no one has ever broken up with him. I'm curious, you know, because girls always break up with me." He pauses, waiting for me to acknowledge his own tragic past.

"You go out with jerks," I tell him.

"Whatever. So I said, 'Man, how come nobody ever breaks up with you?' And he goes, 'It's a question of timing. If I sense that the girl is getting tired of me, I break up with her.' He said there's a major difference in the way it feels. Maybe Dad's doing that. He's just saying, 'Well, then, Shelley, I break up with *you*!' "

"You're sweet, Abe," I say. I have to use the hem of my shirt as a tissue.

"No, really. It works. I'm going to try it next time." He nods like someone at a turning point. "Heidi, I break up with you!" "Cheryl, I break up with you!" "Vanessa, scram!" With each sentence, he holds his finger out like a magic wand, and the girls disappear: Poof! Poof! Poof!

Even though Martin treated me like his children's buddy, I believed that, deep down, he felt something more. On beach days, we would talk for hours, almost completely about my trip. Other than Vietnam and his stopovers in Japan on the way there and back, he'd hardly been anywhere. He read about the world with the serious attention of someone who expected to visit every place himself, but he also told me, without any obvious regrets, that he had kids and a business in Wilmington, and no intention of leaving. I couldn't figure him out. Every few days, I'd throw out some new idea about my itinerary—Bali or Lombok? Costa Rica or Brazil?—and he'd go home and look at maps, then come back with definite opinions on the subject. Sometimes, all this interest gave me absolute confidence in his affections. But, on the other hand, it also showed a serious commitment to my leaving the country.

The day after camp ended, I called him again. "Do you want to go out to dinner with me?" I asked. "Just me?"

He took forever to answer. "I guess so," he said.

That Friday night, we met in the bar of the Pilot House downtown. He wore a pale blue button-down, khakis, and a tie. I had on a sleeveless green sundress with sandals and a purse that matched. I'd pulled my hair back into a loose bun that made my hair frame my face like Meryl Streep's in *The French Lieutenant's Woman*, an effect that seemed both attractive and grown-up. Martin smiled when I came in, but he didn't say anything.

We had to stand by the bar to wait for our table. Without much more than a hello, he launched into a description of an article he'd been reading about the Mayan pyramids in *Smithsonian*. I nodded, pretending to listen. Outside, the sky was turning pink and by the time we sat down at our table, the river had gone dark and the lights on the bridge had begun to twinkle. I tried to remember how good I had felt sitting next to him on the beach, watching the children play in the water. I felt so rigid now, and I couldn't judge his mood at all, except that he seemed determined to wring enough material out of the Maya to carry us through the night. He talked nonstop, barely pausing to look at me or take a bite, as if he'd spent the whole day burrowing into the magazine, trying to memorize it. His behavior might have convinced me that he really didn't care at all, but once, when I looked up more suddenly than he probably expected, I caught him gazing at me so intently that I had to look away.

After dinner, we ordered coffee. I went to the bathroom, where I stared at myself in the mirror, daring myself not to blink. Camp had ended, and if I didn't say something now, I would never see this man again. I turned on the water in the sink, scooped up a handful, and drank as if I were thirsty. Then I left the bathroom and walked back to the table. I felt myself shaking. When I sat down, I looked at Martin and said, "I think I'm in love with you."

His eyes grew wide and he tried to laugh. "You think you are?" he asked. "Well, if you think you are, you may be wrong."

"No, I am. I'm in love with you."

The waiter brought the coffee. Martin looked out the window. When the waiter walked away, Martin said, "I think you *think* you're in love with me and I have no idea why."

"I am. I am in love with you."

His eyes rested on me again. "You're still in college," he said.

"That has nothing to do with it."

"Have you ever been in love before?"

"No."

"Have you ever thought you were in love before?"

"Yes."

"Then how do you know?"

"I know. Don't be so condescending."

He smiled. "Look," he said. "I am twelve years older than you. You're going to change a lot in your twenties. You have no idea."

"So I'm too young for you to be interested in me?"

He gripped his coffee cup, staring down at it. "Well, sort of. It's not you personally. I like you a lot. But you're just a kid."

"You think I'm unsophisticated."

"Well, yes."

"You think I won't ever grow up?"

"No, you'll grow up," he admitted.

"And you don't find me attractive?"

He let out a breath of exasperation. "Of course you're attractive," he said.

I waited a moment. Then I asked, "But you're not attracted to me?"

He rubbed his eyes, and when he looked at me he looked miserable. "Of course I am," he said.

I could have let those words hang in the air a bit longer, but he kept going. "Do you want me to be perfectly honest?" he asked. "Of course I'm attracted to you. Who wouldn't be? You're beautiful, smart, you like my kids. My kids like you. I'm terribly flattered that you would even sit down on the beach and talk to me. But whatever you're feeling, I don't believe it will last. You're too young."

"You don't even know me." I threw the words at him like rocks.

"Exactly. What do I know about you? That the thing you want most is to travel. How long would you last in Wilmington?"

I remembered the golden cities then and, to my surprise, I felt their pull as strongly as I had on the day that I first flew back from Scotland. I met his gaze across the table. I wanted to say, "Come with me," but I didn't. He'd told me already. He wasn't going anywhere.

I spent my first few weeks back at Chapel Hill trying to forget Martin and failing. My future had once seemed so full of possibility. Now it came down to a single choice. Not: Go away or stay in Wilmington. Not even: Go away or be with him. But: Be with him or don't be with him. And when I looked at it that way, I knew that, if he would have me, I'd be with him. My fantasies of New Delhi and Athens and Rio didn't dim, but the need felt less pressing. I began to regard my trip in the same way that I'd felt when my family scattered the ashes of my grandfather in the waters off Wrightsville Beach. I'd felt sadness, but also a sense of completion. I loved those dreams of adventure, but I believed I could let them go. Choosing one thing, I reminded myself, always meant eliminating something else.

Over the next semester, I wrote Martin a couple of letters, never mentioning my trip, or our dinner at the Pilot House, or the fact that I loved him. I made myself sound breezy. I sent comic books to his kids. He wrote back. His letters were breezy, too. At Thanksgiving, I brought Tar Heels baseball caps for the whole family. When I came home at Christmas break, the four of us sat in their living room playing Monopoly. Martin looked the same, and happy in a way that struck me as completely unrelated to my presence in the room. Absorbed by the task of helping both Abe and Theo take their turns, he hardly seemed to notice me. I wanted anything, even the anguish I'd seen on his face in the summer, but Martin talked to me like any visiting friend, and seemed to have forgotten that I loved him. At some point during the evening, he mentioned that the funeral home gardener had quit. I told him that I'd do some mulching and pruning for him over the break. When he said he couldn't accept such a favor, I told him I'd charge an hourly rate. For the next two weeks, I gardened with deliberate slowness and he finally complained that I would bankrupt him to save his shrubs.

During that vacation, I managed to see him almost daily. But I only crossed the line once. For months, Lindi had suffered from a terrible crush on a local actor, Richard. Just after Halloween, in November, she finally got up the nerve to ask him out. They had their first date a few days later and moved in together a week after that. On New Year's Eve, they invited me over for dinner. After three glasses of wine and another of champagne, I decided to spend the night. At three-thirty A.M., I picked up the phone and called Martin.

"Hello?" His voice was a mix of sleepiness and forced efficiency, which I took to be the result of regularly being woken by news of death.

"Happy New Year," I said.

He was quiet for a second. Finally, he said, "Whenever the phone rings this late, I have to tell myself where my boys are."

"They're safe at home with you," I told him.

"Happy New Year, Shelley," he said.

"Good night."

"Good night."

During the next semester, I wrote to Martin every week. My letters were still breezy, but more intimate, too. I made occasional confessions about myself. I worried about whether I had learned anything in college. I worried about money, my relationship with my mother, and that I would grow old and discover that life had no meaning. I even told him that I worried he'd find me trivial and immature. His letters were lighter, but he was never again condescending and he assured me that he didn't find me trivial or immature. Week by week, I felt myself moving closer to him and I felt Martin allowing it. In all those letters, I never mentioned my dream of traveling and Martin never asked.

On May first, at three-thirty A.M., I called to wish him happy birthday.

"Must you always call so early?" he asked.

"I wanted to be the first," I said. "Happy birthday."

"Thank you," he said.

"Good night."

"Good night," he said, then added, "No. Wait."

We stayed on the phone for four hours. I told him about visiting Niagara Falls when I was a kid, and how I'd always been terrified, after that, of accidentally going over a waterfall in a barrel. Martin worried about the impact that his divorce had had on his kids, and he wondered if his constant fear that his sons would die was a negative effect of his profession. At one point, I began to cry, but he didn't seem to know it. We didn't say a word about our feelings. When we finally hung up, it was because I had to get out of bed to go to school.

My 8:00 A.M. class ended at 9:10. I walked home, got into my car, and drove to Wilmington. He didn't even look surprised to see me. We got married two years later.

Clearly, I have a lot on my plate. I'm facing divorce, motherhood, home-lessness, and job loss all at the same time, not to mention, in all likelihood, depression. Over the next two days, I work. I file the death certificates for four new cases, gather the forms together for Albert to deliver to the registrar of deeds, make plans with the cemetery for two burials and one client's purchase of a plot. I have a phone conference with Helen Abernathy from sales at Marsellus about the new casket models for our display. I order fifteen sets of burial clothes—six blue dresses, six red ones, three gray suits—for the deceased who had been ill or aging for so many years that they didn't own anything nice enough to be buried in. I e-mail the updated schedules to my staff. I oversee the memorial service for Marina Eleosoros, a funeral at Freedom Baptist for the former director of the Red Cross, two gravesides, and an early evening visitation. I get the plumber in to fix two leaks. Through all of this, Martin and I communicate primarily through e-mail. We make the adjustment quite smoothly, really, because even during normal times, we would spend our days typing our thoughts into cyberspace and letting them bounce back to the other person's office, five feet away. But now, the tone of these messages has changed. We used to use words like "sweetheart" and "love." We used to use words like "I" and "you." We seldom do that anymore.

Before:

Dear One,

What time can you get the cars back from the McMillan graveside? Can I have Albert for Gonzalez and Peterson? I'm going to run out at three to pick up my mom's birthday present and get back in time for the five o'clock viewing. I'm starving! What should we have for dinner?

xo,

S.

Now:

Where are the records from the Horace Brown cremation last year? It was sometime in March. Thanks.

His answers? Well, they're about the same. But I can't complain about the e-mail. Without it, we would have to talk.

On Thursday morning, Rita comes on the speakerphone.

"Shelley? You there, darling?"

"Rita, I'm so busy. Can you just take a message?"

"I think you're going to want to take this call." She pauses long enough to drive me crazy, then adds, "It's that adoption lady."

I grab the phone. "This is Shelley."

"Hi, Mrs. Marino? It's Carolyn Burns from Southeastern Adoptions."

"Oh, hey." I try to sound normal. Whose turn is it to talk?

Finally, she says, "Mrs. Marino, we've got a date."

"A date?"

"For the giving and receiving ceremony. In Hanoi. It's scheduled for June tenth. I hope you're all set because you've got to work quickly to get there on time. We're only talking about a week."

I glance at my wall calendar, but it takes a while before I can make heads or tails of it. "Ten days," I finally say.

"Yes. Ten days." She starts to laugh. I didn't know she had it in her. Now, like two giddy pals, we chat about itineraries and airline tickets, my documentation, Mr. Phung Van Luan of the Vietnamese embassy in Washington, whom I plan to mention in my will.

By the time I hang up the phone, an hour has passed. I'm inside Martin's office before I remember that he no longer loves me.

He's at the computer, his back to me. The hair around his neck looks two weeks late for a trim, unruly and soft, long enough to curl around my finger.

"Hey," I say.

He swivels the chair to face me. He smiles grimly. "How was Washington?" he asks. It's been three days since I came back.

"Okay." I'm leaning inside the door, but I keep my hand on the knob. If necessary, I could exit quickly. "Actually, it went really well, I guess. I wanted to tell you I just got the call."

Martin's voice sounds almost sarcastic. "The call?"

"About the baby. I got a date for the G and R." I seem to be crying. I wipe my nose with the back of my hand.

He blinks. His chin goes up, then falls toward his chest: a failed nod. After a while, he says, "Any other news?"

"I'll have to go in about ten days. Will you be okay—here in the office?"

He shrugs one shoulder. "Sure," he says, as if such issues are not my problem anymore.

"We could call Carl to come in," I say. It's a recent idea. After the debacle over Sonya, I arranged with our former mortician to step in, on occasion, from retirement.

"Don't worry about it," he says.

"Well." I look at him uncertainly but, really, we have nothing more to say to each other. I should leave him alone, but I am full of joy and sadness and can't seem to move. Is it true, after all, that he no longer loves me? I can't tell. In his face at this moment, I see nothing but defeat. Martin squints at me as if I'm in a hot-air balloon, floating away from him, up toward the clouds.

10

Xuan Mai

We fly in from the east, and Vietnam reaches out to us. I have never seen my country from the air before. At least, not from so far above. Once, when I was twelve or thirteen, our teachers led the class on a hike up Ba Vi Mountain. We were Hanoi children living in the countryside to avoid the bombs falling on the city. Whenever our parents had a chance, they would bicycle out to the village to visit. Most of the time, though, we were on our own, supervised by anxious teachers who couldn't keep track of so many charges. The expedition to Ba Vi must have taken place during a cease-fire, because it's the only time I can remember leaving the village. The hike was long and steep and, even in midwinter, I sweated. At the top of the mountain, we ate a picnic of boiled manioc, dried fish, and jackfruit picked from a tree. From where we stood, our teachers pointed out the bomb craters that ripped a zigzag line across the earth. "See, the American government is cruel," Teacher Lam shouted. "Dropping bombs on children and farmers. But they won't ever win this war!" We children chanted and cheered. From the top of Ba Vi, we could just make out the scattered clusters of simple homes, the swooping roofs of pagodas, neatly planted sugarcane fields, and farmers with their water buffaloes plodding through the rice paddies. It seemed so cruel that a pilot flying overhead would drop a bomb on all of that.

I gaze down through the window, through the bright harvest of clouds, to green and brown patches of farmland, an occasional stand of trees, a muddy river looping like handwriting across the earth. *Quê hương.* My homeland.

The seat belt light comes on. The flight attendant announces in Vietnamese and in English that Vietnam Airlines flight 790 has begun its descent into Hanoi. I glance over, adjust the blanket covering Shelley's arms. Her head, leaning back against the headrest, bobs gently from side to side. Somehow I have managed to doze, on and off, in the time it took for us to travel all this way, but Shelley hasn't slept since Wilmington. Through all those hours, she paced the aisles until a flight attendant told her that she'd be safer in her seat. And then, with less than three hours from Taipei to Hanoi, she fell asleep.

Each of us is half insane already and we haven't even arrived yet.

The landing gear whistles its descent. Villages appear below, metal roofs glinting in the sun, dusty brown roads, a lonely tree, a factory with HONDA painted across its roof. I spoke to Khoi once, but only briefly, in the time between when he came back from Vietnam and my own departure. He told me the country had so many more cars now, and so many more motorbikes. Hanoi had become louder and richer than we ever could have imagined during those poor, silent years after the war ended. He talked about the noise, mostly. You couldn't get away from it. These days, everyone has a radio, or even a TV. Cafés blast pop music out into the street. Vietnam sounds like a nation of the hard-of-hearing, Khoi said, the way they amplify everything full blast.

Khoi kept his word. He stayed away from my family. Through some friend of a friend, he heard that my father remains alive, but suffers from emphysema. Though Bo still manages to play Chinese chess some mornings at the veterans' club, he's grown weak and has trouble walking. And Lan has done well for herself, Khoi said, stressing the "well," as if to convince me that life has gone on and all is forgiven. These days, Lan owns a café on Quang Trung Street, one in a series of three, the closest to Trang

Thi. She also has a new daughter. Well, not so new anymore. Fifteen or so, by now. Khoi didn't say if Lan had remarried and I didn't ask. I didn't want to know too much. I worried that some small piece of stray information might scare me, might make me lose my resolve to go there myself.

The jet touches down on the runway. Shelley's eyes flutter open. "Hello, Vietnam," she says, gazing out the window. "Hello, my little boy."

Over the next few minutes, passengers stand, stretch, gather their carry-ons, push toward the door. I press my face to the window, not quite ready to touch down yet, staring at the concrete tarmac, at the rice fields beyond, at the dusty red earth. I feel frightened, curious, happy, too, but mostly grateful that, despite all these years, despite everything I did, this place still exists.

The airport is new, marble floored, gleaming, and, according to the Hong Kong businessman walking up the jetway next to Shelley, something of a tourist attraction for local Vietnamese. We follow him down a series of corridors to an open area where immigration officials stand studying passports and visas behind a row of chin-high desks. In front of each desk waits a line of passengers: tourists, mostly, looking fidgety and tired, and well-pressed businesspeople who have already transferred their cell phones from carry-on bag to breast pocket. On the far side of the room, diplomats and Vietnamese nationals move through lines of their own, swiftly passing on toward the baggage carousels to scout for their luggage. I feel envious, not for their speed, but for the confidence with which they enter this country.

You forget the things you don't force yourself to remember. I have often thought, over the years, about the Hanoi trees, the way their leafy branches stretched wide, raining drops of shade like cool water down upon the streets. The trees have their place among the details of Hanoi I long ago decided to remember. But I've forgotten so much. Maybe I should say that there's so much I never noticed at all. I was young then, and I knew nothing else. Now, in these first few minutes back, I begin to notice things I'd never thought to remember: the way a man holds a cigarette, pinched between his index finger and thumb, as if it's a dart and he's about to throw it. I notice the cleaning women, squatting in pairs and trios outside the bathrooms, rags spread to dry across the edges of their buckets. In the gleaming confines of this modern airport, they still manage to look like village women waiting out the afternoon heat.

And then, as we approach immigration, I notice the expression on the face of a soldier: eyes narrow, cool, patient, waiting. It occurs to me that I might be arrested for murder. I think of Gladys back in Wilmington, launching into one of her tirades about the government of Vietnam. Police state, she calls it. Commie dictatorship. Red. Red. Red. I try to recall the circuitous route back to the airplane, which will probably soon take off again. Can I beg my way back on? Will they let a coward have a seat?

Over the tops of the passport-control desks, I glimpse the luggage carousel and, farther on, windows and the sky overhead. Somewhere, not so very far away, my father struggles to catch his breath. I have come such a long way already.

Shelley's firm hand takes hold of my arm. "It's okay. Don't worry," she says, her voice tender and teasing.

"Maybe it better your mom come with you," I tell her, though I know it's a moot point now.

Shelley laughs, squeezing my arm. "Believe me. My mom and I are both relieved that you're here and that she's back in Wilmington."

I smile. I'm not used to being needed, and I like it. But, I don't feel competent. I whisper, afraid that someone might hear, "If I have problem, you go see my father." I will write down his address.

Shelley shakes her head, refusing to acknowledge such a possibility. "Stop worrying," she says. "How many Pham Thi Xuan Mais are there in Vietnam? You're just like Jane Doe here."

I close my eyes. "Nobody's Jane Doe here," I mutter.

The line begins to move. Shelley nudges me forward. "Mai," she says. "We're nearly there."

As it turns out, nobody does make a connection between this Pham Thi Xuan Mai and the girl who let her niece stray too close to the lake in

Unification Park twenty-three years ago. The passport-control officer looks at my U.S. passport, glances at my face, then stamps my documents and sends me through. A moment later, Shelley follows. We load a luggage cart and walk through customs with barely a wave of our papers, then step out into the crowd. Women wearing pastel *áo dài* grip limp bouquets of flowers. Small children perch on their fathers' shoulders. Drivers hold up tour-company placards with foreign names written on them.

"Taxi!"

"Taxi!"

"Taxi, madame! I take you cheap." Under his breath, the driver wheedles in Vietnamese, "Lady, I've got air con. What'll you pay?"

He is a short, thick man, reeking of cologne and something I recognize but can't quite place. It isn't a pleasant smell, but I find it comforting. Somehow, it reminds me of my father. The man edges closer. "Lady," he says.

"Someone's meeting us," I mutter, but he doesn't look convinced. His hand rests on our luggage cart. One word from me and he will whisk us away.

I look back toward the arrivals exit, out of which dazed passengers continue to trickle. Shelley huddles close, her hand on my arm. "What now?" she asks. She thinks I understand this scene, but I know so little of this Vietnam.

"What's the lady's name again?"

We look at the letter Shelley pulls from her pocket. "Mrs. Huyen. From IFS, International Family Services. Or, it might say Happy Family Tours."

"Taxi, madame!" the stocky man persists.

We scan the area, our eyes ranging over the placards held in the air by various disembodied hands. Then, on the far side of the crowd, I spot a small hand-lettered sign that says, "Mrs. Marino Shely."

"There!" I yell, pointing across the crowd. Without another glance, the taxi driver dashes off, already targeting a new fare. "Follow me," I say to Shelley, who still hasn't seen the sign. I push the luggage cart forward, plunging through the crowd, all the while calling in Vietnamese, "*Chị ơi!*

Chị ơi! Cô Shelley Marino đây! Chị ơi!" The Vietnamese slips from my mouth as easily as cramped passengers from a crowded plane. Hey, lady, Here's Shelley Marino!

The young woman holding the placard can't be older than twenty, and she looks back and forth uncertainly between the two of us. Finally deducing the obvious, she focuses on Shelley. "You are Mrs. Marino?"

Shelley nods, relieved, then puts her hand on my shoulder. "And this is my friend Pham Thi Xuan Mai."

The young woman zeroes in on me. In a rush of Vietnamese, she says, "Oh, miss! I'm Hong Ngoc. My mother, Mrs. Huyen, sent me here to meet you. The other Americans in your group arrived last night. They're waiting for you to go to the orphanage. My English is so bad. Can you explain it to Mrs. Shelley?" Her hand flutters around her mouth, hiding giggles.

We follow her out of the terminal toward the parking area, and, suddenly, the sun beats down like a weapon. The air feels thick and heavy, impossible to breathe. Hong Ngoc, wearing a wide-brimmed hat, sunglasses, and gloves to her elbows, can handle the glare. But we can't. I put my hand up to shield my eyes. "Do you have a car?" I ask.

"Oh, yes, of course." It takes her a long minute to locate the driver, although in the end he is only a few feet away, leaning against the back of a gray Toyota van. When he fails to hear her call, she runs out to him, points back in our direction, and the two of them hurry toward us.

"This Mr. Lap," she explains. He is a powerfully built man, stiff and unsmiling, who shakes our hands and scowls at our luggage. Within thirty seconds, he's filled the back of the van and we are speeding out of the airport.

From our seat in the back, Shelley leans forward and asks Hong Ngoc, "Have you met my son yet? At the orphanage? A little boy named Hai Au?"

The girl turns around to look at us. Her face is young and fresh and blank, as if nothing she's experienced so far in life has left a great impression. She nods eagerly, though it's not clear that she's understood. "Your group waiting," she says. She holds the MRS. MARINO, SHELY placard in one hand, fanning herself with it.

Shelley looks at me. I explain the plan for the morning and she checks her watch. It is nearly ten A.M., though it's the middle of the night for us. She runs a hand over her hair, which lies matted against her head. "I can't meet my son without taking a shower," she announces. "Those folks had a night to sleep. They can wait for us."

Hong Ngoc understands this statement. She glances at Lap, who seems to understand as well.

"It's always something," he mutters in Vietnamese.

Hong Ngoc offers Shelley an airy smile. "No problem."

Then Shelley whoops, high and happy and hysterical. "I can't believe I'm here!" The car makes the slightest veer toward the shoulder, then corrects itself. Hong Ngoc keeps smiling, but she looks at Shelley as if she's trying to figure out what kind of crazy person they've just picked up. Lap has one eye on the road and one eye on the rearview mirror, fixed on Shelley. She grins. "Sorry about that. Sorry," she assures us. "Oops." She lets her head settle against the seat of the van and murmurs, "I just can't believe it."

I can't believe it, either. I stare out the window at Vietnam. We have moved well past the airport now, beyond the police kiosks and the Sanyo billboards and into farmland stretching in every direction. Lap switches on the radio and the air fills with the roar of a crowd. A voice full of awe and pleasure says, "Spectacular! We won't see that kind of defense very often." It sounds like any announcer on ABC Sports, except that this guy is speaking Vietnamese. The road passes fields filled with fresh green rice. What do I call such a green in English? Vietnamese has no word for green. It's just a place near blue on the spectrum. *Xanh lá cây.* The blue color of leaves. The blue color of fresh new rice. I never knew, or needed, another word for it. It was always there, just beyond the edge of the city, the blue of the rice fields, spreading to the horizon, as present and expected as the sky.

Somewhere in the center of the city, Lap pulls the car up in front of a set of glass doors that have WELCOME TO LUCINDA HOTEL painted in English on them. I don't know where we are, except that this is a hotel foreigners stay at when adopting their babies. We crossed the Red River on a bridge I've never seen before, plunged into the city through streets I didn't recognize. Hanoi seems disguised, determined to confound me. But behind the plastic billboards reading JAPANESE WATCHES and GOLD JEWELRY, I manage to glimpse the familiar sloping tiled roofs of the city, peeking out.

This building is narrow, so narrow that the glass doors stretch nearly the width of the entire structure, which sits between its wider neighbors like the thin edge of a single sheet of paper stuffed between the hard covers of a book. Just inside, Shelley and I stop in front of a wooden half-U-shaped desk with a sign that reads RECEPTION on it. We don't see a soul. Hong Ngoc drifts off deeper into the building, calling back that she'll find someone to help us.

"Well, this is nice," says Shelley, taking in the place with a smile. "All this marble and glass. And air-conditioning!"

Lap, grunting, comes in from the car, his arms full of luggage. In order to let him pass, Shelley squeezes against one end of the reception desk and I squeeze against the other. Even then, he has to pull and shove just to get our luggage past the furniture and pile it at the base of the stairs.

"This place too skinny," I say. "We'd have more room on a city bus."

"Mai." Shelley sighs. "Everyone on the Internet who adopted babies in Hanoi said we had to stay here. I hope you didn't expect the Marriott."

I watch Lap warily. He has already begun to haul our bags upstairs. I still want to find another hotel, but with all our luggage packed inside this building, how difficult will it be to get it out again?

From where we stand, the hallway leads beneath the stairs and then opens onto another long and just as narrow room, with couches and a couple of computer desks lining one side of it. Next to the couches, Hong Ngoc stands talking with a young man. He appears to be trying to edge his way around her, but each time he moves, she launches into another emphatic statement that immobilizes him. Finally, during one longer than usual pause for breath, he slips past her and hurries in our direction. "Ms. Shelley. Ms. Mai." He holds out his hand like a diplomat. "Welcome to our Lucinda Hotel. I am Tri, your manager." The young man is tall and soft-spoken, stooped from the effort of making himself heard by shorter people.

Shelley, tall enough to look him in the eye, grabs his hand and shakes it. "You have no idea how happy I am to be here."

Her enthusiasm disarms him. His face softens and he looks at her with concern. "You must be very tired."

"Tired? No! I'm too excited."

He laughs, then turns to me, becoming more formal again now. "*Chào cô,*" he says, which, literally, means "Hello, ma'am," but which we both understand to mean "You're Vietnamese."

I feel irritated with his hotel for offering such unacceptable accommodations. "Hello," I say in English.

Tri invites us to see our room. Shelley practically skips behind him up the stairs, chattering on about how interesting Hanoi looks, how thrilled she is to see her baby. I follow more slowly, trying to remember where Khoi told me he stayed and wondering if we can get a reservation there.

Our room, on the third floor, overlooks the street. The proprietors have managed to squeeze an astonishing amount of furniture into a space only a shoulder width wider than the double bed. In addition to the bed, it contains a bedside table (which, by necessity, sits at the head of the bed), a television set (at the foot of the bed), a wooden wardrobe, two tiny chairs with a tinier table between them (on which sits an ugly bud vase holding a scrawny little rose), and the mountain of luggage accumulating near the doorway as Lap drags more loads up the stairs. Off the front of the room, a sliding door opens onto a bathroom with barely enough floor space to turn around in. There's a bathtub, small and cramped, that seems to have been placed here merely for show. The most notable feature of the accommodations is a wall-size photographic mural of a deserted island, all ocean and palm trees blowing in the wind, a taunt that the universe contains something better.

The place smells sour and moldy. The noise of traffic makes me feel like we're standing in the middle of a busy intersection.

I look at Shelley. "I didn't say Marriott. But, like, Econo Lodge or something?"

She ignores me. She squeezes—*squeezes!*—along the narrow space between the wall and the bed and pulls open the door to the balcony, which amplifies the noise of the traffic into something no longer bearable. "You're not going to believe the view of the street, Mai!" she yells back in toward me.

Tri picks up two remote controls off the nightstand at the head of the bed. Holding them up in front of me, he instructs in Vietnamese: "Use the white one for the TV. The World Cup's on channel seven. Use the black one for the air con." Like a magician with his wand, he tips the remote in the direction of the air conditioner, situated above the balcony door, and gives it a push. Immediately, the machine begins to hum. Then he pushes the remote for the TV. On the screen, artificial turf appears. Men in yellow jerseys give each other high fives.

"Can I get Star TV?" I ask. An international network might carry *Oprah*.

His face betrays some mild disapproval. "Of course," he says, but then his attention shifts to the game.

Lap walks in and dumps our last few possessions on the floor. "It stinks in here," he mutters, then notices the TV. His eyes on the screen, he pulls out his handkerchief and wipes his neck. "What's the score?"

"Zero to one, France."

"It stinks in here."

"Mildew," Tri says. "The air con will get rid of it." They stare at the television. After all these years being around southern Vietnamese, it sounds strange, but also kind of wonderful, to hear people speaking with northern accents.

Shelley pulls open the door. "Mai! Come see this."

She stands with her hand on the door, waiting. I will tell her that we have to move. I slip past Lap and Tri and along the narrow space between the wall and the bed to reach the door onto the little balcony. I take a place beside Shelley in the hot sun, leaning on the railing looking down. At the street level, I can see a dozen shops, some wide and spacious, hung with bright-colored blouses or lined with sleek cabinets filled with glistening jewelry and watches. Some are as narrow as our hotel, a tiny storefront holding nothing but a thin cabinet displaying batteries and a cheap plastic stool on which a bored-looking teenager perches. Along the road, the traffic flows like a river running in the wrong direction, away from the lake. Hoan Kiem Lake. Now I know where we are. The traffic will continue on toward Dong Xuan Market. I look down at the press of motorbikes. "What's the name of this street?" I ask, merely for confirmation.

"H-a-n-g D-a-o," she tells me. "I don't know how to pronounce it."

"Hang Dao?"

"I guess."

Hang Dao. Why hadn't I noticed?

Below us, the traffic beeps and roars.

Now, I have my bearings. To our right, to the south, I can just make out the trees surrounding Hoan Kiem Lake. And to our left, to the north, lies Ngo Gach Street, which would lead me home.

11

Shelley

By the time we get back downstairs, the narrow lobby has filled with Americans, Hong Ngoc bustling among them like a cheerleader at a pep rally. Mai and I haven't been upstairs much longer than half an hour, but they look at us like we've kept them for weeks.

"Hey, y'all. Sorry," I say. "I'm Shelley. This is my friend Mai."

They introduce themselves quickly and inattentively, pulling together their water bottles and purses, cameras and caps. In one big crowd, they squeeze past us down the hallway toward the door. I hear names but don't have time to pair them with faces. Eleanor Survey. Posie Elder. J. Nathan Survey. Hal Chambers. Marilou Chambers. John Elder. One woman—I guess it's Chambers—tucks a blue stuffed elephant under her arm and, with her other hand, grabs a plastic bag full of what looks like baby clothes.

"Should I run upstairs and get some things for Hai Au?" I ask Mai. I love the way that every sentence I utter points to the fact that I will soon have my baby.

"If you want these people to kill you," she says, nudging me toward the front door. Through the glass, I see some Americans already piling into our van and another one idling behind it. Our driver Lap paces up and down the sidewalk, peering toward the front door. We step into the heat and push ourselves inside the van. Behind us sits one of the couples, a pale-faced and doughy pair, prairie looking. "You're the Surveys?" I ask.

They shake their heads. "Elder," he says. "Posie and John." They have on Adidas track pants and T-shirts to match. He's navy; she's purple. They swish when they move.

"So you got here last night?"

He gives a little nod. She says, "We're still exhausted. Slept through the wake-up call and just had time to eat breakfast and get a taxi over to your hotel."

Mai perks up at that information. "Where you staying?" she asks.

"Hanoi Horison. It's gorgeous. Even nicer than the Hilton we stayed at in San Francisco. The American ambassador got married there."

Mai tries to get my attention with her eyes, but I refuse to get into it with her. I have enough to think about without worrying over our accommodations. I stare out the window at the crowds, the storefronts, laundry hanging on the line, an old woman selling bananas. Isn't it enough, I want to ask, that you are home? That I'm about to meet my son?

I need to settle down. Vietnamese officials won't care that I sailed through my home studies and the American authorities declared me 100 percent fit to be a parent. Somewhere over the Pacific, they'll tell themselves, I lost my mind. Well, could you blame me? There's nothing natural or unstressful about an American woman, newly single, arriving in Vietnam to meet her kid. I do not mean to imply that I don't already consider Hai Au to be mine, or that I don't already love him. I love him so much that I left Martin for him. But—I'm not a fool—I know that it's a fantasy love. I know his statistics: his size and weight (at a certain point in his life, at least), his birth date (as close as anyone can guess), his name (that, at least, seems fairly certain). But, honestly, I mostly love my own idea of him. Essentially, I'm talking about a meeting between two strangers here.

Behind me, the Elders sit silent, engaging, I tell myself, in their own little preadoption freak-out. Hong Ngoc, in the front seat, leans back and tries to converse with Mai in Vietnamese.

Hong Ngoc: Long long long phrases in a breathless, effusive voice. More and more and more. Voice rising. Silly giggles.

Mai: Word. Uninflected. Staring out the window.

Hong Ngoc: Soft thing, like a secret, like we two are the best of friends. Pause. Waiting.

Mai: Word.

Hong Ngoc: Shriek! This and this and this and this.

Mai doesn't answer.

Hong Ngoc: Louder! And fast! Over and over without stopping.

Lap breaks in, over the sound of the radio: Grumble. Short, to the point, effective.

Hong Ngoc shuts up.

After about fifteen minutes, we leave the congestion of the inner city and move into the less dense suburbs, residential areas dotted with small gardens and ponds that appear intermittently between the clusters of buildings. This is not the Vietnam where the little girl ran naked down the road. It's urban and noisy, just going about its business. Bored-looking motorbike drivers pause impatiently in traffic and old ladies squat in doorways, exploring their mouths with toothpicks. The scene is different, but the expressions on people's faces don't look so different from what I'd see inside a Taurus on College Road or on the face of the girl at the guest services desk at Target. I wish Martin were here. I wish I were holding his hand. This is our great adventure.

And then we arrive.

I heard that the orphanage sat on the grounds of a hospital, and somehow, despite all logic to the contrary, I imagined a large Western-style building situated on a wide, green campus, with a homey little orphanage occupying some sunny corner, all picket fence and flowers. In reality, the hospital consists of five or six small concrete one-story buildings. As our van pulls through the front gate, I see that you could walk from one side to the other in less than three minutes. The orphanage itself is a compact, utilitarian, L-shaped structure, five doors opening onto a porch that runs along a front walkway.

When we stop, a woman steps through one of the doors, strides toward the driveway, and, with her hand up to shield her eyes, pauses to watch us get out. "That my mom," Hong Ngoc declares. Mrs. Huyen is robust, perhaps fifty, dressed in royal blue slacks and a matching blouse. Unlike her daughter, who looks perfectly Vietnamese, Mrs. Huyen has copper-colored hair and the round, bosomy body of a middle-aged matron from western Europe. Around her neck hangs a strand of blue pearls and a pair of glasses on a gold chain. She wears the kind of distracted, fleeting smile that people use when they pose for pictures.

"Shelley! And this must be Mai? You're the only two I haven't met." Her accent sounds less European than Vietnamese, loud and slightly nasal, her pronunciation clear, her grammar perfect. Her manner, though brisk and polite, is also faintly impatient, as if to let us know that we've delayed the program. With a flick of her wrist, she ushers everyone along a flagstone path through a scraggly flower garden and into a room at one end of the building. Glancing toward the other end, I glimpse a simple wooden fence enclosing a section of porch. Three or four women, all wearing white jackets and slacks, sit on mats folding diapers. A couple of babies crawl on the floor beside them.

We take seats around a large conference table. The room is musty, yellow, in need of paint. A young woman appears, sets a tray on the desk, and begins pouring tea. Mai and I face the windows along the back wall, which overlook a stand of palm trees and, beyond that, a rice field where two boys coax a water buffalo along a path. A slight breeze ruffles the field, but the air in the room doesn't move at all. The girl switches on a TV in the corner. One of the Americans murmurs, "World Cup." Another adjusts the time on his watch. John Elder leans forward in his seat, his wife's hand resting on his back. A woman with a ponytail pulled high and perky—Eleanor Survey, I think—pushes aside her tea, fishes through her purse, and pulls out a lipstick.

In the doorway, Mrs. Huyen and a bespectacled woman in a white medical jacket talk animatedly, like neighbors gossiping on a porch. The rest of us will the day forward. Finally, the two women break off their conversation and, still smiling, amble into the room. "Ladies and gentlemen," Mrs. Huyen says. "I would like to introduce you to Dr. Le Bich Thuy, who is not only the director of this home for children, but also the person responsible for founding it over twenty years ago. Today you will meet your healthy babies, and you have the dedication and determination of Dr. Thuy and her staff to thank for that."

Mrs. Huyen pauses, gazing out at us. We take the cue to clap. The doctor grins and raises her hand in modest acknowledgment.

For the next half hour, Mrs. Huyen translates a welcome speech by Dr. Thuy that not only includes the story of the founding of the orphanage, but also thanks everyone from the Communist Party of Vietnam to the Hanoi People's Committee to the Ha Dong District official who, twenty-one years ago, first agreed to turn over this small plot of hospital land for use as an orphanage. Over the past two decades, she tells us, the orphanage has taken in over six hundred infants, most of whom have been adopted by Vietnamese families, and some of whom have been adopted by foreign families like ourselves.

I drift in and out. It feels ridiculous, now, to be so close to my baby and not rush directly toward him. I manage, I suppose, through some combination of willpower and a suspicion that I couldn't move even if they let me. Beyond the trees outside the window, the two boys turn at the edge of the rice field and drag the water buffalo back in our direction. The smaller boy pulls it forward by the rope hanging around its neck; the taller one holds the other end of the rope and whacks the animal on the rump. Their skin, in this heat, must be slick from sweat, their breathing heavy. Had his mother not abandoned him, my child might have lived a life in which water buffaloes and rice fields were as familiar to him as cocker spaniels and swimming pools are to the children of Wilmington.

Somewhere out there, maybe just beyond these rice fields, that mother lives. Later, I suppose, I will call her by other names—biological mother, birth mother—but I haven't even met him yet, so she's still more his "mother" than I am. What's she doing now? I imagine her in some cramped house, cooking lunch for a family of ten. Or maybe she's a fifteen-year-old country girl, doing what she needs to do to stay in school. Or maybe she's lying beneath some stranger who will give her a dollar or two for sex. Here's what I'm doing: offering a home to a child who needs one; feeling grateful that her decision led me to my son. Here's what I'm also doing: building my family on someone else's pain. How did that woman feel when she gave him up? I'll always wonder. Poor Hai Au. He'll always wonder.

It is nearly one o'clock when Dr. Thuy finally explains the procedure for meeting our babies. To avoid overwhelming the children and the staff, parents will enter the dormitory one couple at a time. Once each set of parents meets their child, the new family can go into the garden or out onto the porch, making way for the next introduction. The families can stay until four o'clock to give the children a chance to acclimate, and then they can take the children back to Hanoi.

What?

I raise my hand to Mrs. Huyen. "We're taking the children back to Hanoi?"

The other Americans stare at me.

"Nobody told me that," I say.

Mrs. Huyen puffs up with pride. "Oh, yes, of course, dear. I have a very good relationship with my orphanages. Your agency should have explained. Or, would you like to wait until after the giving and receiving ceremony tomorrow?"

Mai and I glance at each other. I wave my hand energetically. "Oh, no. It's great. I'm ready."

Dr. Thuy calls the Elders first. They stand up quickly, then follow Dr. Thuy and Mrs. Huyen. They look graceful and light, dancers leaping across the stage. I cannot move. I cannot walk. I cannot, maybe ever, hold a baby.

Ten minutes later, Mrs. Huyen appears in the doorway and motions to me.

Mai stands and takes my hand to help me up. "Come," she says, smiling.

We follow Mrs. Huyen outside and down along the porch. The Elders sit on a small bench under a tree in the garden. She holds a baby in her lap, its body turned to face her. She speaks softly, smoothing the child's hair back with her fingers. Her husband wipes his eyes.

Dr. Thuy stands in front of the wooden gate that separates the main porch from the mat-covered area inhabited by the children. The mats are empty now, except for a couple of barefoot staff members standing to the side, observing the foreigners. Before allowing us inside the enclosure, Dr. Thuy motions for us to slip off our sandals and leave them outside. Barefoot, I step through the gate. Mai follows. We walk to the second of the three rooms and pause at the door. The dormitory is narrow, with two cribs, head to foot, along the wall on either side and a single one at the far end in front of the window. The space in the middle of the room, covered with mats, is no wider than a double bed. An old metal fan makes slow, creaky turns on the ceiling.

Two toddlers occupy each crib, some awake, some dozing, a few watching the door. One stands, hanging on to the railing, just as Hai Au does in my photo. But it's not Hai Au.

Dr. Thuy walks to the second crib on the right. *"Con ơi, con ơi,"* she coos, leaning over the crib and looking down at someone inside. Then, without looking up, she motions with a finger for me to come closer.

My legs feel heavy, as creaky as a hinge that needs oil. I've spent so much time preparing for this moment, but I never imagined that these last few feet would be the hardest. When I fail to move, Dr. Thuy walks over and takes my arm, then leads me to the crib. Two children lie side by side on a thin gray mattress. One is curled up asleep, its face turned toward the wall. The other lies on his back, his hands resting on his cheeks, looking up. His eyes are large and impassive, the same eyes that I memorized in my photograph, only older now, more well-defined. Beautiful? I couldn't say. Perfect? Yes.

I'd prepared myself for screams and terror. Mine might be the first Caucasian face he's ever seen. But he doesn't scream. He doesn't seem afraid. He doesn't smile, either. For a long time, his eyes move slowly over my face, like someone paging through a book. I don't want to move or scare him, and so we remain in this position, one staring up, the other staring down, until Dr. Thuy finally scoops him up and sets him in my arms. I hold him awkwardly, one hand pressed against each side, maintaining a distance between us. He feels solid. Something in his expression keeps me from pulling him closer. He lifts his hand and touches my face.

Within two minutes of driving away from the orphanage, the Elders' new son—a dark-skinned and sinewy eighteen-month-old they call Granger—dirties his diaper. The van, twenty degrees cooler than the air outside, starts to smell like a Porta Potti. But Granger and his parents don't seem to care. He has a brand-new brightly colored set of PlaySkool keys and he perches on Posie's lap, examining them and cooing amiably.

At least, I imagine him cooing. I can't actually hear anything over the sound of Hai Au's screams. They are livid and ferocious and they tear through his body as he tries to squirm away from me. The two of us had nearly three hours of peaceful coexistence, sitting in the shade in the garden, sometimes alone, sometimes with his caregiver, a sweet and brawny girl named Minh. We played "This Little Piggy," "Pat-a-Cake," "Itsy Bitsy Spider," and a game that Minh taught me where I wiggled my fingers against Hai Au's tummy. He smiled and laughed through all of it, his giggles as fine and precious as works of art. Then it was four o'clock, time to go, and Minh began to cry. I think she tried to hide it, but Hai Au noticed right away and cried, too. He wrapped his arms around her neck and she gently pried him off. Panicked, he grabbed her hair, thick handfuls of it, jerking her head this way and that to hang on. She laughed, which seemed to relieve him, as if he decided she'd only been joking when she tried to hand him off to this stranger. His laugh was loud and strained, half comforted, half anxious. But I still had my arms around his body and he knew it. Minh whispered to him in Vietnamese, serious again and softly urging, and his cries began again, despondent.

Mrs. Huyen hustled up to us from behind. "Come on, dears," she said, her voice cheerful and tidy. "This is the hard part. We make it fast so they don't have time to cry."

Too late for that. Hai Au and Minh and I had nothing in common but tears. Why didn't anyone tell me that, in order to have my son, I would have to break his heart?

Somehow, before we even realized what she was doing, Mrs. Huyen lifted Hai Au out of Minh's arms and out of my grip, then strode away with him. "Shelley, Mai, let's go!"

Mai appeared in the doorway of the conference room, where she'd been stretched out on a wooden couch, napping. She walked over, looked at me, then at Minh, then at Hai Au, his little head peeking over Mrs. Huyen's shoulder, bouncing toward the van. And that was the moment he became real to me, particular, not just some random child assigned to me on a form. A real person, with a real name—Hai Au—that actually does fit him. Would it take any less time to feel that way if he had emerged from my womb?

But the look on his face—both furious and terrified—made me feel like a criminal. "I can't stand this," I said. The caregiver's eyes rested on Hai Au and it seemed she couldn't stand it, either. For some reason, I took her hand and held it in both of mine. I looked at Mai. "Is it wrong? Please, ask her. Is it wrong for me to take him?"

The two of them talked for a moment. Minh gripped my hand, kneading it between her fingers as she spoke. Mai looked at me. "She says he'll be okay. You'll give him his real home. In a few days, he'll get happy."

I read somewhere that infants perceive abandonment. The smells change. The sounds of people's voices shift. On some level, even newborns feel it. And so Hai Au, who had lived through the experience one time already, now faced it again with the loss of Minh. I felt cruel, given his obvious love for her, to torture him this way. I thought of asking, Will *you* take him instead? But she had released me. She had handed me, the thief, the goods.

Now, in the van, between one scream and the next, his head rears back and he throws up. The adults yelp in dismay. I feel the wetness seeping through my shirt, but I refuse to take my eyes off him. He looks so scared. I hold him. From the front seat, Lap, the driver, laughs and explains that the babies, most of whom have never traveled by car, often get nauseated. With Hong Ngoc out of the van (she rode home with her mother), he has become garrulous and demands that Mai translate everything he says. Lightly resting one hand on the steering wheel, he uses the other to point to spots in the van that have, at one time or another, been splattered with vomit.

And so we suffer back to Hanoi. I grip Hai Au while Mai wipes up the vomit with one of Lap's rags. "See if there's anything interesting for him in my purse," I venture. She bends down to the floor and brings up object after object from our bags—a credit card, lipstick, crinkled receipts from the newsstand at the Los Angeles airport—but he doesn't even look at what she offers. My child, my son, just screams and screams, utterly alone in his grief.

Mai refuses to take him. While I sit on a chair, holding Hai Au, now sleeping in my arms, she gets organized. She seems to have abandoned her hope of finding a better hotel, probably because, now that there are three of us, she knows we couldn't manage it. She unpacks my bags, finds ways to fit our belongings into the various shelves and cupboards of the tiny room, supervises three young hotel workers who remove the big bed and replace it with two twins, one on each wall with a narrow path to the balcony between them. Following my instructions, she assembles the portable crib I brought from home, covers the crib mattress with a sheet, fluffs the suitcase-smooshed baby pillow, and sets a Mickey Mouse and a plastic train down inside. Then she sets up a little changing area on the other side of the crib, stocked with piles of Pampers, wipes, and ointments. She handles everything, but she won't hold Hai Au. She barely pauses to look at him.

"He got enough problems without thinking about this Vietnamese lady in the room," she says. "He need time to get to know you." She's right, I suppose. But I wish she wouldn't steer so clear. I want a partner sitting next to me, cross-legged on the floor, someone also anxious and willing to spend hours staring at this little boy. Mai won't do that, and I've had to abandon an older fantasy, the idea that Martin would do that. No one else will do that. Okay, maybe my mother will.

A few minutes before six, Mai decides to go out to buy us some food.

I cradle my sleeping boy, lean close to inhale his sweet, milky breath. His face is strong and sturdy, not at all delicate, expressive even when he's sleeping. He shrugs, sighs, yawns, taps his fingers to the air as if he's playing piano. His lips are full, the color of plums, and his wide, flat nose gives him an expression that is both pouty and determined. He is not yet two, but so substantial. I doze, then wake again when Hai Au stretches, whimpers, opens his eyes. We look at each other. He furrows his brow with mild concern. "What's next?" he seems to ask.

I lift a finger, touch my chest, and employ one of the few words I have mastered in Vietnamese. "*Mẹ.*" Mother. Then I touch his chest. "*Con,*" I say, offering up nearly the last of my vocabulary. Son.

He grins. His eyes are not all-forgiving, but they are tolerant. He pushes himself off my lap and slips over the side of the chair.

By the time Mai returns with bottled water and bags of food, Hai Au has pulled all the newly folded clothes out of the drawers and I have replaced them so that he can pull them out again. He has gnawed on his toy train and eaten two Hershey's Kisses. He has pooped. I have changed his diaper.

Mai looks at the clothes strewn across the floor and laughs. "*Nghịch lắm!*" she exclaims. "He a little rascal!"

Together, we eat dinner. Proving the value of this hotel in addressing the particular needs of the international adoption crowd, the staff downstairs have sent up a bowl of rice porridge for Hai Au. He eats hungrily, then he circles the food that Mai has bought us—pork buns and candied ginger and sticky rice. It's an odd combination, one that wouldn't make sense in any culture. Mai says it's all an "impulse buy." She seems content and I imagine that her successful procurement of dinner has given her more confidence that she can function here. We eat as ravenously as the baby. After we've finished, she looks out the window toward the dusk. "I think I go outside and walk around for a while. Maybe it cooler now."

The lights have come on in the buildings across the narrow street and the roar of rush hour has lessened to intermittent honks and beeps. It's a good sign that she would like to walk outside, and I don't want her to think I will need her every minute that we're here. I grip the back of a chair so Hai Au doesn't pull it over. I say, "I'm hoping to be asleep when you get back." We both look at the baby doubtfully. "Him, too."

After she leaves, I sit down on the carpet. Hai Au moves like a bee traveling from flower to flower. He careens from bed to wardrobe to chair, then back again, pulling and tugging at whatever his little hands can reach. Every time he falls to the floor, he pulls himself up. He smiles with satisfaction, but his smiles are close-mouthed, a little off. He's puffy, swollen around the jaws. Am I only now noticing that something's strange, or has a problem developed? Moving slowly so that I won't frighten him, I edge closer. I lift my hands to his lower jaw, and gently press with my fingers. "Is it okay?" I whisper. "Does it hurt?" My mind races through the symptoms of all the exotic maladies that adoptive parents of Vietnamese children report to each other on the Internet.

Hai Au makes a grimace, then whips his face out of my hands and pulls away. He scrambles silently into the space between the bed and the portable crib. I sit down on the floor, clutch his feet, and pull him toward me. "Wait a minute, buster," I say, setting him into my lap. I take his face in my hands again. He tries to squirm, to throw himself face-first onto the carpet, to shield his mouth from me. I pull him up, as gently as possible. Is he in pain? Clearly, he doesn't want me to touch him there, so I hold his head with a hand at each ear and stare down at him. "What is it, sweetie?" I ask, even though I know he won't understand. "*Con ơi,*" I say. Oh, son!

For a long moment, we stare at each other. He locks his lips together. His nostrils flare. His eyes narrow, fearless and stubborn. And then I understand that he has something in his mouth. Slowly and carefully, I move my thumbs down along his cheeks, slide them into the corners of his mouth, and pry open his jaws.

His mouth is full of porridge. It lines the pockets between his cheeks and gums, lies like buried treasure beneath his tongue, hangs in a clod on the roof of his mouth. I keep his jaws wide open. His eyes burn with rage at me.

Vaguely, I remember a report from some Midwestern mother, describing how her adopted daughter from Vietnam hoarded wads of beef in her mouth for hours. The child had known hunger and she didn't seem to trust that another meal would ever come. I pull Hai Au up. "Eat!" I urge, then drag the Vietnamese from my memory: "*Ăn đi!*" Thank god for Mai and her lessons. Gently, with the tip of my pinkie, I scoop the porridge from its hiding places and set it on his tongue. How long will it take before he trusts me? "*Ăn đi!*" I say, closing his mouth. Eat!

Slowly, resentfully, he begins to chew. I grab the bowl of porridge off the counter. It's still half full, and there's more downstairs. There's always more, I want to tell him. I hold out the spoon and smile encouragingly while he takes another bite. I admire him. He is not yet two, but he has suffered and he has learned to keep himself alive. I see now, among all the other qualities that I am just beginning to recognize, all the things that make him *this* boy, unlike any other. Everything he does gives me more information. I think: This is my son. And this. And this. Sitting here on the carpet, he stares at me, still chewing, his eyes now glazed with fatigue. I listen to his feathery breaths, to the sound of motorbikes puttering past on the street, to the occasional honk of a car, to the wails of babies in other rooms, and to the soft, slightly desperate sounds of new parents trying to soothe them. "You're the sun and the moon to me," I whisper, watching him swallow. "The earth, the planets, every single star." I run my finger across his little chipmunk cheek. For the first time, all the pain I've experienced makes sense. I started trying to have my baby many years too soon. But I had to wait for Hai Au to be born, for this child to be ready for me to come and get him.

12

Xuan Mai

Even at night the heat feels immense, a huge animal wrapping its body around the city. When I leave the hotel, I head down the sidewalk toward Hoan Kiem Lake, walking so rapidly that the cyclo drivers waiting for fares don't even notice me. Out in the street, the river of traffic flows past, more recreational and less hurried than earlier in the day. Even with such unfamiliar noise, the scene reminds me of my youth, of cycling along the shores of the lake with Khoi, or with Lan, or with friends. Somehow, in the darkness, the city seemed so intimate. We chatted with anyone who happened to be gliding along at the same speed and willing to talk. How would it feel now, I wonder, to be so young and free and happy? At the corner, I stop and instinctively lift the hair off the back of my neck. With a quick flick of my wrist, I've tied it in a knot. Funny, I haven't done that since I was a girl.

Even at this hour, the shops remain open. Khoi didn't tell me how bright the city has become. In my memory, Hanoi at night is empty streets, darkness lit only by the moon, the occasional sound of a creaky bike. Tonight, fluorescent lights give the city a glare, turning night into day, as if making up for all those decades of missed opportunity. I could read a book out here. I step up to one of the shop counters, the gold and silver jewelry twinkling in the glare. Twenty years ago, the only gold we saw was in the sparkle of the sun on the lake, the only silver in the underside of clouds. Now, inside the glass cases lie dainty bracelets, jewel-studded necklaces, tie tacks engraved with cursive monograms, and watches that look too heavy to wear. The shopkeeper sits on a stool behind the case, holding a mirror to her face and carefully applying mascara. She doesn't pause in what she's doing. Her voice is flat and bored. *"Cô mua đi."* Lady, buy. I step away, wander here and there until I reach the open plaza that faces the lake.

When I was a child, we'd sometimes see Russians lumbering along these sidewalks. We used to run along beside them, yelling, *"Liên Xô!"*— Soviet! Sometimes we raised our fingers over our heads and wiggled them, pretending we were communicating telepathically with beings from another planet. Come in, Commander Astro! Can you hear me? I'm Commander Astro now, but lacking nerve. I don't even know how to get across the street without being run down by a passing vehicle. I stand for long minutes, stepping off the curb, then back on, then off again. The traffic never even pauses. Finally, two young women, graceful in high heels and tight skirts, appear beside me. Talking, they don't notice me cowering beside them. When they cross, I cross with them. They follow some kind of ritual, an unspoken communion between pedestrian and driver that I can't understand. For so many years in exile, I've considered myself the sophisticated one. I own a house in the United States of America. I get 327 channels on my cable TV. I can turn on my computer and order books over Amazon in dozens of languages. But now I feel like the country girl in the city, uncertain and all alone, nothing to look at, bumbling. Why didn't I get a stylish haircut before I came? Why don't I wear mascara?

On the far side of the road, the girls and I step up onto the sidewalk. They turn one way and I turn the other. The air feels fresher here. I walk to the south and west, along Le Thai To, past a café with blinking lights, past a vendor grilling dried squid, its sharp, rich aroma rising in the air, past a police kiosk where two young officers play *đá cầu,* which—and

I've never made the connection until now—looks a lot like the game Americans call Hacky Sack. Couples wander along the sidewalk holding hands. Small children, even at nine o'clock at night, make wobbly circles on bikes, their parents poised to catch a fall. Hoan Kiem is a good lake, an uncomplicated lake, not the lake with so much grief in it. If I stare out at the twinkling water long enough, I can pretend that I'm eighteen again, that not a single thing has changed.

I walk quickly now, with purpose. I don't lie to myself. I know where I'm going. At the intersection of Trang Thi, I'm grateful to see a traffic light, and I manage to get across. A block farther on, I come to a small open square with a simple playground in the center of it. A policeman, alone in a kiosk, stares out at me. A few yards on, I reach the corner of Quang Trung. In this part of town, the streets are nearly as empty and quiet as the streets of the Hanoi I remember. I stop at the corner and look across.

On the other side of Quang Trung lie three cafés in a neat little row. A teenage boy squats by the curb, washing dirty dishes with a hose. I walk along the curb until I'm directly opposite the first. The sign above the door reads Café Lan, of course. Low wicker chairs and tables are scattered across the sidewalk, lit only by the dim light of a streetlamp. All but one of the tables are empty. Here, three men smoke cigarettes, waiting for the coffee to drip through metal filters into the pools of sweetened condensed milk in their glasses below. I walk across the street, stand in front of the café, gazing in. Now I notice it again, that familiar scent from the airport. Tobacco! Have I always thought it smelled so good? I imagine my father, thirty years ago, smoking a Song Cau cigarette, patiently waiting for his coffee. My father as a younger man, sitting with his friends every morning that I can remember, waiting out the rain or the heat, discussing the latest news, reciting poetry. After my mother died, he did little else, really. She had kept the family going and after she was gone, he left that role to my sister. Lan was twenty-two, a widow already, and capable. But she lacked my mother's ability to accomplish things without seeming petulant and bossy about it. Most days, my father retreated to the Army Club just after breakfast. Sometimes we didn't see him again until dinnertime, when he'd arrive home with a bag full of mandarin oranges, or candied plums, or books—treats rather than necessities—which made Lan seethe.

Inside the café, a teenage girl wipes tables. The three men stop their talking to stare at me. The first few notes of "Let It Be" float from the speakers on top of a small refrigerator in the corner of the room. On the street behind me, a lone motorbike whistles past. One of the men yells to the girl, "Hey, kid, you've got a customer."

The girl looks up. Behind her, the strings of beads that separate the front of the café from the private rooms behind it rustle open and my sister appears. She says something to the girl, then she strides toward the front of the café. She wears a flowered skirt, a string of beads, pumps. She's gained some weight in twenty years and the change makes her curvy and even more alluring. Her gait is slow and unconcerned, confident, the walk of a woman who knows that men often look at her. I look at her. I can't move. I watch Lan glide in my direction. Lan, the orchid. My mother always said they should have named her Phuong. The flower of the flame tree.

As she approaches the door of the café, her little sister runs back across the street, into the park, and tries to disappear.

13

Shelley

My travel alarm clock says 3:27 A.M. I stare out toward the darkened windows of the buildings across the road. Above my head, Hai Au has worked his way up onto the pillow and he sprawls across it sideways like someone climbing, his head nestled in my curls. He and I inhabit the same room now, but not, apparently, the same time zone. My body seems to think it's still in Wilmington, refusing to sleep away the afternoon. From the other bed, I can hear the soft sound of Mai breathing. Could she have adjusted more quickly, simply because she's Vietnamese? I reach up and untangle my hair from Hai Au's fingers, wiggle out from under the covers, and stand up.

Quiet. Not even the sound of a motorbike. I pull on some shorts, and step out onto the balcony. Even at this hour, there's not a trace of coolness in the air, but it doesn't feel as oppressively hot, either. To the left, the street makes a gentle bend, leading, Mai told me, toward the market and the little alley where she used to live. To the right, it goes toward the public square just above the lake. The houses are tall and narrow, wedged against each other. The architecture seems random: The balcony of one house will sit two feet higher than the balcony of its neighbor. Some buildings rise straight up from the street, some taper back, some jut out over the sidewalk with awnings, balconies, metal signs. Even at night, the colors look rich. The deep yellow glow of the streetlights. Blue walls, dark green shutters. Once-white plaster with dark stains of mildew creeping up it. It's three-thirty in the morning, but, still, I see so many signs of life. Below, two lovers stroll, flirting and toying with each other, reluctant to get home. I watch them until they round the bend and disappear. Bats dart in and out of the streetlight. On the roof of the house next door, a yellow cat stands, stretches, then settles again. Geckos chirp. A bare-chested man steps out of a house, pulling on his shirt as he ambles down the street. In the dark silence, I hear the door lock behind him. A few minutes later, a light upstairs flickers out. I have a sudden sense that everyone's making love with not quite the right people.

For two minutes, I'm all alone out here. Then, a group of women peddles past, heading in the direction of the market, their conical hats hanging on straps from their handlebars. A few doors down, a middle-aged man in shorts steps onto the sidewalk, throws his arms into the air, and begins a set of calisthenics. I look down to see two blind people walking in the middle of the street, arms linked, their walking sticks scratching back and forth across the pavement. Night and morning hang in balance. It seems so peaceful. What would Martin think of this city, this country, this Vietnam? And, am I wrong to take Hai Au away from here?

I go inside and take a shower. When I come back into the room, Mai's up on her elbow, her head resting on her hand, watching Hai Au sleep. I sit down next to her on her bed and begin to work a comb through my hair. It's matted and full of snarls. I haven't combed it yet in Asia.

Mai watches me, wincing. "That hurt?" she whispers.

I tug at one complex tangle. "I'm used to it," I tell her. "Ow."

She seems impressed. "If I see hair like that when I'm little, probably I run away, scared."

I keep tugging. "Like I came from another planet?"

She smiles. "Something like that."

Our voices are low, soft. Hai Au sighs in his sleep. Outside, the sky of the Vietnam that I know begins to gray. I say, "I feel embarrassed that I never took the time to learn what happened here. The war and all. I should know. For you. For Martin. For Hai Au."

Mai takes my hand. It comforts me to have her as my friend. She says, "What you see now is better."

"But I don't have to be ignorant," I say. "What was it like for you?"

She lets her head fall back onto her pillow and stares up at the ceiling, still holding my hand. "Here's something. We didn't cry during the war. We cried when it was over. April 30, 1975. In our neighborhood, they invited my father to lead the singing at a rally. After, when we went home, my father start crying. You know, a war over, everyone crying. Even my mother cried, a little. Relief and joy and we don't have to be scared no more. That's what my father said, 'We don't have to be scared no more.' "

"What did your mother say?"

She laughs. "My mom say, 'Now what?' "

I let her doze again. I squeeze back into my bed next to Hai Au, careful not to let my wet hair touch him and wake him up. His breath is warm and sweet and I am glad that he refused to sleep in his crib. Down below, the traffic stirs to life. These sounds must resemble the sounds that Martin heard, all those years ago—honking, engines sputtering, people yelling to each other across streets. What happened to him here?

Hai Au squirms, stretches, rolls over, and looks at me, rubbing his eyes, registering the fact that he's still here. The realization doesn't seem to affect him either way. He scoots across the bed, slides to the floor, totters to his toy train, and sticks a wheel into his mouth.

Mai sits up in bed, her feet crossed, the bottom of her nightgown bunched and tousled in her lap. Together, we watch Hai Au knock the train against the floor. "I saw my sister last night," she says.

I can't read anything in her face. "You okay?" I ask.

She shrugs, staring down at her hands. "I don't say anything. Just stand outside her café. She look like a real business lady now."

"Did she see you?"

She shakes her head and shrugs. "I ran away."

We eat breakfast in a café that Tri from downstairs recommended. It's a Western-style place, long, narrow, and crowded with both foreigners and Vietnamese. The menu boasts European-style items like fresh croissants and "French" coffee. We stand at the counter and order omelets and baguettes, orange juice, coffee, and rice porridge for Hai Au, then find a table near the back. Mai seems distracted. She hasn't said a word about finding her father, and I haven't brought it up. It occurs to me that she might decide to go home without ever seeing him.

While we wait for our breakfast, I entertain Hai Au with the wiggle-finger game that Minh taught me. Around us, the café hums with morning chatter. It is a simple place, furnished with small wooden tables and chairs. Closer to the entrance, a few Vietnamese sit hunched over plates of cake. One young woman sprinkles sugar on hers. I'm surprised, of course, but not disgusted. I wonder why I never thought of it myself. Before I left Wilmington, Lindi warned me that I'd experience culture shock in Vietnam, but what's so different, really? Here we are, a bunch of humans coming together over breakfast.

At a table in the back near us, a Western couple with a sleeping Vietnamese baby quietly argues in French, apparently over whether or not they should wake the child to change a dirty diaper. The baby, hidden inside an infant carrier against the man's chest, has fat pink legs, and every time the man moves they flop against his shirt. He points to the child, then mutters something to the woman. She's anxiously gripping a diaper she's pulled from their gargantuan diaper bag. I believe she says "It's too hot," but I don't know much French. She waves the diaper like a flag. We are compatriots in the means we've used to have our children, but we pretend that we don't see each other.

The waitress brings our food, omelets like yellow half-moons and hunks of French baguette, a small steaming bowl of porridge that Hai Au reaches for with delight. Mai cuts her omelet in half with a fork, stuffs some into a piece of bread, and douses it with chili sauce. I hold Hai Au in one arm, pour some milk into the porridge to cool it down, and begin to spoon-feed him.

Mai watches me and smiles. "You a real relaxed mother," she says.

"You're surprised!" I slide a bite into Hai Au's eager mouth, scrape a few drops off his lips with the spoon. He and I look at each other with mutual understanding. He knows that I am watching. Sullenly, he swallows.

Mai says, "I'm not surprise. I'm impress. Yesterday, he screamed a lot, but you don't mind."

"You've always seen me stressed out," I tell her. "Adoption is a great cure for infertility."

Against the other wall, the French continue to argue. The father shakes his head defiantly. Even a conversation about poop sounds pretty in French.

Suddenly, the man's eyes light up. "Dr. Penzi," he shouts in English toward the front of the café. "Dr. Penzi. Hello! Remember us?"

A tall, Einstein-haired Westerner stands at the front counter. He glances back toward the French couple and waves, then finishes ordering and ambles over. "Yes, of course. Jacques and Sophie," he says in an accent that sounds European. The expression on his face implies that everything is very funny. Leaning over the baby, he says, "Is this little Josephine? Asleep? Cause for celebration, yes?"

The worried mother nods, but explains their predicament. Dr. Penzi listens to her concerns and then, with a wave of his hand, dismisses them. "Let the sleeping baby sleep," he says. "What, you think she has never had this problem before? She's a Vietnamese girl. This is her own climate. Let her sleep an hour in the poopy, then you change her." He sits down at the table next to theirs, picks up the coffee that the waitress has brought him, and takes a sip. "Relax. Take a walk. Read a book or something. She gave you a short rest and so you take it."

It's a strange prescription, counterintuitive to say the least, but the concern on the parents' faces does seem to lessen. How many days does it take to feel that a child is really, truly yours and that your decisions will probably be wise ones? I don't feel it after fifteen hours, that's for sure, but I do feel more confident that, eventually, I will get there. The French couple seem happy enough to have someone else make decisions for them. They grin at each other, relieved, then thank the doctor. A moment later, they have pulled their various bags and bottles together and headed toward the door. Dr. Penzi takes a newspaper from his briefcase and begins to leaf through it.

"Excuse me, are you Dr. Dario Penzi?" I ask. He raises his eyes over his paper and nods, waiting for me to continue. "My name is Shelley Marino. This is my friend Mai, and my son, Hai Au." That word—"son"—comes out more easily now, but I can't imagine when I'll actually feel anything but amazement over it. "We're supposed to see you this afternoon, after our G and R."

The doctor sets down his paper and leans forward, his hands on his knees, looking at Hai Au. "Have I met this child already?"

"You did the preadoption examination a couple of months ago. He had a slight case of anemia."

I can't tell if he remembers, but he focuses on Hai Au. "Hello, sweet boy." Hai Au gurgles happily, his mouth full of porridge.

The doctor's eyes drift to Mai. "And you, a mother as well?"

Mai looks concerned to be singled out. She shakes her head, then vaguely motions toward me with a finger. "I'm just here helping her."

"But you're Vietnamese?" Mai's nod is noncommittal, more of a shrug. Dr. Dario laughs. "I don't think a question like that can have no answer."

Mai is so serious. "I'm Vietnamese"—she pauses—"American."

"Oh, yes. Well, then, I see what you mean. Sort of Vietnamese. Sort of not."

She looks down at her coffee, clearly annoyed. "Can we go?" she asks me.

I stand up. "I'll see you this afternoon, Doctor," I say.

He nods, then picks up his paper again. "Good-bye, then," he says, and opens it.

In the van on the way to the G and R, my dress, a dark blue knit, is already sticking to my skin against the tacky vinyl seat. It's only ten A.M., and bound to get hotter, but I'm not worried. That's the beauty of knit— it absorbs the sweat. One of the other new moms, in a green silk blouse, will not be so lucky. You should never wear silk in the heat, unless you like your clothes attached to your back in great patches of sweat. I'm practical when I dress in the summer. I learned the hard way, at more than one graveside service in July. The men in our van know the rules. They carry their jackets folded neatly on their arms, not garments so much as props that tell the audience: I'm serious.

We're in a bigger van today, with an aisle down the middle, and plenty of room for all of us and our children. The mood of our group shifts between anticipation and anxiety, like a team headed for a game we expect to win but still worry about, a little. My situation is pretty straightforward: married woman, husband waiting anxiously for wife and baby to come home. Two of the families—Chambers and Elder—have it harder. They've got birth mothers to meet, women who've come to sign the final documents relinquishing their children, and, I suppose, to say good-bye.

Mrs. Huyen tries to prepare them for this meeting. "These are poor women," she says. "Some of them have five, six children already. Others are only teenagers. Today is a happy day for them, seeing their babies adopted by loving parents and leaving for America."

No one responds. Mrs. Huyen offers what she thinks these parents want to hear, but, if they're honest with themselves, it can't satisfy them much. Nothing will erase the fact that, given more money, or husbands, or jobs, or a decent education, these women might have kept their babies. Even if they're drug addicts, or insane, you can't deny the heartbreak there. I feel relieved that I don't have to deal with that reminder in person, even though I recognize the downside, the fact that, one day, Hai Au will regret that I know nothing about his mother, nothing of the person who left him, bundled in a blanket outside the Ha Dong Children's Center one night at three A.M. Maybe I'll regret, too, that he has no accurate history, no family medical records, no birth date, even. But he has a name, scrawled on a scrap of paper and tucked between the folds of his thin cotton shirt. Hai Au. A seabird stranded far from the sea. Who knows why she named him that? Maybe it's fate, or some premonition that I would take him to a life at the beach. He comes to me with nothing but his name, and we will keep it.

Right now, he sits sideways in my lap, a dazed look in his eyes. It's ten-thirty in the morning and he may be sleepy. I don't know his rhythms yet.

"Should we talk to the birth mothers?" Marilou Chambers asks Mrs. Huyen.

"No problem. You do what you like. In this province, the ceremony is very genial. You take some pictures of the birth mother, maybe a few minutes of video, save it all for your child to look at later."

Each time Mrs. Huyen turns back around in her seat, someone has another question. "What's the name of this province again?" John Elder wants to know.

His wife, Posie, sighs loudly. "Honestly, John. We even put it in our Christmas cards last year."

"I'm sorry, okay? I forgot."

Mrs. Huyen shifts again in her seat, smiling as if she's talking to a five-year-old. "Ha Son Binh province," she says, distinctly. Very teacherly. Mai called Mrs. Huyen a priss. She told me an even worse word for her in Vietnamese, but she won't translate it into English. I'd like to catch Mai's eye now, but she doesn't seem to be listening. I can't expect much help from her today, but I don't think I need much, either. I've got my boy. If all goes well, he'll be my legal son tonight.

Just as we pull up to our destination, Hai Au vomits across my blue knit top.

At eleven A.M., we enter a dim but spacious meeting room on the second floor of the Ha Dong Justice Department Building. Thankfully, it's air-conditioned. Three long tables form a U in the center of the room. On each table sits a large arrangement of flowers and scattered bottles of La Vie drinking water. I carry Hai Au, who looks less dazed now that he's thrown up. My shirt, rubbed with a handful of baby wipes, feels damp and stinks.

Dr. Thuy and a few of her caregivers meet us at the front of the room. Hai Au squeals when he sees Minh, and as soon as she opens her arms, he

reaches for her. I don't deny him. I want whatever makes him happy. He
rests his head against her shoulder and tries to wrap his little arms around
her. I feel deeply, deeply jealous. Then Dr. Thuy says a word to Minh and
she makes to hand him back to me. At first, Hai Au hangs on, refusing to
let go of her, then, suddenly, he does. He turns in my arms to look at her,
laughs.

We sit on one side of the U with our babies in our laps. The white-
suited caregivers sit in chairs along the wall behind us, Dr. Thuy fluttering from baby to baby, patting cheeks, cooing. At the center table,
five men and one woman page through folders full of documents. I lean
over Hai Au and count through my dossier: the home study form, my
birth certificate, Martin's birth certificate, our marriage license, criminal records, health reports, copies of our passports, our U.S. government
form I-600-A, giving us permission to adopt, our I-171-A, granting us
final approval. I can remember a time, not so long ago, when I felt intimi-
dated by the requirements of so many legal documents. Now, the adoption bureaucracy seems tedious, but straightforward. After all this time, I
know it by heart.

A door opens at the side of the room and more people shuffle in.
These are peasants, clearly, in solid-colored, loose-fitting pants and shirts,
rubber sandals, a few carrying the famous conical hats. They look at us
and we look at them. I count among them four young women who could
be moms. One of the officials directs them to sit on the other side of the
U facing us.

When everyone has taken a seat, a white-haired man at the center table
gets up and makes a speech. He is Mr. Ha, vice-director of something or
other. The audience stares in all directions, parents toward their children,
children toward whatever toy or gizmo they covet, Vietnamese toward
Americans, Mai toward the floor. It goes on for thirty minutes and you
don't even have to pretend to listen. Next to me, Hal Chambers puts his
hand on his wife's knee. The gesture seems both comforting and casual, a
signal passed between a husband and wife a thousand times in the course
of a marriage, silent acknowledgment of mutual need. I miss Martin.

When the vice-director finishes, we clap politely. Somehow, I don't feel nervous anymore. It's oddly fun. The Chamberses go first. Their baby is a little girl, hardly nine months old, dressed, now, in a pink dress with a pink ribbon clipped to her few strands of hair. She'd been whimpering at first, but now, still clutching her bottle, she's fallen asleep. They pick up their daughter, walk around the table, and stand in the middle of the U facing the officials at the central table. Hal reads a prepared speech. He sways as he speaks, gently nudging his wife's shoulder. She gazes down at their child.

The Chamberses, adopting baby number three, have it down: He salutes the People's Committee, the Justice Department, the entire government of Vietnam, thanks the birth mother, too, for trusting them with her child. At this point, after a nod from Mrs. Huyen, a woman steps forward. She's not, as I had guessed, one of the young ones. She could be forty or older, tall and bony, her shirt hanging off her thin shoulders like clothes from a hanger. She stands with her hands behind her back, looking at the Chamberses, but not looking at the baby in Marilou's arms. Then she begins to speak. Her voice is not loud, but it carries. Next to me, Mai looks up for the first time. Everyone in the room listens.

Mrs. Huyen translates: " 'My name is Vo Thi Minh Ha. I am thirty-seven years old. I come from Ha Tan village, seventeen kilometers from Ha Dong. My daughter—I call her Ngoc because she is a precious gem—was born September 3, 2001. We grow rice in our family. I have three older children and my husband died from a malignancy in his leg. In addition to the work that I do in our rice fields, I make tofu to sell in the market. So far I have managed to keep my three older children in school. I relinquish my rights to Ngoc so that she might enjoy an education that I cannot give her. Please take good care of her. If she ever asks about her family in Vietnam, tell her that she is our precious girl, that we will always love and cherish her." When she stops speaking, the People's Committee guy directs her with his chin toward the Chamberses. She walks around the table and approaches the couple and the baby, who stand in the center of the U.

At that moment, Marilou, the baby in her arms, takes the tiniest step

backward. It might not be conscious, because she rights herself immediately, and even asks Mrs. Huyen, in a voice that's only slightly strained,
"Would she like to hold the baby?" She lifts the child a few inches toward
the birth mother, clearly offering.

The birth mother understands Marilou's gesture, because she gives a
little wave, like someone declining a generous gift, and keeps her distance.
Her eyes are on Hal and Marilou, not on the sleeping child.

The Chamberses glance at each other. Hal holds up his camera. "Can
we take your picture, then?" he asks.

Now the woman nods. Her hands hover around her head, working
on her bun. Then she stands, arms at her side, staring at the camera.
When Hal's finished, she makes a request: "Please, send me pictures of
my girl. One every year, if you can afford the postage. If the postage is too
expensive, save your money. Just make sure that she can go to school."

I can't see Marilou's face, but I can hear the cracking of her voice.
"Tell her not to worry. We'll send the baby to school and we'll send pictures."

The woman nods, apparently satisfied. One of the officials opens the
dossier spread out in front of him and instructs her to sign. She leans over
and signs quickly, awkwardly holding the pen. And then she begins to cry.
She keeps crying as she walks back around the table to her family. In a
flurry of whispers and glances at the Americans, they crowd out the door.
The last I see of the birth mother, she is being led by the elbow, her face
in her hands.

Next to me, Mai sighs. She's staring at the floor again, her chin in her
hand.

"Mrs. Shelley. You're next." Without knowing what I'm doing, I stand
up. The officials watch me. With Hai Au on my hip, I page through the
pile of papers on the table in front of me, even though I know there's
no speech inside. After a while, I look up. "I come from Wilmington,
North Carolina," I tell them. "Thank you for considering my applica-
tion to adopt Hai Au. Thank you to the People's Committee and Justice
Department of Ha Dong. You don't know me, but I have been waiting all

my life for this day. I have a big family and many friends back home who are waiting to welcome Hai Au. I promise to do my best for him. Thank you very much. Thank you."

Nobody does anything for a minute. Hai Au's fingers begin to work their way into my hair. I don't know if I should sit down, so I keep standing, trying to keep my hair out of his grasp. Mrs. Huyen, who stands beside me, motions for me to walk into the center of the U. The officials lean forward in their seats, looking through the documents. "Should I give them my papers?" I ask. Mrs. Huyen nods. I pick up my file and walk around the table, into the center of the U. My hands are shaking. Hai Au's attention turns to the ceiling fan.

I hand over my dossier and stand in front of the table. They go through them once, twice, then discuss them again. For some reason, they spend more time on me and Hai Au than they spent on the Chamberses, long enough for people to start whispering among themselves. Posie Elder pours herself some water. The Chamberses and the Surveys, sitting next to them, are cooing over each other's babies. I look toward Mai for information. She shrugs. She doesn't know what's going on, either.

The officials keep talking, moving my papers around, pointing at this and that. Mrs. Huyen walks over and hovers above them. The woman in the spectacles keeps shaking her head, pointing to a line on one page and then a line on the other, then back to the first page, then back to the other. They're taking a long time. I hold Hai Au's hand.

"Mrs. Huyen," I finally say. "What?"

She raises a finger to get me to wait. She and the woman go back and forth again, between one page and the other. I have no idea what the pages are. I am two feet away. The pages are upside down. I have filled out ten million documents in pursuit of my child.

I am patient. But, again, I say, in the most neutral voice possible, "Mrs. Huyen? What?"

Now they all look up at me. The woman picks the two papers off her desk and hands them to Mrs. Huyen, who says, "They've noticed a discrepancy here. In your documents."

"What?" I ask. Over my shoulder, I look back toward Mai. She stands up and hurries around the table toward me.

"Your I-600-A, your original form, with home study, you filled out with a Mr. Martin Marino, your husband?"

"Yes." I shift Hai Au to my other hip.

"But you have no power of attorney for him."

"Power of attorney?" Carolyn Burns never mentioned power of attorney. Mrs. Huyen never mentioned power of attorney.

Mrs. Huyen explains, as if she's told me a thousand times, "In Vietnamese law, both adoptive parents must be present at the G and R, but the authorities waive this regulation if the absent parent signs a power of attorney."

"Why didn't anyone ever tell me that?"

The vice-director draws Mrs. Huyen's attention away. She translates, "You need to contact your husband and have him sign the document. He should send it here immediately."

"I can't."

"Why not?"

I lie. I never lie. I lie now. "He's not at home," I say. "He's out of town."

Mrs. Huyen translates. The officials huddle together, discussing this new information. My mind races from one lie to the next. "He really wants our son," I say.

They tell me that I'll have to wait.

I tell another lie, and this is the one that will break me. "He might be out of town for months." Even the other Americans gaze at me in disbelief. There's something in my tone—I hear it, too—that sounds deceitful. The room is silent now. Everybody stares.

The officials confer again. I stand there gripping Hai Au while these six people decide our fate. Mrs. Huyen leans over the central table. Hai Au sticks his nose in my hair and smells me. I hold him so close. At some point, Mai squeezes my hand. She can understand what they're saying to each other, but I don't ask for a translation. The details aren't relevant.

When the vice-director closes my file on the table in front of him, I'm already hopeless, but I make myself sound determined. "Mrs. Huyen," I ask. I want to say, "Mrs. Huyen, did you fight for me?" but I don't. "Mrs. Huyen." That's all I say.

She turns around and walks over to me and Hai Au. "They've begun to feel suspicious," she says, taking off her glasses. Her voice drops a notch. "Lately, there have been allegations of corruption, even baby buying. The officials want to do everything *aboveboard*. After all, these are documents of international law." It galls me that she's defending them.

"Nobody ever told me about power of attorney," I remind her.

Mrs. Huyen's eyes close and then she opens them again, searching the ceiling. "This is the first time I've had such a problem," she murmurs, as if I care. Mai, in the quietest voice you can imagine, says something in Vietnamese that makes Mrs. Huyen wince.

"What do I need to do?" I ask again.

Now Mrs. Huyen looks at me. "They want proof of the validity of this adoption." She puts a hand on my arm, forcing her voice to brighten: "Don't worry!"

Somehow—I don't know how—Hai Au ends up in Minh's arms. "Make sure he eats!" I cry. "Make sure you feed him." My baby looks back at me and begins to scream. Dr. Thuy hustles the two of them out the door. For so many years, I suffered from wanting a child. Now begins the suffering of losing one.

Once, Martin and I took Theo and Abe to Myrtle Beach for the weekend. They were adolescents then, maybe twelve and thirteen. We spent the day swimming and, after dinner, the boys begged to take a walk alone. I could see the indecision in Martin's eyes. He knew they needed freedom from his worries, but he couldn't bear it. Frustrated with his anxieties, I argued for the boys. What could be wrong with a walk on the beach? They promised not to swim.

Two hours later, Abe came back alone, crying. They'd met some high school girls from Raleigh and Theo had disappeared with one of them.

Abe ran up and down the beach and all through the hotel, calling Theo's name, but he hadn't found him. Martin put his shoes on, instructing me to wait in the room in case Theo returned. "Call the police if I'm not back in half an hour," he told me. He did everything right, but the expression on his face, a mixture of terror and resignation, made me realize that Martin believed his son was dead already. I felt guilty for having supported the boys, but I also thought Martin was overreacting. Why couldn't he relax? Why couldn't he understand that such things happen, that Theo could be irresponsible and also still be alive? Luckily, Abe, sobbing on the bed, didn't see how scared his father was.

The sheriff's deputy arrived about twenty minutes later. He was short, bald, suspicious. He looked at me and Abe. "Did you lose a boy?" he asked.

I nodded, taking Abe's hand. For that brief moment, I did imagine Theo's skinny body floating in the water. "Did you find him?"

"Ma'am." The deputy sighed. "You gotta keep track of your children."

I got angry then. "Do you have to torture us?"

He turned to peer down the hotel hallway. "Okay, boy, come on."

Theo appeared from around the corner, his hair wild, his clothes covered with sand, looking scared and sheepish. "We found him with a girl on the dunes," the sheriff said. "In a state of ill-repute."

Abe looked at his brother. "You asshole," he said.

In our family history, the "Myrtle Beach incident" took on different meanings for each of us. Theo saw it as the night he scored. Abe saw it as the night his little brother surpassed him. Martin saw it as a terrifying reminder—as if he needed it—of the fragility of human life. And I saw it as confirmation that my husband and I perceived our world in different ways. Why couldn't he be more optimistic?

I'm starting to come around. None of us has any rights here.

Sometime in the night, I lie awake with my eyes closed, wishing for morning. If I open my eyes and see darkness, that's one more disappointment, so I keep them shut while I wait for the dawn, wait for the phone to ring.

It took hours, and long meetings behind closed doors, before Mrs. Huyen emerged with their decision. Martin has to come. She informed me that she had convinced the officials not to cancel the adoption altogether. She grinned, wanting credit for her victory, for our success. But what do I have to be thankful for? A stay of execution, merely. A newly signed power of attorney will not suffice, even if I could convince Martin to sign it. They don't want that. They want Martin here, to prove himself a real, live, enthusiastic future father. At stake, Mrs. Huyen explains, is the legitimacy of Vietnamese adoption. Get it? But, she tells me, they will wait, and she will do what she can to get them to change their minds.

Last night, when it was nine A.M. at home, I phoned Martin at the office. Rita promised that he'd call back as soon as he could.

"What time is it over there?" she yelled.

"I can hear you fine," I said. "It's eight P.M. Eleven hours different."

She chuckled. "Never thought I'd be chatting on the phone to someone in Vietnam." Veet-Nam. Rhymes with "ham."

I wouldn't have called it "chatting" exactly. "Can you have Martin call me?" I asked.

"Sure, sweetie. He's got two gravesides, then a viewing at five. I'll get him to call before the viewing." But she's only a receptionist. She could give me Martin's schedule, but she can't make him call.

At this point, I could lose my mind completely. I tell myself that it's too early for that. Or too late. Someday, when Hai Au is ten or twelve, I will tell him the story of how they almost didn't let me have him. No. That might scare him. I'll wait until he grows up. I'll wait until he's visiting me in the nursing home. My grandchildren, cheeks sticky from lollipops, will have dashed into the hallway to marvel at the Christmas tree, and I will pull Hai Au toward me and whisper in his ear. I will tell him about the close call, about how I would have slung him across my back and escaped with him over the mountains into Laos, about how, thank God, it never came to that. That's what I'll tell him. It never came to that.

The phone rings. Mai stirs. I hurry to the phone and sit on the chair beside it. "Hello?"

"Shelley?"

The sound of his voice gives me the sharpest pang of joy. "Hi!" Then, remembering the state of things, I shift to something sober. "Thanks for calling."

"Is everything okay?"

"Everything's fine. I mean, I'm fine. But no. It's not really fine." Mai turns to look at me in the darkness, rubbing her eyes. "I don't even know how to put this. I found out yesterday that I've got a problem with my documentation."

"What is it?"

"I need your help."

"What is it?" I imagine him staring out the window, on to Market Street, his eyes guarded.

"They won't let me adopt the baby unless you come and sign the papers."

I wish that I could hear him breathing. Something. But I hear nothing. Finally, he says, "I can't do it, Shelley. You know that."

Between us lies the failure of our marriage. But doesn't he remember all the happiness we brought each other, too? Don't we have any goodwill left between us? "Yeah. I know. But I need your help. It's the last thing I'll ever ask of you. Just adopt him from Vietnam. You won't have to readopt in the U.S. Just for the Vietnam part. It means nothing. Please." I'm trying to sound reasonable, but he knows that I'm desperate.

"No." One single syllable. A steel wall. Not a single speck of light shines through.

"Can you think about it for a few days?"

"No. I've got to go now, Shelley." Sometime later, I will recall a sound of pain—raspy and broken, like someone choking—but nothing registers now.

"Okay," I tell him, and because I don't want to hear the phone click off on his end, I rush to hang it up on mine.

14

Xuan Mai

On the first night after the debacle of the G and R, I threatened Mrs. Huyen. Shelley lay in bed upstairs. The other Americans with other children were finalizing their adoptions at the U.S. embassy and getting ready to fly home. I cornered Mrs. Huyen in the lobby. At first, she tried to wiggle out of any responsibility for Shelley's problems. She argued that Shelley's agency had made the mistake and that Shelley's agency should fix it. I told her that she was responsible for supplying Vietnamese bureaucratic information to the agencies in the States, so she shared responsibility. In case that didn't convince her, I mentioned that I know an official at the Vietnamese embassy in Washington, D.C. If she didn't help Shelley, I told her, I would put her out of business. Of course, I'm not actually so well-connected. But she doesn't have to know the truth.

As time passes, I know that Mrs. Huyen would rather be rid of us, but my threat has made her eager to help.

The possibility of Martin flying over quickly receded into hopeless fantasy and, since then, it's all I can do to get Shelley out of bed. She moves slowly, like someone old or sick. I squint at myself in the mirror, put on lipstick, brush my hair. I look hopeful, chipper. I am firm as well. I say, "If you gonna give up, then go home right now. I'll change your ticket myself."

She stares at me, one hand on a sandal she hasn't managed to get on her foot. She's never seen me angry before, and so she listens.

"You ready to leave that child in Vietnam?" I ask.

She looks at me, her eyes wide and sorrowful. "I don't have any choice."

I laugh. "Sure you have a choice," I tell her. I put my hands on my hips. I say, "Fight."

Downstairs, Tri hands us a note from Mrs. Huyen:

Dear Shelley,

    I have been awake all night worrying about your predicament. Today, I will make appointments with three officials whom, I believe, can advance our cause. We will meet with them tomorrow. This morning, Mr. Lap will pick you up at nine A.M. and take you to spend the day at the orphanage with Hai Au. The officials have given you open access to the boy and Dr. Thuy is anxious to make sure that you two continue to see each other.

> With especially warm regards,
> Nguyen Thi Huyen
> Executive Director
> International Family Vietnam

Shelley seems pleased to know that Mrs. Huyen has not given up, but nothing cheers her like the fact that she can see Hai Au. Her face comes alive again. "Let's go eat!" she says, grabbing my hand and pulling me out the door. She seems relieved, too, to have an excuse to feel better. Shelley can live with anxiety, but not with despair.

We head toward the same café where we ate breakfast our first morning. It's hot, hotter than Wilmington even. We pass an open door and I catch the scent of bamboo shoots stewing in broth. I have no logical reason to feel happy, but I do.

"Since when did you use lipstick?" Shelley asks.

"Since I saw Hanoi ladies my age looking younger and prettier than I do."

"Since you saw all the cute guys over here."

I'm surprised that she's noticed. "Since I live in the States and I'm supposed to look beautiful."

Shelley pauses at a shop and leans over to examine a pair of child's shoes with a mouse face on the toe. The shop owner picks one up and presses the heel, demonstrating for Shelley how, when the child walks, the slippers will squeal. Shelley laughs. She squeezes the heel herself, then buys two pairs. "One for Hai Au now," she explains, "and one for when he's bigger." Fake hope is better than no hope at all.

When we reach the café, that doctor stands ordering at the counter. He smiles at us when we walk in. "Hello, Shelley. Mai." I'm impressed, with so many adoptions going on here, that he remembers our names. I can't remember his. "Will you join me for breakfast?" he asks.

We order, then follow him to the back of the café and pull up stools around a table. It's funny seeing Western men try to sit on Vietnamese-style furniture. They twist into contortions to fit. The doctor, being tall, looks especially silly, but he seems mostly amused by the challenge, like a clown taking pleasure from his own tricks. He's the first foreigner I've seen in Vietnam who appears perfectly at ease here, even content.

The waitress arrives with the coffee tray, with glasses of orange juice for each of us. The doctor turns to Shelley. "I expected to see you and the baby the other afternoon."

She rubs her forehead with the tips of her fingers. "I'm having some problems with my documentation, so they've postponed the G and R," she says.

The doctor's face turns serious. "Sorry to hear that."

Shelley looks at him. "Do these things usually get settled okay?" she asks.

"Of course. Very, very common," he says. "Don't worry." But he's a doctor. He sees what she needs and makes the right prognosis.

Shelley pours some milk into her coffee, then stirs it with a spoon. "I'm trying to be optimistic." She gazes down at the coffee cup, her voice low, as if she's giving herself a lecture.

No one says anything for a moment, and when I glance up, I see that the doctor is looking at me. His eyes are large and unblinking, a melancholy green, but also amused. He lifts his orange juice. "Here's to a quick solution," he offers, then drinks it in a gulp.

Shelley grins, but she doesn't look up. The waitress arrives with our omelets. For a few moments, we fuss with butter and jam, chili sauce, napkins, refills of coffee, our forks. Then the doctor says, "I have a proposal for you, Ms. Mai."

I stare at him. Why me? I'm just the friend here. He must notice the look on my face, as if he's the police coming to arrest me. He hurries to explain. "It's a favor. You see, I spend Wednesdays conducting primary-care clinics in the countryside. Today my nurse, Ngoc, had to stay home to care for her mother. I'm left without a translator. I'm wondering—" He leaves off here, gesturing with his hand in the air, letting us guess the rest.

Shelley jumps in. "You need Mai?" She pats my leg with her hand. "Go ahead!"

Under the table, I pinch her thigh. Is she crazy? I stare at her. "I have go with you." I let her know in a dozen different ways that she should mind her own business.

She shakes her head. "I'm only going to the orphanage today. Tomorrow I'll need you. Today I'll be fine." She grins pleasantly, like I'm the problem.

The doctor has his eye on me. "I no good translator," I argue. "My English terrible." Okay, maybe I'm dropping a few more verbs than usual. But the basic point is true. I don't know how to do that work. I don't know how to spend a day with a strange foreign doctor. I can't even remember his name.

"I'm not worried about your English, Ms. Mai," the doctor says.

"Go with Dr. Penzi!" Shelley exclaims, supplying me, at least, with that.

I look away from both of them. Outside, an army truck full of pigs wheezes past in traffic. "My English bad," I mutter.

With Dr. Penzi's driver, Long, we head west out of Hanoi in a new white Toyota. The road is narrow and full of traffic, even five, ten, fifteen kilometers beyond the city. We pass long stretches of farmland, with no sign of a building or a shop. Every few kilometers, we go through a village. Along the edges of the road, women in bare feet or plain rubber sandals bob along with poles slung across their shoulders, carrying cabbages, bananas, lychees. They move in mass, too many for the narrow road, and Long veers around them, honking, as he passes. Out here in the countryside, I see few cars, more trucks, mostly motorbikes. The road is thick with them, low to the ground and drifty, like cats racing after their dinner. We are so far from I-40, and I am so glad.

Out beyond the road, over the rice fields, the air already shimmers in the heat. It's cool inside the car. Dr. Penzi and I sit in the back while Long sits alone up front, humming to the music on the cassette player, drumming his fingers against the steering wheel. Behind Long, Dr. Penzi dozes, his head resting against the window, his arms folded like a make-shift blanket across his chest. I'm grateful that he doesn't want to talk. I'll do what I can for the man, but he should know that I'm no translator. If he complains about my skill, I'll remind him that I am a shopkeeper. I can say "bandage" and "antibiotic" in both English and Vietnamese. He shouldn't expect more than that.

I do like the solitude. For the first time in days, I don't have anyone pestering me for assessments of how the country has changed since I left. People seem obsessed with the subject. Mrs. Huyen, Dr. Thuy at the orphanage, Tri at the hotel—give them two minutes with me and they're spouting statistics about Honda sales since 1990. If I'm slow to demonstrate that I care about such things, they'll say, "Haven't you noticed how many more motorbikes we have in this country since when you went away?" They are polite toward me, but slightly resentful, too, as if I'm a member of the family who went on vacation and left them with the chores. They want me, the *Việt Kiều,* to understand that they have done just fine since I abandoned them.

Khoi must have given his family and friends great satisfaction when he was here. He considered the motorbikes a sign of an economic miracle. Two thousand dollars a pop, he told me. People are rich! But I have seen a more impressive sign of wealth in Vietnam. I have seen fat children on the streets of Hanoi. Imagine it: fat children. I think of My Hoa and the paltry spoonfuls of rice gruel we managed to offer her. In those days, we considered a piece of dried fish a special treat. Now I see fat children slurping crème caramel, licking ice-cream cones, picking at cake. Picking at cake! I can see, right out the window of this car, proof that poverty in this country still exists, and that the gap between rich and poor has grown vast, but why talk about motorbikes when there are children in Vietnam who are picking at cake? What symbol of wealth is more effective than that?

Dr. Penzi shifts in his seat, stretching his legs diagonally across the floor. His worn sandals rest only inches from mine and I find myself staring at his long, knobby toes. They're clean, but rough and callused, like feet that have never worn real shoes.

"I have a theory." He's talking to me. I turn my eyes away from the doctor and his toes. "Imagine that our feet or hands were simple blocks," he says. "Like paddles."

Am I supposed to respond to that?

"How do you think we would feel about toes then, Mai? Or fingers?"

I turn to look at him. "I beg your pardon?" In Wilmington, rich ladies say "I beg your pardon?" to let you know you're rude.

"Toes. Fingers. I believe we'd find them very ugly."

"I don't know what you're talking about," I tell him. His toes are ugly now.

He slides a foot from a sandal and places it against the back of the front passenger seat, directly in front of me. I should be insulted, but mostly I'm just shocked by his foot. Now, in the sunlight, it looks even worse, a rice farmer's foot. He contemplates it for a moment. Then, he says, "The human form. We speak of it as if it's beautiful. But, if you look at it objectively, a foot seems strange, even ugly."

I don't know why he's talking about the human form. This is not an issue of the human form. To prove my point, I pull my foot out of my clog and press it against the seat, a few inches from his. The doctor looks at me and smiles. Now there are two bare feet resting against the passenger seat in front of me. Through his rearview mirror, Long tries to figure out what we're doing. Dr. Penzi points a finger at our feet and says, "Look, both yours and mine are natural. No polish. Bluntly clipped. We were born with these feet. I see nothing wrong with either one. I state this opinion to you as a fellow human being. But, if I step away from my species for a moment, they're rather ugly, don't you think?"

My feet are well-proportioned, the toenails uniform and even, the skin smooth and pink. "My feet aren't ugly," I tell him, "but yours are."

The doctor looks at me sideways, grins, and lets his foot drop to the floor. "Okay, then, hands!" His right hand shoots up and both of us look at it seriously, as if we're contemplating a work of art. Long is having trouble keeping his eyes on the road. "I have nice hands," the doctor announces, lifting the other for me to see.

He does have nice hands. His fingers are thin, nimble, delicate but sturdy, adequate for his profession. "Now, yours," he orders.

I hold up my left hand, but only reluctantly. I bite my nails. I have a poorly healed scar on the thumb from rushing too fast while cutting carrots. And I have the remains of a deep gash, years old now, on the tip of my index finger from the morning I miscalculated the distance between my hand and a cleaver. I would hold up the right hand instead, but the scars from two bad burns make that one even worse. "I cook," I explain.

"A clumsy cook," he says. "My hand is prettier. That makes us even now."

In the front seat, Long turns on the radio: a blaring crowd, announcers cracking jokes. Dr. Penzi leans forward and rests his arm against the driver's seat. "Long, can we have a little quieter World Cup, please?" I slide my hands beneath my thighs, not knowing quite what to do with myself. Long reaches over and fiddles with the volume, but the difference is barely noticeable.

Dr. Penzi leans back into his seat. "Why did you return to Vietnam?" he asks.

He's caught me off guard. "For Shelley," I say. My voice is flat, uninviting. I concentrate on what's outside the car. Ahead of us, I can see the dim outline of hills. The sky is milky white. In Wilmington, the sky is almost always blue, but I can recall so few blue skies from my life in Vietnam. We pass a truck full of prisoners, built like a cage. I can see hands, gripping bars.

The doctor whistles softly as we pass. Then he turns his attention to me again. "You have no family here?"

"I do. In Hanoi. Where you from?" I want to change the subject.

"From Italy. And the reunion? Has it been a happy one?"

We drive through a town. Black stains of mildew cover the garish new concrete buildings. In front of a store filled with ruffly evening gowns, a hand-painted sign reads RENT WEDDING DRESSES HERE. I say, "My father has emphysema."

The doctor responds quickly. "If he needs any kind of examination, please feel free to bring him by my office."

"Thank you," I say. Then he leaves me in peace.

Fifteen minutes beyond the town, an old French road marker says we're seven kilometers from the provincial capital of Hoa Binh. I've never been to Hoa Binh. When I was a child, this part of the country seemed dark and mysterious, the gateway to the mountains and the border with Laos. These were the homelands of the *người dân tộc,* minority people, the Thai and Muong, whom I only read about in school. Once or twice, when I was a girl, I'd see a group of them walking through Hanoi. They wore intricately embroidered costumes, heavy silver jewelry, and carried their babies in pouches on their backs. My friends and I would chase behind them on tiptoe, shy but curious, trying to catch snippets of their language. When I was even younger, and had been bad, my mother would threaten to send me to the mountains to live with the *người dân tộc.* This warning could always make a bad girl try to be better.

"I like the idea of a town named Peace," Dr. Penzi says.

I look at him. "Peace?"

"My nurse, Ngoc, told me that the name of Hoa Binh City means 'peace' in Vietnamese."

"Oh. Yes. I guess it does." Just like Americans with Chapel Hill, or Los Angeles—"the Angels"—we Vietnamese don't give much thought to the literal meaning.

"Hoa Binh," he repeats, then he sighs. "Only a country that has suffered war as intensely as Vietnam would think to name a city 'peace.'"

I nod. I don't want to be rude, but, really, what would an Italian know of peace? He's too young to remember World War II. Peace, to him, would be a romance, like those few minutes of elation my friends and I felt when we first heard that the war was over. The boys jumped onto their wooden desks and shouted with joy. The girls hurled themselves into a teary mass embrace. We expected so much. But what did we get, really? Just emptiness. Hunger. Cleaning up the mess. Every trouble of life—the violence, the deprivation, the loneliness—had been endured in the name of war. And when it was over, nothing took its place. Just more deprivation, more national struggle, but fewer people believed in it.

What could I say that an Italian would understand? "Peace," I say. "It's a very pretty name."

He continues to look at me. Perhaps he's guessing from the tone of my voice that I suffered deeply. I won't deny him that pleasure. There's something epic about tragedy on such a scale as Vietnam's. But my little disaster? Well, nothing's epic about bad judgment and bad luck.

Although it's only ten-thirty when we reach Hoa Binh, we pull to a stop on a wide tree-lined avenue in order to have lunch. As we get out of the car, Dr. Penzi explains that there's nothing to eat in the tiny village where we'll hold our clinic, so we need to stop before we go there. "My appetite is very enthusiastic," he tells me. "If I'm too hungry, I might sew one person's foot onto another person's arm."

I stop, my hand resting on the car door. "You do that," I say, "and the

Muong people will sew your brain to the back of a donkey and haul you up to China."

Dr. Penzi faces me across the hood of the car. He cocks his head, quite genially, and looks at me for so long that I have to laugh. "That could be a problem. Could you and Long find your way home without me?"

"I think we manage," I tell him.

At the end of the block, the town comes to an abrupt end and the hills rise above us, blocking huge portions of the sky. My grammar school had a book of photographs of Vietnam, and the one of Hoa Binh was spooky. The town nestled among craggy, mist-laced hills, a place of wandering spirits, beautiful and bleak. I dreamed of visiting, then. I dreamed of traipsing through the hills, a rucksack on my back, unafraid of ghosts. Now that I'm here, though, it just looks grim and poor.

We go inside a noodle shop, empty at this hour. Most of the tables sit low to the ground, surrounded by stools, and Dr. Penzi picks the only Western-style one, which sits near the curtained door to the kitchen. Even on these larger stools, his tall frame looks awkward. Long has left us for some shop down the street. I take a seat across from the doctor.

Within a few seconds, a stocky middle-aged woman in a pink summer pantsuit emerges from behind a curtain at the back of the room. When she sees Dr. Penzi, she breaks into a grin and claps her hand.

"*Chào bác sĩ!*"—Hello, Doctor!—she bellows. She has the voice of a produce seller at the market.

"Hello, my old friend," says the doctor. He stands again and shakes her hand, causing her all kinds of embarrassment and pleasure. "I'm very happy to see you." Both of them turn and look toward me expectantly.

Of course, I'm supposed to translate. But, with the two of them staring at me, I find myself unexplicably stumped. It's as if one of my hands had suddenly stopped working. I will it to move, but it won't.

Eventually, the restaurant proprietor and the doctor move away from each other awkwardly. He sits down. She motions toward a row of bottles on the bar and mimes the sign for drinking. Dr. Penzi points to a 7-Up. She looks at me and I nod. She takes two 7-Ups off the shelf and carries them with her into the kitchen. Dr. Penzi leans back in his chair, clasping his hands behind his head. He doesn't say anything. He watches me.

The toe of my clog rubs against a dark patch on the bare concrete floor. "Maybe I'm little nervous," I admit.

"I would like a bowl of beef *phở* and a pâté sandwich, please," he says.

I nod. I feel like an idiot.

The proprietor reappears, having opened our two bottles of 7-Up and filled two glasses with ice. "Tell the doctor that I made the ice from boiled water, just the way he likes." She whispers now, as if it's a secret between the two of us that I understand Vietnamese.

I tell the doctor about the ice, then turn to the proprietor. "We'd like two bowls of beef noodle soup. And the doctor also wants a pâté sandwich," I say, in Vietnamese. The sentence comes out accurately, each word distinct, but I feel as if my mouth were stuffed with cotton.

The proprietor goes back into the kitchen and neither of us says a word. Instead, we stare out the open door toward the quiet street. The town seems slow and lazy after the raucous energy of Hanoi. Dr. Penzi sighs and stretches his legs across the floor. His body is nothing but angles. I like that he doesn't feel obligated to talk.

When our food arrives, the restaurant owner brings an old wine bottle as well, refilled with homemade rice wine. Dr. Penzi takes the bottle by the neck and gazes at it fondly. "This dear woman makes the best *rượu* in Vietnam," he says. The proprietor, delighted by the satisfaction on his face, hurriedly grabs two glasses from behind the bar.

When the doctor sees the glasses, he raises a hand and waves them away. "Please explain about our task for the afternoon," he tells me. "We'll drink the *rượu* later." Then he turns back to his soup.

The woman has paused uncertainly, waiting for me to tell her why the doctor has refused to drink. "He has to see patients this afternoon," I explain. "He'll save it for later."

Realizing that he hasn't rejected her offer entirely, she laughs, then sets the glasses down on the bar again, pulls up a chair by the table, and sits down next to me, leaning over her knees. "So, do you live in San Francisco or Paris?" she asks.

I glance at Dr. Penzi, but of course he can't understand. "How do you know I'm *Việt Kiều*?" I want to know.

The proprietor throws back her head, letting out a howl that is slightly derisive. She reaches forward and grabs a handful of my Levi's. "Girls here don't wear blue jeans," she begins. "And they don't cut their nails so short. And they tuck their shirts in. And they don't like flat shoes. We Vietnamese girls like to wear heels these days," she says, proudly holding up a pudgy foot stuffed into a tattered pump. I consider telling her that I've seen women in Hanoi wearing jeans, and even sneakers, but we're in the provinces now, and fashion might be different. Anyway, my blue rubber gardening clogs, a recent purchase from Land's End, seem to be the clincher.

"Those are ugly," she tells me. "How long since you left Vietnam?" she asks, as if the answer might help her assess the time it took me to lose my fashion savvy.

"Twenty-three years."

She laughs and then gets that sneaky look of pride on her face. "A lot more motorbikes now, don't you think?"

Dr. Penzi watches us, but when he sees me glance at him, his eyes drop back to his soup. His hands move over it nimbly, tossing the noodles through the broth, and I remember my father hunched over a bowl of *phở*, saying, "Girls, we eat our *phở* with finesse, like a maestro conducting a symphony."

It takes an hour to travel from Hoa Binh to the village, heading deeper into the mountains. Long has brought back to the car the strong smell of tobacco and an urge to chat. "What's it like in America?" he asks in Vietnamese. He's maybe twenty-five, with slicked-back hair and a crisply pressed button-down shirt that probably cost more than the doctor's. "How much money do you make every month? I bet you own a car. Is it true?"

"Yes," I tell him. I'm getting nervous about the afternoon. I don't want to make some horrible mistake that kills somebody.

The road winds higher and higher. We turn off the air-conditioning and let the fresh, cool air float in through the windows. To our right, the rocky hillsides are dense with leaves, ferns, and bright bursts of wildflowers. To our left, the ground drops off sharply. Sometimes, I can see villages and fields far below. At other times, we drive through the clouds themselves and I can't see more than a few feet beyond the windshield of the car. Long shifts into low gear. "I bet you have a TV in every room of your house. Is it true?" he asks. With every syllable, his head jerks back over his shoulder toward me, but he somehow manages to keep his eyes on the road.

"No," I tell him.

"But you know people like that, don't you? Vietnamese people with that much money."

I think of Gladys and Marcy's two-bedroom apartment at Oakwood Manor. It's a cheap, slapped-together complex populated by students and itinerant construction workers. But, yes, Gladys and Marcy do have a TV in every room. "I guess I do," I say.

Long snorts with satisfaction. "Tell the doctor that. He says that in Italy no one has two TVs. He wouldn't believe me about the States." He throws his chin backward, talking louder to the backseat. "Hey, Dr. Dario!" he says. His English is loud but merely passable.

The doctor has been dozing again. He doesn't open his eyes. "Yes, Long?"

"In America, they have TV in every room."

The doctor opens one eye and looks at me. "True?"

"No."

"Sometimes true!" Long declares.

I shrug.

"Long, why do you care so much?" The doctor sighs.

Long flips one hand off the steering wheel, but he keeps the other in place. "This subject is interesting one," he asserts, but his voice trails off, defeated by the fact that no one else agrees.

The road descends a bit and we enter a valley marked by small hamlets and cultivated fields. We turn off the main highway, drive for a few kilometers down an unpaved road, then pull to a stop in front of a house, one in a cluster of thatched-roof buildings, all rising on stilts eight or ten feet off the ground. Below the house, chickens and the occasional pig nose about on the bare, dusty earth. Children, some wearing tattered shorts, others wearing nothing, soon surround the car. Near the steps to the house, twenty or thirty people stand watching us. We're a long way from the poverty of Oakwood Manor. We're a long way, even, from the poverty of Hanoi.

We get out of the car. The children squeal with excitement and I can't understand a word they say. I walk over to the doctor, who is bending over the open trunk. "I don't know their language," I tell him.

He glances up for a moment, then immediately turns back to the trunk, which is filled with medical supplies and pharmaceuticals. "Don't worry. Some of them speak Vietnamese."

Within a few moments, two men appear from down the road, jog to the car, and shake hands with each of us. Then they lead us through the crowd and up the stairs into the house. At the threshold, we slide off our shoes and step inside. The building consists of one enormous semidark room. At the far end lies a freestanding hearth stove. At the other end, a pile of rolled-up mattresses sits against a wall of glassless windows, simple wooden screens pulled down to keep out the light. The floor is made of long, narrow slats of wood, smooth to the touch. Sunlight shines up through the spaces between the slats, which give a little as you step on them.

Long heads directly to the hearth and sits down on the bench beside it, pulling his cigarettes out of his breast pocket. I follow the doctor and the two Muong men toward the front of the room and we sit down on a wide mat that covers a broad section of the floor. A woman, wearing one of the traditional long skirts that I remember from my childhood encounters with the *người dân tộc,* appears out of the darkness and walks toward us. Without looking at any of us, she sets a tea tray on a mat on the floor, then carefully opens the windows, letting the light flood over us.

I can hear shouting and the murmur of people down below. Two or three teenage boys step through the door, each with one of the boxes from the trunk on his shoulders. They set the boxes down and the doctor begins sorting through them.

"Do you know, in all the time that I've been treating patients in the villages," he tells me, "I've never had any supplies stolen. Not a single box of bandages."

One of the two young men leans forward and says to me, "My name is Bac. I'm the village council leader." He speaks Vietnamese with an accent I've never heard before, but I'm grateful to find that I have no trouble understanding him.

"I'm Mai. I've never translated before."

He smiles kindly. "It doesn't matter. We always double-check every instruction two or three times." He turns and introduces the young man by his side. Close up, this one looks to be about sixteen. "This is Sinh. He's had some medical training, so the doctor tells him what to do for the patients in the coming weeks." Sinh grins shyly, staring at the floor.

The sounds of voices now waft in through the wall that runs beside the stairs. Although I can't see anybody, I can distinguish, between the slats, flashes of color, a play of shadow and light that suggests the presence of a growing crowd. "Let's begin," says the doctor. I nod at Bac and he stands up, walks to the doorway, and leans out. I can hear him making an announcement in his strange language. Then I hear the sounds of more rustling and movement on the stairs. An old woman appears in the doorway and hobbles toward us.

Bac motions for her to sit down. With some effort, she lowers herself onto a stool. She has a badly disfigured foot, twisted almost 180 degrees, with the toes bunched together and pointing like a ballerina's toward the floor.

"I remember this lady," says the doctor. He waves.

The old woman breaks into a toothless grin, nodding and chuckling.

"What's her problem?"

I look at the doctor. "Her foot?"

Dario lifts his hand and lets it drop again, rejecting that idea. "No, no.

She was born with that foot. She's very agile with it. She walks a couple of kilometers just to get here. Find out what her problem is today."

As it turns out, the old woman is suffering from a gastric disorder. She hasn't been able to eat anything but plain rice for weeks. After a few minutes of questioning, the doctor gives her a bottle of pills and tells her to boil her water before drinking it. She grabs his hand and jerks at it like the handle on a water pump before limping out.

Next comes a man who scorched his leg while burning off the stubble in his rice field. Then, a child with a broken arm, a pregnant woman showing signs of preterm labor, a man suffering from unexplainable headaches, a teenager with alcohol poisoning. The doctor gives each of them several minutes of focused consideration, listening to their symptoms, making his diagnosis, then prescribing a course of therapy. It's a complicated process. Between us, we have three native languages. Every question has to go from English to Vietnamese to Muong, then the answers come back the same way. To be certain, we repeat every question twice.

"What do you do if you see someone very sick?" I ask during a pause while a new patient shuffles forward.

The doctor shifts his legs from one side to the other. He's clearly not used to sitting so long on the floor, and I catch the slightest wince as he unbends his knee. "That can be a problem," he says. "As you've probably noticed, this Socialist Republic of Vietnam is not so socialist anymore. My services today are free, but the hospital isn't. We try to do the best we can right here."

Over the course of the next few hours, a steady stream of ill and wounded make their way up the stairs and through the door. On the way in, I saw only ten or twelve houses in the entire village, but dozens of people wait their turn. According to Bac, some walked for hours from distant hamlets, just to have a moment with us. Dario methodically examines each of them. The line, which sounds from the clatter of voices as if it trails down the stairs and circles beneath the house, slowly dwindles. The light from outside grows so dim that Bac has to light a kerosene lamp so that the doctor can read the boxes of medication and look at the patients' bodies. Across the room, the owner of the house fans the flame of the fire and sets a pot on to cook. Soon, the smell of rice drifts across the room. Long, who has spent his time napping on a mat in a corner of the room, paces a few feet away, clearly anxious to start back to Hanoi.

At six o'clock, we're finally packing up Dario's instruments and a few remaining medications when the sound of distraught voices comes through the door. Bac walks over to investigate, then leads a young couple, no older than twenty, toward Dario. They are barefoot, their faces sweaty and smudged with dirt. The girl wears a traditional skirt and a thin yellow T-shirt, despite the fact that the mountain air has grown chilly. The boy wears army khakis and a torn button-down. On his back, he carries a sleeping child in a canvas sling.

Bac squats down next to me and Dario. "They've come from a village about ten kilometers away. It's their daughter. She's three. Several days ago, she stepped on a piece of metal that cut open her foot."

As I explain the situation to Dario, the mother is gently lifting the child from the sling. A putrid smell fills the air. The lower half of the child's right leg, severely swollen, has been tightly wrapped in dense layers of fabric. Dario murmurs something in Italian. He stands up and takes the child out of her mother's arms, then lays her down on the mat. For a moment, he ignores the foot, pulling at the child's eyelids and getting no reaction, then taking her pulse. He continues his examination and, without looking up, he says to me, "This fabric has cut off the circulation to the foot. The infection is severe. She's lost consciousness. I'm going to unwrap the fabric. Get the parents outside."

I give Bac the information, but the parents, squatting a few feet away, refuse to move, keeping their eyes on their child. Bac brings forward another kerosene lamp. In the dim, smoky light, Dario slowly unwraps the fabric. At first, it comes off easily, but as he gets into the deeper layers, they begin to stick together. The smell becomes almost unbearable. The mother begins to cry. Using a pair of scissors, Dario carefully cuts through the remaining fabric. At first, it seems endless. He'll never get to the child's skin. But then I realize that much of the foot has been revealed already, and the skin itself has turned as black and mottled as the cloth. A few seconds later, the mother, probably realizing the truth, begins to scream, standing up, holding her hands to her mouth, lunging toward her daughter. Her husband holds her, and Sinh leads them to the other end of the room.

The child begins to stir. Her eyes won't open, but her head moves from side to side and her arms flail about her. "Mai, hold her," Dario instructs. I move closer and crouch beside the little girl, gently holding down her arms. The child's head flops back and forth, and I lower my lips until they're just beside her ear. From out of nowhere comes the wordless tune of one of my mother's lullabies. I close my eyes and I can hear nothing but the sound of my song and the doctor quietly speaking to himself in Italian. The child's thrashing slows. I'm crying, but I can't let go of her arms to wipe my tears.

After a long while, I feel a hand touch mine. Dario is smiling at me gently. "Okay. It's okay," he says. "Her pulse is up, but if we don't get her to the hospital, she will die tonight." He pulls a blanket out of one of his boxes, picks up the little girl, and bundles her in it. "Come," he says. "We'll go now."

On the way to the hospital in Hoa Binh, Dario sits in the front of the car with Long. I sit in back with the parents and the baby. No one says a word. The mother holds her lips against her daughter's head and murmurs chants that sound like prayer.

We leave Hoa Binh at nine-thirty. By now, the child is hooked up to a hospital IV and a Vietnamese doctor has taken over her case. In the hallway just before leaving, I see Dario hand the parents a wad of U.S. dollars. Then, as our Toyota heads back toward Hanoi, Long asks the doctor, who's returned to his old place in the backseat, for a prognosis. The doctor leans against the door, rubbing his eyes. "I believe she'll live," he says, "but they won't be able to save her foot."

We managed to get out of the mountains while a bit of light remained in the sky, but now we don't even have a moon to guide us. Bicyclists and pedestrians continue to travel along the shoulder, weaving in and out of our headlights. The car passes through a small village. A couple of children toss a ball back and forth at the very edge of the road while their parents, seated in folding chairs, watch from their gravel-covered yards. Life is nothing but accidents waiting to happen.

"Opera, please, Long," says Dario, and Long pushes a cassette into the tape player. Within a few moments, music fills the car. No one says a word, then Dario reaches down to the floor by his feet and picks up the bottle of rice wine and a bag of sandwiches that Long bought while the two of us were in the hospital. "I would have invited you to have dinner with me in Hanoi tonight. After all you've done, I'd like to be able to thank you. But now it's so late I'll be lucky to get you home before tomorrow." He unscrews the top on the bottle and offers it to me. "Can we consider *rượu* and a sandwich a substitute for an evening out?"

I don't even hesitate before taking the *rượu*. Maybe he's just tired, but his voice is kind and I feel grateful, after the trials of the afternoon, that he's pleased with my performance. I don't know why such a thing would matter to me, really, but it does. I wouldn't have imagined that sitting on a mat for five hours could exhaust me so completely, or give me such a sense of satisfaction. Without looking at him, I hold the bottle and take a sip. The liquor tastes sweet as it slides down my throat and within seconds I can feel its warmth all over my body. We eat our sandwiches, passing the bottle back and forth. "What this music?" I ask. It sounds forlorn.

"*La Traviata*. It means 'The Lost One.' It's a love story, a tragedy, of course. When I was still in Italy, I never listened to our operas. They seemed so silly and old-fashioned. But now, so far away, I find them very beautiful. Sometimes, I just need something from home." He pulls a second sandwich from the bag and takes a bite. "And you? In America do you sometimes need something from Vietnam?"

"I cook."

Dario takes another sip of wine. Two or three men sing back and forth, but I can't understand a word of it.

"Why you not live in Italy?" I ask.

He shakes his head, passing me the bottle. "It's been almost ten years since I've lived there."

"Why?" I'm finished with my sandwich now. I roll the paper napkin and the plastic bag in a ball and, not knowing what else to do with them, stuff them in my pocket.

"My wife and I practiced emergency medicine in Sienna for years."

I can't decide if he's deliberately ignoring my question or if he isn't listening. Then, he begins again. "I had been reading about the war in Bosnia and I decided that we should go and help. My wife didn't want to. She wanted us to start our family. But I wanted adventure. 'We can always start a family. How many opportunities do we have in life to help people who are suffering?' You know? I gave her the whole bit. It sounded so exciting. I can be very convincing, or very stubborn, so finally she agreed to volunteer for six months, Medicins Sans Frontieres. They call it Doctors Without Borders in English. It turned out that she really liked it. I liked it, too. We felt like we were superheroes—you know?—saving the world. At least, I felt that way. You get sort of swept up in a life like that. It feels good to help people, even if maybe you do it for the wrong reasons."

I nod, though I don't understand, exactly. I've had enough of war, myself, but I suppose I could see how someone else might find it thrilling. My body feels warm and sleepy. "Why Vietnam, then?" I ask. "You and your wife got tired of war?"

Dario shakes his head. He takes another sip of wine, then says, "My wife died over there."

I look at him. "I don't know that. Sorry."

His second baguette, half eaten, sits forgotten on the plastic bag in his lap. He stares out the window. Then, he says, "When you go to a war, you know something bad like that can happen. But you think of it in a general way—I could get hurt someday, maybe. Day to day, though, you forget about it. And that day, we were leaving for vacation, going to Italy for two weeks. Who thinks about danger then? We got a lift in a twenty-seat UN plane headed from Sarajevo to Zagreb, but there's engine trouble on the way. The pilots must make an emergency landing in a field. No one dies." He turns and smiles sadly. "We thought it was a miracle." Then he looks back out the window toward the night. "Julianna, the seat in front of her had smashed down on her legs. She couldn't move. Other people on the plane, same thing, trapped. Julianna and I cried. It was a miracle. We were all still alive. Many injuries, but everyone was alive."

Dario picks up his sandwich as if to eat it, then pulls the plastic bag around it, and tosses it to the floor. His voice has grown flat, like someone reading a script without intonation. "The pilots crawled out through the front window. We could see them out there, trying to fix the radio to call for help. Julianna told me to go talk to them, find out their plan, and then see if I can find some medical supplies somewhere in the cabin. So I kissed her—sometimes I forget the details, but I do remember this—I kissed my wife, then I crawled out of the plane. It was just a big field, in a valley. We could not see any town or any farm or car or village, but the radio was working. The pilots and I stood there, trying to radio for help. That's what I was doing. Looking down at this radio. I don't know, one minute, two minutes. I'll never know for sure. And then we heard this *whoosh!* And heat, air like boiling water, and it threw all three of us across the field. When I looked up, I saw the plane was only fire, nothing but fire. And my wife was inside."

His hand has been resting against his face. Now it drops to his lap again. "Silly, to tell this story now. I don't know why I tell this story now."

"Sorry," I say.

His head falls back against the seat. "It's many years already, you know. In some ways, it's not so bad anymore. But I don't go back to Italy."

We pass the bottle a few more times. Dario sighs. I close my eyes and soon I feel like I'm swimming through the sad voice of the opera singer. The sound is water, air. I don't even need to breathe. At some point, I may feel his hand touch mine, but by then my mind is floating between wakefulness and dreaming.

15

Shelley

I can't account for what I did today. It started bad—or sad, I don't know—and then got worse. I lost my head, I guess.

After Mai left with the doctor, I walked back to the hotel and found, on the reception desk, a FedEx envelope addressed to me. The way the hotel staff lurked around the package, you might have thought I had received a commendation from the president. FedEx deliveries, the manager Tri explained, arrive rarely. Apparently, even insubstantial envelopes have a sort of glamour to them. The young women who work behind the desk looked at me with enhanced respect.

I saw immediately that it came from Martin. Even though the hotel employees were clearly waiting to watch me open it, I grabbed it off the counter and rushed upstairs. Only a small part of me held out any hope that the envelope contained good news, an itinerary for a flight to Vietnam, perhaps. But I was anxious to touch something that he had touched so recently. I felt angry, hurt, finished with him forever. But, I missed him, too.

I closed the door, sat on my bed, and tore the envelope open. It contained a sheaf of papers from the yellow legal pads that Martin uses at work, paper-clipped together and folded in half. In his spare, teacherly handwriting, he had covered nearly a dozen pages. I got up to pour myself a glass of water, then sat down and read it.

Dear Shelley,

Listen. Listen, please. In the beginning, you asked about my time in Vietnam and I couldn't tell you, even though I knew I should. A couple of times, I planned to bring it up on my own. Once, I spent an entire Saturday at the office (I don't remember my excuse), and wrote you a letter that included everything. Then, I threw it away. We'd only been married a year. You made me so happy. I guess I was terrified that I could mess it up somehow. Obviously, I was a lousy student of human nature. Pain comes back anyway, even after years and years. I never told you anything because I was afraid. Now, I'm afraid that you will never understand me, that I missed my chance. When you called and asked me to go over there, I refused. I refused to do the last thing that, as you said, you'd ever ask of me. And now I have the nerve to ask something of you. Will you do this for me, Shelley? Will you read this?

I'm sitting in the study. Outside, the rain has turned our entire yard into limp grass and mud. You would love it. Remember the time you pulled me outside during a thunderstorm, and insisted that we both wash our hair? Remember how loud it was, and the way you started singing? I had never seen anyone as happy as you were. We were so wet and so happy, soaked right through.

It's a grim night here. I guess I'll begin.

They stationed me in Danang, at the base at China Beach, like the TV show. It wasn't a bad place really and I didn't suffer there. Not physically, at least. When people thought of Vietnam back then, they thought of kids on patrol, eating rations out of cans, dirty, sick, stepping on mines, putting their lives on the line every day. You were young, but I know you remember. You might think of me that way, but here's what I did: I worked in air-conditioning. I faced fewer risks than nurses, generals, number crunchers in Artillery who had to keep track of bombs.

No one considered the morgue a top priority on the enemy hit list. Why waste ammunition on people who had already died? I did go to Vietnam, but I didn't do anything heroic.

For a long time, I wished I had never let on about the family business. I was safe, but I had no social life. The other guys my age wouldn't come near me. They couldn't see me as a normal nineteen-year-old. I listened to Creedence. I got hot for Raquel Welch. I would have been happy to smoke weed, if anyone had offered me any. The grunts I met in Basic called me "Chilly" or "Chilly Long Hands." One kid named Pepper, from Arkansas, called me "Sneed." I never figured out why.

The guys were superstitious. Pepper wouldn't change his underwear. Supposedly, he planned to go through his whole tour in the same pair of Fruit of the Looms he had worn the last night he slept with his girlfriend back in Little Rock. I heard that Pepper had hired a call girl from the Queen Bee Bar and she walked out on him right in the middle of his hour. After that, none of the other Queen Bee girls would go near him. I never knew if that was true or not, but he always looked depressed to me.

I suppose I was depressed as well, maybe not clinically, but unhappy and discouraged. I had regular hours at work, and during my free time I just wandered around. I didn't have any friends. I avoided the guys in Graves. The morticians I knew from home were decent people who cared about their communities and tried their best to help people through pain. These Graves guys, though, never had any personal contact with the families of the dead. They were career military morticians, just patching up bodies and sending them back to the States. They didn't plan funerals or memorial services. They didn't hold widows' hands and stand at the back of the church, watching mourners grieve. In my memory, they didn't do much besides drink. When they talked at all, they discussed football stats and compared brands of formaldehyde. From what I could tell, four years seems the outside limit on how long most military morticians could last there. By that point, they had become incurable alcoholics and made one too many dumb mistakes. The military shipped them stateside, where they finished out their careers at some VA hospital, embalming vets who'd died of heart disease and liver ailments. I kept a distance from them. I had a twelve-month tour and I counted the days until I could go home.

The only one who lasted longer than four years in Vietnam was an old guy, Avery. Avery. I like that name. I had heard that Avery served in World War II and Korea both, so he must have been about sixty. Old enough to retire, for sure. He was tall, balding, thin but sturdy. Remember the butler, Hudson, on the old *Upstairs, Downstairs* videos we used to watch on TV? That butler reminded me of Avery. They both had that same expression: firm, wise, serious but cheerful. (This comparison will probably explain why I acted so ambivalent when you brought home the videos—I'm sure you remember. I didn't want to watch, but I did, too.)

Avery behaved like Hudson as well. I don't mean that he would bring me coffee or anything. I mean he had a butler's style. He was discreet, well-mannered, knowledgeable on a wide range of subjects, and curious about everything. He asked me so many questions about Wilmington, my family, the beach. He gave me his old *National Geographic*s and, because of him, I read them. He had excellent posture. He was older than the rest of us by at least twenty years, but he could work like a horse. I imagine he embalmed thousands of bodies during the course of his career. When I think of the wall of names at the Vietnam Veterans Memorial in Washington, I wonder how many of those guys he prepared for burial. He never seemed phased by the load.

Basically, I was alone there, and I wasn't used to loneliness. Back home, my friends liked to visit the mortuary. If they managed to spot a dead body, even better. In high school—I've probably told you this—the only time I had a problem was in tenth grade, when Mrs. Hicks thought the experience of visiting Marino and Sons would help my classmates "grow more comfortable" with the idea of death. Maybe she was right, but after that I couldn't get a date for months.

In the States, people consider death kind of creepy. But they also think of it as far away, unlucky, something that happens to grandparents, kids who dive into the wrong ends of swimming pools, and bankers with

weak hearts. In the U.S., people can spend the first fifty, sixty, even seventy years of life ignoring death. In Vietnam, though, you couldn't avoid
it, just like you couldn't avoid the heat, or bad dreams. I think guys
had a hard time forgetting about death. They saw me as an unwelcome
reminder of where they could end up: refrigerated in the big gray building at the far end of China Beach. Everyone wanted to avoid Graves
Registration. So they avoided me, too.

I remember on New Year's Eve I went to the USO show and sat at a
table by myself. It strikes me as funny now. Why should it matter, really?
But I was only nineteen. New Year's Eve seemed like a big deal then.

Other than my social life, or lack of it, the hardest thing about
Vietnam was the fact that I had to prepare the bodies of people I had
known. Thousands of U.S. soldiers went to Vietnam, the equivalent of
a good-size city—bigger than Wilmington, for sure—but, still, it wasn't
that unusual to find yourself staring down at a familiar face on the gurney (it's just that so many people died over there). It took me a while to
get used to that. Back home, whenever we had a case that Dad knew
would upset me, he took care of it himself. After my friend Ben Anson
died of leukemia, I just sat with all the other New Hanover students
crammed into that little church.

I wished my dad was with me at China Beach. Some weeks, I recognized two, three, even more of the names rolling in on the gurneys—my
basic training sprint partner, Ellis, who stepped on a mine near Doc Lai;
Jackson, my seatmate on the flight from Okinawa, who accidentally set
off his own grenade when he was horsing around, pretending to pull the
pin out; and Pepper, who lost his head, literally, when he stood up too
fast after his lieutenant announced that Charlie had cleared out of the
area. I found myself able, then, to settle the rumors about Pepper's Fruit
of the Looms. They were a bit gray, and worn thin from so much hand
washing, but they didn't stink any more than mine did. (I know that this
kind of information is "off topic," as Theo would say, but somehow,
now that I've started, it all seems relevant. I should probably go see a
psychiatrist.)

One day, I embalmed Holcomb, the clown who sang a bawdy

"Rudolph the Red-Nosed Reindeer" during the holiday talent show. Poor Holcomb took a sniper shot through the left eye. He wasn't even fighting at the time. He was sitting on the ground, writing a letter to his sister. I kept trying to imagine what kind of person would shoot a guy writing a letter. War has no limits. Not a single limit.

Part of me felt glad to be the one to clean them up and ship them off, to make them as presentable as possible for their families. But I also felt ashamed to see them like that. In life, these guys were tough and swaggering. The base counselors talked about our "soldier's armor." You didn't see the "real" person, which felt fine to me. Whatever got these boys through the weeks and months before they could turn around and go home again. I didn't care if I didn't see the "real" side of any of them. I would have been satisfied to spend the rest of my life thinking of Holcomb as the joker who stuck out his foot and tripped Tony Morton headfirst into the C barracks latrine. I would have been fine with that.

Then Holcomb—loudmouthed Holcomb—came in on the gurney and I had to spend a couple of hours with him. Holcomb was a big guy, with Popeye muscles and carefully tanned skin. I'd seen him surfing on his days off, or just dozing out there in the sun, one arm stretched up over his eyes and the other hand gripping a bottle of government-issue Bud. If I had had my choice, I would have remembered Holcomb like that. But instead I remember his nails. Chewed down to the quick. Even the skin around the cuticles was bitten until it was raw and red, like something worked by sandpaper. No, like meat. I wondered if it hurt. I wondered when he found the privacy to do it. I couldn't help seeing Holcomb, sitting there in the dark on patrol, awake and listening, chewing and chewing, wishing for the night to end. And I've always remembered the wound on him, the hole where his eye had been, and the expression on what was left of his face—lips pursed in concentration, right eye squinting.

After I finished up with Holcomb, the old guy Avery looked him over and said, "Nice job, Martin. That was a tough one." Avery was very polite, and I appreciated it. Nobody else in Vietnam ever called me Martin. "Could you pass me that scalpel, please, Martin?" he would say.

He was a gentleman. A gentle man. As I saw it, he made everyone else in Graves seem like brutes. The physical demands there could be crushing. Much harder than what I did back home. You had to be strong enough to maneuver a two- or three-hundred-pound corpse into proper position on the table, all by yourself. You were constantly hauling heavy gallons of chemicals from the storage areas to the preparation rooms. And on a bad day you'd stand in the exact same spot for hours at a time. A "bad day" might bring a dozen or more bodies rolling through the door. The physical exertion could knock you out, but you needed more than stamina to do the job. The colonel who ran Graves talked about our patriotic duty to make these Lost American Heroes go home looking human again. But what could we do with a guy like Pepper, who came in without a head? America called itself the leader of the free world and we couldn't even make Pepper recognizable to his girlfriend back in Little Rock. I often felt beaten down by the challenge. Out of all of us, Avery was the only one who came close to getting it right. He would spend a whole afternoon smoothing over the face of a burn victim, trying to simulate healthy skin. He scrubbed out the crud-filled nails of guys who hadn't been able to shower in weeks. He focused on those tiny details that the rest of us, too busy or overwhelmed, were always neglecting.

I don't want to paint myself as completely pathetic and depressed. I wrote letters, mostly to Janet and my mom. I received a lot of letters, too, which kept me going. I remember feeling startled by how little happened back home, but I read every word, often twice. On Valentine's Day, I got a valentine from some church lady in Indiana, but that just seemed weird.

I guess I was weird, too. One day, probably out of bored desperation, I followed Avery to the base front gates. Out of all the guys in Graves, Avery was the only one who seemed to have a life. I wondered about him. When he left the building after completing his shift, he had on well-pressed trousers and a clean polo shirt. He might have been sixty, but the guy moved like a kid. By the time I reached the road outside, all I saw was the back of his bald head as he sped away in a hired cyclo (a three-wheeled bicycle taxi. That was the main way to get around at that time. Maybe it's the same way there now, for you.).

That day, I didn't follow him. I wouldn't have admitted it to anyone, but I hadn't left the base since I got to Vietnam. Three months. I was too afraid. I always felt edgy. I spent my days around the bodies of so many guys my age that I couldn't stop thinking about ending up on the gurney myself. You never knew. The VC could be anywhere at any time. One guy told me he always checked before he sat down on the toilet—someone might be hiding down there—and the idea didn't seem completely unreasonable to me either.

Still, it looked kind of interesting out there past the main gates. I realized that there was only so long that a guy could hang around by himself playing pinball. Finally, one afternoon when the heat had eased a bit, I left the base. I'd been thinking about it for days. I decided I'd just go out for an hour or so, take a ride in a cyclo, get a look around, and be back by supper. It sounded fairly simple.

The cyclo drivers parked in a line to the side of the main gate, lounging in their battered wicker passenger seats. When they saw me, four of them jumped up and ran over.

"Queen Bee?"

"Queen Bee?"

"You like Queen Bee? I take you there cheap."

They formed such a tight cluster around me that I had to step back. I shook my head. "I just want to take a look around the city," I told them.

Three of the cyclo drivers started talking to each other, trying to decipher what I'd said. Apparently, their English didn't go beyond "Queen Bee." The fourth, who was wearing a Dodgers baseball cap, grinned at me and said, "City tour?"

I nodded.

His smile got broader. "Let's go, fella!" he said.

I remembered what they'd told us in the "Customs and Culture" lecture when we arrived. You're supposed to bargain. "How much?" I asked.

The cyclo driver bunched his eyebrows and rubbed his chin. He had a greasy face and a lazy eye. "Five dollar," he said. He didn't even want my piasters.

"One dollar," I replied.

He laughed energetically. One eye looked at me; the other gazed at a button on my shirt. "Three dollar. One hour!" he said. I followed him to his cyclo.

We headed north along the main road, which was lined with small stalls selling sodas and souvenirs. Within a few minutes, we turned left and started across the bridge that led over the river and into the city of Danang. From there, I could see the city stretching along the shore in both directions. The skyline was low, with only a few taller buildings and the spire of a church jutting up toward the sky. In the river below us, rickety wooden fishing boats and small gray U.S. naval vessels plied the water. A breeze blew across my face. I'd never ridden in a cyclo before. I wondered if the driver thought I was heavy.

"What's you name, fella?" He bent toward me to ask. His breath on the back of my neck smelled of cigarettes and garlic.

"Martin," I told him.

"Marty!" he said. "You know Marty Kansas? Big guy, Marty Kansas?"

It was awkward to turn around and talk to him, so I just shook my head. "What's your name?" I asked, yelling into the wind.

"Charlie!" he answered, letting out a cackle. He spoke in distinct syllables, rather than words: Cha-Lee. Ma-Tee. Kan-Sa. I leaned my head back, cocked to the side so that he could see the edge of my smile. Charlie. Very funny.

At the end of the bridge, he made a sharp turn to the right, heading up a road that followed the river. The street here was quiet, lined with shady trees leaning out over the water. "You Yankee, Marty?" Charlie asked.

I shook my head.

"Aussie?"

"I guess I'm Yankee," I said.

Charlie gave my shoulder an appreciative shove. "America. Beautiful America," he said. We arrived at an intersection and turned down a wide commercial road that led away from the river.

Danang wasn't what I expected. For one thing, it was filthy. I'd never imagined that a city could be that dirty. Open sewers ran along the sides of the road, full of knotty plastic bags, dead rats, the rinds of watermelon. Mangy dogs roamed the sidewalks, nosing through garbage and fighting each other over food. Children, wearing nothing but tattered underpants, raced barefoot through the sewers in the same way that Abe and Theo used to run through the waves at Wrightsville Beach. The place smelled like gasoline and rotting fruit.

The city was clearly poor, but also surprisingly peaceful. If you'd just landed in Vietnam from Mars, you might not have known there was a war going on. Cars and trucks, buses and bicycles filled the streets. Shoppers crowded the stores. Mothers perched on the front stoops of their houses, nursing their babies. Old men sat on lawn chairs, drinking tea and watching the traffic. I might have forgotten the war altogether were it not for two things: the military vehicles and the refugees. The military vehicles were loud, and the refugees, well, it seemed like every out-of-the-way corner was full of them. Whole families sat sheltered inside abandoned concrete pipes. Children slept on cardboard spread across the grassy medians of the road. Unlike the busy city dwellers, the refugees didn't do anything at all. If they were awake, they just sat there.

The streets all seemed the same. Most of the buildings were two-story concrete structures, newish but not pretty, painted pastel pinks and yellows, and tinged, already, with mildew and dirt. Shops filled the bottom floors. Upstairs, the balconies were cluttered with potted plants, bicycles, folding chairs, and laundry drying on lines. We passed a large open-air market, and the women selling fruit out on the sidewalk motioned for me to come over. Charlie hummed "Big Old Jet Airliner, Don't Carry Me Too Far Away." We moved very slowly, slower than I could walk, but I had never ridden in a cyclo before, so I thought this speed was normal. After passing the market, we turned off the main road onto a side street, then turned down another one, then another one. We kept turning. We passed a florist. A pharmacy. A few dress shops. A tailor sitting at a sewing machine right out on the sidewalk. A florist. A pharmacy. A few dress shops. A tailor on the sidewalk. That's how I realized that Charlie was peddling me around the same block again and again.

I turned around. "What about my city tour?" I asked.

Charlie grinned. He leaned forward. His sweat splattered my face. "You want see Cham Museum?" he asked.

I nodded.

"You want see Danang Cathedral? Cao Dai Temple?"

"Yes," I said. I'd seen the names in the Rec Facility guidebook.

"Five dollar," Charlie said.

I looked at him. "What's the three-dollar city tour, then?"

"This!" Charlie grinned, as if it were the punch line of a joke. One eye was watching to see how I'd react. The other eye looked unconcerned.

I leaned back in my seat. We passed the tailor one more time. "Take me back to the base," I yelled.

"Five dollar," said Charlie.

Now, on our fourth rotation, the young woman at the florist's waved. Behind me, Charlie's breath sounded wet and heavy. I tried to remember the survival tips I'd learned in basic training: maintain rational thought, consider all your options. But I didn't even know if I was in danger. Was this guy VC or just any old lunatic? Either way, he sat at the perfect angle to slit my throat. Quickly, I glanced around. I'd never been lost in a foreign city before. I had no idea what direction the base lay in, and no idea how to ask directions in Vietnamese. On the other hand, five dollars equaled half my spending money for the week, and I wasn't willing to fork it over to a thief.

"Take me back to the base or I'll have you arrested," I said, using my harshest military bark.

Charlie shoved my shoulder. "Five dollar or I keel you," he said. Then he laughed. "Ha! Ha! Funny?"

I don't know if I can explain how I felt at that moment. I can only say that the world around me broke apart. Everything looked distorted, as if I were gazing out through a shattered window. Even my body felt like it didn't fit together properly. I couldn't move.

I might have sat like that the rest of the afternoon, but then Charlie shoved me again. The gesture pushed me forward, changing the vehicle's balance and dragging the metal frame against the ground. "Hey, fella! Sit!" Charlie complained. His tone had shifted. He didn't sound menacing so much as whiny.

At that moment, without thinking about what I was doing, I pushed my hands against the armrest and leaped toward the pavement. With the sudden shift in weight, the cyclo reared back, and the metal rim slammed against my shin. I felt my legs come out from under me as my shoulder twisted to absorb the fall. I landed on my side. Pain shot up my leg and across my back.

Charlie's good eye glared down at me from the cyclo. He began to yell in Vietnamese. I couldn't understand anything but "dollar," "city tour," and "Yankee," but it sounded vicious. People came out of the dress shops to look. Charlie gestured wildly. I pulled myself up and began to limp away. He turned his cyclo around and followed me, peddling against the traffic, yelling and pointing at me as he rode. I ignored him. I looked down at my hip. The muscles throbbed with pain. My shirt had a rip along the right sleeve. I didn't know if I was walking toward the base, or farther away.

"You pay money!" Charlie yelled. A military jeep slowed down to look at us. Five South Vietnamese soldiers were crowded into the vehicle's open seats, their rifles pointed into the air. One of them asked a question. Charlie, speaking in Vietnamese, pointed to me, then to his cyclo.

"I'm not paying you a damn thing!" I yelled at him.

The soldiers looked at me, then back at Charlie. The driver said something that made his colleagues laugh, then he gunned the engine and sped away.

Charlie was quiet for a few seconds, then he screamed, "I call police!"

I kept walking.

By pure luck, I ended up back at the market. With Charlie still yell-ing and causing everyone in the vicinity to stare, I ducked inside. The sound of Charlie's voice grew weaker behind me. I looked over my shoulder. I could see him perched on the seat of his cyclo, unwilling to abandon it, but screaming down the aisle anyway, as if he expected me to turn around. I hurried on into the market.

I wandered for a long time. In the depths of the dark building, the air was stale and at least ten degrees hotter. My blue jeans felt like damp cardboard against my legs and my shirt stuck in patches to my shoul-ders. I walked down an aisle lined with meat vendors. Slabs of pork and beef lay in pools of blood on wooden tables, dotted with flies, stinking of decay. The vendors sat on stools a few feet away, smoking cigarettes, playing cards, or napping. As I passed, a few looked at me, gestured toward their wares, then gave up. It was too hot to do anything energeti-cally. Sweat dripped into the corners of my eyes. I was thinking about Britt's Donuts out at Carolina Beach. Crunchy on the outside and light as air on the inside. On a summer night I could eat a dozen, and wash it all down with a quart of milk.

When I emerged from the market, dusk had fallen. Lights shone inside the buildings, and street vendors had lit candles next to the little wooden display cases holding their goods. I walked down a side street hoping to find my way. None of the buildings looked familiar, but they didn't look unfamiliar either. Inside the homes, on TV, a man read the evening news. Women squatted in front of stoves, stirring food in large, smoking pans. The scents floating through the doorways were succulent and indistinguishable. For a moment, I forgot where I was going.

Around that time, I spotted Avery. Maybe I'd started hallucinating. I don't know, but I had the sensation that I was floating, that nothing around me was real, and that I wasn't real either. The sight of him made everything clear again. He was sitting at a table on the sidewalk, looking down at a chessboard, his back as butler straight as ever. His chess part-ner, an elderly Vietnamese in pale blue pajamas, leaned so close to the board that, if he'd breathed too heavily, he would have knocked over the queen. Neither of them saw me.

Avery made a move. And then, a minute or two later, the old man countered.

"Hi," I said.

The old man didn't look up. Avery did, but chin first, and very gradually. When his eyes finally lifted and focused on me, he smiled briefly, then immediately dropped his gaze back to the chessboard in front of him. "Hello, Martin," he said. "We're just in the middle of the game. Why don't you have some refreshment?"

A glass sign that said "Ca Fe" hung from a wrought-iron hook above the building. I walked inside, then took a seat near the door. The front half of the room was filled with low tables and stools of the same type that Avery and his chess partner sat at outside. The back half of the room contained simple furniture and a television showing a man reading the news, the same man reading the news on all the other televisions in all the other houses. Travel posters sporting pictures of Vietnamese beaches covered the walls, and from the ceiling hung a dozen wire cages filled with green, yellow, and ruby red birds. Sounds of fluttering, chirping, and hopping filled the air. I was the only customer.

A moment after I sat down, a girl of about eight or nine came in through a beaded curtain at the back of the room. She wore a ruffled dress and green rubber flip-flops. Instead of picking up her feet as she walked, she shuffled them back and forth on the floor. When she arrived at my table, she sat down on the stool across from me, kicked off her shoes, pulled her knees up, and hugged them. Then she grinned at me. I grinned back. She looked up at the birdcages and began to whistle.

After a while, I said, "Can I get a beer?" The word was easy to remember in Vietnamese. "*Bia?*" I asked.

The girl looked at me and nodded. "*Bia* Pepsi? *Bia* Fanta? *Bia* Bud?"

"*Bia* Bud," I told her.

She pushed herself up off the seat and shuffled back behind the curtain. I glanced outside. The opening to the street was as wide as the entire room. A retractable metal gate, which served as the front door, had been pulled open. Avery and his chess partner were sitting beneath a blue awning that stretched out over the sidewalk. They hadn't moved.

I leaned back, let my head fall against the wall behind me, and closed my eyes. The girl's voice, light and musical, floated in from the back room, mixing with the twittering of the birds.

When I heard her shuffling back toward me, I opened my eyes. She had a can of Bud in one hand and an ashtray in the other. She put the ashtray down on the table, then held the Bud up so that I could see it. She said a word in Vietnamese. Her grin got even wider.

I looked at her.

The girl continued to hold the beer in the air in front of me, refusing to give it up. She said that word again. She seemed delighted, but I couldn't understand what she was saying. As if to demonstrate what she was telling me, she set a finger against the side of the can and drew a line down through the moisture that beaded it. I still didn't get it. She stared at me for a moment and then, in a flash of inspiration, took a step closer and touched the can to my cheek. The shock of the cold metal against my skin made me gasp. Then she said that word again, even louder.

"Cold." I laughed, and then, in almost the same breath, I started crying. I mean, really crying. It's pathetic, but true. I must have shocked that little girl. She handed the Bud right over, which made me laugh again. Then she ran away, picking up her feet this time. I think that was the first physical contact—with a living human, at least—that I had experienced since I arrived in Vietnam.

After I composed myself, the girl ventured through the curtain again and returned to my table. She sat back down in the seat across from me and tentatively reached for the metal tab I'd pulled off the top of the beer can and left in the ashtray. With a few expert flicks of her hand, she broke the tear-drop-shaped tab off the ring, folded it over, hooked it back onto the ring, and slid the whole thing onto her index finger. Then she held up her hand and considered it as if she were a jeweler. The two of us sat there like that, beneath those dazzling noisy birds.

By the time Avery stood up, stretched his legs, and ambled into the café, the night had turned completely dark. He carried the chess set to the back of the room, opened the cabinet, and neatly set it inside. That's when he said, "What's gotten you so upset, Martin?"

The old man was trying to drag the table and stools in from the sidewalk. I got up to help him and, together, we carried it all inside. The old man nodded his head genially. "*Merci beaucoups, monsieur,*" he said, then he motioned to the little girl and the two of them disappeared back behind the curtain.

Avery picked up a pitcher sitting on the cabinet and poured himself some water. He walked over, sat down at my table, and looked at me, waiting for an answer. "I don't want to go back out there," I told him.

"Out where?" Avery asked.

"I don't know."

Avery took a sip of water, turned, and looked out at the street. The traffic on the alley had picked up as workers headed home for dinner. Now that even more people had turned on their TV sets, the sounds of the programming drifted in from all directions, and I could hear the voice of the news announcer coming at me in stereo. That noise, mixed with the blare of the traffic and the cacophony of the birds, gave the otherwise empty room a noticeable clatter. But Avery didn't seem to mind. He may have been sixty, but his face was still handsome, unwrinkled, and tranquil as a child's. I couldn't understand how a face could remain so youthful through three wars, and countless corpses.

"How can you stay so calm through all this?" I asked.

He turned to me. "Calm?" He looked back out at the street again. "What have I got to be nervous about? We're not here to save lives, you know, Martin. The stakes are very low in our profession." Then he pushed himself up out of his chair and, turning to me, said, "Feel like getting a bite to eat?"

I shrugged. "Sure." The throbbing in my leg had finally eased and it didn't hurt when I stood up.

Avery paused for a moment in front of one of the birdcages. He made a little cooing sound, then blew gently through the bars. Two red birds lifted off their perches. "Lovely, aren't they?" he asked.

"Yeah," I said. We stood watching them for a long time, because they looked like they were dancing through the air.

So. I wish the story ended there. Unfortunately, it doesn't. For a while after that, my life got bearable. I considered Avery my savior. Nearly every free day, we'd go into Danang together. We visited pagodas and temples. Wandered through markets. In my memory, it seemed like we mostly just ate. I could eat four, five meals a day and then eat more. Grilled shrimp. Steamed catfish. Big bowls of noodle soup. I couldn't get enough of the food. I felt like kicking myself for spending the first three months of my tour eating meat loaf and hot dogs. Avery could not believe that one person could eat so much.

One day the two of us found a famous pagoda at the end of an alley near the market. Not far from the entrance sat a small statue of the Buddha, described as a "Must See" in Avery's old guidebook. It was slate black, carved from a single piece of stone, with a face that was peaceful and pitiful at the same time. Avery lifted the tip of his finger and traced a line along the Buddha's brow. "Is it worth it to you, Martin, to see this?" he asked.

I looked at the Buddha, and then at Avery's own calm features. We'd had a lot of people die lately, and I was worn out. "I don't know," I said. "Is it worth it to you?"

He stared at the statue. "I come from Akers, Texas," he said.

I was curious. He had never mentioned his past.

"Sixty miles from the county seat. Desolate little town. No one I knew had ever traveled farther than Abilene. But, from the time I was a kid, I wanted to live somewhere else. Not just another part of Texas, or another state. I wanted to live in another country." He turned and I followed him farther back into the pagoda. "When Pearl Harbor happened, I was already thirty years old, working in my uncle's funeral home in Akers, and I saw my chance to get out of there. My family couldn't argue with patriotism. Two days later, I left. That was it. I've never been back. While my mother was still alive, I bought her tickets so she could come meet me when I took leave in the States. We had wonderful visits together. San Francisco. Chicago. New York. Mother hated Akers as much as I did."

We reached the central altar of the pagoda. A bronze Buddha, surrounded by a ring of dull yellow lightbulbs, stared down at us. "Mother died about ten years ago," Avery said. "I haven't had a reason to go back to the States since then."

Neither one of us said anything for a while. At this moment, the United States seemed impossibly exotic. I asked again, "Is it worth it?"

Avery laughed. "Well, it's worth it not to spend one's life in Akers, Martin."

We spent most of our time at the same café where I first spotted Avery. He and the old man, Mr. Quang, would sit over their chessboard for hours, while Mr. Quang's granddaughter, Thuy Linh, and I played round after round of Vietnamese "Go Fish." Once Avery had introduced me to a few trustworthy cyclo drivers, I got around town quite easily. I never saw that Charlie again. Some days I stopped at the market on my way to the café. I always bought birdseed. And fruit. I wanted to try every variety while I had the chance: mango, star fruit, guava, rambutan, pineapple, dragon fruit, papaya, even durian (they said it smelled like hell and tasted like heaven). "Breast milk fruit" was green and round and firm, I remember, with a juice as white and creamy as mother's milk. I discovered five different kinds of banana, some no bigger than my thumb. When I arrived at the café with my purchases, Thuy Linh took the bags from my hand. First, she filled all the little feeder boxes with seeds, which sent the birds into flutters of pleasure. Then she disappeared into the back room, and returned a few minutes later, holding two plates piled high with cut-up fruit. After she delivered one plate to her grandfather and Avery outside, she and I dug in.

I was halfway through my tour. If anyone had asked me, I would have said I was almost happy then.

You're expecting worse, of course. So here it is: Avery died. Even after all these years, I have a hard time writing the words on the page.

It's morning now. I had to take a break last night. The rain has stopped, but the pavement is covered with puddles. I can see dark thunderclouds coming in from the west. The paper says we'll get more rain later. I should take a walk or something while I can.

I'm going to try to finish now.

We were in the market. I loved that market. I had a favorite vendor for every fruit I bought. The pregnant lady for jackfruit. A gray-haired woman with black teeth for bananas. And I always bought mangos from an old man who sat near the exit heading to Thuy Linh's café. Why did I buy from him? I liked the long black hair that grew out of the mole on his chin.

That day, Avery came with me, hoping to teach me the right way to pick a mango. I thought I knew already. I'd been buying them for months, but Avery, Mr. Quang, and Thuy Linh laughed about the ones I brought to the café. My mangos were either too soft or too hard, too sour or too pulpy, or so stringy that, after eating them, you'd have to spend an hour picking your teeth. "I'll go over there with you, Martin," Avery told me. "Introduce you to my vendor. I've been going to her for a year. She always has the most delicious fruit."

So we went. I walked right by my man with the mole, following Avery to his special vendor located closer toward the center of the market. She was no older than thirty, well dressed and pretty. She was sitting on a small plastic stool, painting her toenails. When she saw Avery, she grinned with recognition. "Hey, mister," she said. "Buy from me."

Avery smiled. "I always do," he told her quietly, then he squatted down beside her pile of mangos, spread out on a burlap sack. I squatted next to him.

"It needs to have a give to it, Martin," Avery told me, his hands moving lightly from fruit to fruit, pressing here, pushing there. "They should be pliant, but firm, like the muscle on your arm."

"Mister, mister," the vendor said. I wasn't paying attention then, but later, when I thought back on it, I remembered how she spoke. She wasn't looking at us. She seemed to be talking to herself, but louder. She put down her polish and craned her neck, looking here and there around the market. Then she started talking loudly in Vietnamese.

At that moment, I was just squatting on the dirty market floor, pressing the muscle on my arm, pressing the mangos. Avery had three before I'd even decided on one. He pushed them to the side of the mat and stood up. "Bow New?" he asked (I remember the phrase, but I don't know how to spell it). "How much?"

The woman was turned around, looking backward, into the next aisle of vendors. Avery stood waiting. "Mister, mister," she said.

I heard a yell, then firing. I dove into the mangos. Something exploded. I felt an intense heat, then debris and ash poured down on my head. And something like rain. Hot rain. I didn't move. Then I heard screaming, screaming mixed with yelling, and more gunfire. I opened my eyes and turned my head. The first thing I saw was that the vendor had disappeared. Her nail polish lay next to her newspaper. The next thing I saw was Avery, stretched out on the market floor. Most of his chest was gone. I put my head back down on the mangoes.

It took me most of that night to prepare Avery's body. He was one of those "tough jobs," where there was too much left for cremation, but not enough to supply a solid foundation for the work. I tried to do the things he would have done himself. I cleaned the nails on his remaining hand, even though they were clean already. I shaved his face. The shrapnel had ripped through his chest, and so, before putting on his dress uniform, I padded the cavity, being careful not to pad too much, which would have made him look like a weight lifter, or too little, which would have made him look like he'd been sick. I didn't have to do anything to his face but close his eyes. His face looked as handsome and peaceful as ever and, because he had such rigid posture to begin with, he actually looked quite natural in death. When I was nearly finished, I pulled a ring out of my pocket. It wasn't a real ring, just one of the beer tab rings that Thuy Linh had given me. It was the only souvenir I had from any of them, and just before I closed the zipper on the bag that held Avery's body, I lifted the breast pocket on his dress uniform, and slipped it in.

After Avery died, I didn't leave the base again, even though I knew that I should go back to Mr. Quang's café and say good-bye. Time has passed in strange ways since then (I've never told you this, either). Sometimes, I feel like each moment lasts hours. Sometimes, I feel like I close my eyes and open them to find a week or two has passed. For a while, I worried that something was wrong with my brain, but I wasn't injured and you can't call messed-up time perception a symptom of anything, really. I felt some consolation when I learned that a lot of vets found their thinking altered in some way after leaving Vietnam. We're the lucky ones. I came home in one piece, so I can't complain at all. And my story is such a little one, just another moment of guerrilla warfare, back-page news compared to worse things that were happening all over Vietnam.

When I think of those last few months in Vietnam, after Avery died, I think of the earth there as acid, bubbling, sending out black fumes that made it impossible to breathe. When I remember the day I finally got on the plane to leave, I imagine myself running across the tarmac, stepping lightly, my feet seared, my lungs burning. Of course, it didn't happen that way. Nobody attacked us. I got out fine. But that's how I remember it. When I think of going over there to help you, I find it difficult to breathe.

I don't expect you to forgive me. I don't.

Martin

For a long time after I finished Martin's letter, I lay on the bed, the yellow pages scattered around me. Now, with the blank of his life filled in, some of the puzzles of our marriage become easier to comprehend. Those days when he could barely speak. The days he wouldn't get out of bed at all. Were those the days he would wake up later to find he'd missed entirely? I felt sad for him, and angry that our country had put him through that trauma, and for no good reason either. I knew that Martin expected me to feel angry at him, as well, but I didn't. I don't doubt that those emotions might come later, when I am forced to abandon hope that I will ever get my boy. But, lying there on the bed, I merely thought of the way he'd damaged our marriage (and, probably, his first marriage, too) because he could never talk about it. How many lives do we get here? I wanted to ask him. I even said it out loud, just to hear it myself. "How many lives do we get, Martin?" I whispered, willing the words out through the walls of my skinny hotel, up into the sky above Hanoi to merge with a cloud that would carry them, within seconds, across the Pacific, across North America, to Wilmington and into Martin's ear. How many lives do we get here, Martin? If death is so easy, so imminent, why are we wasting our time?

And then I thought of Mai, wasting her time, too. After that single creeping peek at her sister, she'd stopped. She hadn't mentioned her father in days. She approached this city like a jumpy cat, edging close to the door of the house, to the light, to the milk, and then, at the slightest sound, racing away. How many lives does Mai have? How many lives does her father have, sick and coughing?

And so, because Mai refused to do it, because Martin refused to do it, I got up and entered the house myself.

It is one A.M. when I hear the key jiggle in the door. I have left the lights on but fallen asleep anyway. Mai comes in almost silently, switches off the light, then stands there, her purse dangling from her hand, slipping off her shoes with the quiet care of a teenager returning late from a date.

I sit up on my elbows. "How was it?" I ask.

She looks at me, sets her shoes and purse by the door, then sits down on her bed. Her body sags sleepily, but I can see in the light from the street that she's smiling. Apparently, she's no longer annoyed with me for making her go. "Better than I thought," she says. She leans back onto her hands. "I should have been a nurse or a doctor. Learned to help people, do good in my life."

I switch on the little light by the bed. "Mai," I say. "I have to tell you something."

She sits up again. "Martin's coming!"

I shake my head. Not that good. Really. "I saw your sister."

An almost imperceptible tremor crosses her face, then passes, like an earthquake just below the surface. "When?" she wants to know.

At this point, she may still believe in accidents. But I operated with a clearer purpose than that. "Today. At her café," I say. "She wants us to come over tomorrow morning."

Her eyes turn suspicious. "Why you go there?"

I can only tell the truth. "I thought I could help you."

"Help me?" she demands. She makes it sound like a crime.

"You've done so much for me. I just wanted to make things better."

She glares at me, completely exasperated. Then she stands up and goes into the bathroom as if she can't stand to be in the room with me a moment longer. Minutes later, she comes back, slips on her nightgown, and gets into bed. I switch off the light. Even in the darkness, I can see that her eyes are open, staring at the ceiling. "Can you forgive me?" I ask, but she refuses to answer.

In the morning, I suggest that we skip the appointment, but she insists on going to meet her sister. At eight o'clock, we are walking beside Hoan Kiem Lake. The road that runs beside the lake is thick with commuters on motorbikes and the air is a lethal mix of dust and exhaust. A thin veil of clouds spreads across the sky, and the air, already, is very hot. We walk next to each other, but not together, really. I can feel her disgust with me. I feel disgusted with myself for meddling, for believing I could solve her problems on my own. I'm not sure that our friendship is old enough to withstand this kind of betrayal.

"Mai, I'm sorry," I tell her again. I'd like to tell her what happened, but she won't even look at me.

At first, my mission seemed to go so smoothly. I simply walked into the café and ordered a Coke. I thought maybe I would just check out the place, gather information I could report back to Mai to let her know that her sister's life seemed good now. I didn't expect Lan to bring over my drink herself and then sit right down to chat. "Where you come from?" she wanted to know, pulling up a chair. She leaned forward, eyes bright and full of curious anticipation. Her knee touched mine. She looked at me like we'd been intimate for years already.

"America." I found myself glancing around the room wildly, looking for an exit in a smoking building.

"You come by yourself all the way Vietnam?"

"You speak good English," I said.

"You flatter me!" She laughed, patting my arm. She had an easy, good-natured way about her, not at all what I'd imagined. Then she got back on track. "You married?"

I sipped my Coke, so cold, clinking with ice. My mother read some Centers for Disease Control warnings about how ice in Vietnam could carry cholera and she made me promise to stay away from it. But the cold Coke tasted so delicious. Just a few more sips, I told myself. "Is this ice from boiled water?" I asked, trying to take responsibility for my health, my life, my presence in this place. To be honest, though, she could have told me that she made the ice by mixing water with cholera spores and I would have kept drinking. The world was so hot, the drink so refreshing.

She looked at my Coke. "This ice? You no worry about this ice. We boil. We have lots foreign customers here. We take good care you. Don't you worry."

In some subtle way, she did remind me of Mai. They have the same fine-boned and delicate beauty, the same bad accents, the same way of pursing their lips when they listen. But Lan seems alive, and Mai acts like someone trying to be alive. "Is that your daughter?" I asked, looking at the teenager watching the TV.

She laughed and nodded. "You a mom?"

Maybe I made a mistake. Maybe I'd come to the wrong place. They might not look alike at all. What do I know about Asian faces? "What's your name?" I asked.

She touched her finger to her chest. "My name Lan," she said, eliminating one possibility. "What your name?"

Her face was so gentle, confident, serene. I felt like I'd discovered something unexpected. Without contemplating what I was doing, the words came out. "I'm Shelley. I came to Vietnam with your sister, Mai."

Her hand dropped. Her eyes closed, then opened, darted around the room, then closed again. For a long time, she said nothing. When she looked at me, her face had turned completely hard. "Why you come here?" she whispered.

We talked for an hour. Other customers entered the café and she ignored them. Her daughter took their orders, served them, glanced at us to try to figure out what was going on. Lan didn't take her eyes off me.

Now, in retrospect, I realize that I did almost all the talking. I started out describing Mai's life in Wilmington, then slowly moved backward: the grocery store in San Francisco, the refugee camp in Hong Kong, the boat trip out of Vietnam. Somehow, I couldn't bring myself to go farther back than that. Farther back than that, Lan knew already.

"You bring her here," she said. Her face had closed completely. "Tomorrow. I be here seven o'clock. Waiting."

I nodded.

Now I understand what I've done.

At first, the café seems closed. The metal accordion doors are opened only wide enough to allow a single, small person to squeeze through, and, from the bright sidewalk, the room inside looks dark and empty. I lean through the door. "Hello?" I hear voices inside, then movement, the clatter of dishes. Mai stands behind me.

After a moment, Lan appears from the back room, hurries forward, and pulls back the gate. She glances at Mai but her face shows no expression.

Mai whispers, "Lan."

Lan looks at me. "Come inside," she says in English, ushering both of us in. "You want something drink?"

I shake my head. Mai hovers behind me like a shadow. When she doesn't move, I take her arm and lead her to a chair, then gently nudge her into it. "Actually, yes. I think we'd both like some tea."

Lan stands beside the counter, getting the tea ready. Her daughter peeks her head through the door of the back room, assessing her aunt. Mai looks at the floor. After a minute, Lan carries a tray to our table, pours us each a cup of tea. I take a sip of mine. It seems wrong that I should be sitting here, witnessing this reunion. I'm an outsider, really. And it's all my fault.

Lan begins to speak. Her Vietnamese is slow and rhythmic, like the recitations I hear from women praying in the pagoda. From somewhere deeper inside the building, I can hear the sound of a radio, running water, a bouncing ball. Through it all, Lan's voice continues to drone.

Mai doesn't move. I can't understand the Vietnamese, of course, but I'm beginning to guess about the content. Lan stands above us, her body stiff, her face impassive. She doesn't take her eyes off Mai. And she keeps talking, never raising her voice, never lowering it. Mai puts her hands to her face. Her shoulders begin to shake and you can make out the quiet sounds of sobbing. Lan keeps talking. Mai pulls her knees up to her chest and her head drops against the top of them. She reaches her arms around her legs, hugs herself, rocks. Lan continues.

I push my hands against my knees and stand up. Enough is enough. "I'm going to take her home now," I say. "I didn't bring her here for this."

Lan's eyes remain on Mai. She keeps talking.

I lean over and rest my hand on Mai's shoulder. "Come on, sweetie. I'm sorry. Let's go." Mai doesn't move. "Mai, let's go."

Lan continues. She's waited twenty years for this moment. Nothing's going to stop her now.

"What are you saying?" I demand.

She doesn't even look at me.

Mai has shriveled into a ball in her chair. Her body shakes, but when I try to get her to stand up, she refuses. Lan keeps talking.

I raise my voice. "That's enough. I don't know what you're saying, but you're wrong." Somehow, I've managed to drown her out. She pauses, looking at me. "You don't know what you're talking about," I tell her.

"I know my baby dead," she says, offhandedly, as if she's giving me directions. "I know my sister kill my baby, then go live in America. You tell me I wrong about that."

"She didn't kill your baby. It was an accident."

Lan's gaze is a finely sharpened knife. "You want adopt your little boy," she says. "When your little boy drown one day because someone not watching, then you come back here, lady. You tell me about accident."

I pull at Mai. "Come on. Let's go."

She won't move.

"You come back here your baby dead, you tell me about accident," Lan says.

I let go of Mai and look at Lan. "Okay, then. Let me tell you a few things about your sister. This girl who killed your daughter. Here's what she did: She closed her eyes and kissed her boyfriend. At the wrong moment. And your daughter died because Mai wasn't looking. Then she got scared and ran away. She was nineteen years old. A kid. I'm lucky. I don't have to live with having made a mistake like that. You're lucky, too. You can live your life hating her because of those mistakes. And Mai? What does she do with her life? She pays for it every single day. All day. Every single day."

Lan is breathing heavily now. She grins. "She pay for it in America. Very sad life."

"Yes. What do you know about life in America?" I could hit her. "Do you remember that when Khoi first decided to leave for America, Mai planned to go with him? That's right. But then she changed her mind at the last minute. She loved her family. She loved Hanoi too much to leave. On that day, during that kiss, she was saying good-bye, she thought forever, so she could stay with you. And then your daughter died. She lost her mind. They both did. They went to America. And Mai's been paying for it ever since."

Lan shakes her head. She looks suddenly exhausted.

"You don't have to believe me," I tell her. "But it's the truth." I make a gesture that takes in the café, the pretty paintings on the walls, Lan's fashionable clothes, her daughter in the back room, and Mai, sitting in her chair sobbing. "After all these years, you have joy. I saw you yesterday. You can smile and laugh with a stranger. You have a daughter, your father, your home here in Vietnam. Mai has nothing in her life that gives her joy like that. She has tortured herself every day for twenty years. It's time for her to stop."

I pause, waiting for Lan to speak. When she doesn't, I say, "Let her stop now. Let her stop!"

Lan looks down at Mai, whose face remains buried in her lap. No one says anything. Then Lan lifts her hand, waves it dismissively, and walks away, disappearing behind the curtain that leads to the back room.

I pull Mai off the chair. She lifts a hand to her face, looks at the door, looks toward the back room, looks at me. She doesn't seem to know what to do with herself. I take her arm, lead her out the door and onto the sidewalk. Somehow, she manages to walk across the street and around the corner, out of sight of the café. Then she stops. She shivers in the heat. "You hold me?" she asks. "Okay? Hold me?"

I pull her toward me, wrap my arms around her. Her body feels like rods of glass. "It's okay in Vietnam," she sobs. "It don't matter here. Nobody think we're lesbian."

"I know." I stroke her hair with my hand.

"Girls hold hands in Vietnam. It don't mean nothing."

"I know," I tell her. "I know."

Mai insists on coming with me to all of my appointments. She may not have forgiven me entirely, but she refuses to leave me, and she seems calmer now, a woman purified by fire. She translates, quietly, while Mrs. Huyen talks to officials at the Ministry of Justice, the Ministry of Health, the Ministry of Transportation (don't ask me why—they chat with each other as if they're friends). When, in the afternoon, Lap offers to drive me out to see Hai Au, Mai insists on coming along. I don't think she wants to be alone. She doesn't seem angry. She seems blank now, like someone who had one emotion left, and used it up.

Two days pass. Three. Four. I haven't called Martin since I received his letter. There was a time when we might have helped each other through grief, but we're on our own now. The officials have given me two weeks, and the time wastes away. Five days pass. I will wait my two weeks. And then I will refuse to leave without my son. Of course, I don't fool anybody. The government will throw me out whenever it's ready. I will become the first American dragged kicking and screaming from Vietnam.

I continue to visit Hai Au. I realize that I may simply be torturing myself, that I may be torturing him as well, but I refuse to give up hope. I do the only thing that I can do: I continue to act like I'm his mother. I fall into a routine. Every day, I bring food, not just for him, but for all the children and their caregivers, too. Great big bags of rice. Bananas, water morning glory, meat. I keep an eye on the staff, make sure he gets as much as he wants at every meal. He responds by eating voraciously and, perhaps, gaining a bit of weight. He also continues to hide extra food. Once, I uncurled his fingers and found that his little hands were full of rice. How much good can I do for this poor country? Very little. But, today at least, I can keep these children fed.

Time with Hai Au gives me hope, a dose of reality, or the reality I choose to accept. I used to dream about my child, but everything looked wispy then. Now that I've met him, I don't think of him as wispy at all. I'm accumulating facts and details. Here's one, for example: He loves cats. You can set a cat in front of him and he will grab it and lick it if you let him. Maybe it's the fur. I don't know. The word for cat in Vietnamese is *mèo* (perhaps they allow their animals to name themselves here). *Mèo* is one of his five words, along with Co (his cribmate), bottle, more, and "*ba.*" I don't know the actual meaning of that word. He uses it as an all-purpose signifier for any animal other than a cat.

The boy is fickle, too. On Wednesday, when I got to the orphanage, he smiled when he saw me. Then he cried. Later, he smiled again. Now, I have lost count of his smiles. He also has a scream like an electric drill, which he uses as a weapon. And he pulls my hair. I should have expected as much. Vietnamese don't have red hair, and they don't have curls. At first, Hai Au liked to grab handfuls and jerk. Now he pulls just a few strands, hard, without letting go. It takes forever to unknot his fingers from my hair, and the expression on his face—eyes squinched, face turning red—reminds me of a boxer knocking the hell out of his opponent. Later, he lies asleep in my arms, his fingers entwined once again in my curls. He fights so hard against sleep that it seems like the peaceful and uncomplicated resolution to a silly war. At those moments, I run my lips across the top of his head. His smell is some sweet mix of soap and milk and sweat. This is my son, I tell myself. It couldn't be some other baby in some other country or some other crib. This boy. This one.

I'm a bit insecure about his love, and pained by the idea that so many days of his life have passed without me. I regret that I never nursed him, that I never saw him in those newborn months, his hands and feet like little birds, flying this way and that above his head. I would like to have felt him stirring in my belly, but, funny, I don't feel any less his mother for not having given birth to him. It just took us longer to find each other, and now we have. I think less about the days we missed than the ones we could miss, still ahead of us.

Mrs. Huyen continues digging and prodding for a solution. Each day, she arrives at the Lucinda with a new plan. Once, she decided to approach some high-level official, a distant cousin of her neighbor. Another day, she found a loophole in the law. Yesterday, she proposed hurriedly pulling together a whole new set of documentation. Nothing has panned out. Nothing has even remained a possibility between the time I leave for the orphanage in the morning and the time I arrive back at the hotel in the afternoon. The first time I called Martin, I held a small, bright hope that I could pull it off without him. As time goes by, I know that I can't pull it off without him. I'm just waiting for a miracle now.

16

Xuan Mai

After his initial suspicion of me, the manager, Tri, downstairs, has come to like the idea of a Vietnamese American returning to her homeland. He insists that I sample every famous local delicacy, especially those that weren't available during the time before I left. "The food is so much better now," he asserts, as if nothing else has changed at all. He directs me toward a popular shop for *bánh cuốn* rice pancakes on Cam Chi Street: "Go toward the great big Sanyo sign, turn right when you pass the second Fuji Film store—not the first. The place is at the end of the alley, near the Disco Super Beauty." We stand at the desk, his pencil hovering above a hastily drawn map, measuring distances, discussing routes. I say, "What Sanyo sign? What Fuji store? What disco?" His Hanoi is a different one from mine. The city is a thousand years old, but, to him, the most significant landmarks are neon. Somehow, I do find the *bánh cuốn*, and the *bánh cốm,* a bright green candy made of new rice, and *cháo cá,* a famous fish porridge, fragrant with cilantro, white pepper, and mint. But I'm not sure how to measure my success. If I do taste these foods, if I do write down recipes to re-create back in Wilmington, will that mean I have accomplished something important on this visit?

My main satisfaction comes from pestering Mrs. Huyen. I have followed her to the Ministry of Labour, Invalids and Social Affairs; the Ministry of Health; the People's Committee of Ha Dong. But the sight of a lurking *Việt Kiều,* one with no family connection to Shelley Marino, does nothing but incite suspicion among officials. Now, I wait for Mrs. Huyen at the hotel instead. As soon as she steps through the door, I am a dog with my mouth around her ankle. I don't trust her at all. She professes allegiance to Shelley's cause, but there's a sense of aimlessness to her activities that indicates she's just biding her time until we leave. With Shelley, she is calm and bright. "We will find a way," she says in a voice that soothes but lacks conviction. Shelley doesn't seem to notice. She grasps at any hint of hope. And Mrs. Huyen, duty done, grabs her purse and clipboard and heads for the door. I follow, trapping her in the lobby or on the stairs. My Vietnamese takes on a military cadence then. I use words like *must* and *absolute*, and *fight*. If we were in America, I would use another word, and liberally: "sue," "sue," "sue." But such a word is ineffective here.

At night, Shelley and I lie in our beds, too worn out from strategizing to say another word, too anxious to sleep. We are on the third floor, above the neon line, but the lights below reflect off the buildings, sending flickers of yellow and purple and orange into the room. The deserted island mural, beckoning to me from the wall beside my bed, looks like a landing strip for creatures from a distant planet. Despite everything that's happened, I would not be anywhere but here. We extended our plane tickets once, then again. We will stay as long as they let us. When I e-mailed Marcy to give her the news, she told me that she has opened the lunch business again, and sent back her menus from the past week: beef shanks with a red wine infusion, pasta Bolognese, sauerbraten, barbecued-chicken pizza. It's not exactly Vietnamese, but it seems to work. In her spare time, Marcy goes on the Internet and researches culinary schools. "Forget chemistry," she writes. "I'm going to be a chef." I've gone from being indispensable to being irrelevant.

Every day or so, the doctor leaves me a message. At first, his messages related to his offer to examine my father. "Dr. Penzi called. Wants to make the appointment tomorrow." Then, "Dr. Penzi called. Wants to make the appointment." Then, "Dr. Penzi called. Please call." I don't. How would I tell him that my father may not even know I'm here? Some days, I think of riding my bicycle, borrowed from the hotel, to my neighborhood. Maybe I'd get a glimpse of him, old now, using a cane for support, feebly navigating the uneven sidewalks. His days pass, I imagine, in intervals of coughing and chess. Can he still sing? Does he still tell jokes? Has Lan even told him that I'm here? If one of Tri's maps takes me too far in that direction, I turn around, head back to the hotel, announce that I can't find the way. Tri is a student at the Foreign Trade University, impressed by a woman who made it to America and back. My inability to locate a certain famous rice shop baffles him.

Between Shelley and me, conversation revolves around topics discussed and avoided. Shelley will talk about tactics to secure Hai Au—institutional, diplomatic, and criminal. She can chat with abandon about the boy's personality, his eating habits, his health, his caregiver, and Co, his cribmate, who is scrawny and ill and will probably be adopted sooner. We can talk about shopping, food, traffic, and Shelley's refusal to ride a bike. We can talk about the other Americans, the French, the Swedes, who arrive with suitcases full of sanitary wipes and diapers and leave with badly tailored silk pajamas, conical hats, busts of Ho Chi Minh, and kids. We cannot talk about Martin, or his letter, or the fact that he refused to come. We cannot talk about going back to Wilmington and starting over. We cannot talk about Hai Au's being adopted by another family. We cannot talk about running out of time.

My rules are less eclectic and, I suppose, less clear. One afternoon, sitting through a rainstorm in a café on Ba Trieu Street, I laid out for Shelley a detailed picture of the house I grew up in. She listened to every word, asking questions about the kitchen, the garden, the bucket and drain we used as a toilet. And then she put her hand over the little diagram I'd drawn and said, "Mai, why don't we go over there? It's been so long. You'll make your father happy." I put the pencil down, pulled my rain poncho over my head, and walked right out, leaving her with a half-finished cup of coffee and no idea how to find her way back to the hotel. Of course, a few minutes later, after I walked around the block, I returned, sat back down at the table, and ate more cake. Shelley didn't say anything and I didn't say anything either.

In some ways, I'm still trying to deal with absolute truth here. Now that I have seen my sister, I know the thing for certain. Every now and then, in Wilmington, the thought would occur to me that perhaps I got it wrong. Maybe My Hoa didn't drown. Maybe some doctor rushed up to save her. Maybe she grew into a happy, healthy teenager, a college student, a young woman, an adult. My family, relieved but desperate that I had gone, had done everything to find me. Later, after many years had passed and Vietnamese began to return to Vietnam, I imagined that My Hoa had won a scholarship to the States. On quiet, lonely days at the store, I would sometimes stare out the window toward the parking lot and imagine her getting out of a car, staring up at my sign, the Good Luck Asian Grocery. She would pull her sunglasses off her beautiful young face and, after a moment of hesitation, step inside. I would look up from the cash register, and immediately I would know her.

Shelley believes I'm refusing to see my father out of the fear that he might reject me. That would be easier, in a way, because I could leave decisions about forgiveness to him. But I know my father. He's forgiven me already. He forgave me on the very day. My father sees life as a series of accidents. A war, a typhoon, my mother's illness, My Hoa's death—all tragedies in a long, sad string of them. His friends called him an idealist, a romantic. He wasn't either, really. He'd lost the best years of his life to the wars and he simply didn't have much fight left in him. He refused to judge and hoped to avoid judgment, that's all. So, although his love means everything to me, his forgiveness means very little. To the extent that my mind, full of reproach and grief, moved with any sort of logic on that day in Unification Park, I believe I had the vaguest awareness of that. Lan could never forgive me and my father could do nothing else. I ran from both of them.

How would he feel to know that I am here and haven't gone to see him? Every day I plan to go, and then, too scared, I don't. Little sins pile on top of big ones.

It's been eleven days since the G and R. Shelley calls it the K and L, the Keeping and Losing Ceremony. Time passes and we've had no breakthroughs. At first, Shelley called home every morning, but she did it like a person checking the winning lottery numbers—out of habit, not out of any expectation that she could win. After she received Martin's FedEx, she gave up. Nothing gets her out of bed except the chance to see Hai Au. Eventually, we will have to get on a plane and go back to Wilmington. We both know it, but we don't discuss it.

Most mornings, I buy us *xôi,* sticky rice, from a street vendor who parks her bike at the corner at dawn. When I go back to the room, I hand Shelley the sticky rice wrapped in a banana leaf, and she finally sits up in bed, breaks off clumps with her fingers, and eats, staring toward the window. "We should go to the art museum," she will say, but it's a statement, not a suggestion.

On Saturday morning, on my way out to buy the *xôi,* I come upon Dario in the lobby.

"I meant to call you back," I say. I only slow down a little, as if I don't recognize that he's waiting here for me. He is tall and his eyes are greener and more beautiful than I remember and he blocks my way. I grip my money in my fist. I look like someone in a hurry.

"I don't think you did," he says, a grin on his face. He keeps up with me without any effort.

I stop by the door. If we're going to have this conversation, we might as well have it in air-conditioning. "It's not a good time examine my father. He's not well."

Dario laughs, as if he finds the excuse purely funny and nothing else. He says, "I wanted to show you something." He reaches into his satchel, pulls out an envelope, and hands it to me. "Look."

Inside the envelope is a photograph of the little Muong girl. A bandage covers her foot and she is smiling. I stare at him over the top of the photo. "She okay?"

He nods. We look at the photo together. It might contain evidence of reincarnation, or life on Mars. "A miracle," he says in a voice that is low, startled, grateful.

In the picture, an adult hand holds the child around the waist. It is a woman's hand, small and calloused, gripping firmly. I wonder how it feels to experience that kind of relief.

"Let's go have coffee," the doctor says.

I look down at the money in my hand. "I got to get Shelley breakfast."

"I'll wait."

It's still only seven-thirty by the time the doctor and I step outside together. The sky is cloudy, threatening rain. We head west along Hang Bo Street, passing shops selling fabric, lace, spools of thread. Shopkeepers stand on the sidewalks tossing buckets of soapy water out across the dirty pavement. Even at this hour, the water evaporates in little wisps of steam, and the air feels heavy with humidity. Later today, the heat will turn aggressive. Now it feels silky and inviting, like the fur on a sleeping lion.

On Bat Dan Street, we go into Café Phuong, all wicker chairs and greenery and soft-focus photographs of landscapes and beautiful women: another spot on the Hanoi map that didn't exist when I was young. A couple of men sit at a corner table with coffee and cigarettes. One of them raps his finger against an item in the morning paper. The other is shaking his head. A teenage girl stands behind the counter, wiping it with a rag. She's tall and graceful and wears her hair in pigtails, a new style that Marcy has adopted back home. "Dr. Dario," she says in English. "What's up?"

"Not much. Two black coffees, please, Stephanie, with fresh milk." He looks down at me, then explains, "She studies at the International School."

We take a table by the window. Outside, the rain begins, loud and sudden, like the overture of a symphony. Inside the air-conditioned room, the temperature feels artificial, almost too cold. On the wall beside us hangs a photograph of a woman wearing a white *áo dài* and sitting on the beach. She hugs her knees and cocks her head so that the wind blows her long hair off her face and into the air behind her. Unadorned and glamorous, she is half peasant, half beauty queen, vaguely familiar. I wish I'd put on lipstick.

"That's Phuong," the doctor tells me. "I delivered her daughter." Stupidly, I glance at the girl behind the counter. "No. Stephanie is Phuong's older daughter. I'm talking about the baby, Christina. Phuong's an actress. Did you see *Indochine*?"

I shake my head, but I remember Gladys talking about it. She complained that it made the Communists into heroes.

"Phuong played the wife of a mandarin in Hue," the doctor says. I shrug. "Look—" He makes me get up and examine another photo farther down the wall, a black-and-white still from the movie, the beauty queen as colonial princess.

"Maybe I've seen her in some other movie," I say.

He pulls out my chair and I sit back down. Stephanie has delivered our coffee. "Phuong's husband, Dat, is a photographer," he says. "Actually, quite a good one."

I'm Vietnamese. I should be the one explaining the facts of contemporary culture. "They have sugar?" I ask, glancing around the room. I'm looking for what I've found in all the other cafés I've visited here: a clump-filled bowl with an ant or two crawling through it, a spoon encrusted from too many dunkings in too many cups of coffee. Dario pushes a little wicker box across the table. Inside, I find sugar cubes wrapped in rose-colored paper. Imported, the label indicates, from Japan. As I said, this is not my Vietnam.

Dario picks up his coffee and leans back in his chair. "Why haven't we gone to see your father?" he asks.

The cigarette smokers have begun to debate Argentina's odds in the World Cup. From somewhere in the rooms behind the café, I can hear the sound of running water, shrieking and laughter, the movie star's baby taking a bath. I stir one, then another, sugar cube into my cup. Dario sips his coffee and watches me. We have come to a crossroads and perhaps he knows it. If I lie—"Actually, his health improved. He doesn't need anything"—I would discharge his debt to me for serving as a translator at his clinic. We could finish our coffee and say good-bye and never have to bother each other again. It's a convincing answer, more or less, and satis-fying, too. It frees him of awkward obligations and frees me of the humiliations of the truth. I open my mouth, but I don't lie. I look at the doctor. "It's a long story," I tell him. And the route that I choose is the one that takes us past every single ugly thing.

Now that I'm initiating the second in my string of confessions (two in less than two months), it should be easier. I should be able to distance myself—perform it, so to speak. Actually, it's worse. The first time, I knew Shelley well enough to trust her, and so, sitting in that van in Virginia, I told her my story as if I were alone there, as if I were speaking to the clouds above our heads. Today, I am a guilty person standing before a judge. But why this man? Why here? Why now? Because he seems capable of hearing it. Because I'm not ready to say good-bye yet. Because he seems to want to know me, and this story is me.

And so I talk. I don't skip anything. The man listens without responding. At one point he nods, but only to indicate that he hears. A while later, as Stephanie wipes a nearby table, he orders a bottle of water for each of us. When I finally finish, the rain has stopped. Sunlight pours over the street outside, making all the wet things sparkle. I feel as if I've exposed every inch of my body. My worn-out body, panting, alive, and surprisingly thankful, more or less.

Dario lifts a hand and massages his eyes. He looks very tired—not old, but not young, either—and disappointed, too. I may have snatched from him the hope that I'd be different. But I don't know for sure. The man is three continents away from me, at least.

The clock on the wall says 8:47. I unscrew the top from my water and drink the whole thing without a pause, not so much out of desire as out of a need to focus on something else.

"Sorry," I say. "You just ask me to come have coffee."

He shrugs. "Maybe you always tell this story over coffee."

I smile, shake my head. I press my bottle cap into the skin on my arm, lift it, and look at the circle left on my skin.

"Why did you tell me?" he wants to know.

I make another circle on my skin. Then another. "You didn't understand me right," I say.

"Now I understand you because I know that story?"

"Something like that."

I would like to find a way to leave, or find a way to let him leave, but the door opens then with a blast of hot air and a woman bursts inside, her arms full of shopping bags, and spots Dario. "Hello there! Finally, you've come to visit me. How long has it been since you promised?" She calls toward Stephanie behind the counter, instructing in Vietnamese, "Child, go get the rest of the things off the motorbike." The bags slide to the floor and then she is standing over our table and I recognize her.

Dario says, "Phuong, meet my friend Mai, from North Carolina, U.S.A."

"Xuan Mai?" she asks.

"*Chị Ánh*?" I stand up, slipping into the old form of address: Older Sister Anh. As if it's only been a day or two since I saw her.

"You've grown up," she says, wrapping her arms around me.

Anh sits down in the chair next to mine, holding my hand. She was pretty then, and is beautiful now, as if it took her a decade or two simply to grow into it. Now, just back from the market, sweaty and mussed, her beauty seems thoughtless, more destiny than art. Still gripping my hand, she turns to the astonished Dario and explains, "We've known each other since we were children."

"But you don't even seem surprised to see her," he says.

She puts a hand to my cheek, then lets it drop to her knee, smiling at me gently. "I'm happy, that's all. But, no, not so surprised. We Vietnamese miss Vietnam. People come back. Even Xuan Mai came back, eventually."

He looks at me. "Xuan Mai?"

I say, "That what everybody always call me here." I can't even describe how it feels to hear my name again. Xuan Mai. My whole name.

Anh says, "Mai is just a plain old apricot blossom, but *Xuân Mai* means 'apricot blossom blooming in the spring.' It's almost like a poem, you see?" Before he can answer, though, she continues, "Xuan Mai's sister, Lan, and I are best friends. We used to play Hai Ba Trung—Vietnam's warrior queens—out on the dykes beside the river. Xuan Mai would follow us and beg to play. Remember, Xuan Mai? If we were feeling nice, we'd let you be our chief ambassador."

I nod. "And if you not feeling nice, you make me be the horse."

"True, true!" she admits. She drops my hand, then cradles my chin in her palm. "You've gotten so lovely," she muses. She turns to the doctor. "She was a scrawny thing. Isn't she a beauty now?"

I stare down at my knees, willing the conversation to shift in a different direction. Dario says, "She is." His voice sounds thoughtful, as if he's actually considered the question.

Anh pokes at my shirt. "But these clothes!" she laughs. "Hanoi girls are so modern now. They wear short skirts and tight blouses. They want to be like Hong Kong starlets. Xuan Mai goes to America and comes back looking like 1975!"

I force myself to look at Anh. "Why you change your name to Phuong?" I ask.

She leans back in her chair, waving away the question. "You can't be Anh and be an actress," she says, as if merely asserting the obvious. But the doctor looks confused. "Xuan Mai, tell him. Anh—what's a similar name in English?"

"Gladys."

"And Phuong? What's something glamorous?"

"Gwyneth."

Anh likes that. "Yes. Definitely. Gwyneth!" She looks at the doctor. "Now you understand?"

"In Italy, Gina would change her name to Eleanora."

"It's only common sense," says Anh, as if the Italian names actually mean something to her. "I always planned to be an actress."

Anh and my sister were among the smartest and most ambitious of the girls chosen to study in the Soviet Union in 1973. Anh had a knack for languages and was being groomed for the diplomatic corps. Lan, unlike anyone else in my family, excelled in the sciences, and the Vietnamese government picked her to travel to Moscow to study physics. Then, a few months before she was scheduled to leave, Lan fell in love with Tan, whose family lived a few doors down. We'd known him, I suppose, my whole life. But Tan, who was two years older than Lan, never joined the neighborhood children who roamed the streets as guerrillas or cops and spies. Instead, he used to sit on the front stoop of his house, constructing buildings out of scraps of cardboard, wire, and wood. Then, when he turned seventeen, he left for the war. Three years later, in 1973, when he returned on leave, he was taller and more muscular, as quiet as ever, but confident, too. I think that Lan was drawn to the things he knew but wouldn't tell her, the ugliness of whatever was going on in the south. Despite our familiarity with bomb shelters, evacuations, and the occasional low, booming rumble of airplanes or bombs, Lan and I had never seen the war itself. She complained that we were watching a play from backstage: You knew what was going on, but you never got to see it. The night before Tan was scheduled to go back to the front, they found an official to marry them. The next morning, Lan went to the station to see him off. Then she enlisted as a sapper along the Truong Son Trail, which the Americans called the Ho Chi Minh, and she left a week later. Two months after Lan left, Anh and the other students went to the Soviet Union. I never saw her after that.

"So you changed your name in Russia?" I ask.

"In Paris. I started doing theater, comedy mostly, in Moscow. After the war ended, I met some diplomats from France and they got me a scholarship to study in Paris. I made a passionate appeal about wanting to perform on behalf of my country and somehow I managed to convince the Vietnamese authorities to let me go. What did they have to lose? I already spoke Russian and, through no cost of their own, I could learn to speak French. So I went to Paris in 1976 and immediately met an American named Joe, who ran the French office of American Express. We had a love affair, totally Romeo and Juliet, you know? He taught me English. My French is awful, really."

"When did you come back to Vietnam?"

She turns around and calls to Stephanie, "Darling, bring us some croissants, and that bunch of lychees!" Then she grabs her stomach. "I'm starved. Tonight's my father-in-law's death anniversary and I've been at the market for hours. So? Oh, I came back in 1980. I'd split up with Joe, then Mike, then—what was his name?—Hal; for some reason, I liked the American guys. And Paris wasn't a bad gig. I got plenty of work in theater and even some in film. But, I just thought, enough already. I'm sick of playing whores, you know? The whole Madame Butterfly bit gets old after a while. I came back so I could get some serious roles. And my mother was sick. After eight years, you know, it was time."

Stephanie delivers the lychees and the warm croissants. Anh has hers in her mouth before the plate is even on the table. She says, "Eat. Both of you. They're fresh, this morning." She looks at Dario. "Even the European will be satisfied." He and I taste our croissants, which are so fresh and light that each bite disintegrates into nothingness as soon as it touches the tongue.

Anh rests her hand on mine. "Have you seen Lan?"

I nod.

She takes another bite of croissant, glancing at the doctor, then back to me.

"He knows everything," I say.

"Everything?"

He lifts a hand into the air and lets it drop against the table, saying, "Only recently." I am so afraid that he will leave, but he doesn't.

"I just saw her yesterday. She seemed kind of distracted, but she didn't tell me you're here," says Anh. She pulls a couple of lychees off the bunch, peels them open, and hands one to the doctor and one to me.

"She not happy about it."

"No. She wouldn't be," she says. "Come on. Eat."

The lychees are plump and sweet, heavy with juice. The three of us devour them as if it were our occupation. Our eyes focus, our hands move efficiently, peeling, tearing the flesh with our teeth, depositing the smooth brown pits and rose-colored skins into a growing pile amid the dirty plates, the cups of cold coffee and empty water bottles. It's convenient. No one has to look at anyone else.

By the time Anh returned from France in 1980, she tells us, My Hoa had been dead a year. At that time, Lan worked as project manager at the Institute for Marine Sciences. There, she ran a Swedish-funded study of shrimp farming that, as Anh remembers, was expensive, unpromising, and likely to continue for a decade, at least. Lan didn't complain. In fact, she seemed perfectly content to fill her days with work and caring for my father, who, frail but also newly ambitious, had decided to learn Chinese so that he could translate into Vietnamese a famous dictionary of Chinese idioms. "The two of them were like robots," Anh tells me. "Their bodies moved, but their brains didn't have anything but data in them."

Then, in 1986, Australia and the Institute for Marine Sciences launched a joint-venture partnership based on preliminary results of the shrimp-farming project. Lan was sent to Sydney on a three-month study tour and, while there, fell in love with an Australian colleague, a Vietnamese-born man named Chung who happened to be married. Lan returned to Vietnam pregnant and gave birth to their daughter, Lien, the next year. "That's when she finally came out of it," Anh says. "I don't mean she got over My Hoa's death. She'll never get over that. But she acted as if she were under a spell for seven years. Lien woke her up."

I can feel Anh's eyes on me. I stare at my hands, sticky and smudged with lychee juice and dust. It is one thing to imagine, all these years, how I made my sister suffer. It is another thing, entirely, to hear about it.

"Lan stayed at the institute another few years," Anh continues, "until the economy began to improve. Then she quit her job and opened her café. She kind of blossomed then. She adored Lien, and her café was a great success. Dat and I would never have opened this one if we hadn't seen how well she did with hers. Life has gotten better, really. And then, last year, Chung showed up. Fourteen years later! He'd gotten a divorce and he wanted to meet his daughter. One thing led to another—again!—and they got married. He can't leave Sydney because he owns a big seafood processing plant somewhere on the coast there. Of course, he wants Lan and Lien to move there. But Lan refuses to leave your father."

I finally have someone to ask. "How is my father?"

"He's dying, I suppose." Anh was always frank. "How old is he now?"

"He'll be sixty-six this year."

"He can't breathe. To be honest, he could die tomorrow or he could die next year. I think he'd rather die tomorrow."

For more than half my life—yes, it's been that long now—I have wanted to go back in time, to live it again, and better. But that's a lot to desire. Let me consider the possibility of something simpler. Giving my lungs to my father.

"You should go and see him," Anh says.

I stare at her.

"He's alone during the day. There's a padlock on the metal gate of the house, but people come and go, to visit him. It looks locked, but it's not, really."

At some point, I realize, we have slipped into Vietnamese. Dario, however, seems intent on following the conversation anyway, through tone, expression, the gaps between our words. "I'm sorry," I tell him. "We're rude."

"No." He shakes his head. He looks kind of embarrassed, as if he's heard too much already.

Dario and I walk back to the hotel over the same route, but not quite together, like two people who became intimate too quickly and now try to put distance between themselves. I struggle to focus on the day around us: the feeling of the sun on my skin, the glare in my eyes, the crankiness of the traffic. But I can't ignore the fact that I am not a better person. For so many years in America, I have been a failure to myself, and I came back to Hanoi knowing I'd face the disappointment of others. But this new shame comes unexpectedly. Two weeks ago I didn't even know this man existed.

Amid the noise of the street, I almost don't hear him. "Can I tell you something, Xuan Mai?" he asks.

I smile, but I'm worried. "I guess." No criticism could be worse than how I feel already.

"Do you remember when I described my wife's death?"

"Of course."

"In the airplane, right after the crash, I worried about the plane exploding. I mean, I am not an idiot. I knew such a thing could happen. I tell my wife I am going out to look for supplies, but, also, I want to get out of the plane. Very quickly. When I tell my story to other people, I omit that piece of information."

Kind, but unconvincing. "It's not same."

"You're competing."

"No. Why you want me to hear this?"

"What do you call your crime?"

"I don't know."

"I call it negligence. And abandonment. For negligence and abandonment, you get twenty-three years."

"And you?"

"For being a coward, I get nine years."

"You try to make it easy."

He sighs, then stops, right in the middle of the sidewalk. The woman behind us, hauling a load of bananas, curses and walks around us, glaring. The doctor takes my arm and holds it, looking down at me and speaking Italian—two or three sentences, maybe, not a single word that I can understand. The phrases roll into each other, up and down, languid but emphatic, like opera. Then he releases my arm and we begin to walk again. I don't ask for a translation and he doesn't offer one.

I grew up on Nguyen Sieu Street, just down from Ngo Gach, the Brickmaker's Street. It used to be a quiet neighborhood, the focus of which was the Thanh Ha Pagoda. Now, every building houses a shop selling paint. It's a rainbow of house paint, my old street. And brushes, turpentine, tarps. I can't think how such a thing has come to pass. My mother taught history at the Tran Phu Middle School a few blocks away. When she died, I remember, the students filed through our house in waves, class after class after class, all braids and jitters, eyes on the floor, unsure of themselves, embarrassed. My father insisted that he and Lan and I shake every single student's hand. At the time, I resented it. I didn't want to shake hands, accept condolences, or look into the eyes of children who would, ten minutes later, rush home to confirm that their mothers still existed. I wanted to escape, too. I wanted another family. A whole one.

I head down Nguyen Sieu, bags of groceries hanging from the handlebars of my borrowed bike, and it takes me a minute to figure out where I am. The street-level doorways have changed. These days, they all contain the same displays of paint and paint products, none of it familiar. I have

to position myself by looking across the street, and locating myself in relation to the pagoda that I walked past every day for the first nineteen years
of my life. Then I see the familiar entry, the narrow passageway leading
between two street-front buildings. I step inside, and follow it twenty
feet, where it jogs to the left, then straightens again and plunges deeper.
The air smells of mildew, kerosene, and something new, too: incense. Yes.
I pass the doorway of the tiny room where Old Mrs. Nhung used to live
and the steps leading up to the Le house, the floor by the bottom step still
cluttered, as always, with bicycles and shoes. And then, at the end of the
passage, the old gate and the padlock in it. I jiggle the lock and it opens. I
slide back the gate and I'm home.

The house was old, even when my parents first moved into it. A family of Chinese merchants had lived in it for fifty years or more, finally
abandoning it in 1954 when they fled to the south during the cease-fire.
When my parents arrived in Hanoi soon afterward, they were homeless
and unsure of where to go. The government granted them a lease on the
house as an acknowledgment of the service they'd provided in the war.
Unlike some of the ornate villas in the city, it wasn't big or grand in any
way, but it had one memorable feature. In one corner of the courtyard,
facing the passageway leading from the front gate, a banyan tree grew
out of a small square of dirt, up the side of the wall, and opened its great
green arms over the courtyard, making the space quiet, cool, and shady,
even on the hottest days of summer. The tree had existed longer than
the house, sending its long vines toward the ground, where they grew
thick and hard as trunks. I was raised believing that banyan trees, including ours, are homes to the spirits of the dead. We weren't particularly
happy to have one growing so close by, but we wouldn't dream of cutting
it down, which would risk angering the spirits and inciting them to haunt
us. Our family and that tree always lived together in peace. Even during
the most stringent years of Communism, we could manage to find a stick
of incense to leave there as an offering. My mother would have liked to
do more, worrying that failing to make the requisite offerings showed dis-
respect. My father always said that you couldn't make an offering if you

had nothing to offer. And, besides, the spirits weren't blind. They could see the barrenness of our lives. They wouldn't expect much.

The first thing I notice when I step into the courtyard is the hundreds of bright red incense sticks, spent now, stuck into the crannies of the tree. The second thing I notice is my father, seated in a wicker chair in the shade beneath it. A folded newspaper lies across his lap, his glasses rest in his hand and his eyes are closed, his head tipped back. I lean the bike against the wall, set my groceries on the ground, then step inside the courtyard, moving closer. With each breath, his chest rumbles to life, then dies again. My father's skin is pale, bluish, veiny, and spotty. His hair, nearly white now, forms a silky mass of short, thin curls around the base of his head. After twenty-three years, he looks different, of course, but not radically so. He was old when I left, although not much past forty. He aged enormously after my mother died. People talk about growing old, but he didn't "grow" old. He—the optimist who had believed beyond reason that she would recover—"turned" old, in about five minutes. That can only happen once in a person's life. Afterward, there's nothing to do but get older, which he has done. Part of me feels sad to see this once strong and agile man look so frail and exhausted. The other part just grieves for the years I missed with him.

An empty second chair sits next to my father's, positioned close, as if inviting conversation. On a table between the two lie a worn deck of cards, a copy of *The Tale of Kieu,* three medicine bottles, a mug, a fan, and a pile of crumpled tissues. Quietly, I pick up the stray tissues, straighten the table, then take the mug, which is half full of lukewarm coffee and ringed with dried milk, and carry it to the spigot in the far corner of the courtyard. When I squat and turn on the valve, the water bursts out, spraying my clogs. It's a deluge compared to the trickle I remember, the moments when my mother would scream at the spigot, as if it bore responsibility for the fact that it produced so little water. Why didn't Khoi give me this information when he talked to me about his visit to Hanoi? Why didn't he tell me about improvements in the plumbing?

Next to the spigot, I find a basin containing a pile of clothes, soaking in water, a thin soapy ring making rainbows on the top. I take off my watch, push it into my pocket, then thrust my hands into the cool water and begin to scrub, one item at a time, firmly enough to get at the dirt, gently enough to keep from tearing the fabric. These are old man's clothes: nothing but white undershirts and faded pajamas, thin from so much scrubbing. I glance over my shoulder, but my father hasn't stirred.

It takes me longer than it should to finish the laundry. After so many years of washing clothes in machines, my hands and arms feel awkward and weak. Finally, I hang each item to dry on the line, then unpack my groceries and begin to prepare lunch. I've brought water morning glory, which is a darker green and tougher than what I can get in the States. I've got eggs, a piece of pork, tofu, a small bag of tiny pickled eggplants, which I know he loves, and rice. Sometimes, in Wilmington, I cook the food my mother told me she'd eaten during her childhood—fine pork sausages, ginger prawns, even French specialties like crème caramel and pâté. I never had a chance to taste such delicacies during my life in Vietnam, but in America I learned to make them. Today, though, I'll cook simple food. I remember how much my father loved the dishes he grew up with. I think they reminded him of his youth, his days in the war, when he could survive on so little. Now I squat over the old stove, preparing a meal for a peasant: a simple omelet with chunks of pork; boiled water morning glory; fried tofu stewed in tomatoes; a plate of pickled eggplant; a bowl of vegetable broth; and rice. I have not smelled anything so delicious in years. When I'm finished, I clear the table by my father's chair, pull out the round aluminum tray, set the bowls and chopsticks on it, and carry lunch to where he sits. Perhaps it's the sound of the tray brushing across the table that, finally, wakes my father. Perhaps it's the smell of the food in front of him. He rubs his eyes and opens them, gazing for a moment at the sky. Then he picks up his glasses, sets them on his nose, and sees me, standing there in front of him.

"*Bố,*" I say. Father.

I think he tries to speak, but the words catch in his throat. "Cough" seems too insignificant a word for what happens to his body then. Wave after wave of spasms begin in his gut, move up through his chest, shoul-

der, back, and neck, erupting from his mouth in loud and cacophonous
bursts, like air bellowing from a broken machine. How can such a weak
and fragile body produce such noise? I rush across the courtyard to pour
a glass of water from a pitcher by the stove. But when I offer it to him, he
waves it away, still coughing, still staring at me when he gets the chance.
Five minutes later, as the spasms subside, he points to the bowl of broth.
I perch on the other chair and spoon some of the liquid into his bowl.
He takes it between his shaking hands and slowly brings it to his mouth
to drink. I would like to hold it for him, but I don't. He sips slowly, but
without stopping, finishing every drop.

"Can I give you some rice?" I ask.

He nods. "I came after you," he says in a voice that's stronger than I
expected.

I spoon the rice into a bowl, put a couple of pieces of omelet and tofu
on top of it, push the plate of pickled eggplant in his direction.

"The omelet might be a little burned," I tell him. In fact, it's golden
brown, crispy outside and soft and moist inside, the way my mother made
it. But I have to say something, and I can't bring myself to acknowledge
the fact that I've been away for a very long time.

He takes a bite of the omelet and chews. "I came after you," he says
again.

I spoon some rice into my own bowl, take a small piece of tofu and eat
it. Leaning across the table, I lift an especially large and succulent cube
of tofu and place it in my father's bowl. "The omelet's not good," I say.
"And the tofu is too chewy. And the rice—it's a little dry. I'm sorry."

"I knew you would go on the boat," he tells me. "I went after you.
Uncle Binh had a motorbike, remember?"

I nod, but I don't look at him. I push the plate of eggplant farther across
the table. I lift a grain of rice from my bowl and put it in my mouth.

"Your boyfriend's brother told us where to go. We found the village
easily, only a few miles south of Hai Phong. We made good time on the
motorbike. I don't think I arrived more than an hour after you did on
the bus. But those fishermen move fast. As soon as they saw you had the
money, they let you on the boat, and pulled away." I'm surprised that he

goes on for so long, talking and breathing simultaneously. His bowl is full and forgotten. I put a piece of tofu on top of all the tofu there already.

"Bo," I say. "Eat."

"I stood on the pier. I could see the boat. They didn't even lie about it, the women on the dock. They said the boat was headed for Hong Kong. Did you hear me when I called to you?"

I shake my head.

"I called to you."

I shake my head.

"I said, 'Xuan Mai. Come back, child. One is enough. Don't make it two.' "

I shake my head. I shake my head. I didn't hear a thing.

My bowl is in my lap. The chopsticks dangle from my hand, toward the floor. "I'm sorry, Bo," I whisper. Maybe he hears me, maybe not.

"One was enough. Why did you have to make it two?" he asks, his voice forlorn, and it's not a question so much as a demonstration of the way he stood there on the dock, calling after the daughter who had killed his granddaughter, then disappeared.

"I didn't hear," I say.

He nods. He's crying now, and the crying sets off another coughing spell, this one worse than the first. I manage to get the rice bowl out of his hand, then I squat beside him, my hand on his knee. When he finishes, he's panting. His arms go around my shoulders and he leans over, kissing me the old Vietnamese way, bursts of short, quick sniffs against the top of my head. I haven't been kissed like that in so many years. It makes me see that I had a whole life ahead of me, and skipped it.

17

Shelley

Lap, the driver, has plans of his own. He speaks very little English. But he's got a clue, unlike Mrs. Huyen and Carolyn Burns. They expect (and want?) me to throw up my hands and head for the airport. Vietnamese tradition seems to require that I, the customer, sit in back, but I sit up front with him. In the mornings, on the way to the orphanage, we share cigarettes and listen to tapes of Vietnamese rock and roll, or the World Cup on the radio. In the afternoons, he brings his kid along, a twelve-year-old named Binh who speaks pretty good English and uses it, mostly, to speculate about life aboard airplanes. Binh leans forward from the back of the Toyota, dangling his arms over the front seat as if he's catching fish.

"My friend say, you have to go toilet in airplane, you go in cup. For man, no problem. For lady, big problem. Many lady die. On airplane, they die." He speaks sadly and with conviction. I imagine him at school, relaying this information to his buddies on the playground.

"That's not true," I tell him.

He nods his head. "True. True!"

Lap nudges his son's arm with an elbow and says something in Vietnamese.

"My father say my cousin can help you," Binh relates. "He minister of interior. Very good."

I look at Binh. "He's the minister of the interior?" Today's dialogue concerns plan number five. The first four plans washed out, through no lack of diligence on the part of Lap, so I can't believe we didn't approach this guy already.

Binh stares at me. His ability to express himself surpasses his ability to understand.

"The *minister* or the *ministry*?" I ask. "Person or place?"

The boy blinks. "Ministry! Ministry!" he says, making the *y* sound like the yips of a puppy.

"Oh."

Lap talks. He drives with his hands hovering above the steering wheel, gesturing, fiddling with the lighter or the volume on the cassette player. When needed, his hands will alight for a moment to make a turn, or to pound on the horn, then fly up again, more necessary for communication than steering. His voice is emphatic. He repeats his sentences two or three times, as if he doesn't trust Binh even to follow the Vietnamese.

"My father say we go to my cousin house right now, if you like. Okay?"

What do I have to lose? It is six o'clock. Mai will be glad to have the room to herself. And I, having run out of other options, will try anything. "Sure," I say. "Why not?"

The boy grins and relays the information to his father, who gives me a thumbs-up and completes a U-turn across three lanes of traffic while dialing a number on his cell phone.

Ten minutes later, we pull to a stop in an alley lined with ornate-looking contemporary town houses, all three and four stories high but not much wider than the length of our car. Compared to the Lucinda, the space seems palatial, but in the States people have wider closets. Land is expensive here, but air is free.

We slip off our shoes at the doorstep and walk into a room that, though narrow, is spaciously deep. In the front half of the room, three men sit on two wooden couches, facing each other across a coffee table with a white cloth over it. Behind the couches, a large set of glass-fronted cabinets juts perpendicularly into the room, serving as a partition between the front of the room and the back.

"Hello!"

"Hello!"

"Hello!"

The men stand up and surround us at the door. One is burly and unkempt. A second is slight and looks like a teenager. The third has white hair and hobbles toward me. Behind them, two women appear from the part of the room behind the cabinets, drying their hands with rags. They stop before they get too close, smiling and waving shyly.

The men laugh awkwardly, as if, simply by entering the house, I've told a funny joke. Then everyone falls silent, glancing around, trying to figure out what to do next. Luckily, my professional experience kicks in. "Shelley Marino," I say, grabbing a hand and shaking it, then another and another, moving efficiently around the room. "Shelley Marino. Shelley Marino." I go through all the men. And the women, too, who look surprised and pleased. Their handshakes are limp and unpracticed, but game enough.

I take the burly man, Duc, to be the owner of the house. He ushers me to a seat on the couch. On the table in front of me sit about a dozen unopened cans of 333 beer, a tray of glasses, a tower of bowls, and a pile of chopsticks. Duc, who is humming quite loudly, opens a can of beer, pours it into a glass, and offers it to me. I accept it, but look around. "Binh?" I ask. Lap may save me, but his son keeps me afloat. The boy, throwing his chin into the air, makes his way past his elders and takes the seat next to mine.

The women have disappeared into what I suspect is the kitchen. Here in the front of the house, the beer flows freely. The conversation becomes loud, witty, and, judging by the glances in my direction, focused on me. It's hard to know for sure because my translator, concentrating on the prospect of pilfering sips of his father's beer, forgets to pay attention. Lap hands me a small ceramic cup with a clear liquid in it. He points to the cup, then at me, and says something that makes the others laugh.

"Binh." I speak loudly and firmly enough to make the boy look up. "What is it?"

Binh lifts the cup off the table and sniffs it. "Our Vietnamese whiskey. My father say you like cigarettes and Vietnamese lady don't like cigarettes. So my father think you like our whiskey, too."

Whatever. I pick up the cup, taste it with my tongue, and swallow it like a shot. The men applaud. The liquid burns in my throat, but it goes down smoothly. "Not bad," I cough.

"On airplanes, people drink whiskey only this big," Binh holds up his hand to show a space between his finger and thumb about as wide as a pencil. "And, because they in the air, they very tipsy. So tipsy, sometime people die because they drink too much."

I don't bother to answer. The men keep talking. From the kitchen, I can hear the low voices of the women and I suddenly feel the need to see them. Pushing myself off the couch, I cause the men to pause in their conversation, but they don't seem to mind my stepping over Binh and walking around the cabinets to investigate. The kitchen is a small space, off the back of the main room. I peek through the doorway, and find the two women squatting on the floor, one over a cutting board, chopping tiny red chilies, the other over a frying pan balanced on a small portable stove. She's turning spring rolls sizzling in oil. The air is so full of the smells of the food I could almost lift my hand and catch them.

When the women see me, they grin. The one at the frying pan, who appears to be in her early twenties, says, "How you?"

"Just fine," I say. "And you?"

She seems to have used up her English. Instead of replying, she giggles, using the back of her arm to push her hair off her forehead, then looks back down at what she's doing. *"Binh oi!"* she calls to my translator in the other room.

A moment later, the boy ambles around the cabinets and leans into the kitchen. He spies the spring rolls, squats down to snatch one draining on a plate, and receives a slap to the hand with a chopstick. He and the younger woman bicker until she reluctantly lets him take a spring roll. Then he stands up and leans against the other side of the door, gingerly biting into it, then letting the steam escape.

The women ask Binh a series of questions, which he answers disinterestedly. In the midst of their labors, they continuously glance at me. Finally, they ask him something he can't answer.

"Mrs. Shelley," he says. "You don't speak Vietnamese. They want know how you going teach that little baby Vietnamese."

The older woman is chopping chilies now. The younger one stirs the spring rolls aimlessly.

"He may not learn Vietnamese," I say. "Or he may learn when he's older, if he likes."

They absorb this information, cook for a while. Then, the older one wants to know, "How you going to feed him?"

"I'll cook."

"You know how cook Vietnamese?"

"Not well."

"You know how cook rice?"

I nod, which seems to convince them that, at least, the child won't starve. Still, it's hard to tell if they approve. Binh only translates the questions he feels incapable of handling himself, and the women mutter under their breaths in a way that makes me feel like a member of an international criminal ring dedicated to baby snatching. Have a little pity, I'd like to say, for our situation. Our. Hai Au and me.

The older woman, perhaps in her mid-forties, deep voiced and chubby, points her wrist in my direction and mumbles another question. "Why you no baby here?" Binh asks, pointing at my belly.

How to explain such a thing? I open my hand and wave it back and forth over my stomach. "Not possible," I say.

The women stare at me, nodding and murmuring between themselves. The younger one pulls a golden spring roll out of the pan, shakes off the grease, and lays it on paper to drain. The older one finishes chopping the chilies. Then she pushes herself up, rinses her hands at the sink, and slips out the door, motioning for me to follow. She stops in front of a bureau, yanks it open, and begins to pull out clothes: tiny pants, hats, mittens, a little shirt with a purple doggie on it. "*Mấy tháng?*" she wants to know.

"How many months the baby?" Binh asks.

"About two years old."

The woman squats on the floor with the clothes, sorting them, creating piles here and there, tossing the frilly pink dresses and rainbow pajamas into one heap, carefully folding the sailor pants, the choo-choo shirt, the soccer shorts, and the purple dog, then stacking them beside her. When she's gone through everything, she dumps the heaps back into the drawer, then picks up the stack of folded clothes, stands, and pushes them into my arms. I look down at them, then back at the girl in the kitchen.

The girl in the kitchen urges me with her chin.

I think of my suitcase full of Baby Gap, Carter's, and Gymboree. I think of the poor women I see every morning outside the windows of the orphanage, slogging through the rice fields. Certainly, they have children. Certainly, they could use a bag of hand-me-downs. I mean, face it: I don't even have a baby. But I hug those clothes to my chest as if there is a shivering infant at my hotel. The woman lifts the clothes out of my arms, stuffs them into a plastic bag, and roughly pushes me back toward the dinner table, urging me—I know this much—to eat.

The men respond to the sight of the baby clothes with a little burst of applause, a few thumbs-ups, and a toast to my baby. Lap, who seems to have been holding the floor, bangs his hand against the table as if it were his steering wheel, and continues to talk. It's stirring to hear him speak at such length, so eloquently, so capable of holding other people's attention. I've already grown so fond of him, but now I'm filled with admiration, too. The women return to the room carrying bowls of rice noodles, platters of lettuce and herbs, plates full of spring rolls. Everyone squeezes closer together on the couch to give them room to sit down. Lap, still talking, picks up a set of chopsticks, fills a bowl with noodles, greens, and a spring roll.

"*Xin mời,*" he says, inviting me to eat. He holds the bowl with two hands and passes it to me as if it were a precious gift.

"*Cám ơn,*" I say. Thank you. After all those weeks of practicing Vietnamese with Mai, *thank you* is the only phrase I never forget.

I also recognize the word *em bé*—baby—and they say it so often in the next few minutes that it would take a dolt to miss the fact that they're discussing my future. Next to me, Binh's hand makes slow progress toward his father's beer. I watch the others eat and, following their leads, hold my bowl in one hand, lift the spring roll to my mouth with the other, and take a bite. It's long and fat, solid as a banana, and doesn't deflate like the egg rolls we used to eat thirty years ago at Joy Young's—oily, balloonlike things, full of wilted lettuce and only good as missiles aimed at distant objects

"Binh," I say, nudging him. "Which one works at the ministry?"

The boy has half a spring roll in his mouth. He motions with his chopsticks toward the man sitting across from him: the teenager, the child. "How old is he?" I ask.

"He my cousin Quang. He nineteen year old." At twelve, Binh is clearly impressed.

The pimply-faced Quang listens attentively to the conversation, his eyes flicking back and forth as he follows the discussion of his elders. He looks excited and somewhat tense, as if he's finally allowed to sit with the grown-ups and he doesn't want to blow it. Even the way he drinks his beer makes the gesture seem new and thrilling. Unlike the others, who grab their glasses and swallow without looking, he pours carefully, watches the foam subside, fingers the glass.

"What's his job at the ministry?" I want to know.

Binh answers through another mouthful of spring roll. "Driver!" he says.

"Driver?" Okay. Maybe not a problem. Maybe there's a connection to the real minister here. "Who does he drive?" I ask.

"Worker bus! You know, worker bus?"

"Yes, sure," I say. For this, we are here? I look at Lap. His plans are ridiculous. Maybe he's only brought me here because I'm an interesting object to invite over for dinner. A conversation starter. Something new.

The older woman, who I guess now is Duc's wife, leans across the table to put fresh spring rolls in people's empty bowls. She announces something, tipping her head to indicate the front door or the street outside.

The others speak at once, motioning to the door, nodding, pointing.

"What?" I want to know, but Binh is too focused on the conversation to notice.

The older woman nods. She points to the telephone. She seems convinced of something.

Lap claps his hands together, looks at me as if he has a prize to offer.

"What?" I ask again.

Binh looks at his father, then at me. "The neighbor daughter," the boy explains. "She sixteen year old and pregnant. Her father very angry. Her mother very angry. Whole family, very unhappy. What to do with baby?"

A brief exchange ensues between Binh, Lap, and Duc's wife. She makes a gesture with her hand at her stomach that I take to indicate late stages of pregnancy.

Binh looks at me. "Very soon," he says.

The room grows quiet. Seven pairs of eyes on me. I've heard of private adoption. It's rare, and somewhat complicated bureaucratically, but people do it. A couple in my adoption support group back in Wilmington met a child in Guatemala, completed the paperwork on their own, and six months later that kid was a first-grader at Wrightsville Beach Elementary. Before I got into this process, putting an adoption together without the help of Carolyn Burns or Mrs. Huyen would have seemed impossible, but now, I think, who needs them?

Lap grins. Despite his debatable reasons for bringing me to his cousin's house for dinner, I know that my predicament disturbs him. He seems to think he's solved it now. So I feel a little bad that I have to disappoint him. I shake my head at their hopeful faces. "No. I don't think so, thanks."

You don't have to speak English to understand what I'm saying. Lap's eyebrows bunch together in confusion. His hands fall open on his lap. Why not?

I don't know how to explain that the idea of adopting some faceless infant has no appeal to me anymore. Two months ago, I merely wanted to be a mother. Now I want to be a mother to Hai Au, this little boy who hoards food, likes cats, enjoys the feel of grains of rice rubbed across his face. He needs me. My son. My child. If I can't bring him home with me, I'll go alone, and I'll stop trying. I feel sure of this fact, though I've only just recognized it.

The food lies forgotten on the table. Everyone sits watching me, waiting for an explanation. I say, "I want Hai Au."

Binh translates and my answer sucks all the energy out of the room. Lap toys with his noodles using the tip of a chopstick, but can't seem to remember to put the food in his mouth. The women start to collect the dishes, dumping leftovers onto the empty spring roll platter, stacking the bowls, grabbing up the chopsticks in their fists. Duc gets up and flicks on the stereo. The first few notes of "I'm on the Top of the World" float across the room. The old man scowls and rubs his ear; the teenage bus driver jiggles his knee like someone ready to disco. I sip my whiskey. Your love's put me on the top of the world.

Lap tips his head in my direction, says a word to Binh.

"You feel okay, Mrs. Shelley?" the boy asks.

I manage to nod, but I'm woozy. I realize I'm slouching in my seat and I try to sit up. "What time is it?" I ask.

Before I have a chance even to wipe my mouth with a napkin, Lap is standing, keys ready, helping me up, grabbing the bag of clothes, and ushering me out the door. One of the women finds my shoes. Good-bye is a set of nods, waves, and smiles, both anxious and sympathetic. My son's culture, I tell myself, is a warmhearted and generous one. At least, the ones who want to help.

During the drive home, I focus on the blur of lights and the honking. Lap and Binh help me into the Lucinda. Even in my drunken state, I sense that this man is worried about his job, bringing his charge home drunk and reeling, and so I do my best to stand tall and walk efficiently. For some reason, at that moment, I remember the original goal of the evening. "And the minister?" I ask. My voice sounds loose and far away.

Lap looks at his son, who doesn't seem to understand.

"The minister?" I want to know. "Can he help?"

Father and son confer for a moment. "It's possible. Don't worry," little Binh says.

My wave is kite high and circular. "Don't worry," I tell them, spinning toward the stairs. "No problem."

"Tomorrow. Nine A.M.?" Lap asks in English. Given the demands of his job, he is capable of scheduling. "See Hai Au!"

"Yes!" I say, all loud and peppy. Linguistically, Lap and I have almost nothing in common, but we understand each other very well. We're both committed to confidence, if only because hopelessness is too pathetic.

I am drunk enough to consider throwing myself off the balcony, but not so drunk, perhaps, that I would do it.

Upstairs, I find the door unlocked. I can hear Mai in the bathroom, running the water. I stumble inside, drop the bag of hand-me-downs onto the floor, then lower myself back against a pillow and close my eyes. Mai must have just come in herself. Her bed looks untouched. When the water goes off, I call out, "I'm back. I ate dinner with Lap. I'm drunk."

I hear the sound of water being poured from a bottle, the creak of the bathroom door, a step. I open my eyes. Martin stands above me, a glass of water in his hand.

"Here," he says. "Drink this."

Any observer witnessing the interaction that takes place in my room over the next few minutes would not mistake it for a reunion of long-separated lovers, or even for that of a no longer ardent but still affectionate married couple. We hug, but only briefly and because it would feel even more awkward if we didn't. I sit back down on my bed and drink the water he's offered me. Martin sits on the chair by the window, gazing at the building across the street. His face looks thin and exhausted, his hair tousled, his cotton shirt bearing all the wrinkles of too many hours on airplanes. We talk, but our conversation focuses not on the purpose of Martin's journey here, but its mechanics: flight itineraries, fatigue, the details of bringing Carl in from retirement to help at the office. Other than the fact that we are discussing such matters in Hanoi, and that I'm still slightly tipsy, we could be sitting in my office in Wilmington, arranging burials.

Besides simply trying to absorb the shock of his arrival, I'm also distracted by the realization that I can, after all, take Hai Au home. If someone had prepared me for this moment in advance, I might have expected the joy to hit me suddenly, like a cool splash of water on a hot day. But, in fact, it seeps through my body drop by drop, moving from my brain to my neck and shoulders, into my heart and back out through all my veins to my fingers, to my toes. I am nothing but happiness, sitting on this bed.

I lie. I am happiness, and more. I am grateful to Martin, and angry, too. Should I apologize for leaving him? Should he apologize to me? Who, exactly, is responsible for the mess that we've made of our marriage? The air in the room fairly swirls with guilt and anger, but no firm emotions seem able to take root in either one of us.

Finally, all other topics spent, I allow myself to ask: "Martin, why did you come?"

At first, he merely shrugs, stretching his feet in front of him and staring at his shoes. Then he says, "I didn't want to ruin your life." His voice is firm and without emotion, but not unkind.

"What about the letter? What about everything that happened to you here?"

He slides his hand through his matted hair. "It helped some, just to write it down. After I sent it, I thought about how little it would take, really, just to travel over here. It wouldn't kill me. All I have to do is sign the papers and go home."

I'm grateful that the room is dim, that he refuses to look at me. I whisper, "Thanks."

"Mostly," he continues, "I didn't want to have to live with the fact that you lost another baby because of me."

He lets his head fall back against his chair and closes his eyes. I am full of wonder over what he has done for me. I remember some TV documentary we watched years ago, maybe on the History Channel. A scholar was talking about courage among soldiers during World War II. She said that almost every soldier she interviewed had experienced fear. Courage wasn't lack of fear, she argued. It was the willingness to go on, despite the fear.

I say, "I think you're brave."

Martin laughs, but there isn't much pleasure in it. He pulls himself up from the chair, then looks down at me on the bed. "I'll let you sleep."

"Where are you going?" I try not to sound frantic.

"I've got a room upstairs."

"Oh." I don't know what I expected. There's not space for all of us here. But I'm not ready for him to go yet. "Do you want to get something to eat?" I ask, starting to get up.

He shakes his head, waving away my offer with his hand. From down on the street, I hear the now familiar sound of one of the vendors who wander the streets with glass cases full of popping corn and horns that blare the tune "Lambada."

I remind myself that I am happy. Really happy. I would like to throw open the window and yell out to all of Hanoi: "I'm getting my boy!" I would like to rush down the stairs and tell the old babysitter ladies who sit in the lobby that I could, if I wanted, book them tomorrow. I would like to pick up the phone and give my news to the useless Mrs. Huyen. Part of me also wants to cry, because I have lost Martin.

He opens the door. "Okay, then. Good night," he says, already stepping out into the hall.

"Martin?" I can't bear to see him go already.

He turns halfway around, but keeps his hand on the door. His eyes are guarded. "What?"

I don't have anything to say, actually. He looks at me, waiting. "Okay, then," I say, forcing myself to sound enthusiastic. "Good night." Then I shut my eyes tight so that I see nothing but black.

18

Xuan Mai

At eleven-fifteen, I try to slip in without being noticed, but Tri spots me coming in through the front door. "*Chị ơi!*" he calls—Hey, Older Sister! He's completely abandoned whatever formality he once reserved for communication between himself and me.

"What?" I support myself against the empty reception desk while he charges toward me. "I need to go to bed," I tell him.

He moves like Maury Povitch—hearty and sly at the same time—nudging me toward some unexpected drama in the back lobby. "Come see!"

In the back lounge, a Western man gets up from the couch. A game of Monopoly sits half completed on the cushion beside him. "Hi, Mai," he says, waving almost shyly, "I'm Martin."

I've only seen him twice—once at a long ago funeral, but I don't remember him at all, and once sitting on the sidewalk in front of my store, when I didn't see his face. I can't have expected to recognize him, but I also shouldn't feel so shocked that he is here. Ever since we lost Hai Au, I have constantly hoped for his arrival. Now that he's arrived, though, I feel completely unprepared. For one thing, I never actually expected him to come. But, also, the timing compounds the surprise. My day has been so strange and miraculous that, I realize now, I've forgotten Shelley's predicament completely. Suddenly, I feel as if I have to shake myself awake again.

I run my fingers through my hair, which could stand to be brushed. "You came," I tell him.

He holds up his hands and stares at them as if he can't believe it himself. "Apparently so." He laughs. He looks dazed, but sort of pleased as well, like someone who has just realized that the oddest things can happen. For a moment, we simply stare at each other, sheepishly, but frankly, too. I feel like I'm glimpsing the face of someone I have heard on the radio for months. Now that I actually see what Martin looks like, I realize that I had unconsciously conjured up in my head a particular image of him: the dour face of the farmer in the painting *American Gothic,* which my teachers at Hanoi University showed us as a demonstration of the severity of the American people. Martin doesn't look like that at all. He's younger, for one thing, with considerably more hair. He has a round and pleasing face, a wry smile, and eyes that don't seem to miss a thing.

Tri puts his hand on the Monopoly board, uncertain if the game will continue. "Later," he asks, "I can whip your butt, sir?"

Martin grins, then looks at me. "Did you teach him that?"

I shake my head. "A lot of Americans come through here," I explain, then tell Tri in Vietnamese, "Watch it with the slang."

The young man nods enthusiastically, grateful for another mini lesson, then puts away the game. "Please, Older Sister, take a seat," he says, returning to his version of textbook English.

I perch on the couch next to Martin, who is the first person I would choose to have come here, of course, but not the first I would choose to converse with right this minute. "We didn't expect you," I say.

He shrugs. "How could I *not* come?"

"Still." Shelley told me the story of his time here. I want him to know that I recognize what it's cost him to come.

"Still," he admits.

Tri settles down at the computer and soon the whirs and pops and zings of some battle for the universe blast through the room. I look at Martin. "Did you see Shelley?" I ask.

He nods. "A few hours ago. She's happy," he says, as if it's as simple as that. I pick up my purse. I'd like to get upstairs to check on her myself, but Martin looks at his watch. "Eleven-thirty. The time has absolutely no meaning for me now. You want to take a walk or something?"

No. "Okay."

"Maybe we can get something to eat."

We walk around the corner to No Noodles, a trendy little restaurant that attracts foreigners with its international ambience and cold German beer. Even at this hour, a certain subset of young Hanoians demonstrate their determination to forge some kind of nightlife here. We find a table near the bar and Martin glances through the menu, then orders a tandoori chicken sandwich and a Heineken for each of us.

"How's it been for you, being back?" he asks.

"Great and terrible," I tell him.

He nods. "I can understand that." Around us, groups of well-dressed young people fill the restaurant, Vietnamese and foreigners, many of them in mixed groups, speaking English, French, German, and Vietnamese. "I didn't expect it to be so convivial here."

He's the first person, I realize, who might understand the feeling I've had since I came back to Vietnam. I lean across the table toward him. "It's like a different country," I explain. "Another country with the same name."

He nods, then smiles. "I guess I'm a little relieved." He sets his elbows on the table, massages his chin with a hand. "You get a picture in your head, you know? Some weird mix of memory and nightmare." His eyes settle on a boisterous table of Vietnamese yuppies. He stares as if there's something supernatural about it. "I was just playing Monopoly with a boy whose parents might have tried to blow me up."

"That true."

He shakes his head. "It's a little hard to absorb."

"You look pretty satisfied," I point out.

He shrugs. "It's not what I expected. I guess it's kind of invigorating, actually."

"Shelley told me what happened to you here."

He doesn't take his eyes off the Vietnamese. "A lot of people went through bad stuff."

"That don't change it," I tell him.

"Maybe not," he says and shrugs.

The waitress brings his sandwich and sets a beer in front of each of us. Martin takes a bite of the sandwich and then begins to devour it. "I'm starving," he says. "I had no idea."

I laugh. He motions to the waitress to bring him another sandwich. "It's jet lag," I tell him. "You a mess." He looks at me, smiles, keeps eating. I feel a wave of joy pass through me. One part of me relaxes in this chair. Another part hangs back, cowering in the corner, amazed that I could sit at this table with some American I don't even know, chatting as if it's the most natural thing in the world. This is the kind of life that you see on TV: busy, complicated, painful, stressful, happy, too. It bears no relation whatsoever to the life of the woman who runs the Good Luck Asian Grocery in a town in North Carolina on the other side of the world. I take a sip of the cool, bitter beer. "You done a wonderful thing for Shelley," I tell him. "I know she so happy now."

He settles back in his chair, his plate empty, waiting for the next sandwich to arrive. He looks at me. "You understand her pretty well, don't you?" he says.

"Maybe. I like her. I learn from her."

He nods, his fingers idly playing with his can of beer. "I've learned from her, too. I've always loved her determination. That's how she got this baby, you know. It's not because I came here. It's because she never gives up. I remember how, when we first got married, she decided she'd go into the business with me. It seemed crazy. A history major going to mortuary school—she hadn't planned that for her life, and I didn't need her to do it. But she insisted. The first time she came with me on a removal—an old man had died alone in Pender County—the decomposition was severe and she had to run out into the woods to throw up. Later, in those first few years, she often came home from funerals in tears. She wasn't depressed—actually, we were really happy then—but she got sad a lot. She acted like a person who spent her days watching tragic movies. I made some shifts in scheduling, gave her the easier cases, but, I don't know, basically she just got used to it. She became really good—efficient, compassionate, sincere. We were all so surprised. I mean, I grew up in this business, so everything about it seemed normal to me. But Shelley had never even seen a dead body before."

He glances at me, stressing the last sentence for emphasis, as if Shelley had never seen an airplane, a monkey, the sea. Then he seems to recognize the assumption he's made—that I, a Vietnamese, *have* seen dead bodies. "I mean, I don't know your history, of course."

"I have," I tell him.

He nods. A look passes between us, an acknowledgment that we share something. "She got along fine," he said, the slightest trace of bitterness in his voice, as if he believes that death shouldn't be so easy. "I guess it's possible to work in our industry without really understanding what it means to lose someone you love. But I've been through it myself, and lately I've started to feel like every day in this business scrapes off a little more of me. I mean, I had to bury a bride a few months back. A bride. She had a heart attack a month after her honeymoon. Shelley thinks that's sad and all, but when we were driving back from the memorial service, she pulled out this big sheaf of papers and started reading me documents explaining immigration regulations."

"Is that a bad thing?" I ask. "That she can do the job and want a baby, too?"

He shakes his head. "I've got two boys myself. But I was young when I had them. I wasn't so worn out, I guess."

"You promised her."

"I know," he admits. He lifts his hands and rubs his eyes.

His second sandwich comes. We talk about the war in Vietnam. Little of it pertains to Shelley, but, then again, it all does. We don't tell each other secrets, or even stories, really. I already know what happened to him here, but he doesn't mention it. At one point, he says, "Our guys were so young. We sent them back in pieces."

I say, "My father's brother died." He ended up in pieces, too.

He looks at me, but doesn't say anything. There's nothing, really, to say about a thing like that. We lapse into silence. At one end of the room, a raucous group of young people starts to dance between two tables. They're about the age I was when I left this place, but they live in a different world. I look at Martin. "Could you be glad you came?" I ask.

He stares at his beer. "I'll get a lot of satisfaction from helping Shelley," he says. "It's the least I could do, I guess."

"You make her very happy," I tell him.

He looks up at me, puzzled. For once, I like the ambiguity of my English. Make her happy? Made her happy? It isn't clear.

He doesn't take his eyes off me. "What does 'forgiveness' mean, anyway?"

He looks at me as if he believes I have an answer. "Giving up anger?" I ask.

"Maybe. I can imagine spending the rest of my life mad at her. After all, when she had to choose between me and a child, she chose the child. But what will that get me? I'm still angry with my first wife. I don't want to feel that way about Shelley forever."

"That bad for the heart," I tell him.

"But what's left after you forgive someone? People say love is strong, but it's not that strong, to be honest."

When I don't respond, he laughs. "I know I sound like a cynic."

I tell him, "I'm a cynic, too," but I say it more out of habit than from any real conviction. In fact, I'm suddenly distracted. At the table across from us, a blond European man tucks a strand of hair behind the ear of a lovely Vietnamese woman. The sight of people touching used to offend me, but I find the gesture completely charming now.

I suppose that my perspective on a lot of things has shifted. I spent a single afternoon with my father and, despite two decades of powerful evidence to the contrary, I left his house convinced that the world is beautiful, and merciful, and full of love. I assume that I'm unlikely to feel this way forever, but it breaks the monotony after twenty-three years.

My father didn't want me to leave at all, but I became anxious, knowing that Lan could return at any moment. Once I'd washed the dishes and made sure that Bo was comfortable, I picked up my purse to go. He reached out to take my hand. "If you leave, I'll think it was a dream," he said.

I squatted down beside him, grinning. "Then you'll dream it again tomorrow, Bo."

He kept his grip on my hand. "I don't want one daughter hiding from the other."

I had told him about my meeting with Lan. "She hates me," I reminded him.

He sighed. "Maybe. But you ran away once. What good did that do for any of us? Try something different now."

I looked at him, contemplating the possibilities. My father stroked my cheek. "You need to take your place in this family again," he said.

I left him listening to the World Cup, the radio against his ear, his eyes closed to conjure up the speed of the players, the green of the field, or, maybe, the face of his daughter, returned after so many years. As I walked to the door, I kept looking back, not quite ready to take my eyes off him. My place in this family, I thought. My role in this world.

Out on the street, I paused with my bicycle to consider what to do. The late afternoon remained hot and sultry, but I didn't mind. I had responsibilities now and news to relate. Shelley wouldn't return from the orphanage for an hour, at least. I got on my bike and began to peddle in the direction of Giang Vo. I would make an appointment, finally, for Dario to examine Bo. I had the telephone number somewhere on his card, maybe in the room, maybe in my purse. But the clinic itself was not so very far away. I'd go tell him. And I wanted him to know, too, that I had seen my father.

There is no easy route between my father's house and the doctor's clinic on Giang Vo Street. Afternoon commuters clogged the roads. The air was hot and sticky, stinking of diesel, loud with the roar and honk of traffic. But still, my arms and legs felt strong and impatient—not nineteen, but something like it. The energy in my body was almost more than the bike could absorb, and I whipped through the traffic. I fairly flew.

The clinic faces a small frontage road that runs parallel to Giang Vo. It occupies the first floor of a modern apartment building, just up the road from the Swedish embassy and a few doors down from the World Food Program. On balconies above, I could see the barbecues and plastic pool toys of foreigners. And racing bikes. Funny, when I was young, only foreigners and high-level officials rode in cars or on motorbikes. Now, most Vietnamese in Hanoi drive motorbikes and the foreigners—the health nuts—ride through the city on bicycles. So, what am I—Vietnamese or American? Vietnamese American can mean you're a little bit of both. Or, as Dario said, I'm sort of Vietnamese, sort of not.

His clinic has shiny marble floors. The reception desk separates the medical staff from the waiting room, just like in clinics in the States. In the waiting room, a Western couple, an Indian woman, and a Vietnamese mother and her children sat on the dark blue upholstered armchairs. Another Vietnamese child played with a puzzle in a corner filled with toys. "Can I help you?" A young woman behind the counter smiled professionally.

"I need to see Dr. Dario Penzi," I told her. I was out of breath, sweaty, unable to remember why I'd come.

"Do you have an appointment?"

"Can I use your bathroom?"

The receptionist pointed toward a door on the other side of the waiting area. Her eyes had already refocused on her computer screen. I made my way across the room, opened the door of the bathroom, and locked myself inside. Turning on the water, I splashed my face. It took a long time before I began to feel cooler and, even then, my skin in the mirror looked red and splotchy and my hair stuck to my neck in little patches of sweat. If I'd known a back door to get out of that place, I would have used it. I grabbed a paper towel and rubbed it under my arms to absorb the sweat. I reached to the back of my head, yanked the hair elastic off my ponytail, turned upside down and tried to dry my hair by swishing around and letting the air flow through it. Then I stood up, fluffed it out, and pulled it back once more. I patted my face, splashed it again, trying anything to get the red out. My mother would have scolded me. Mai, she would have said, Vietnamese ladies wear hats.

Finally, after ten minutes, I was dry, at least, and paler. I walked back to the desk and the receptionist looked up again, waiting.

"I need see Dr. Penzi." This time I said it in English.

"If you don't have an appointment, it won't be possible."

"Not for appointment. I'm his translator."

She looked at me suspiciously.

"When the regular one was busy. In Hoa Binh."

The receptionist shook her head, but then, from behind me, I heard his voice. "Mai?"

He stood in the doorway, looking at me. I'd never seen him in a lab coat before. He looked like someone on *ER.*

"Hey," I said.

"What are you doing here?"

"I saw my father."

He smiled and walked over. He set his hand against my back and we both leaned against the counter to face the receptionist. "How many more patients today, Thuy?" he asked.

Thuy clicked across the computer screen. "Three. Mrs. Seth. Mr. and Mrs. Miller. Tra Bingham and her little boys."

He glanced out toward the waiting room, took in its inhabitants, then looked down at me. His hand remained on my back. "Can you wait?" His voice was just above a whisper.

"I just wanted ask about the medicine for emphysema. And also, about maybe you examine my father. But no problem. I just call you tomorrow."

"No. Wait. Half an hour. Are you in a hurry?"

I shook my head.

"Wait." He turned, took a clipboard off the reception desk, and, without looking back at me, walked over to his patients. "Mrs. Seth?" he asked. The Indian woman stood up, he opened the door for her, and they disappeared down the hallway of the clinic. Behind her reception desk, Thuy had already begun clicking away again at her computer. I walked over to the waiting area and took a seat, picked up a month-old copy of *The Far Eastern Economic Review,* and began to page through it. In the corner where the toys lay, the little boy squealed. He had completed his puzzle.

At five forty-five, only one woman remained behind the reception desk. The other staff had pulled on their sunglasses and hats, hung their purses over their shoulders, and called out their good-byes. From where I sat, I could see them rev their smart little motorbikes and ride away. If I had stayed in Hanoi, I might have had a job like theirs.

Dario reappeared out of the clinic and walked the Vietnamese woman and her sons to the door. "With a sinus infection, please be careful about the smog," he told them. The mother nodded. In her hands, she carried two bottles of medicine. He opened the door for them and let them out, then turned and walked toward me.

I was cooler now but only slightly more relaxed. He stood above me with his hands on his hips. "You saw him?"

I nodded. I couldn't think of a thing to say that would explain it.

"Come." He motioned toward the door that led into the clinic. I followed him through it, down a long hallway, past a technician bent over blood samples. We walked into his office and he closed the door. It was a sunny room, full of bookshelves, with windows facing a small pond behind the building. At this hour, the sunlight streamed in sideways, making the whole room yellow. "Will you drink some water?" he asked. "You look so hot."

I shrugged, glancing around the room. I had no reason to be here, really. He pulled a bottle of water out of a small refrigerator, opened it, and handed it to me. I stood there in the middle of his office, drinking from the bottle. The doctor leaned back against the edge of his desk, watching me. "Can you tell me about it?" he asked.

I shook my head. I offered him the water. "You want a sip?"

He accepted the bottle and started to put his mouth to it. Then, changing his mind, he set it down on the desk beside him. He leaned forward, took my hand, and pulled me closer.

I have tried to remember when I felt this way before. Only with Khoi.

Or maybe not with Khoi. It's really quite hard to remember. For so long, I sifted through memories so precise that I believed I could feel the breath on them. But maybe I just imagined it. I think of the pencil drawings and photographs of the ancestors that my mother used to place on the altar in our house. The pictures perfectly captured the likenesses of those people's faces, their eyes, their grins, but the people themselves never moved again, or talked, or breathed. Hannah Ellis's drawing of my mother didn't change anything, but seeing my father did. Nothing makes the past alive again, and nothing can change it. Change only happens now, or tomorrow, or next year, or next week. Why has it taken me so long to understand that?

Dario looked down at me.

"Hello," I told him.

He laughed. "Hello."

He kissed my hand. Then he lowered it and let his thumb move up my fingers, along my open palm, and press against the veins of my wrist.

"What?"

"I'm feeling your heartbeat," he said.

"My heart?"

He let go of my hand, lifted his stethoscope from around his neck, and placed it in my ears. "You, listen," he suggested, setting the end of the stethoscope against my shirt. "Do you hear it?"

I shook my head.

He put his fingers on the top button of my shirt. "Is it okay?"

"Yes."

He unclasped the button. Then his hand slid the stethoscope beneath the fabric and laid it firmly against my chest. "Now?"

I closed my eyes and listened. I had never heard my heart before and I was surprised by its steadiness, its persistent beat. How faithful it had always been. Ignored and unencouraged, it kept beating. What a wonder. Even dead, I was alive.

While I listened to my heart, his cool hands moved across my face, down my neck, and along the ridge of my shoulders beneath my shirt. I felt his lips against my forehead. My hand reached up to touch his cheek.

That might have been the moment I gave myself to this man, but this morning, in Anh's café, I had given myself to him already.

I'm just a little bit flustered and tipsy by the time I finally say good night to Martin and make it to my room. In the darkness, Shelley sits up on her elbows and looks at me.

"I saw him," I tell her.

In the dim glow that filters in from the street, her expression looks as peaceful and content as a Buddha's, but I suspect it's merely an interesting trick of the light. "I'm a mother now," she says. Her voice sounds rough and tired.

I sit down next to her on her bed and smooth her curls. "Congratulations," I whisper.

She lowers her head to the pillow, reaches up and takes my hand. "I worked so hard to get him."

"You got him."

"No. Martin."

My hand in hers turns firmer. I could encourage her with some prediction about Martin eventually warming to her and Hai Au, but I couldn't make it sound convincing. "Come on!" I tell her. "It too late to think about that now."

"Oh, Mai," she moans. "I can say it, can't I?"

"When you drink down a glass of beer in Vietnam, you say 'One hundred percent!' " I tell her. "You don't say 'Sixty percent!' Or 'Eighty-seven percent!' "

"One hundred percent," Shelley says. And then, "Ninety-two percent."

19

Shelley

Hai Au is a traitor. At times, he has clutched me. *Clutched* me. At times, lying in his crib for a nap, he has kept his arm in the air for fifteen minutes just to grip the end of my shirt while he falls asleep. I am the only person in the world, other than Minh, whom he would allow to hold his bottle while he drank from it. I will not say that I was cocky about his affections, but I did feel enormously relieved by them. My boy was ready to come home with me. He demonstrated that at the aborted G and R, when he screamed after Minh lifted him from my arms. He told me so that morning. He was ready.

And now, whom does he scream for in this new life? Whom does he cling to? This child, who absorbed my attentions so calmly, so willingly, in the orphanage; this child, who rejects them so absolutely now, far away from the only home he has known or counted on? This child. Whom does he turn to in his hour of deepest agony, and terror, and need?

Martin.

I hold Hai Au in my arms, pacing. I try to console him myself. I stand by the window, pointing to a bicycle, a tree, a light. It doesn't matter.

He screams. Tears smear his cheeks. His nose produces a clear stream of liquid, which pours down over his lips, into his mouth, and pools there, mixing with saliva, before it overflows again, covers his chin and separates into thin threads that attach to his shoulder, his chest, my hair. His head bobs back and forth, up and down. It's hard to believe that such a small package can emit such energy. He's nuclear. He seems to understand that the move, this time, is real.

I try: "Shhh. Shhh. Shhh," which sounds soothing, but does not soothe him.

I try: "Sweetie. Honey." He doesn't even pause.

I try: "Hai Au," in every tonal combination I can muster. He will not react to his own name.

I try: "*Cún. Cún. Cún.*" The nickname Minh gave him: Puppy. You would think that it would do the trick. It does not.

His screams grow hoarse. I imagine his throat hurts, but if so, pain doesn't stop him.

Martin stands up from his chair and walks over. "Want me to try for a while?"

I don't. But Hai Au is already reaching over my shoulder, grabbing for him. What is with this child? I let him go.

The boy's head falls onto Martin's shoulder. The screaming stops. His breathing comes in little gasps.

"It's just a change," Martin says, trying to console me. "He needed a shift in momentum before he could stop. Theo was the same way."

I sit down on the bed. After carrying him for forty-five minutes straight, I feel like a truck hit my side.

"He didn't act like this at the orphanage," I insist. "He didn't act like this when he slept over the first night. He was upset, but not like this."

"Do you want me to go upstairs and leave you two together?"

"I don't know." I look at him. "What do you think?"

Hai Au hangs in Martin's arms like someone who has given up entirely. Martin sways. He pats the baby's back again and again, firmly and loyally, offering him something to depend on. Hai Au yawns. "Let's wait a few minutes, see how he does."

Despite my resentment, I'm grateful that Martin and I show good-will toward each other now. We've managed tragedies together for twenty years, so it seems fitting that we respond to our personal situation ("trag-edy" would be too strong a word) with even tempers and some degree of grace. In that respect, I didn't doubt him. And from the moment he came downstairs this morning, he has been nothing but good-natured and help-ful. I can't say that the tension between us has evaporated entirely, but we have, at the very least, repressed it.

It wasn't yet seven as Martin and I walked with Mai to have break-fast. We had called Mrs. Huyen as soon as we got up and she promised to arrange the G and R for the afternoon. Mai and I walked together, oblivious to the persistent drizzle on the street, distracted by anticipation. Martin walked behind us and every thirty feet or so we had to stop and wait for him. He ambled slowly, taking in the vendors on the streets, the traffic, the morning smells of chicken broth and soap. His face bore that same look of wonder and absorption that I'd seen so many times at home, in the lamplight of the study, while he pursued a course of knowledge on wedding rituals in Madagascar, or horse racing in Tibet. That expression on his face gave me the urge to share something with him. Nothing per-sonal, but some tidbit he might enjoy, the kind of random but satisfying fact that he could find in *Discover*. I slowed down, letting Mai wander on up ahead. "They have words for all different kinds of rain here," I tell him. "This kind of rain, I can't remember the word for it in Vietnamese. Mai said it's called 'dust rain.' "

Martin kept his eyes on the sidewalk, but let me fall in beside him. "I liked the sound of the language. It's nice to hear it again after all these years."

The note of pleasure in his voice silenced me. I didn't want to say the wrong thing and startle an emotion that, like some edgy wild animal, could disappear at any moment.

He continued, "I remember, if someone asked if I was married, I couldn't just say no. I had to say 'Not yet.' I thought that was the funniest thing. Even for questions where the answer could never be yes—Have you ever been to Mars?—you couldn't say no. You had to say 'Not yet.' "

"It's so odd," I said, laughing.

"It's so optimistic."

At the café, we followed Mai toward the back. The place had become familiar by now, made even more so by the exotic sight of my husband pulling up an extra chair. Although I had longed for him to come, I hadn't actually expected it. Now he sat only inches away, his body folded to fit on the tiny stool. I pulled a plastic-covered menu from between the salt shaker and the sugar bowl and handed it to him.

Martin ordered coffee and a croissant. Mai and I ordered coffee, orange juice, our usual mix of omelets and cake, yogurt, croissants, and toast. As we ordered, Martin stared at us as if we were playing some weird cross-cultural practical joke, as if restaurants operated in some different way in Hanoi. But I just shrugged and told him the truth: "We've turned into pigs here."

On this day that I would—barring some new unforeseen disaster— finally become a mother, I felt both elated and jumpy. It seemed easiest just to focus on Mai. "So, how was your day yesterday?" I asked her.

Her eyes had settled on the door of the café and now she turned back to me with a grin. "I saw my father."

I must have just stared.

"It's no problem." Her eyes were bright, her smile fresh and grateful. "He very happy."

I was about to explain to Martin, in some simple and evasive way, Mai's relationship with her father. Then I spotted Dr. Penzi up at the front counter, buying a paper. "Dr. Penzi's here," I announced.

Martin squinted toward the front of the café. "Who's Dr. Penzi?"

Mai reached across the table and poured some milk into her coffee.

The doctor had already begun to head back in our direction. "He's going to examine Hai Au," I said. "He eats breakfast here."

"Good morning. Shelley. Mai." He glanced at each of us, then, focusing on Martin, he reached out his hand. "Dario Penzi."

Martin, the polite American funeral director, pulled himself up off that tiny stool and shook. "I'm Martin Marino."

The doctor looked at me. "Shelley's husband?"

"Well, yes," Martin said.

"Wonderful!" he said, as if Martin had taken a spontaneous vacation to meet up with us for breakfast. The two men adjusted stools to make room at the table. "Good morning," he said to Mai, again, as he sat down beside her.

"Good morning." She gave him a brief glance, then stared down at a menu as if she planned to order something else.

The doctor looked at Martin. "Well!" he said, grinning broadly.

Martin looked at the doctor, clearly wondering what the doctor knew. I wondered, too. Mai wouldn't look at any of us.

"We're hoping to complete the G and R this afternoon," I said.

"All of you?" He looked at me, then Martin. He patted Mai's arm and leaned closer to her, his voice gentle. "You will go with them?"

It occurred to me that he was flirting. Mai must have realized it, too, because her face turned red and her eyes raced around the room, looking at everything except him. Poor Mai. She doesn't know how to handle such attention. In Wilmington, she managed to bury her looks beneath lousy clothes and a grumpy demeanor. But Hanoi has thrown her off completely. She borrows my clothes. She smiles. Sitting there in the café, she looked beautiful, like a flower you never expected to bloom. No wonder the doctor noticed.

He turned to me. "Shall I come by this evening, then, to take a look at your son?"

I laughed. "That's service. We don't get house calls anymore at home."

"Oh," he said, waving his hand through the air. "There are many wonderful things we manage here in Vietnam. You'll have to come by the clinic for the tests. But tonight, at least, we can make a start."

I looked at Martin. He said to the doctor, "Around six?"

When Martin, Mai, and I got back to the hotel, Mrs. Huyen and Lap were already standing in the lobby, waiting for us. Mrs. Huyen raced up to Martin first. "Mr. Marino, at last!" She gasped. "I was pulling every string I had, but sometimes even our best efforts fail us. I'm so sorry to have put you out in this way."

She was practically wringing his hand. Mai had told him, over breakfast, about Mrs. Huyen. "No problem," he replied, his voice just chilly enough to let her know he was on to her.

Lap stood behind Mrs. Huyen, shy and elated, his hands behind his back, rocking on his heels. I walked around her, took him by the arm, and presented him to Martin. "I want you to meet my friend Lap," I said. I looked to Mai to translate for me, ignoring Mrs. Huyen. "He's our driver, and he stuck with me when everyone else wanted to give up."

Martin's smile turned friendly as he shook Lap's hand. "Thank you," he said.

"I am very, very lucky," I said, to no one in particular, to me.

Lap turned to Mai and began to talk, his voice loud and breathless.

"He say it almost broke his heart," said Mai. "He see adoptive parent all the time, but he knew there something special between Shelley and Hai Au."

Martin's expression flattened. I guess he'd had enough. "Should we go?" he asked.

On the way out to the orphanage, Martin didn't say a word. He stared at the passing scenery as if every single noodle shop, every family on a motorbike, every roving vendor hauling a load of empty bottles both startled and fascinated him. Or maybe he didn't see these things at all. Maybe he was thinking about meeting his future—what do you call it when you go backward with a child? Not a stepson. An ex-son.

Mrs. Huyen and Lap and Mai went into the reception room to wait for us. I led the way toward Minh and Hai Au, who sat on a blanket in the garden. When Minh saw us, she must have realized immediately who Martin was, because she began to grin and yell to the other caregivers in Vietnamese. Hai Au, sensing something wrong, pulled himself up and hung to her neck like a baby monkey, screaming. I thought: I missed my chance with him. One chance to take him calm and happy. And I blew it.

I froze.

Martin continued across the grass and sat down. Hai Au screamed even louder. Minh looked up at me, then back at Martin. I didn't move. Martin leaned over and ran his hand across the top of the grass, then started picking through it. Hai Au, sensing something strange, leaned out, away from Minh but maintaining his grip on her, to see what Martin was doing. Martin took his time. He sorted through the grass inch after inch, here and there, deep and shallow. Hai Au continued to cry, but he seemed distracted now. Then Martin found what he wanted. He picked a long, wide blade of grass and held it up to the light.

"Aaaah," he said.

Hai Au reached for it.

Martin held the grass away from Hai Au's hand. He placed it between his thumbs, adjusted it a bit, lifted his hand to his mouth, and blew. The noise made the caregivers at the far side of the orphanage stop their talking. A cat woke up. An old man riding down the drive on his bike turned to look. Hai Au squealed. Minh started laughing. Martin blew again and again. Hai Au threw himself across the blanket toward Martin, who caught him in his arms.

"Hello there," Martin said.

Hai Au wiggled away to the edge of the blanket, thrust his hands into the grass, and banged it emphatically. The two of them began to dig through the grass, then, together. They spent the next hour blowing blades of grass.

By the time we reached the People's Committee Building, Hai Au had forgotten Minh. He had forgotten me. He had eyes for no one but Martin. The ceremony was as quick and efficient as, the last time, it had been slow and heartbreaking. Martin signed on all of his dotted lines. The officials signed on theirs. I signed on mine. Martin held my hand the entire time, ostentatiously, until the moment I received Hai Au, and then he let it go. No one bothered with the speeches. And then we were outside, in the van, a family.

It's nearly four. Hai Au's eyes are drooping. "Aren't you tired?" I ask Martin. "The jet lag and all. You two could sleep."

"I guess. Yeah. Okay," he says. He perches on the edge of my bed. I fluff some pillows behind him and he lowers himself back against them. Hai Au straddles Martin's body like a drunk in an old Western, hauled home on the back of a horse.

Martin's eyes are closed. "How long will the passport take?"

I would like to run my hand across his cheek, but I don't. I say, "Maybe another few days. Mrs. Huyen also has to find out if you'll have to sign forms at the embassy."

"I'll stay for that. It'd be pretty dumb if I left and the U.S. denied a visa because your husband wasn't there." His hand runs lightly over Hai Au's little body, smoothing down his shirt. "Why don't you tell Mai to sleep upstairs tonight and I'll stay here? He might wake up a lot. Might as well let her sleep."

I gaze down at them. "I won't jump to any conclusions," I assure him.

He keeps his eyes closed. "Right," he says.

For a long time, I stay there, watching them sleep. Of course, it's too late now to make a different set of decisions. Now that I have Hai Au, I have to have Hai Au. But before, when he was nothing more than a four-by-six-inch photo, why did I choose that photo over the man I'd slept with, worked beside, made love to, cooked for, dreamed with, loved—yes, honestly loved, even when he really pissed me off—for twenty years? That's what Martin doesn't understand. No one can understand it, and I can't understand it, either. I lost my mind. I see that now. And so did he. It became a test of wills between two stubborn people. And if winning means you never give in, then we both won.

"Is there any way around it?" I whisper to the sleeping man, the child, myself.

They respond with breath. One, deep and familiar as the grooves on a mattress, an old sheet, the right bed; the other, soft and fragile, morning, the first few steps. I am perfectly quiet, listening to them, but it is too much for me, this closeness between them that will not last, and so I leave and let them sleep.

Downstairs, a new group of Americans sits on the couches, clutching their guidebooks and waiting for Mrs. Huyen. Seeing them, and knowing I've got my boy upstairs, I feel suddenly euphoric, like the girl who won the spelling bee. This joy washes over me in waves, mixed with sadness, too. I'm experiencing the instability of PMS, without the cramps.

I sit down at the computer and check my e-mail. Work messages are supposed to forward directly to Bennet, but, still, I see a few from Batesville Casket, a couple from our plumber, one from a client with a subject heading "bill for urn." I ignore those for the time being, and open messages from my mother, Lindi, Rita, and one for Mai from Marcy (subject heading: "Cuisinart?").

My mother writes:

Dear,

I imagine you have him by now. Do you have him? Is he healthy? I am so worried about you. On the golf course yesterday, Sue Dalby told me that a friend of her daughter adopted from China. The child seemed fine but turned out to have hepatitis C. I don't want you to worry about such a thing, but if you need to know the symptoms, tell me and I'll call Sue. Everything's fine here. We're just waiting, desperately, to hear. Be kind to Martin. I know you can work something out.

Sauly might need to get his tonsils removed, maybe next month or the month after.

I love you, my darling. And, already, I love the little one, too.

Mom

Lindi writes,

Shelley—I can't believe what Martin has put you through. Don't worry about anything. As soon as you get back, you and Hi Ho can stay with us.

Love, Lindi, Richard, and the kids
P.S. This is Sauly writing. I have to get my tonsils out maybe. You eat nothing but Jell-O for a month.

Rita writes:

To: Shelley and Martin Marino, Lucinda Hotel, Hanoi, Vietnam
From: Rita P. Hayes, Administrative Assistant, Marino and Sons, Funeral Directors

Dear Shelley and Martin,

I hope that this reaches you in Vietnam. For all I know, it might be flying to Finland (this is only my third time on the E:Mail, you know?). Everything's quite all right here at the home. We have two funerals scheduled for the next few days and, with Carl's help, Bennet is on top of both of them. By limiting our number of cases, we do just fine. He has impressed all of us. Despite his youth, when it comes down to it, he's stepped up to the plate. We have had not a single complaint. So it is not a problem for Martin to turn this into a vacation like he said he might. We all of us are fine, so don't you worry. In a pinch, I can dress cadavers. I did it for Martin's daddy, and sometimes hairdressings, too, and I was none too bad at it, either, although I prefer the phone.

Let us know about the baby. We are waiting to hear.

Most sincerely,
Rita P. Hayes

I spend the next hour and a half sitting at the guest computer, typing e-mails in reply, offering my good news, finally, after so many weeks and months and years of bad.

"Hey."

Martin and Hai Au stand above me, sleepy-eyed, their hair mussed from the bed. Hai Au's hand rests against Martin's cheek. His expression is not happy, or sad either, just mildly curious as he observes the room. "Hey," I say. "We got an e-mail from Rita." I shuffle through the pages I've printed out and hand it to him. I want to see his response.

He holds the paper in one hand, the baby in his other arm. He reads it, then crumples it and tosses it into the trash beside the desk. "Well, good for Bennet," is all he says.

"Do you want to take a vacation?" I ask. I'm thinking: the three of us, the beach.

"No," he says, yawning.

The front door opens and Dr. Penzi appears. He's carrying his medical bag and a bunch of flowers. "Hello!" he calls across the lobby, striding toward us. The Americans turn to look at him. "Hello!" he says, nodding to each of them. "Hello. Hello."

When he reaches us, he is breathless. The flowers tip out of his arm to the floor and he bends down to collect them. "What a day. Too stressful," he says, but his face doesn't show it. "Here." He offers me the flowers. "For you, the three of you, the new family."

They are red roses and white mums, a thick and fragrant bunch. I think, He must not know we're not a family, not really.

Martin grins. "Our doctor at home doesn't bring us flowers."

The doctor grins. "Again, our Vietnamese system." He cocks his head, focuses on Hai Au, and says, as if to the boy, "Have I kept you long?" Hai Au's expression registers nothing. His finger hooks on Martin's ear.

We walk upstairs to the room. The unavoidable deserted island draws the doctor's eye. "Mai," he asks. "She is here?"

"She's gone to do some errands."

"Oh." He takes another look around. He steps into the bathroom to wash his hands, then, stepping back out, says, "I suppose we should begin."

We lay Hai Au across the bed and he begins to scream again. Martin and I sit on either side of him, holding his arms, cooing, kissing, singing, but he doesn't even hear us. Even Martin has betrayed him. Even the guy who plays grass.

"No worries. I'm quick," the doctor assures us. And he is. He listens to Hai Au's heart and lungs, checks his reflexes, his throat, his ears, the shape of his head, his scalp. "Strong heart," he says, speaking loudly, above the screams. "Strong lungs, but you know this already."

I look up and see Martin gazing at me. For the first time since he's gotten here, his eyes are focused just on me. I manage a smile. "It's scary," I tell him.

He nods. "It'll be okay." The tone in his voice reminds me of how kind he can be.

We hear the door click open and Mai slips into the room. The doctor only pauses for a moment to glance at her, then returns to Hai Au, steady and efficient. I have never spent much time agonizing about Hai Au's health, but now the anxiety clouds the room like sudden bad weather. Hepatitis C? Each pause, each second touch or gesture that might be different from normal, makes me jump.

"Is he okay?"

The doctor presses his finger into Hai Au's side. Kidneys, perhaps? "You, Mommy, do not worry."

Mommy. Mama. Mom. Ma. Mother. Mommy.

"I worry," I tell him.

"We're funeral directors," Martin explains. "We worry."

The doctor keeps his eyes on my boy, pressing a finger into the other side. Hai Au, like a toy with a magic button, ratchets up his screams. The doctor pulls down the pants and unfastens the Velcro tabs of the diaper. Martin, I see, has managed to change it. Hai Au begins to kick. Martin and I each hold a leg.

"At my lab tomorrow," the doctor says, "we will check his blood and, if you can manage, his stool."

"What are you looking for?" Martin asks.

"Oh, the usual parasitic infections. Plus, I check thyroid. Hemoglobin. White blood count. More. I'll give you a list." The doctor's hands continue, expertly. Groin. Penis. Testicles. After resecuring the diaper, the reflex of the knees. The calves, the balls of the foot. "Martin and Shelley, I believe you have a healthy son. But did you bring Elimite?"

I cringe. "I forgot."

Martin looks at the doctor. "What's Elimite?"

"For scabies." The doctor points to a couple of red bumps on Hai Au's groin, and a couple of others between his fingers. They look like mosquito bites.

"Scabies?" Martin looks concerned.

"Like lice," I say. My elbows suddenly feel itchy.

The doctor sees me scratching and smiles. "If you have gotten them also, you won't have symptoms for several weeks. But I'll give you some cream for all three of you to use tonight. You spread it on before bed, then wash it off in the morning. Wash all your sheets and clothing very carefully, too, or you'll make a great big circle of infection. You came here to adopt a boy, only. Leave the bugs in Vietnam, eh?" He leans over and gently brushes a lock of hair off Hai Au's forehead. "It's okay now, little one. All finished." Hai Au's screams have turned to whimpers, like a child who has abandoned hope.

I pick him up and, for the first time today, he doesn't reach for Martin. He holds me, tight, wiping his nose on my shoulder. Mai, laughing, gets a tissue and wipes his face. "There's an e-mail for you on the table," I tell her, then I look at the doctor. "I was planning on giving him a bath tonight. Should we still do it?"

"No problem. It might calm him. But you'll have to wash him again in the morning."

Martin is already squatting beside the changing area, pulling out the soap and a towel. We have slid so easily, he and I, into the tasks of caring for this child together. But I never doubted his ability, only his will. He stands up, pulls his room key out of his pocket, and holds it out to Mai. "Do you mind sleeping upstairs tonight? It might be easier, with Hai Au and all. I had them change the sheets."

She looks up from her e-mail, glances at me. It doesn't mean anything, I want to tell her. She lets the key drop into her hand—"No problem"— then goes back to the paper. A moment later, she reports with a laugh, "Marcy ask, do I mind she sells cakes now? She say that she make a caramel cake and the owner Port Land Grille buy them to sell at her restaurant. And she say Gladys been making tortes. You believe that? Tortes! She wants to know can she buy a Cuisinart."

I'm holding Hai Au, patting him on the back. His fingers lace through my hair and I'm trying not to think of scabies. "What will Marcy do when you get back?"

The doctor looks over at Mai. "When do you go back?"

Mai looks up at him over the top of the e-mail. "Next week." And then, as if she's answering some question he hasn't even asked, she adds, "Well, we got the baby now," as if that's the only reason she's here.

It takes Hai Au a while to realize the bathtub's function and, until then, he likes it. Holding himself up on the edge, he cruises along the side, leaning over to peer into the water like someone checking for goldfish. But when I start to pull off his clothes, he screams. It's not like I can reason with him or anything. He lies sprawled across a towel on the floor, twisting and kicking to get away.

As I struggle to untie Hai Au's shoes, Martin sits on the toilet seat, the tube of Elimite in his hands, reading the instructions on the package. "We rub his whole body with the cream, from the neck down. We concentrate on the areas between his fingers and toes, all the cracks and crevices, too. His genitals and anus. And then we do ourselves."

"How pleasant." One shoe off. I grip the other kicking foot. "It'll be one of our lovely memories of Vietnam."

I glance over and see the slightest smile on Martin's face. Maybe he remembers that I can, in a pinch, be funny. But then Hai Au kicks me in the nose. "Ouch!" The force takes the breath out of me, but it's only the foot with the sock on it. Martin continues to grin, not so kindly. I rub my nose with one hand, catch the wayward foot with the other. "I'm going to get in, too," I announce to Hai Au. The sight of me, pulling off my own clothes, surprises him enough to make him pause. I let my clothes drop to the floor, then rip off his diaper, sweep him up, and climb into the water.

Martin keeps his eyes on the box of cream. A vision of my naked body will not drive him wild. I can remember the years, of course, when it did. It hasn't been so long since a certain pair of flowered panties would utterly distract him. But I don't expect that he and I will experience moments like those again. I ease down into the water, holding Hai Au against my chest. His body is smooth and slippery, a baby seal. As soon as he feels the warm water, he begins to giggle, then squeals with delight, leaning forward and slapping his hands against the surface.

Martin looks up and watches both of us. "You like it!" he tells Hai

Au. He pulls himself down off the toilet seat and kneels on the towel on the floor, filling his cupped hands with water and letting it spill over Hai Au's head. I can't see Hai Au's face, but his shoulders jump with pleasure. His skin ripples at the folds of his neck. I take some soap and rub his back, which makes him wiggle more. His laugh is loud and ecstatic, the laugh of a human being who has discovered something great and totally unexpected: air-conditioning, whipped cream, cats. Yes, it's his cat laugh. When I look up, Martin is smiling at me.

Then Hai Au dives. My hands, slick with soap, can't catch him, and he ends up headfirst underwater before my mind even registers what he's done. Martin grabs him, pulls him upright, holds him while he gasps for air, spits, turns red. At first, he doesn't scream. He looks too shocked, and shattered, and mad. The silence only lasts a second, then he wails again.

After the bath, after we uneventfully administer the Elimite, after Martin and I acknowledge, without words, that each of us, in private, will spread the cream on our own lonely bodies, we sit on the bed, snapping the baby into his pajamas. Hai Au watches Martin slide the feet of the PJs over his toes. He doesn't fight it now. He just gazes at these feet of his, all pink and strange smelling and greasy.

"Martin?" I ask. I smooth a last bit of cream into Hai Au's shoulder, then pull the sleeves up around his arms.

Martin has miscalculated the snaps on the legs and has to pull them apart to try again. "You need a doctorate for this," he mutters.

"I don't expect you to forgive me," I tell him.

He keeps his eyes on the snaps, lining them up in pairs before squeezing the pairs together. "Don't worry about it," he says. "We both made mistakes." Though the words are gentle enough, the tone is willfully disinterested. I'd rather he felt any emotion than nothing at all.

It takes everything I can muster to plow forward. I don't do it for myself, because I have to assume that my marriage is over. I do it for my little boy. "I'm just wondering. Hai Au seems to love you. I'm wondering." I find it hard to continue.

He finishes the snaps and looks up. "What?"

We gaze at each other over the sleepy baby. Martin looks curious, and slightly vulnerable, too, as if he wants to trust me but can't. I want to make this request as simple as possible, without begging or crying or any other kind of manipulation. "When we get home, do you think that maybe you could let him be in your life, a little?"

He looks down at the floor, pushes a stray baby sock across the rug with his toe. Hai Au, noticing our distraction perhaps, begins to whimper and squirm. Martin picks him up and walks to the window. Hai Au's ear rests against Martin's shoulder, his arm dangles like a pendulum. He stares at the wall, at the palm trees, the surf trailing in fine little fingers down the beach. He blinks, then blinks again, not fighting sleep so much as observing its arrival.

"What would you like if you could have anything?" Martin asks.

"You and Hai Au," I tell him. He doesn't respond, just continues swaying, staring out the window toward the street. I'd like to ask the same thing, but the thing he ultimately wanted—no child—is no longer mine to give. I have two things to offer—Hai Au and myself—and, though he seems surprisingly fond of Hai Au, I'm pretty sure that he doesn't want either one.

After a while, he asks, "Do you remember that woman, a couple of years back, her ex-husband died of lung cancer—I think he owned Cape Fear Plumbing or something?"

"Sort of," I tell him. We see some ex-wives and ex-husbands, but they seldom announce their relationship to the deceased. At funerals, they stand in the shadows, alone and unconsoled.

"Well, she came by one afternoon before the funeral and sat by herself near his casket. We talked a little. She said that they'd been divorced for years—he'd had an affair when they were still pretty young and she left him. Then, after his diagnosis, he contacted her and asked her, straight out, to marry him again. He said he was dying and he wanted to be her husband when he died."

"What did she do?"

"She refused. Of course. She'd gone on with her life by then, and she had never forgiven him. Why should she marry him again? But then, after he died, the loss hit her in some really weird way. She was devastated. And she was so angry with herself for not marrying him."

"She still loved him?"

"I don't even know if she still loved him. Maybe. Mostly, she felt like she'd failed because she'd never managed to forgive him. That's what I remember most. She said it's a big burden, not to forgive somebody."

Martin lays Hai Au in the crib, pulls the blanket over him, then turns off the top light, leaving only the lamp. He sits down on Mai's old bed, facing me, and leans forward, his palms on his knees. He looks deeply tired. "Which do you think is harder, forgiving or not forgiving?" he asks, staring at me across the gulf of these two beds.

"I have a different set of problems," I say. "But I'd like to believe that not forgiving is harder."

"You're biased."

"Of course," I say. "When I die, I want to be your wife."

He lies down, his head against the pillow, and closes his eyes. After a while, he says, "I guess I like to hear that."

I slide from the bed to the floor, take his hand from his chest, and lay it against my cheek. He doesn't resist. I ask him, "Can I hold you?"

He doesn't open his eyes. He says, "Not yet."

For the longest time, we don't move at all. The room is dark but dappled with light. I watch him. I remember once, years ago, probably after we had to bury another person who died too young, I decided to memorize Martin's body. I had photographs of him, of course, but I needed my hands to remember his features in case I ever lost him. Despite his laughter and protests, I finally succeeded in getting him to lie on the bed and be still. Then I straddled my legs across him, closed my eyes and set my hands on the top of his head. Little by little, my fingers traveled through his hair, down his brow, over his eyelids, along the bridge of his nose, across the curve of his mouth, over his chin and down his neck, along every surface of his body. I felt like I was reading him. You would think that after making love with someone for so many months or years you would really know their body very well, but you don't know it absolutely.

You never can. That night, though, I saw my husband in a way I'd never seen him before. I learned his body as only a blind person could know it. Even now, after all these years, I can still close my eyes and travel in my mind over every muscle of his body, every shift of surface, every feature.

He looks asleep, but I know he's not. I whisper, "When you say 'not yet,' do you mean the Vietnamese not yet? Like when people say 'Have you ever been to Mars?' and you say 'Not yet,' but, really, of course, you know it's never going to happen. Is that what you mean, Martin, when you say 'Not yet'?"

He doesn't open his eyes, but he's smiling now. His finger moves, ever so slightly, along my cheek. "I'm American," he reminds me. "For Americans, 'not yet' just means 'not *yet*.'"

We don't say another word. I close my eyes. On the street below, the honks of the motorbikes sound rhythmic, even kind of jazzy.

20

Xuan Mai

Upstairs, Dario confronts me. "You go next week?"

Until this moment, he hasn't mentioned it. We have taken my bags to the new room, eaten *phở* down the block, and made it all the way back to the Lucinda without mentioning the subject. Now, he asks. His eyes still have that sweetness in them, but they look wounded, too, as if he's surprised, despite all evidence supporting it, that I would leave. I'm surprised that he's so willing to let me see his disappointment. I mean, we've only just met. I think we're supposed to play more sophisticated games than that. I read a book called *The Rules*, which Marcy, an expert at dating, had left by the register. I've also seen a lot of Sally Jessie on TV. Hasn't he heard about "self-protection"? Hasn't he heard of "playing hard to get"?

I play for both of us. "They got the baby," I remind him. Then I turn away from him to close the door. My stomach feels full from the *phở*, satisfied in a way I never feel from eating Big Macs. I think of all the things I'd like to show him in Hanoi. "Have you ever eaten *bánh cuốn* rice pancakes?"

He nods. I sit down on the bed, crossing my legs. There's room for him, but he prefers to stand.

"The kind with the rice paddy beetles in them?"

He nods again. It's my city, but I can't impress him with it.

He crosses his arms. From this angle, he's all limbs and misery. He tries another tactic. "What about your father? You're going to leave him now?"

I shrug, say nothing, look a little tortured, maybe. To be honest, I'm not tortured at all. Dario doesn't need to worry. If I had to, I would find an excuse to stay here. But I don't need an excuse: I won't abandon my father again. Bo understands that, but Dario doesn't. I should tell him, but I'm so astonished by the look of pain on his face, and so pleased by it, that I can't quite give it up. "I don't live here," I say.

"Why not?"

"I got a business back there."

"And anything else?"

I think of my store, my van, my house filled with cases of spring roll wrappers and chili sauce. I think of Gladys and Marcy. "Not really," I admit. He smiles as if he's won a point, takes a seat on the edge of the bed, picks up my hand.

"So stay," he says. He holds my hand against his cheek, then kisses it, then kisses the inside of my wrist.

"Hey!" I say. My head is on the pillow now. He presses his lips against my ear. "Stay," he whispers. "Stay. Stay." Then, with each word, he moves his mouth to a different part of my body. Stay. Stay. Stay. Here. Then here. Then here. "Okay," I finally tell him, and he can view it as acquiescence, if he likes. But I made this decision already. Maybe when I met him. Maybe when I saw my father. Maybe even when that plane touched the ground and I found that I could breathe again.

We lie naked together on the bed, not even under the sheets. Just naked, as if we have been lying naked on beds together for years and years and years. I feel both surprised to find myself in this position and surprised that I don't feel more awkward about it. I stare at the ceiling, which is pale yellow and seems to glow from the lights outside. "Do you know the heavens give each person one spectacular gift in life?" I ask.

Dario smoothes back my hair with the tips of his fingers. "No, but it's interesting."

"That's what my father told me when I'm little girl. He has beautiful voice. You'll hear it. And my mother had dark gray eyes. Very unusual in Vietnam. Silver eyes, my father called them. If you saw them, you wouldn't forget them." On this upper floor of the hotel, I can see the lighted windows of rooms across the street, but in my mind I see my mother.

"Your spectacular gift is your accent," he tells me.

I swat his arm. "Really!"

"But I like your accent."

I relax again, smile at the ceiling.

"Okay," he says. He turns on his side and rests his head in his hand. "What was heaven's spectacular gift to you?" he asks.

I've known for days already. "I get two lives," I announce.

He grins, runs a hand along my arm. "Very nice. And me? I can't think of anything spectacular there."

I turn to look at his beautiful face. "You get two lives, too."

We doze. When I open my eyes, I'm surprised to see him gazing at me. Conscious, I can think of little else, but, like a dream that vanishes when you wake, in my sleep I forgot he existed. "What?" I ask.

"Go see your sister."

My initial impulse would be to reject the idea out of hand, but I don't. I glance at the clock. It's nearly ten. My father said she keeps her café open late on weekend nights. "Now?" I ask.

"Why not?" He puts his hand on my cheek. "I'll go with you or wait here."

I look at him. "Wait here."

I see my niece, Lien, first, wiping tables out on the sidewalk in front of the empty café. Without pausing, I walk up to her. When she looks up, she recognizes me immediately and freezes, the rag in her hand. "*Chào,*

Liên," I say. The fact of her name on my tongue drags me from the past into the present.

"*Chào, cô,*" she stutters. In the context of our blood relationship, she should really call me "*dì,*" the term for a mother's younger sister, but she calls me "miss," instead.

"Could I sit down?"

She hurriedly pulls out a chair. She doesn't take her eyes off me, as if I'm a ghost who could disappear again at any moment.

"Will you join me?" I ask.

Nervously, she perches on a chair. Now, the light from the café bathes her face, offering my first chance really to look at her. On some level, of course, I hoped and feared that I would see My Hoa in this girl, but I see no hint of that stubborn gaze that charmed and exasperated me so completely. Instead, I see my mother in Lien, my mother's eyes.

"You look like your grandmother," I tell her.

Her expression shifts to a smile. Clearly, she takes it as a compliment.

I laugh. "You've heard about her, then?"

Lien nods. "She spoke beautiful French. She was almost like a princess, but her parents died—she saw them die!—and then she became a soldier at the front." She leans toward me, warming to the subject now. "They met on the side of a mountain. They were in terrible danger and he protected her. They fell in love at first sight."

I smile. Without my mother around to temper his exaggerations, my father's stories have evolved into myth. But Lien's version seems close enough. "She was lovely, too," I tell her and her face crinkles with delight. Here's the difference, then: My mother's eyes always contained at least the hint of sorrow. But this girl has never known war. I imagine that a fifteen-year-old, in any culture, suffers all sorts of complicated emotions, but at this moment I see only joy there.

"Lien!" a voice calls from inside the café. We turn quickly, like thieves caught exchanging jewels, and see Lan striding toward us.

She shows no surprise to find me sitting here with her daughter. "Go wash up the dishes," she orders and Lien scampers back into the café. "What do you want?" she asks.

Strangely, I don't feel frightened now, maybe because I haven't come to beg for mercy. I merely have a proposition for her. "Sit down," I say.

To my surprise, she sits. For a while, we simply look at each other. It's interesting, after all these years, to gaze at Lan's face and have her gaze back at mine. "I have a suggestion to make," I say.

She looks wary but also mildly curious. "What?"

"I'm planning to stay here. I might have to go back to the States to arrange my business, but, basically, I'm moving back to Vietnam. If you like, you can join your husband in Australia now. Lien can go to school there. I'll take care of Bo in Hanoi."

I am prepared for any reaction. She could throw back her head and laugh in my face. She could deride me with insults. After all these years, why should she trust me? But, she doesn't do any of that. She calls over her shoulder back into the café, "Lien, bring us some tea." Then, she turns to me and, for the first time, her face lacks any hostility. "I know you've suffered, too," she says. "Khoi told me."

It takes a moment for me to understand what she means, and then I'm stunned by Khoi's betrayal. "I didn't know he came to see you," I stammer.

She shakes her head. "He didn't. The news got around that he'd come back to Hanoi. I went to see him myself."

I stare at the sidewalk beneath my feet. Lan continues. I notice the sound of struggle in her voice as she forces herself to speak. "Shelley didn't tell me anything I didn't know already. Khoi told me, too. He said you moved to this little town where no Vietnamese live. You don't have any friends. He said you kept yourself miserable there. He said you've spent your whole life like that." I look up at my sister. She is doing the unthinkable. She has put aside her pain in order to acknowledge mine.

I shift in my seat. Above our heads, the leaves of the chinaberry tree twist in the breeze. My life sounds so pathetic. I ask, "Why did you say all those things to me the other day?"

She sighs. "I spent so many years rehearsing that speech. When I finally got the chance, I had to say it."

Lien brings us tea and we sip in silence. We've said everything we're capable of saying tonight. I feel no sudden warmth between us—I may never feel warmth between us—but I experience a kind of comfort in this silence, at least. We've lost so much in our lives that I think we've grown to accept very little. I feel grateful, and maybe Lan feels grateful, too. We have this, I tell myself. We have *this*.

My father has consulted his calendar and discovered that Tuesday is the death anniversary of my mother's paternal grandfather, Nguyen Thai Son. Seventy-three years. Seventy-three? That's no auspicious number I've ever known. My father never knew Nguyen Thai Son. My mother never knew him either. We didn't celebrate his death anniversary when I was a girl. But I have returned to Vietnam and, in my father's eyes, any anniversary occurring during the period of my homecoming must, of course, become auspicious. So he decides that we will honor him on Tuesday. We will cook our feast, burn our offerings, and remember this man whom none of us knows a thing about. In this way, we bring the entire family together. Not just Nguyen Thai Son, but my mother, too. And My Hoa. And Lan. And me. My father insists upon it.

From his wicker chair in the courtyard, he supervises everything, from the cooking in the kitchen to the arrangement of mats in the main room, where we will eat. He breathes more easily now that Dario has set up an oxygen tank and shown him how to use it. We keep it in a little cart and he pulls it behind him like a traveler dragging a suitcase through the airport. In the early mornings, I walk with him to Thanh Ha Pagoda and back. It takes us an hour, not only because of my father's speed and the trouble he has maneuvering the contraption on the uneven sidewalk, but also because he likes to show off his new appliance and his newly rematerialized daughter. We visit with Ba Nguyet, the tea stall lady at the corner, the paint shop proprietors down the street, the gatekeeper at the pagoda, the neighbors he hasn't seen in months. My father made Dario explain every knob and valve and tube, once, then twice, then again one more time. Certainly, he wants to be sure he uses it correctly, but he also wants to understand the machine in the most absolute and detailed way.

He is a man who loves technology but never had a chance to use it. If, by some different stroke of fate, he'd been born an American instead of a Vietnamese, he might have spent his youth tinkering with computers instead of hiding out in the forests, memorizing old poetry.

I had forgotten how much my father loves to be in charge. He has a list in his hand and, every hour or so, he goes through the whole thing, checking items off. If my mother were still alive, they would have spent the day bickering over exactly how to accomplish each task. They never fought over anything significant, like money, or the children, or politics, or whose relatives caused more trouble. But they could argue for hours over where to put the rattan mat, dinnertime, who more accurately remembered the day's price of rice in the market. This afternoon, with eight people expected for dinner, my father seems delighted that no one has questioned his right to run the show. He wants three mats instead of two. He wants stuffed mushrooms in broth, not chicken with baby corn soup. He wants two trays of food, so no one has to reach for anything. He wants Heineken, not 333. He wants Courvoisier, and Old Hiep's rice wine, too. He wants all of these things, and I make sure he has them.

By five o'clock, though, he has fallen asleep. The tubes of his oxygen tank fill his nostrils, and he sits with the radio on his lap, a cool wet rag draped around his neck, luxuriantly breathing. I've turned a fan on him and the breeze makes the silk strands of his white hair dance around his head. Air. The man has come to love air like the rest of us love food, or sleep, or sex, or water. He delights in it. He savors it like a fine wine. If I could, I would perch at his feet and feed it to him with a spoon.

Lien and I squat in the kitchen, just off the courtyard, each of us hovering over a wooden chopping block. This morning, she and I walked to Hang Ma Street to buy ceremonial goods to burn as offerings for Nguyen Thai Son, and, while we were at it, My Hoa and my mother. When I was a girl, if we wanted to burn *vàng mã* to offer to our ancestors, we could only find the old-style paper hell notes, or maybe gold coins made from disks of cardboard and a little orange paint. Now, the shops sell money in two currencies, Vietnamese dong and U.S. dollars, plus the old-fashioned gold coins and hell notes. The gold coins, though still cardboard, now have the shiny tint of real value. These days, I discovered, the *vàng mã* shops sell all sorts of fancy paper outfits, fashioned like clothing for a set of life-size paper dolls, as well as cardboard houses and VCRs, computers and refrigerators—in short, all the luxuries that we want on earth are now available for the ancestors to enjoy in the next life. Because Lien and I imagined Nguyen Thai Son to be an old man, we bought what seemed appropriate to his age: a man's traditional *áo dài,* complete with tunic and pants and hat; a pair of simple slippers; and, because Lien is silly, a cardboard motorbike. "An old man is not going to want a motorbike," I reminded her. But she insisted. "Maybe old men drive motorbikes in the next life," she argued and, since I had no reason not to, I relented. For my mother, we bought a pretty purple *áo dài,* with shiny yellow swans glued on to look like appliqué. To match the outfit, we found a pair of cardboard purple high-heeled shoes, light and sturdy as papier-mâché. My mother, who came of age during the era of military fashions, never wore heels herself, but she was a person who appreciated beautiful things, so we bought them for her. For My Hoa, who would have turned twenty-five this year, we started with a dress, light blue with navy diamonds around the hem and the cuffs, a youthful but sophisticated look, the closest we could find to Western fashion. "My mom wouldn't let me wear a dress like this," Lien said uncertainly, fingering the deep V of the collar. "Do you think that grandmother will let My Hoa wear it?" I considered for a moment. To be honest, it wasn't hard to imagine the two of them, standing in front of some netherworld mirror, my mother telling My Hoa that she couldn't step out of the house in that outfit. Lien and I unfolded the paper dress and held it up for inspection. It seemed likely to fall well below the knee, we agreed. "Let's let her have some fun," I said, then picked out a pair of heels to go with it.

Now, squatting in the kitchen, Lien pulls apart the cloves from three heads of garlic, sighing over the fact that I have asked her to peel and mince every one. On the altar by the banyan tree lie all the offerings, including a box of cardboard cosmetics for My Hoa that Lien grabbed as an impulse purchase. Above the courtyard, the sun is bright, but the shade from the banyan makes the hot air mild. I could grow to like these

Hanoi summers. I perch on a low wooden stool with a knife in my hand, peeling the cellophane-like skins off a kilo of raw shrimp, then using the knife to pull out the blue-black veins and wipe them onto the sheet of newspaper we've laid out to catch our scraps. From my father's lap on his chair in the courtyard, the radio sends the unmistakable cadence of the afternoon news in a volume that is soft, bleating, and incomprehensible.

"Does Marcy wear those short shirts?" Lien has chosen Marcy for her role model.

"Short shirts?"

"I saw it in last week's issue of *Young People*. In America, there's a pop star named Britney and she doesn't even cover her navel."

I have often seen Britney on *Entertainment Tonight*. That girl is trash. "Marcy wears jeans with holes in them," I say.

Lien, forgetting the garlic, looks at me excitedly. "I know those jeans. The holes are just below her butt? Big rips. And she wears them tight, right? So she can be sexy?"

She says the word in English. "Sexy."

"You don't know what that means."

"I do," she says, nonchalantly, pulling the skin off another clove.

"What, then?"

"It's like the word 'cool.' It has to do with the way you walk. You never laugh and everyone thinks you're beautiful."

I lift another shrimp out of the basket.

"Right?"

"Right," I say, then I add, in English, "You are going to kick ass in Australia."

"I know 'kick ass,' too."

"Terrific."

"It means really perfect. Like, *kick-ass* steak. Everyone loves steak in Australia, did you know that? So, when someone invites you over to their house, you say"—she switches to English—"Thank you very much for this delicious *kick-ass* steak."

"Good!" I tell her.

"I didn't know a person could be kick ass, too."

"Now you know."

The sound of voices coming along the entryway makes both of us pause and look around. My father stirs at the commotion and we see Shelley and Martin come through the doorway with Hai Au.

"Oh!" Lien leaps across the room. "The baby!"

Martin carries Hai Au in one arm and their diaper bag in the other. Shelley balances three bakery boxes in her hands. I stand up, crouch for a moment to rinse my hands in the spigot, then go help Shelley with the boxes.

"Did you have hard time finding the place?" I ask.

She shakes her head, looking around the courtyard. "The taxi driver came right here."

I lead them to my father. Lien stands behind Martin's shoulder, making funny faces at the little boy, who alternately hides his face and peeks.

"Bo," I say. "These are my friends Shelley and Martin, and their new son, Hai Au."

My father lifts his hand. Sometimes, he seems to enjoy the invalid thing, the holding-court aspects of it, at least, and he looks like gracious royalty now.

Shelley takes his hand. "*Chào bác,*" she says. Hello, uncle.

He looks at me, raises his eyebrows, then back at her. "*Chào cô. Xin mời vào. Hôm nay vui quá.*"

Shelley looks at me. Her Vietnamese, impressive as it may be, is spent.

"He says, 'Welcome. Today a very happy day.'"

Shelley nods, smiles at my father, seems not quite sure of what to do with herself. "Isn't it a death anniversary?" she mumbles.

I wave the idea aside with a flick of my wrist. "The ancestor died seventy-three years ago. We didn't even know him. My father just needed an excuse for celebration."

My father gazes up at me, obviously delighted by my English. I introduce him to Martin, both of them to my niece. Lien seems captivated by Hai Au, but he is unwilling to relinquish the arms of his father. Father? Who knows?

By six, everyone has arrived but Lan. The guests and my father have moved inside. Lien sits on a stool at Bo's feet, translating for Martin, Dario, and Bo. Ever since Dario helped to set my father up with the oxygen tank, Bo has watched him with particular interest. I haven't said a word to him, so maybe it's the way that Dario looks at me, or the sound of his voice when we talk. I'm not sure, but I can see that my father knows. And I can see that he's pleased by it.

Hai Au has fallen asleep on a mat in the corner, the fan turned now in his direction. Shelley and I watch them from the kitchen. Shelley sits on a low stool next to mine, filling the mushroom caps with minced sausage. Each time she completes a plate of them, she hands them to me and I slide them gently into the boiling broth, where they sink, then rise, bobbing in the bubbles. From where we sit, we can hear the conversation in the courtyard, but we can also have our own.

"Martin's surprised that people here don't seem to hate him," Shelley says in a low voice. "Everyone's so gracious. Look at your dad. He knows Martin's a vet. And so does Lap, who spent three years eating wild roots in the jungle. Yesterday, when he took us out for shrimp cakes at the West Lake, he asked Martin all sorts of questions about the war. After a while, they acted like buddies. It was as if they'd been through it together. Martin seems relieved that they're nice to him. I thought he might be angry at the Vietnamese, but mostly he just talks about how he doesn't understand their attitude. I mean, Martin hasn't gotten over the war. Why should Lap?"

"It easier to be nice if you won," I remind her. I lay out three plates and use my chopsticks to build a pyramid of spring rolls on each one.

Shelley stares down at the mushroom in her hand. "Well, that's true," she admits. She smooths the filling across the top with a spoon, surveys it, then works it over one more time, a sculptor perfecting her art.

I pick up a spring roll, choose its prettiest side, then set it on the dish. "It complicated, really," I continue. "One day they feel one way. One day they feel something else. Now they're curious. They never have a chance to speak with Americans before." Earlier in the week, I told my father that Martin had seen his friend killed in Danang. Bo just nodded. There's a point, I think, when the details of war cease to startle a person who has experienced too much of it. Bo reached that point a long time ago. I imagine that Lap did as well. It's not that they've gotten over the war, though. How can you get over something that shapes your entire life? An evening's chat with Martin might be interesting, but it won't affect my father in any way that's fundamental.

I can see that he's enjoying himself, however. He seizes the opportunity to ask all sorts of questions. How did the postal system work? What did the GIs do to keep up their morale? How's Jane Fonda getting on these days? Martin answers each question with great thought, like a diplomat sure that a single word could make or break the negotiation.

"You think my dad too nosy?" I want to know. "I can say something to get him to stop." He doesn't know the whole thing about American vets. Post-traumatic stress disorder and all that. They don't have *Oprah* here.

Shelley shakes her head. "Martin's okay," she says. "I think he's enjoying himself, actually."

We look over at Martin just as he leans forward and says to my father, "I wish that you could just see the movie *Barbarella*. Mai"—he calls over to me—"do you think you should try to translate the word 'hot' for him?"

Lien turns and looks in my direction. "I know what 'hot' means," she says, apparently insulted by this underestimation of her skills as a translator. "*Nóng*," she announces, offering the adjective for the temperature, but not a synonym for the kind of heat generated by Jane Fonda. My father gazes back and forth between us, puzzled. Dario looks at me and grins.

I wave the idea away with a chopstick. "I'll explain later," I tell Martin. I know my father will get a kick out of such information, but, really, what with Lien's notion of "sexy" and all, I just don't want her to hear it. The conversation shifts as my father launches into some kind of question about C rations, which he sampled when, after liberation, a cousin brought a can back to Hanoi. "What were the options?" he wants to know. As Martin begins to answer, I pick up a spoon, stir the broth a bit, then lower the heat. "How you two doing?" I ask Shelley.

She hands me the last plate of mushrooms and I slide them into the boiling broth. "It's strange," she says. "He didn't want another baby, but now I think he loves Hai Au too much to abandon me entirely."

"He love you, too," I tell her. I have seen the way he gazes at her when she isn't looking.

She smiles, idly poking at the bobbing mushrooms with a chopstick. "Well, it seems sweeter between us," she says. "Somehow."

"Did you ever see that *Oprah,* 'Couples at a Standoff'?"

She rolls her eyes dramatically.

"You could do worse," I snap. "I'm not talking about Jerry Springer." Why are Americans so down on *Oprah*?

I'll miss *Oprah*. I remember how I felt when Rosie quit.

Across the room, the men are laughing. My father smiles beatifically. He must have made a joke. Dario reaches over and fiddles with something on the oxygen tank.

"Could you love him?" Shelley asks.

"Who?" I ask.

She cocks her head and smiles, revealing to me that she has known everything for a long time. "The doctor," she whispers.

I pick up my ladle and move the mushroom caps around in the broth, carefully turning them to make sure that they cook evenly. "Yes," I say, not just because she has pushed me into a corner, but because I want her—Shelley—to know. My sister was wrong in one important way about my life in Wilmington. I did make one friend there.

When everything is ready, I ladle the soup into a bowl and arrange a dish of each type of food on the offering platter, then carry it to the altar in the main room of the house. "Come on," I announce in English and Vietnamese. "We each got to pray."

Only my father does it properly, and even he lacks the stamina to stand for long in front of the altar. Everyone else comes up with their own odd method. Lien, distractedly, races through the gestures before skipping over to where Hai Au sits now, groggy eyed, reaching for a foam rubber soccer ball that has rolled into the wall. Martin holds his incense uncertainly, as if he's afraid he'll do the wrong thing. Shelley stands there for many long minutes, eyes closed, perhaps going through every prayer she's ever known. Dario holds the incense above his head, like he's seen them do at the pagoda. He, too, closes his eyes, and whispers words that sound like chants, resolute and steady, in Italian. I raise my incense when all of them have finished and wandered off to take their seats around the mats laid out across the floor. I can hear them, speaking softly behind me, but when I look up I see the photographs of my mother and My Hoa, looking down at me. I lose myself, not in the images on paper, but in my memories of who they were. Mother, I pray, watch over us. And My Hoa? I ask her for nothing. I've taken too much already.

When I hear sounds of greeting, I turn around and see Lan standing in the doorway. Apparently, someone has already introduced them all because she moves, without looking at me, toward the altar herself, picks up three sticks of incense and lights them. We stand there side by side, staring up at the photos of the dead. Lan doesn't say a word, but I can feel the force of her prayers. What would it mean, I have to ask myself, for her to forgive me? Neither of us moves. I close my eyes. I am concentrating on the two women in front of me and the one who stands a few inches away.

Later, after Shelley and Martin have taken Hai Au back to the hotel, after Lien has gone to study, and Dario has headed to his clinic to check on a patient sick with bronchitis, my father sits out in the courtyard again, listening to the World Cup while Lan and I wash dishes. My sister and I have done this together so many times, after so many days and so many meals. I remember singing on cold winter nights, loudly and quickly, to keep ourselves warm. I remember hissing beneath our breaths, not wanting our parents to hear us fighting over whose turn it was to scrub the pans. I remember telling each other secrets there, secrets we didn't want anyone else to know. And now we move through the motions, silent and awkward.

We set the dishes to dry on the rack, then Lan gets up and goes over to the altar. She picks up all the offerings, still folded neatly in their plastic sleeves. "We should burn these now," she tells me. "Go get the metal bucket and some matches."

We move my father's chair close to where we've set the bucket and help him get comfortable again. Lan sits on a stool on one side of the bucket, a pair of iron tongs in her hands. I set down a stool on the other side and pull the plastic off the *vàng mã*. My father sits quietly, just watching us. Lan picks up Nguyen Thai Son's paper *áo dài,* bunches it into a ball, then stuffs it into the bucket. She lights a match, touches it to the paper, and starts the fire. The flames sputter and pop in the air.

"Lan," I say, glancing back and forth at both of them.

"What?"

"Do you remember Mother's last words?"

She stares down at the flames. "Of course," she says. "Don't you?"

"I wasn't there." Bo wasn't there, either. Only Lan was there.

She nudges the paper with the tip of the tongs. "Yes, you were."

"No. I ran home to cook dinner. She hadn't spoken for days. And then, when Bo and I came back to the hospital, you told us she'd spoken. She died the next day. Tell me again."

She looks down at the flame.

I'm sure my father remembers, but, still, he wants to hear it. "Tell us, child," he says.

Lan's voice sounds irritable and impatient, but she doesn't refuse the request. "I could barely understand her. She said, '*Lan, Xuân Mai ơi!*' as if she were calling us home for dinner."

I look at my father. He just shrugs. After a while, I say, "It's not always very meaningful."

Lan lifts the burning paper and turns it in the basket to expose it to the air. "It can't always be meaningful," she reminds me. As the *vàng mã* begins to burn down, she points with the tongs to our mother's *áo dài* and I hand it to her across the top of the bucket. She crumples the *áo dài* and pushes it in. Immediately, the flames dance up again.

Next, I hand her one of our mother's high heels. "Shelley told me that once there was a guy who started counting in the last week of his life. He had Alzheimer's and he couldn't count in order. Seven, one million, sixty-three. Like that. Until he died." Some chemical in the shoe turns the flame a deep blue, then it hisses and shifts back to orange. The smoke makes your eyes burn, like onions do.

Lan looks at me across the top of the bucket. "Do your friends really bury people for a living?" She sounds somewhat appalled.

"Yes," I say, "but it's considered a respectable profession in America."

I hand her another shoe. The flames sputter blue again. The entire shoe catches fire, but holds its shape for long seconds, glowing and popping, before suddenly disintegrating into a heap of burning embers. My father has left on the radio to hear the World Cup and you can tell by the sound of the announcer's voice that someone has scored. From the neighbors' houses in all directions come the echoes of other football fans, clapping and shouting, "Argentina!" which is, apparently, a favorite. My father grins with pleasure.

"My Hoa now," Lan says. I hand her the dress. She unfolds it and considers it for a moment, then without a word she crumples it and sets it in the bucket, turning it with the tongs to catch the flames. The dress burns. The first shoe burns. The second shoe burns. Then the cosmetics. The smoke rises in a thin column up through the branches and leaves of the banyan toward My Hoa and the sky.

Lan rubs her eyes. "They must think about death differently in the U.S.," she says. I remember people making similar remarks as we sat in the shelters, waiting for the Americans to drop their bombs on our heads.

Slowly, the box of cardboard cosmetics disintegrates in the bucket, sending embers like gray moths flying through the air. "Not really," I tell her. "They're pretty much like us."

We have nothing left to burn. The air smells of carbon and something slightly sweet. My father looks tired, but refuses to go to bed. The sight of his two daughters burning *vàng mã* together seems to give him exquisite satisfaction. Lan sets the tongs down and holds her arms around her knees. For so many years, I have wished for nothing in my life, and so it strikes me as surprising to realize that, had I given myself the chance, I would have wished for exactly this.

For a long while, Lan's eyes scan the upper reaches of the branches. "What's it like over there?" she asks.

I gaze at my sister and my father across the smoldering ashes. And then, without any other fanfare, I begin to tell them about it.

ACKNOWLEDGMENTS

For helping me to understand the experience of Vietnamese Americans in an out-of-the-way corner of the United States, I thank Nga Erdman, Solange Thompson, and Lan Washington, proprietor of one of Wilmington's great treasures, the Saigon Market. Also in Wilmington, I benefitted from the information provided by the Andrews family of Andrews Mortuary and Bernie Kantowitz of Coble Ward Smith Funeral and Cremation Service. *American Funeral Director* magazine and the books of Robert G. Mayer and Mary Roach supplied additional helpful information. I am deeply grateful to Helen Lane, whose life as a funeral director in San Jose, California, provided me with the first seeds of an idea that eventually grew into this book. Thanks, also, to Allison Martin, Lael Martin, and the members and moderators of the Internet e-mail list Adoptive Parents Vietnam for their willingness to share, both privately and publicly, their experience and knowledge.

A number of people helped me with this book, either by reading drafts or through other kinds of support. Thank you, Dwight Allen, Karen Bender, Ginny Berliner, George Bishop, Wendy Brenner, Nguyen Nguyet Cam, Vern Cleary, Amy Damutz, Sherry Goodman, Peggy Hageman, Carolyn Jones, Amy Keith, Andrew Lund, Alison Lurie, Sarah Messer, Hope Mitnick, Barbara Namerow, T. T. Nhu, Celia Rivenbark, Robert

Siegel, Kathy Steuer, Mark Street, Eric Vrooman, and Kathryn Winogura. I am grateful to Bui Hoai Mai for the beautiful drawings that grace the interior of this book. Thanks to the entire Sachs family, especially my brother, Ira; my sister, Lynne; my mother, Diane; my father, Ira, Sr.; and my grandmother Rose for your love and support. Thank you to Douglas Stewart, my agent, for sticking with me and for being so smart, and to my editor, Marjorie Braman, who is wise and patient and has an excellent temper.

Thanks, and love, to my husband, Todd Berliner, not only for reading innumerable drafts, but also for putting up with me and inspiring me in countless ways. And thanks to my sons, Jesse and Samuel. I lucked out when I got you.